ELLERY QUEEN
in IPL Library of Crime Classics® editions.

ELLERY QUEEN

DRURY LANE'S LAST CASE

A CRIME CLASSIC ®

INTERNATIONAL POLYGONICS, LTD.
NEW YORK CITY

DRURY LANE'S LAST CASE

This novel was originally published with the author listed as Barnaby Ross, who was later revealed to be Ellery Queen.

Library of Congress Card Catalog No. 87-82441
ISBN 0-930330-70-6

Printed and manufactured in the United States of America by Guinn Printing, New York.
First IPL printing October 1987.
10 9 8 7 6 5 4 3 2 1

Author's Note

It is with the revitalized relish of the professional gourmet—who, having nibbled wearily at the morbid comestibles at his command, suddenly encounters a rare and delicious delicacy —that I record herewith the last case to which that grand old man of the theater, Mr. Drury Lane, lent his exceptional efforts.

It has been a privilege to serve as the silent stenographer of Mr. Lane's exploits; and surely no one will question——if differing about the man himself——the remarkable plasticity of thought which he displayed in those investigations which I have entitled *The Tragedy of X, The Tragedy of Y,* and *The Tragedy of Z.* But it is more than a privilege, it is a duty, to record this extraordinary man's last investigation, which I have subtitled *The Tragedy of 1599* for reasons which will be apparent on a reading of these pages. I say "duty," for, if Mr. Lane astounded his contemporaries and his public by the loftiness of his thinking processes in the three explorations into crime already recorded, he positively staggered them by his investigation of the case which terminated his career as self-appointed guardian of the law. And to withhold this amazing adventure from those who have followed Drury Lane's fortunes so patiently, encouragingly, and, at times, enthusiastically would be a lamentable cruelty.

It is my admittedly biased opinion that for sheer wonder and rarity there is no precedent in criminological history for the case set down between these covers.

—ELLERY QUEEN

Dramatis Personæ

Dr. Alonzo Choate, *retiring curator of the Britannic Museum*

Hamnet Sedlar, *incoming curator of the Britannic Museum*

Mrs. Lydia Saxon, *patronne des arts*

Crabbe, *the Saxon librarian*

Gordon Rowe, *a young scholar*

Dr. Ales, *a bibliophile*

Maxwell, *his servant*

Donoghue, *special guard at the Britannic Museum*

Joe Villa, *a thief*

George Fisher, *an omnibus driver*

Bolling, *Chief of the Tarrytown Police Department*

Inspector Thumm, *retired Inspector of Detectives*

Patience Thumm, *his daughter*

Mr. Drury Lane, *who makes his last bow*

Incidental Characters: Samuel Saxon (*who is dead*); Sir John Humphrey-Bond (*who is dead*); James Wyeth (*who is alive but does not appear*); museum employees, police, a district attorney, employees of the Rivoli Bus Company, 17 elderly Indiana schoolteachers, *etc., etc.*

Place: New York City and Environs

Time: The Near Future

Joseph's Beard

It was a curious beard, an unorthodox beard, almost a humorous beard. Shaped like a Frenchman's spade, it fell in the quaintest wave, rippling from his invisible chin to two prim points below his invisible collar. There was something at once girlish and dignified in its series of perfect ringlets, like the majestic statuary brush of Zeus. But it was not its sharply two-pronged beauty nor its rhythmic volutions that caught the goggling eye. The true marvel was its colors.

It was a veritable Joseph's beard, dappled and pied and streaked like Joseph's coat, glinting in unexpected blacks and blues and greens. Had it faded under a playful sun? Or had its wearer for some inscrutable purpose of his own deposited his solemn length on a laboratory table and bathed his remarkable beaver in a pool of chemicals? Such an Olympian beard could have had an origin no less fantastic. This was, one felt, historic hair; a beard for a museum, to be preserved for admiring posterity.

Now Inspector Thumm, lately of the New York Police Department, at present retired and soothing his restless spirit with the balm of private detective agency work, was after forty years of policing inured against the surprises of mankind. But even he was first horrified, and then frankly fascinated, by the extraordinary brush on the chin of his Monday visitor this mild May morning. There was no precedent in the Inspector's experience for that amazing collection of multicolored filaments. He stared and stared as if he could not see enough of it.

Finally he said: "Sit down," in a feeble voice, glanced at his desk calendar to see if by some alchemy of forgetfulness it might not be All Fools' Day, and then sank into his own chair to scrape his broad blue jaws and regard his visitor with awed astonishment.

Rainbow-Beard sat down with perfect equanimity.

He was a tall thin man, Inspector Thumm observed—precious little to go on, for the rest of him was clothed in as cryptic a mystery as his chin. He was heavily attired, as if his body were swathed in fold after fold of thick cloth; for the

7

Inspector's trained eye caught the slenderness of the wrists peeping above the man's gloved hands and the leanness of his legs—undisguisable indications of thinness. Blue-tinted spectacles concealed the man's eyes. His nondescript fedora, which he had with charming insouciance failed to remove upon entering the Inspector's office, effectively disguised the shape of his head and the color of his hair.

And he remained, quite like Zeus, supremely silent.

Thumm coughed. "Yes?" he said encouragingly.

The beard waggled, as if in amusement.

"Yes? What can I do for you?"

Very suddenly the lean legs whipped across each other, and the gloved hands clasped over one bony knee. "You're really Inspector Thumm, I fancy?" the apparition said in a slightly rusty voice. Thumm twitched nervously. It was like hearing a statue speak.

"That's me," said the Inspector faintly. "And you—?"

A hand waved. "Unimportant, Inspector. The fact is—how shall I say it?—I've a rather extraordinary request to make of you."

It would be extraordinary, thought the Inspector, if you didn't—with that get-up! Some of his normal shrewdness banished the astonishment in his eyes. His hand moved lightly behind the shelter of his desk and flicked a little lever. An almost inaudible hum developed which the gentleman with the motley beard apparently did not notice.

"People who sit in that chair generally have," said the Inspector jovially.

A pointed little piece of tongue appeared in the hairy forest about the man's lips and, as if frightened by the strange hues of the underbrush, retreated hastily. "I may tell you, Inspector, I've been looking you up. What appealed to me was the fact that you seem not to be the—ah—usual sort of private detective."

"We aim to please."

"Quite so. Quite so. . . . Ah—you're *strictly* private? I mean to say, you've no connection now with the police, Inspector?" Thumm stared at him. "You see, I must be *sure*. My business with you must be kept severely confidential."

"I'm so close-mouthed," growled Thumm, "that I won't tell even my best friends. If that's what's worrying you. Unless it's something off-color. I'm death on rats, mister. The Thumm agency doesn't play around with crooks."

"Oh, no, no," said Rainbow-Beard quickly. "Nothing like

that, I assure you. It's just that it's something—somewhat peculiar, Inspector."

"If it's about your wife and the boy-friend," observed the Inspector, "nothing doin'. I'm not that kind of agency, either."

"No, no, Inspector, not a domestic entanglement at all. Nothing of that sort. It is—well, in a word," said Rainbow-Beard, his breath agitating the flora on his chin, "I want you to *keep* something for me."

"Oh," said Thumm; he shifted a little. "Keep what?"

"An envelope."

"Envelope?" The Inspector scowled. "What's in it?"

Rainbow-Beard exhibited unexpected firmness. His lips clamped together. "No," he said. "I won't tell you that. Surely it doesn't make any difference?"

The Inspector's cold gray eyes stared at his remarkable visitor for some seconds. The blue spectacles remained impenetrable. "I see," said the Inspector, although it was quite evident that he did not. "Just what d'ye mean—keep it for you?"

"Hold it for me safely. Until I call for it. In trust, as it were."

Thumm yawned. "Hell, I'm not runnin' a safety-deposit vault. Why not go to a bank? It'll be a damn sight cheaper, too."

"I'm afraid you don't understand, Inspector," said Rainbow-Beard cautiously. "That wouldn't do at all, you see. I must have it in safe-keeping with a *person,* you see, a person of integrity," and he examined the hard chunky face of the Inspector very closely, as if to reweigh that doughty gentleman's trustworthiness.

"Heard you," said Thumm. "Heard you and got you. Well, let's see the evidence, Mister Anonymous. Let's see it, let's see it!"

For some time the visitor did not respond; but when he did it was with swiftness, as if he had made up his mind after due deliberation. His gloved right hand groped within the folds of his swathings and emerged after a moment clutching a large long brown manila envelope. Thumm's eyes gleamed, and he extended his hand. The envelope dropped into it, reluctantly.

It was an ordinary manila envelope such as may be purchased in any stationery store. Both front and back were innocent of markings. It had been sealed not only by its original adhesive flap; evidently the visitor had taken certain precautions against the frailties of human nature, for six small bits of ordinary cheap white paper cut into odd shapes had been pasted over the flap for additional protection against tampering.

"Neat," remarked the Inspector, "neat and not gaudy. Hmm." He fingered the envelope without seeming to do so. His eyes narrowed. The visitor sat quite still. "What's inside? You can't expect——"

There was presumptive evidence that Rainbow-Beard smiled, for the hairs on the corners of his mouth suddenly twitched in a northerly direction. "I like your persistence, Inspector, like it enormously. It confirms what I've heard of you. You've a very fine reputation, you know. Your cautious attitude——"

"Yes, but what's in it?" growled Thumm.

The man—if it was a man, for a preposterous suspicion crossed Thumm's mind suddenly—leaned forward. "Suppose I told you," he whispered hoarsely, "suppose I told you that inside that very envelope in your hand, Inspector, there's a clue to a secret, a secret so important, so significant, so *tremendous*, that I daren't trust anyone in the world with the whole truth!"

Inspector Thumm blinked. He might have known. The beard, the spectacles, the heavy disguising clothing, the antics of his strange visitor—why, the man was obviously an escaped lunatic! Clue. Secret. Anyone in the world. . . . The poor nut was cracked.

"Uh—take it easy," he said. "No need to get excited, mister." He felt hastily for the tiny automatic he carried in his armpit holster. The crazy fool might be armed!

He was startled to hear Rainbow-Beard utter a cavernous chuckle. "You think I'm mad. Can't say I blame you, Inspector. I suppose it does sound a bit—er—thick. But let me assure you," and the queer rusty voice became very sanely dry, "that I've told you the exact truth without any dramatic coloration. And you needn't finger your automatic, Inspector; I shan't bite you." Thumm snatched his hand out from beneath his coat and glared, red-faced, at his visitor. "That's better, really. Now please listen carefully, because I've very little time, and it is important that you understand clearly. I repeat that that envelope contains the clue to a colossal secret, Inspector. And let me add," he said in calm tones, "a secret worth *millions!*"

"Well, if you're not balmy," growled Thumm, "then I am.

You'll have to tell me more than that if you expect me to swallow that yarn. What d'ye mean—secret worth millions? In this skinny envelope?"

"Precisely."

"Political secret?"

"No."

"Oil strike? Blackmail—love letter? Treasure? Jewels? Come on, mister, come clean. I'm not going to handle anything I'm in the dark about."

"But I can't tell you that," replied Rainbow-Beard with a trace of impatience in his voice. "Don't be stupid, Inspector. I give you my word of honor there's nothing nefarious about the contents of that envelope. The secret is quite legitimate. It has nothing to do with the very ordinary things you've just mentioned. It concerns something infinitely more interesting and of infinitely greater value. Remember, too, the envelope contains not the secret itself, if I make myself clear; it contains merely a clue to the secret."

"You'll have me going nuts in a minute, too," groaned Thumm. "Why all the mystery? Why do you want me to keep the damned thing?"

"For a very good reason." Rainbow-Beard pursed his red lips. "I am on the trail of—well, let us say the 'original' of the clue in the envelope, the secret I've mentioned. You understand, then, that I haven't found it yet. But the trail is extremely warm, extremely warm indeed! I fully expect to succeed. Now, if anything should—ah—happen to me, Inspector, I want you to open this envelope."

"Ha," said the Inspector.

"In the event that something happens to me—and when you open the envelope—you'll find my little clue. It will lead you by a rather devious route to—me. Or rather to my fate. I'm not providing against this contingency in any spirit of revenge, I'll have you understand. If anything happens to me I'm not interested so much in being avenged as in having the original of the secret *preserved*. Do I make myself clear?"

"Hell, no!"

Rainbow-Beard sighed. "The clue in this envelope is just that and nothing more; it tells little *of itself*. But that's precisely as I want it! Its very incompleteness will protect me against—no offense meant, my dear Inspector!—against even your curiosity, or the curiosity of anyone else in whose hands the envelope might fall. If you should open it before I intend you to, I assure you that what the envelope contains will be quite meaningless to you."

"Oh, cut it out!" cried Thumm, rising. His face was darkly red. "You're trying to make a fool out of me. Who the hell put you up to this crazy kid's trick, anyway, damn it all? I can't waste——"

Something buzzed insistently on the Inspector's desk. The visitor did not stir. Inspector Thumm cut short his explosion of annoyance and snatched up the receiver of his inter-office communicator. A feminine voice snapped in his ear. He listened bitterly for a moment, replaced the receiver, and sat down.

"Go ahead," he said in a choked voice. "Go on. Give it to me. I'll bite. I'll swallow it hook, line, and sinker. What's next?"

"Dear, dear," said Rainbow-Beard with a little cluck of concern. "Really, Inspector, I'd no intention. . . . That's really all."

"Not on your life, it isn't," said the Inspector grimly. "If I'm going to fall for this, I'll do it proper. Must be somethin' else. Crazy as it is, it can't be as crazy as you've *left* it."

The man stroked his extraordinary beard. "I like you better and better," he murmured. "Yes, there is something more. You must promise that you won't open this envelope unless —" He paused.

"Unless what?" growled Thumm.

The visitor licked his lips. "Today is the sixth of May. Two weeks from today, on the twentieth, I shall telephone you here. I'm confident that I shall telephone you here on that date. And also on the twentieth of June, and the twentieth of July—on the twentieth of each month until I've found—it. My telephoning on a schedule this way will tell you that I am still alive, that I've run into no unexpected danger." A brisk note sprang into his rusty voice. "While that condition continues, you are merely to keep the envelope in your safe until I call for it. On the other hand, if by midnight of any twentieth I have failed to telephone you, you will know that I'm probably beyond calling altogether. Then—and only then—are you to open the envelope, read what it contains, and proceed as your very good judgment, I'm sure, will dictate."

Thumm sat, hard-bitten and sour, deep in his chair; there was a cynical twist to his smashed pugilist's nose, a stubborn air about him mingled with a rather bitter curiosity. "You're going to a hell of a lot of trouble, mister, to make sure of this secret of yours. Somebody else is after it, hey? Somebody you think may bump you for it before or after you get it?"

"No, no," cried Rainbow-Beard. "You misunderstand. As far as I know, no one else is after the—the secret. But there's always the possibility that someone is after it, someone whose intentions or identity I'm unaware of. I'm merely taking precautions against that remote contingency, that's all. It's so remote that I won't tell you my name or—or anything! Because if nothing happens—and I don't expect anything to happen—I don't want you or anyone else to come into possession of a clear clue to my secret. I'm sure that's frank enough, Inspector. . . ."

"By God," groaned the Inspector, "hasn't this gone far enough? Listen, mister." He pounded on his desk. "First I thought you were a nut. Then I thought somebody put you up to playin' a joke on me. Now I don't know what to think except this: I'd be a whole lot happier if you'd get the hell out of here pronto. Scat! Shoo!"

The beard sagged in honest bewilderment just as the communicator buzzed again. Thumm started, flushed like a small boy caught stealing apples, and jammed his fist into his pocket. "All right, all right," he muttered to the buzzer, and said aloud: "Excuse me. I—I got up this morning with a grouch. Guess I'm not used to your kind of"—he groaned aloud—"case. I'm just a plain dick, and I s'pose I can't get used to the idea of becoming wet-nurse to an envelope. . . . All right, I'll be crazy, too, just to be sociable! When you ring me up on the twentieth, how will I know it's you?"

The visitor sighed heavily with relief. "I'm so glad—Hmm. Very clever, Inspector, very clever indeed. I hadn't thought of that." He chuckled and rubbed his gloved hands together. "Really, this is quite exciting! Like that mad chap Lupin's adventures!"

"Whose?" demanded Thumm suspiciously.

"The immortal Arsène. Hmm. Password. Password, of course! That's the logical answer, Inspector. Very well, when I call you I shall say—let me see—ha! 'This is the man from Nowhere. Millions!' and by that, as Matthew didn't say, ye shall know me. Ha, ha!"

"Ha, ha," said the Inspector. " 'This is the man from—' " He shook his head warily. Then a gleam of hope scurried to the surface of his eyes. "But maybe my fee wouldn't——"

"Ah, your fee," said Rainbow-Beard. "Yes, yes, I'd almost

forgotten that. What would your retainer be, Inspector, to take this odd little case of mine?"

"Just for holdin' this damned envelope in my safe?"

"Quite so."

"That will cost you," said the Inspector desperately, "just five hundred smackers."

"Smackers?" repeated Rainbow-Beard, apparently puzzled.

"Iron men. Simoleons. Bucks. Five hundred of 'em!" cried Thumm. He searched his client's face eagerly for signs of consternation; that jaw with its horrible foliage should drop, and there would be relieved triumph when the visitor beat a precipitate retreat in the face of so preposterous a demand.

"Oh, dollars," said the visitor with a vague smile. He did not appear unduly alarmed. He fished among his swaddling clothes, took out a fat wallet, extracted a stiff bill, and tossed it on the desk.

It was a crisp new thousand-dollar banknote.

"I think," said Rainbow-Beard briskly, "that a thousand dollars is more nearly the proper remuneration, Inspector. This is an unusual and—ah—unorthodox assignment, to be sure, and besides it's worth all of that to me. Peace of mind, a sense of security——"

"Uh-huh," gulped Thumm, touching the bill with dazed fingers.

"That's settled, then," continued the visitor, rising. "There are just two conditions more. I must insist upon your observance of them, Inspector. First, you are not to have me—what is the colloquial term?—shadowed when I leave this office, and unless I fail to telephone on a twentieth you must make no effort to trace me."

"Sure, sure," said Thumm in a trembling voice. A thousand dollars! Tears of joy gathered in his stony eyes. These were lean days. A thousand dollars for keeping a skinny envelope in his safe!

"Second," and the man went swiftly to the door, "if I should fail to call on a twentieth, you must not open the envelope *except in the presence of Mr. Drury Lane*."

The inspectorial mouth gaped like the Cavern of Doubt. It was the finishing blow. The rout was complete. Rainbow-Beard smiled deprecatingly, trotted through the doorway, and vanished.

Miss Patience Thumm, free, white, over twenty-one, female, honey-haired and, horticulturally speaking, the apple of her father's eye, snatched the ear-phones from her head and swiftly replaced them in the bottom drawer of her desk in the anteroom, the drawer serving as the receiving end of the detectograph apparatus in the Inspector's very modern office. An instant later the Inspector's door opened and the tall bundled man with the blue glasses and impossible beard appeared. He did not seem to see Patience, which was a pity, and indeed seemed intent only on one course: to remove his glasses, his beard, and his incredible self from the premises of the Thumm Detective Agency with the greatest expedition. The outer door snicked shut behind him and on the instant Patience, who was possessed of fewer moral scruples than most females—after all, *she* had given no promise!—sped to the door and peeped out just in time to see one prong of the wonderful beard whip around a corner of the corridor as its wearer, disdaining the elevator, fled down the emergency stairs. Patience wasted three precious seconds sucking at her lower lip; and then she shook her head, virtue having triumphed, and hurried back into the anteroom. She burst into her father's sanctum, her blue eyes warm with excitement.

Inspector Thumm, still dazed, sat limply at his desk, in one hand the long manila envelope and in the other the thousand-dollar bill.

"Pat," he said hoarsely. "Pat, did you see that? Did you hear that? Is he shovin' the queer? Am I crazy, or is he, or what?"

"Oh, father," she cried, "don't be an *idiot*." She seized the envelope, her eyes dancing. Her fingers pressed it, and something crackled inside. "Hmm. There's another envelope inside this one. Not the same shape, either. It seems squarish, father dear. I wonder——"

"Oh, no you don't," said the Inspector hastily, taking the envelope from her. "I've accepted that bird's dough, remember. Pat, it's ten C's, a grand!"

"I think you're mean," complained Patience. "I can't imagine what——"

"Listen, dovey, this means a new dress for you, and that's *all*." The Inspector grunted and tucked the envelope into the remotest corner of his office safe. He swung the steel door shut and returned to his desk, where he sat down and wiped his damp brow.

"Should have let me kick him out," he muttered. "I never saw such a loony business. And I would have, too, if you hadn't buzzed me on the communicator. Cripes, if a guy put this interview in a book, nobody'd believe it!"

Patience's eyes were dreamy. "It's a lovely case. Lovely!"

"For an alienist," grumbled the Inspector. "If not for that grand, I'd——"

"No! He's—oh, he's *quaint*. I never imagined a grown person with unaddled brains—he's *not* a maniac, father!—could dress himself up like someone out of a fairy tale and . . . I suppose you were properly impressed with the beard?" said Patience suddenly.

"Beard! More like dyed wool."

"A work of art. Whimsical art. Those cunning ringlets! No, there's something decidedly queer about this," murmured Patience. "I can understand a man feeling the necessity of disguising himself——"

"So you saw that, too? It was a phony, all right," said the Inspector glumly. "But the queerest phony *I* ever saw."

"No question about it. And the beard, the glasses, the heavy clothes—all meant to conceal his true appearance. But why the *colors* in the beard, father?"

"He's a nut, I tell you. A green and blue beard!"

"Is it possible he meant to convey something? . . ." Patience sighed. "But that's preposterous. Divested of his camouflage he should be a tall, thin man with sharp features, probably middle-aged, with a twangy voice——"

"Disguised his voice, too," muttered the Inspector. "But you're right. There *was* a nosey quality about it. But he's not a Down-East Yank, Patty. Not that kind of twang."

"Of course not. Surely you got it? He's English, father."

The Inspector slapped his thigh. "By God, Pat, that's right!"

"He couldn't conceal it," said Patience, frowning. "And some of his locutions were British, too. His accent was Oxford rather than Cambridge. And then he tripped up on your salty synonyms for 'dollars,' although that may have been deliberate." She shrugged. "I don't think there's any doubt about his being a man of culture. There was something even professorish about him, don't you think?"

"Something *screwy* about him," growled Thumm. He stuck a cigar into his mouth and scowled at his daughter. "But there's one thing he said," he went on in a quieter voice, "that bothers me. If he shouldn't call up on the twentieth and we have to open the envelope, we've got to call in old Drury for the unveiling. In the name of little Cæsar, *why?*"

"Yes, why?" repeated Patience oddly. "I should say that's the most significant feature of your man's visit."

They sat in silence, staring thoughtfully at each other. The extraordinary parting request of the disguised Englishman overshadowed the other mysteries. Mr. Drury Lane, while a colorful figure, was the least mysterious old gentleman in the world. Over seventy, for more than a dozen years retired from the stage, he lived the secluded life of the opulent and aging artist in upper Westchester on an estate of broad acreage, its castle and gardens and little manorial village all charming reproductions of Elizabethan England, which he loved. The Hamlet, as he called his estate, was fit setting for the man. In a past generation Drury Lane had been the world's most distinguished Shakespearean actor. At sixty, in the full vigor of his incredible career, he had suddenly and tragically been stricken stone-deaf. Philosophically, for he was supremely sane, he had set about learning to read lips—an art in which he became remarkably proficient—and had retired to The Hamlet to live on the income of his vast personal fortune and to provide a refuge for outcasts of his own profession and indigent members of the allied arts. The Hamlet became a shrine of learning; its theater a laboratory for the experimental drama; and its library of Elizabethan folios and Shakespeareana the Mecca of ambitious scholars. Purely as a hobby, the grand old man of the stage had turned his sharp restless intelligence to the investigation of crime. It was in pursuit of this hobby that he met Inspector Thumm, then in active service in the Detective Bureau of the New York Police Department, and their odd friendship sprang up. They had co-operated effectively in numerous murder investigations both before and after Thumm's retirement from the Department to open a private detective agency. And then they had been joined by Thumm's daughter Patience who, returning to the land of her birth after an adolescence spent in wandering about Europe with a chaperon, had at once and with characteristic zest plunged into a practical detective alliance with her father and the old actor.

The eyes of the Thumms were troubled. What connection could exist between their mysterious, faintly raffish visitor with his Oppenheimish insinuations of a secret worth millions and their deaf, ailing—Lane had of late years succumbed to the ills of aged flesh—upright, dearly beloved, and brilliant old friend?

"Shall I write him?" murmured Patience.

The Inspector flung his cigar away in distaste. "I wouldn't. Patty, I tell you this whole business is cock-eyed. Old Drury's connection with us is pretty common knowledge, and this funny galoot with the phony chin-whiskers may be just using Lane's name to impress us. That bird's playing a deep game! No sense in bothering Lane about it now. We've got till the twentieth. I tell you, kid, on the twentieth Whiskers *won't* call up—doesn't intend to call up. He *wants* us to open that envelope. Something's primed, and I don't like the smell of it. . . . Time enough to let Lane in on it."

"As you say," said Patience meekly; but her eyes wandered to the locked door of the safe, and a deep pucker appeared between her brows.

As it turned out, the Inspector was a poor and therefore bitterly astonished prophet. Promptly at noon on the twentieth of May, Thumm's telephone rang. A slightly rusty English voice said: "Inspector Thumm?"

"Yeah?"

Patience, listening on the extension telephone, felt her heart leap.

"This is the man from Nowhere. Millions!" said the rusty English voice; there was a chuckle from the other end of the wire and, before the Inspector could recover from his stupefaction, there was a click and the line went dead.

1

The Man in the Blue Hat

On the twenty-eighth of May, which was a Tuesday, Miss Patience Thumm, whose office hours were elastic, entered the anteroom of the Thumm Detective Agency at a few minutes of ten, smiled cheerily at the sad, moon-eyed Miss Brodie, the agency's official stenographer, and burst into the inner sanctum to find her father listening intently to the heavy earnest tones of a visitor.

"Ah, Patty," said the Inspector. "Glad you came so early. This is Mr. George Fisher and he's got an interesting little story. My daughter, Fisher. Sort of her father's keeper," he chuckled. "The brains of this outfit, so you'd better spill it to her."

The visitor scraped his chair back and rose awkwardly, fumbling with his cap. It was a visored cap with a soft crown; a small enameled plate above the visor said: *Rivoli Bus Company*. He was a tall, broad, pleasant-looking young man with unholy red hair; a smart uniform of blue-gray fitted his bulky figure snugly; his chest was bisected obliquely by a black strap which met his broad belt at the waist; and his stout calves were encased in leather.

"Pleased to meet you, Miss Thumm," he mumbled. "Ain't much of a case——"

"Do sit down, Mr. Fisher," said Patience with the smile she reserved exclusively for good-looking young clients. "What's the trouble?"

"Well, I was just givin' the Inspector an earful," said Fisher, his own ears reddening. "Don't know if it's anything, y'see. But it might be. This bird Donoghue's my pal, see, and——"

"Whoa," said the Inspector. "We'd better start at the beginning, Fisher. Fisher drives one of those big sightseeing buses that park around Times Square, Patty. Rivoli Bus Company. He's worried about a friend of his; and the reason he's come to see us is because this friend, fellow by the name of Donoghue, often mentioned my name to him. Donoghue's an ex-cop; I seem to remember him as a nice husky old boy, good record on the force."

19

"Is Donoghue employed by your company, too?" Patience asked, inwardly sighing at the prosaic beginning of the story.

"No, ma'am. He retired from the force about five years ago an' took a job as special guard at that museum on Fifth an' Sixty-Fifth—the Britannic." Patience nodded; the Britannic Museum was a small but highly esteemed institution for the preservation and exhibition of old English manuscripts and books. She had visited it several times in the company of Mr. Drury Lane, who was one of its patrons. "Donoghue an' my old man were together in harness, see, an' I've known him all my life, ma'am."

"And something's happened to him?"

Fisher fumbled with his cap. "He's—ma'am, he's disappeared!"

"Ah," said Patience. "Well, father, that seems to be more in *your* line. When a staid and respectable gentleman of past middle age vanishes it's generally a woman, isn't it?"

"Oh, no, ma'am," said the bus-driver, "not Donoghue!"

"Have you notified the Missing Persons Bureau?"

"No, ma'am. I—I didn't know if I'd ought to. Old Donoghue would be sorer'n a pup if I raised a fuss for no good reason. Y'see, Miss Thumm," said Fisher earnestly, "it may be nothin'. I don't know. But it looked damned funny to me."

"And it *is* funny," said the Inspector. "Queer set-up, Pat. Go ahead and tell Miss Thumm what you told me, Fisher."

Fisher told a strange tale. A party of schoolteachers from Indianapolis, in New York on a combined group vacation and educational tour, had chartered one of the Rivoli Bus Company's mammoth machines to conduct them about the city on an itinerary arranged by mail in advance of their visit. Fisher had been told off to drive the party about the city on the previous day, Monday. They had embarked promptly at noon from the company's starting-point, Forty-Fourth Street off Broadway. The last destination on the day's itinerary had been the Britannic Museum. The museum was not on the bus company's regular sightseeing route for obvious reasons: it was a distinctly "highbrow joint," remarked Fisher without rancor, and most sightseers were content with viewing Chinatown, the Empire State Building, the Metropolitan Museum of Art (from its classic exterior), Radio City, the East Side, and Grant's Tomb. However, the party of visiting schoolteachers was not composed of the usual sightseers; they were teachers of Fine Arts and English in the hinterland and, in Fisher's unadmiring proletarian phrase, were "a bunch of highbrows." Inspection of the famous Britannic Museum had long been contemplated by the visiting æsthetes as one of the features of their New York tour. At first it had seemed as if they would be doomed to disappointment; for the museum for several weeks past had been shut down pending extensive repairs and alterations of the interior, and indeed was not scheduled to be reopened to the public for at least two months to come. But finally the curator and the Board of Directors of the Britannic had granted special permission for the party to visit the museum during its restricted stay in the city.

"Now here's the funny part, Miss Thumm," said Fisher slowly. "I counted 'em as they climbed into my bus—didn't have to, because on a special like this the bus-starter takes care of the arrangements and all I have to do is drive; but I counted 'em out of habit, I guess, and there were nineteen of 'em. Nineteen men and women. . . ."

"How many of each?" asked Patience, her blue eyes kindling.

"Can't say, ma'am. So there were nineteen when we started from our terminal. And what do you think?"

Patience laughed. "I haven't the faintest of brainstorms, Mr. Fisher. What do *you* think?"

"Plenty," said the bus-driver grimly. "When we gets back to the terminal, see, late afternoon—company rule always to start and finish at the Forty-Fourth Street station, ma'am—when we gets back there and my passengers start gettin' out, I counts 'em again and by God if there wasn't only *eighteen!*"

"I see," said Patience. "Very odd, to be sure. But what has that to do with the disappearance of your friend Donoghue?"

"His friend Donoghue," drawled the Inspector, "comes in later. You notice the plot's thickening. Go on, Fisher." He stared out of the window at the gray walls of Times Square.

"Who was missing?" asked Patience. "Did you check up with the party?"

"No, ma'am. It all happened so fast. But in thinkin' it over I thought I knew who the bird was that hadn't come back with me," replied Fisher, hunching his big torso forward. "I'd noticed him on the trip up because he was a queer-lookin' duck. Sort of middle-aged, and he wore a big bushy gray mustache—the kind you see in the movies. Regular soup-strainer. Tall gent. And he wore a funny hat, too—kind of blue color. He'd kept to himself all day, now that I came to think of it—didn't pal with the others or talk to 'em. And now he was missing—hadn't been on the return trip with us."

"Queer, hey?" said the Inspector.

"Very," said Patience. "And what about Donoghue, Mr. Fisher? I still fail to see the connection."

"Well, ma'am, it was this way. When we got to the Britannic, I turned my passengers over to Dr. Choate——"

"Ah, Dr. Choate," said Patience brightly. "I've met the gentleman. Curator of the museum."

"That's right, ma'am. He took 'em away and started showin' 'em around. My part of the job was done until we were due to go back, so I stopped at the door for a friendly word with Donoghue. Hadn't seen him for a couple of weeks, so we made a date to go to the fights last night at the Garden——"

"The fights, Mr. Fisher?"

Fisher looked puzzled. "Sure, ma'am, the fights, the—the boxin' matches at the Garden. I'm pretty handy with my mitts m'self, see, and I like a good fast bout. . . . Well, anyway, I told Donoghue I'd stop in for him last night after supper. He's a bachelor, see, an' he lives in a roomin' house downtown in Chelsea. Well, then I went off after my passengers, followed 'em around, and when they were all finished I took them back to the terminal."

"Was Donoghue at the door when you got your party out of the museum?" asked the Inspector thoughtfully.

"No, sir. At least I didn't notice. Well, after work last night I had a bite to eat—I'm a bachelor m'self, ma'am," said Fisher, coloring, "and I called for Donoghue at his roomin' house. But he wasn't there, and his landlady said he hadn't come back from work. I thought maybe somethin' kept him overtime, so I hung around there for an hour. No sign of Donoghue, so I rang up a couple of his pals. They hadn't seen nor heard from him all evenin'. By that time I was gettin' a little scared."

"A big chap like you," murmured Patience, watching him keenly. "And?"

Fisher gulped in a boyish way. "I buzzed the Britannic. Spoke to the caretaker—nightwatchman, ma'am, name o' Burch—an' he told me he'd seen Donoghue beat it out of the museum that afternoon, before my party left an' while I was still there; but Donoghue hadn't come back. I didn't know what to do, so I went to the fights alone."

"Poor boy," said Patience sympathetically, and Fisher eyed her with suddenly aroused manhood. "And that's all?"

His big shoulders drooped, and the roosterish look went out of his eyes. "That's the whole blamed story, ma'am. This mornin' before I came here I went around to his roomin' house again, but he hadn't been home all night; an' I called the museum an' they told me he hadn't reported for work yet."

"But what," persisted Patience, "has your friend Donoghue's disappearance to do with the missing passenger, Mr. Fisher? I'm afraid I'm a little dull this morning."

Fisher's big jaw hardened. "That's what I don't know. But," he went on in a stubborn tone, "this bird with the blue shappo disappears, an' Donoghue disappears around the same time, an' I can't help feelin' there's a connection somewhere." Patience nodded thoughtfully. "The reason I come here, like I said before, ma'am," continued Fisher in a heavy tone, "is that if I went to the police Donoghue might get sore. He's no trustin' babe, Miss Thumm; he can handle himself. But—well, damn it, I'm worried about him and I thought I'd ask the Inspector sort of for old time's sake to try an' find out what happened to that thick Irishman."

"Well, Inspector," murmured Patience, "and can you resist such an appeal to your vanity?"

"Guess not," grinned her father. "No dough in it, Fisher, and times are hard, but I s'pose we can scout around a bit."

Fisher's boyish face lightened magically. "Swell!" he cried. "That's real swell of you, Inspector."

"Well, then," said Thumm in brisk tones, "let's get down to cases. Ever see this man in the blue hat before, Fisher?"

"No, sir. Absolute stranger to me. And what's more," said the bus-driver with a frown, "I'm pretty sure Donoghue hadn't, either."

"How on earth could you know that?" asked Patience, astonished.

"Well, when I came into the museum with my nineteen chickadees, Donoghue got a good look at the lot, one by one. He didn't say anything to me about knowin' any of 'em, and he would have if he'd recognized one."

"Doesn't exactly follow," remarked the Inspector dryly, "but I imagine it's true just the same. Suppose you give me a description of Donoghue. I don't remember him any too well —haven't seen him in about ten years."

"Husky build, about a hundred and seventy-five," replied Fisher rapidly, "stands around five foot ten, sixty years old, strong as a bull, red Irish pan on him with a bullet-scar on his right cheek—you'd remember that, Inspector, I guess; couldn't ever forget it if you spotted it even once—walks like a slouch, sort of . . ."

"Swaggers?" suggested Patience.

"That's it! Gray hair now and damn' sharp gray eyes."

"Good boy," said the Inspector approvingly. "You'd have made a swell cop, Fisher. I remember now. Does he still smoke that stinkin' old clay pipe of his? That was one of his worst vices, I recall."

"Sure does," said Fisher with a grin. "When he's off duty. I forgot that."

"Fine." The Inspector rose abruptly. "You go back to your job, Fisher, and leave this to me. I'll look into it and if I find anything screwy about it I'll turn it over to the police. It's really a police job."

"Thanks, Inspector, thanks," said the bus-driver, and bowing jerkily to Patience he pounded out of the office, causing Miss Brodie's heart as he passed her in the anteroom to beat quite rapidly in maidenly tribute to his muscular bigness.

"Nice lad," murmured Patience, "if a little on the uncouth side. Did you notice those shoulders, father dear? What a line-bucker he would have made if he'd cut his teeth on a Latin book instead of an emergency brake!"

Inspector Thumm sniffed mightily through his smashed nose, hunched his own wide shoulders, and consulted a telephone directory. He dialed a number. " 'Lo! Rivoli Bus Company? This is Thumm speaking, of the Thumm Detective Agency. You the manager? . . . Oh, you are. What's the name? . . . What? Oh, Theofel. Say, listen, Mr. Theofel, have you got a wheel-wrestler on your payroll by the name of George Fisher?"

"Yes," said a slightly alarmed voice. "Is anything the matter?"

"No, no," said the Inspector genially. "I'm just askin', that's all. Is he a big lad with red hair and an honest map?"

"Why, yes, yes. One of our best drivers. I'm sure nothing——"

"Sure, sure. I just wanted to check up, that's all. Say, he took out a party of hick schoolteachers yesterday. Can you tell me where they're stoppin' in the city?"

"Certainly. The Park Hill, off the Plaza. Are you sure there isn't—?"

"Goo'by," said the Inspector, and hung up. He rose and reached for his topcoat. "Put some powder on your nose, kid. We've got a date with the intell—intell——"

"Intelligentsia," sighed Patience.

2

The 17 Schoolteachers

The intelligentsia proved to be a group of assorted ladies and gentlemen, none of whom was under forty; they were predominantly female, with an awkward scattering of dry and dusty males; and they sat along a festive breakfast board in the main dining-room of the Park Hill twittering and chirping like a flock of sparrows on the first leafy bough of spring.

It was late morning and except for the teachers' party the dining-room was empty. The *maître d'hôtel* indicated the ladies and gentlemen of the sabbatical ensemble with a negligent thumb. Inspector Thumm, unawed, stamped into the *salle à manger* (the Park Hill had Gallic pretensions in addition to its French *cuisine*) and plowed his way through the underbrush of gleaming idle tables followed by a faintly giggling Patience.

At the Inspector's formidable approach the twittering wavered suddenly, peeped a little, and then stopped altogether. A host of startled eyes—the glass-protected mournful eyes of tutorship—swung like a trained battery to observe the intruders. The Inspector's visage had never been one to inspire sweet trust in the hearts of little children and shy self-conscious adults; it was big and red and hard and massively bony, and its well-smashed proboscis added a slightly sinister note.

"You the schoolteachers from Indiana?" growled Thumm.

A tremor of apprehension shivered down the board; elderly maiden ladies groped for their bosoms and the men began to lick their dignified lips.

A fat-faced man of fifty, painfully dressed—apparently the Beau Brummel and spokesman of the group—scraped his chair back from the head of the table and half-stood up, twisting about and clutching the back of the chair. He was quite pale.

"Yes?" he quavered.

"I'm Inspector Thumm," said Thumm in the same savage growl; and for a moment Patience, half-hidden behind her father's broad back, thought there would be a general swooning of females.

"Police!" gasped the spokesman. "Police! What have we done?"

The Inspector swallowed a grin. If the fat gentleman chose to leap to the conclusion that "Inspector" was synonymous with "police," so much the better. "That's what I'm here to find out," said the Inspector sternly. "You all present and accounted for?"

The man's eyes wavered down the table dazedly; they returned, round and large as quarters, to the Inspector's forbidding face. "Why—uh, yes, certainly."

"Nobody missing?"

"Missing?" echoed the spokesman blankly. "Of course not. Why should there be?"

Necks strained back and forth; two ladies with gaunt scarified features uttered horrified little noises.

"Just askin'," said the Inspector. His cold eyes swept up and down the board, beheading glances like a scythe. "You people took a little joy-ride in a Rivoli bus yesterday afternoon?"

"That's right, sir. Yes, indeed!"

"You all went along?"

"Oh, yes!"

"You all came back?"

The obese gentleman sank into his chair, as if overwhelmed by the suddenness with which tragedy had struck. "I—I think so," he whispered piteously. "Mr. F-Frick, didn't we all come back?" Thus appealed to, a thin little man with a high starched collar and watery brown eyes gripped the cloth with a start, looked all about as if for consolation, and mumbled: "Yes. Yes, Mr. Onderdonk. We did indeed."

"Now, now," said the Inspector. "Come, boys, you're shieldin' somebody. Who's missing?"

"It's barely possible," murmured Patience in the appalled and palpitating silence which instantly fell, "that these good people are telling the truth, father."

Thumm winked in ferocious prohibition at his daughter, but she smiled sweetly and continued: "You see, father, I've been counting them."

"Well?" he snapped, and ran his eye swiftly down the table.

"There are *seventeen*."

"What the devil have we run into?" muttered the Inspector, forgetting momentarily his role of ogre as he verified this startling intelligence. "Fisher said nineteen. . . . Here, you," he bellowed in the spokesman's ear, "were you *always* seventeen?"

Mr. Onderdonk could only nod, although he swallowed bravely.

"Hey, waiter!" roared Thumm across the dining-room to the *maître d'hôtel*. The *maître d'hôtel* looked up, startled, from a menu he was studying. "Come here, you!"

The *maître d'hôtel* stiffened. He eyed the Inspector with disfavor. Then he stalked over like an annoyed grenadier.

"Yes?" he said with a musical hiss.

"Look this bunch over." The *maître d'hôtel* complied with a bored inclination of his elegant head. "Is this the whole party?"

"Mais oui, m'sieu'."

"Talk United States," said the Inspector disagreeably. "Seventeen right?"

"Seventeen is the precise number, *m'sieu'*."

"They've been seventeen since they checked in?"

"Ha," said the *maître d'hôtel*, lifting a sleek eyebrow. *"Un gendarme.* I think I shall summon here the manager."

"Answer my question, you idiot!"

"Seventeen," said the *maître d'hôtel* firmly. He turned to the quaking ladies and gentlemen about the no longer festive board. "Compose yourselves, *mesdames*. I assure you this is a trifle, a nothing; something of a surety mistaken." *Mesdames* and *messieurs* uttered little cautious sighs of relief. He faced Inspector Thumm with the brave dignity of a weary shepherd feeling the responsibility of his duty. "Please to be very brief, *m'sieu'*. This is most indecorous. We cannot permit our guests——"

"Listen, Lafayette!" howled Thumm, beside himself with rage, as he gripped the impeccable lapel of the *maître d'hôtel*. "How long have these people been stoppin' here?"

The *maître d'hôtel's* body gave an outraged little wriggle, and then froze with horror. The ladies of the party paled, and the gentlemen rose nervously and whispered to one another. Patience's pert little face went through a series of contortions.

"S-since Friday," said the *maître d'hôtel* with a gulp.

"That's better," grunted the Inspector, releasing the crushed lapel. "Beat it, you."

The *maître d'hôtel* fled.

"Now let's talk this over," continued the ogre, dropping into the spokesman's vacated chair. "Take a seat, Patty; this looks like an all-day job. God, what slugs! Here, you, did you count your people when you got into the bus yesterday noon?"

The spokesman, thus perilously addressed, said with haste: "No, sir, I did not. I'm really sorry— You see, we didn't think —I can't understand——"

"All right, all right," said the Inspector in a gentler tone. "I'm not going to bite you. I'm just looking for information. I'll tell you what I want to know. You people say there are seventeen in your party. You were seventeen when you left Bohunkus, or wherever you come from; you were seventeen when you landed in New York; you were seventeen when you checked into this dump; you've been seventeen on your jaunts around the city. Right so far?"

There was a unanimous nodding of heads, executed with rapidity.

"That is," continued Thumm thoughtfully, "up to noon yesterday. You'd chartered a bus to take you around. You went over to the Forty-Fourth Street and Broadway terminal of the Rivoli company, and you got into your bus. Were you seventeen on the way to the terminal?"

"I—I don't know," said the spokesman helplessly. "I really don't."

"All right, then. But one thing is sure. When that bus started out there were *nineteen* people in it. How do you account for that?"

"Nineteen!" exclaimed a stout middle-aged lady with *pince-nez* glasses. "Well, I noticed— I *wondered* what that man was doing there!"

"What man?" snapped the Inspector; and Patience dropped the spoon she had been toying with and sat very still, watching the mingled triumph and perplexity on the stout lady's face.

"What man, Miss Ruddy?" echoed the spokesman, frowning.

"Why, the man in that *outlandish* blue hat! Didn't any of you notice him? Martha, I believe I mentioned him to you before the bus started. Don't you remember?"

The bony virgin named Martha gasped: "Yes, that's right!"

Patience and the Inspector looked at each other. It was true, then. George Fisher's story had been based on verifiable facts.

"Do you recall, Miss—er—Ruddy," asked Patience with a winning smile, "other details of this man's appearance?"

Miss Ruddy beamed. "Indeed I do! He was middle-aged, and he had an *enormous* mustache. Just like Chester Conklin's, in the movies." She blushed. "The comedian, you know. Except that it was gray."

"And when Lavinia—Miss Ruddy pointed him out to me," added the raw-boned lady named Martha excitedly, "I saw that he was tall and thin, too!"

"Anybody else notice him?" demanded the Inspector.

There were blank looks.

"And didn't it occur to you ladies," continued Thumm sarcastically, "that a man you didn't know had no right being in your privately chartered bus?"

"Oh, it did," faltered Miss Ruddy, "but I didn't know what to do. I thought he might have had something to do with the bus company, you see."

The Inspector rolled his eyes ceilingward. "Did you notice this bird on the return trip?"

"No," said Miss Ruddy in a trembling voice. "No, I looked especially. But he wasn't with us."

"Fine. Now we're getting somewhere. But," said the Inspector with a grim smile, "that only makes eighteen. And we know there were nineteen of you yesterday in that bus. Come on now, folks, think hard. I'm sure somebody here must have noticed the nineteenth person."

"I believe," murmured Patience, "that that charming lady at the end of the table remembers something. I've seen a speech trembling on her lips for the past two minutes."

The charming lady gulped. "I—I was only going to say," she quavered, "that I *did* notice somebody else who—who didn't belong. Not the man in the blue hat. A different man——"

"Oh, a man, hey?" said the Inspector quickly. "What did he look like, madam?"

"He—he . . ." and she stopped. "I think he was tall."

"Oh!" gasped an Amazonian woman with a wart on her nose. "Miss Starbuck, that's *wrong!*"

The charming lady sniffed. "Perhaps it is, but *I* saw him and——"

"Why, I noticed him, too!" cried the Amazon. "And I'm sure he was rather stocky!"

Light dawned in several pairs of eyes. "I remember now," volunteered a chubby gentleman with a bald head. "Yes, indeed. I'm positive he was small and thin and—er—fortyish."

"Nonsense!" said the Amazon sharply. "You've always had a notoriously poor memory, Mr. Scott. I distinctly recall—"

"Now that I come to think of it," ventured a little old lady timidly, "I believe I saw him, too. He was a tall stout young man——"

"Time, time," said the Inspector wearily. "We'll never get anywhere this way. It's pretty evident none of you knows what this nineteenth bird looked like. But do any of you remember if he made the return trip to the bus terminal with you?"

"I do," said Miss Starbuck instantly. "I'm *positive* he came back with us. He got off just in front of me. After that I didn't see him any more." And the charming lady glared at the Amazon as if daring her to contradict *that* statement.

But no one did. Inspector Thumm scraped his jaw in noisy meditativeness. "All right," he said finally. "At least we know where we stand. Suppose I delegate you—what's your name again—?"

"Onderdonk. Luther Onderdonk," said the spokesman eagerly.

"Suppose I delegate you, Mr. Onderdonk, to keep in touch with me for your party in case anything turns up. For instance, if any of you should see either of the two men who were on the bus with you yesterday, tell Mr. Onderdonk and he'll call me at my office." He dropped his card on the cloth and the spokesman picked it up with cautious fingers. "Keep your eyes open, all of you."

"You'll be acting as detectives," said Patience brightly. "I'm sure it will prove the most exciting part of your stay in New York."

The seventeen Indiana schoolteachers beamed as one.

"Yeah, but don't go messin' around," growled the Inspector. "Just sit tight and watch. How long you staying in the city?"

"We were scheduled to leave for home," said Mr. Onderdonk with an apologetic cough, "on Friday."

"Week's vacation, hey? Well, before you check out here, be sure and give me a ring, anyway."

"I shall most certainly do that, Inspector Thumm," said Mr. Onderdonk earnestly. "I really shall."

The Inspector stamped out of the Park Hill's *salle à manger* followed meekly by Patience, scowled fiercely at a pale and deflated *maître d'hôtel* in the foyer, and led the way through the lobby to the Plaza.

Patience's meekness vanished. "I think you're horrid, father —frightening those people that way. The poor things were scared half to death. They're like a group of children."

Unexpectedly, the Inspector chuckled. He winked at an ancient cabby drowsing at the curb above a patient old nag. "Technique, kid, technique! With a woman it's just a matter of turning on the big baby lamps and smiling. But when a man wants something he's got to holler louder and make worse faces than the next guy, or else he doesn't get anywhere. I've always felt sorry for the little skinny guys."

"How about Napoleon?" said Patience, linking her arm with her father's.

"Don't tell me he didn't have a loud voice! Listen, sweetheart, I've got those poor old schoolmarms eatin' out of my hand."

"You'll be bitten one of these days," predicted Patience darkly.

The Inspector grinned. "Hey, taxi!"

3

The 19th Man

The taxicab deposited them precariously in a clutter of monster buses lined up at the curb on the south side of Forty-Fourth Street near Broadway. They were vast gleaming machines decorated whimsically in a motif of pink and blue, like acromegalic infants primped out by a sentimental mother. Their nurses, to a man young stalwarts attired in smart blue-gray uniforms, sleek-calved and military, lounged on the sidewalk outside a little pink-and-blue booth, smoking and talking.

Patience stood waiting on the sidewalk before the booth while the Inspector paid off the taxicab driver, and she was not unconscious of the frank admiration in the eyes of the young men in uniform.

Apparently she pleased one of them considerably, a blond-haired giant, for he tipped his cap forward over his eyes, strolled over, and said pleasantly: " 'Lo, babe. Hahzzit?"

"At the moment," said Patience, smiling, "uncomfortable."

He stared. A young brute with red hair gaped at her, and then turned angrily upon the blond giant. "Lay off, you," he growled, "or I'll clip you one. This lady——"

"Why, Mr. Fisher!" exclaimed Patience. "How gallant! I'm sure your friend meant no—er—disrespect. Did you, you big male Venus?" Her eyes twinkled.

The giant's mouth fell open; after a moment he blushed. "Sure not, ma'am." And he effaced himself in the group of bus-drivers, who broke into guffaws.

George Fisher removed his cap. "Don't mind these guys, Miss Thumm. Just a bunch of wisecrackin' gorillas. . . . Hullo, Inspector."

"Hello yourself," said the Inspector shortly. His shrewd eyes swept the crowd of young men. "What's been going on here? Hey, Patty? One of these pups been gettin' fresh?"

The young men became very silent.

"No, no," said Patience hastily. "How nice to see you again so soon, Mr. Fisher!"

"Yeah," grinned Fisher. "Waitin' for my call. I uh——"

"Hrrmph!" said the Inspector. "Any news, bub?"

"No, sir, not a thing. Been callin' Donoghue's roomin' house and the museum ever since I left your office. No sign of that thickheaded old Mick, blast him!"

"Seems to me those museum people ought to be getting kind of worried," muttered the Inspector. "How'd they sound, Fisher?"

Fisher shrugged. "I only talked to the caretaker, Inspector."

Thumm nodded. He took a cigar from his breast pocket and casually bit off one end. As he did so he permitted his eyes to travel from one face to another before him. The drivers continued to preserve a discreet silence; the blond giant had slunk to the rear of the group. They seemed a rough honest lot. Thumm spat the snip of tobacco on the sidewalk, looked directly in the open pink-and-blue booth, and met the eyes of the man who stood in there clutching a telephone. The man looked quickly away; he was a white-haired, red-faced customer in the same uniform as the others, but the inscription above the visor of his cap displayed in addition to *Rivoli Bus Company* the word *Starter*.

"Well, maybe we'll find out something," said the Inspector with sudden geniality. "Keep your shirt on, Fisher. Come along, sis."

They stepped by the silent group into the doorway of one of the disreputable old structures with which the Times Square section is infested, and mounted a flight of creaking black stairs. At the top they came to a glass door inscribed:

J. Theofel
Manager
RIVOLI BUS COMPANY

The Inspector knocked, a man called: "Come in!" and they entered a small dusty office illuminated by the rays of the typically feeble New York sun which crept in through a high-barred window.

J. Theofel proved to be an oldish young man with deep lines incised in his face. "Yes?" he said sharply, looking up from a chart. His eyes lingered over Patience, and then turned upon the Inspector.

"Name's Thumm," growled the Inspector. "Miss Thumm. I'm the guy called you this morning about Fisher."

"Oh," said Theofel slowly, leaning back. "Sit down, Miss Thumm. Just what's the trouble, Inspector? I'm afraid I didn't get it straight this morning over the 'phone."

"No trouble. Not even a case." Thumm stared hard. "How'd you know I'm an Inspector?"

Theofel smiled briefly. "I'm not as young as I look. I remember the time when your picture was in the paper darned near every day."

"Oh," said Thumm. "Cigar?" Theofel shook his head. "Well," continued Thumm, seating himself with an expansive grunt, "we're just looking into something that smells a little rotten. Tell me, Mr. Theofel. Who arranged for the rental of a bus for that party of schoolteachers from Indiana?"

The manager blinked. "I believe— Here, I'll make sure." He rose, rummaged in a bulging file, and picked out a memorandum. "I thought so. Gentleman by the name of Onderdonk. Seemed to be acting as manager of the party. He wrote us a letter a couple of weeks ago and on Friday 'phoned me from the Park Hill Hotel."

"To arrange for yesterday's tour?" asked Patience, frowning.

"Not exactly, Miss Thumm. That was only part of it. He wanted us to give his party bus service for the entire week they were in town."

"So they went out Saturday and Sunday, too?" demanded Thumm.

"Oh, yes. And they'll be going out today and tomorrow and the rest of the week as well. Quite an itinerary. Little unusual, in fact. We gave them a special rate, of course."

"Hmm. There were seventeen from the beginning, hey?"

"Seventeen? That's right."

"No more than seventeen went Saturday or Sunday?"

Theofel stared at him. Then he said grimly: "No more were supposed to go, if that's what you're driving at. Wait a minute." He picked up one of the several telephones at his elbow; apparently it was a private line that did not go through the central exchange, for he said at once: "Barbey. Send Shalleck and Brown up here." He replaced the receiver, slowly.

"Barbey," said the Inspector. "The starter, hey?"

"Yes."

"I see," said the Inspector, and applied a match to his cigar.

The door opened and two of the stalwarts in uniform marched in.

"Brown," said Theofel sternly to the first, "you took out that Park Hill schoolteacher crowd on Saturday. Count 'em?"

Brown looked startled. "Sure. Seventeen, Mr. Theofel."

The manager gave him a sharp glance, and then turned to his companion. "You, Shalleck?"

"Seventeen, Chief."

"You're positive, now, both of you?"

They nodded confidently.

"All right, men."

They turned to go. "Just a minute," said the Inspector pleasantly. "I think you'd better send that starter Barbey up here when you get downstairs, boys."

The manager nodded at the men's inquiring looks. "You think—=?" he began fretfully when the door had closed upon the two men.

"I know," grinned the Inspector. "You let me handle him, Mr. Theofel. This is my meat." He rubbed his hands and looked sidewise at Patience, who was frowning. Thumm had never quite conquered the colossal wonder of paternity; for fatherhood had struck home to him late in life when his daughter returned from abroad after an absence which had extended from pigtails to shaven eyebrows. But on this occasion his mute appeal for approval went unheeded; Patience was cogitating upon a multitude of things, and feeding her massive father's vanity was not among them. The Inspector sighed.

The door opened and the white-haired man of the downstairs booth appeared. His lips were rather tighter than they should have been, and he ignored the presence of the Thumms pointedly.

"Want me, Mr. Theofel?" he said gruffly.

The Inspector said in the calm magisterial tone of the professional policeman: "Spill it, Barbey."

The man's head turned unwillingly, and he blinked once at Thumm and then shifted his gaze. "What—I don't get you, mister."

"Inspector to you," said Thumm, hooking his thumbs in the armholes of his vest. "Come on, Barbey. I've got you with the goods, so there's no sense in stalling."

Barbey looked about quickly, licked his lips, and stammered: "I guess I'm dumb. What goods? What d'ye mean?"

"Bribery," said the Inspector with a vast unsympathy.

The starter went white in a slow ebbing of facial blood. His big flabby hands twitched feebly. "How—how'd you find out?"

Patience expelled her breath in a slow noiseless stream. A rising anger animated Theofel's lined face.

The Inspector smiled. "My business to find out. I'll tell you right now, mister, I'd as soon throw you in the can as not; but Mr. Theofel, now—well, he's inclined not to press the charge if you'll come clean."

"Yes," said the manager hoarsely. "Well, Barbey, you heard the Inspector! Don't stand there like a dumb ox! What's it all about?"

Barbey fumbled with his cap. "I—I got a family. I know it's against the company rules. But the dough looked sort of—tempting. When this first guy come over I was going to tell him nothing doing——"

"Guy with a soup-strainer and a blue hat, eh?" snapped Thumm.

"Yes, sir! I'm going to tell him nothing doing, see, but he shows me the corner of a ten-spot," faltered Barbey, "and so I says okay. I let him climb in with the rest. Then about a minute later up comes another guy, and he gives me the same proposition as the first one. Wants me to let him go with Fisher's bus. So, well, I'd let the first one on, so I thought while I was doin' it I might's well get the benefit of another five-spot. He gives me a fin, see. So this second guy, he climbs in, and that's all I know."

"Was Fisher in on this?" asked Theofel harshly.

"No, Mr. Theofel. He didn't know anything about it."

"What did the second bird look like?" asked the Inspector.

"Greaseball, Chief. Face like a rat. Black. Eyetalian, I'd say. Dressed sporty, like the bunch that hangs around the

Palace. Flashed a funny kind of ring on his left hand—he was a southpaw, Chief, or at least he handed me the fin with his left——"

"What d'ye mean funny?"

"It had a little horseshoe where you'd expect a rock to be," mumbled Barbey. "Looked like platinum or white gold. And it was set with diamond chips."

"Hmm." The Inspector rubbed his chin. "Never saw this man before, I suppose?"

"No, sir!"

"Know him again if you saw him?"

"Yes, sir!"

"He came back with the crowd of schoolmarms, didn't he, but the bird in the blue hat didn't?"

Barbey's eyes widened at this omniscience. "Why, that's right."

"Swell." The Inspector heaved to his feet, and stuck his hand out across the desk. "Thanks a lot, Mr. Theofel. And don't be too hard on this lad." He winked at the manager, pounded the astonished starter's shoulder in friendly fashion, tucked Patience's gloved hand under his arm, and made for the door.

"The moral of which is," he chuckled as they descended the groaning steps, "always smell trouble when a guy keeps looking at you and then when you look at him looks away. I knew that bird had a finger in this the minute I spotted him in that barber-pole dinky!"

"Oh, father," laughed Patience, "you're the most incorrigible exhibitionist. "What *shall* I do with you? And now——"

The Inspector's face fell. "It's true," he said gloomily, "we haven't made any progress toward finding old Donoghue. . . . All right, Patty," he sighed, "let's pay a visit to that blasted museum."

4

Young Mr. Rowe

The Britannic Museum was housed in a tall narrow four-story edifice squeezed between two severe apartment buildings on Fifth Avenue near Sixty-Fifth Street. Its high bronze door faced the greenery of Central Park and on north and south lay the prim canopies of the apartments.

The Thumms mounted the single stone step and stared at the bronze door. It was austerely decorated in bas-relief; the dominating decoration on each panel of the double-leafed portal was a heroic head of Shakespeare. It looked severely solid —a most unfriendly door. There was no mistaking its attitude, for an equally unfriendly sign hung from the bronze knob, and it stated without equivocation that the Britannic Museum was "closed for repairs."

But the Inspector was made of stern stuff. He closed his right hand and with the resulting fist pounded formidably on the bronze.

"Father!" giggled Patience. "You're walloping Shakespeare!"

The Inspector grinned and redoubled his pounding upon the Bard of Avon's nose. There was a frantic scraping and squealing of bolts; and an instant later out popped the gargoylish head of a bulb-nosed old man.

"Hey!" snapped this apparition. "Can't you read English?"

"One side, brother," said the Inspector cheerfully. "We're in a hurry."

The doorman did not budge; his nose continued to protrude from the crack like a shy lily-bulb. "What d'ye want?" he asked surlily.

"Want to get in, of course!"

"Well, you can't. Closed to the public. Repairs." And the crack began to vanish.

"Hey!" bellowed the Inspector, making a futile effort to prevent its vanishment. "This is—Hey, this is the police!"

There was a ghostly chuckle from behind the head of Shakespeare, and after that silence.

"Well, I'll be damned!" exclaimed the Inspector wrathfully. "Why, the old fool, I'll break his damn' door down!"

Patience leaned against the door, doubled up with laughter. "Oh, father!" she gasped. "You're so funny. That's retribution for having laid irreverent hands on the proboscis of the Immortal Will. . . . I've an idea."

The Inspector grunted.

"And you needn't look so skeptical, you old sorehead. We've a friend in the enemy's camp, haven't we?"

"What d'ye mean?"

"The imperishable Drury! Mr. Lane's one of the patrons of

the Britannic, isn't he? I'm sure a call from him will be open sesame."

"By God, that's right! Patty, you've got your old man's brain. Let's hunt up a 'phone."

They found a public telephone booth in a drug store on Madison Avenue, a block east. The Inspector put in a long-distance call to The Hamlet.

"Hello! This is Thumm speaking. Who's this?"

An incredibly ancient voice squeaked: "Quacey. Hello!" Quacey was an old, old man who had been with Drury Lane for more than forty years; originally his wig-maker, now a pensioned friend.

"Lane around?"

"Mr. Drury's right here, Inspector. He says you are a criminal."

"Guilty. We sure feel ashamed of ourselves. How is the old duck? Listen, you little monkey. Tell Mr. Lane we want a favor of him."

There was a mutter of talk from the other end of the wire. The old actor's deafness, while it did not handicap him in *tête-à-tête* conversation—his lip-reading ability was uncanny—effectually prevented him from conducting telephonic conversations; and Quacey for years had acted as his master's ear.

"He wants to know if it's a case," piped Quacey at last.

"Well, yes. Tell him we're on the trail of something mighty mysterious and we've got to get into the Britannic Museum. But that nut of a caretaker won't let us in. Closed for repairs. Can Lane do anything for us?"

There was a silence, and then Thumm was startled to hear the voice of Lane himself pour into the receiver. Despite his age, the old gentleman's voice still retained the miraculous quality of mellowness and rich flexibility that had made it, at one time, the most famous speaking organ in the world. "Hello, Inspector," said Drury Lane. "You'll have to content yourself with listening for a change," and he chuckled. "As usual, I'm in the throes of a monologue. I hope Patience is well? No, don't answer, you old Masai; it would fall literally on deaf ears. . . . Something up at the Britannic, eh? I can't imagine what it might be, really I can't. It's the most peaceful place in the world. Of course I'll telephone the curator at once. Dr. Choate, you know—Alonzo Choate, a dear friend of mine. I'm sure he's there, but if he's not I'll locate him and by the time you get back to the museum—I take it you're near by—you'll be granted permission to enter." The old gentleman sighed. "Well, good-by, Inspector. I do hope you'll find time—you and Patience, I miss her very much!—to run up to The Hamlet for a visit soon."

There was a little pause, and then a reluctant click.

"Good-by," said Inspector Thumm soberly to the dead wire; and scowled in sheer self-defense as he avoided his daughter's inquiring eye outside the telephone booth.

Shakespeare's beard looked less grim on the return visit to the portals of the Britannic Museum; and indeed the door actually stood ajar. In the doorway, awaiting them, stood a tall elderly man with an elegant goatee *à la mode du sud,* his dark face smiling, teeth shining above the resplendent beard; while behind him, like an apologetic shadow, hovered the bulb-nosed old man who had defended the door.

"Inspector Thumm?" said the bearded man, extending limp fingers. "I'm Alonzo Choate. And this is Miss Thumm! I remember quite well your last visit to our museum with Mr. Lane. Come in, come in! Frightfully sorry about Burch's stupid little mistake. I dare say he won't be so precipitate next time; eh, Burch?" The caretaker muttered something impolite beneath his breath and retreated into a shadow.

"Wasn't any fault of his," said the Inspector handsomely. "Orders are orders. You've heard from old Drury, I guess."

"Yes. His man Quacey just had me on the wire. Don't mind the condition of the Britannic, Miss Thumm," smiled Dr. Choate. "I feel like a conscientious housewife apologizing for the mess in her kitchen to an unexpected visitor. We're going through a long-deferred process of redecoration, you know. General housecleaning. Including your humble servant the curator."

They stepped through a marble vestibule into a small reception room. The reception room smelled pungently of fresh paint; its furniture was collected in the center of the chamber and covered with the strange color-washed shroud that house painters supply in the performance of their duty. Members of the guild crawled about scaffolds swishing damp brushes over walls and ceiling. Looking on sightlessly from niches were the draped busts of the great English literary dead. On the far side of the room stood the grilled door to an elevator.

"I'm not sure I'm charmed, Dr. Choate," remarked Patience, wrinkling her small nose, "at the idea of—er—gilding the lily in this fashion. Wouldn't it have been more reverent to permit the bones of Shakespeare and Jonson and Marlowe to molder undisturbed?"

"And a very good point, too," said the curator. "I was against the idea myself. But we've a progressive Board. We had all we could do to keep them from getting somebody to do a series of modern murals in the Shakespeare Room!" He chuckled and looked at the Inspector sidewise. "Suppose we go to my office? It's right off here and, thank heaven, no brush has touched it yet!"

He led the way across the smeary canvas to a door in an alcove. The wood panel was chastely lettered with his name. He ushered them into a bright large room with a high ceiling and oak-boarded walls comfortably lined with books. A young man reading with absorption in an armchair looked up at their entrance.

"Ah, Rowe," boomed Dr. Choate. "Sorry to disturb you. I want you to meet some friends of Drury Lane's." The young man rose quickly and stood by his chair with a friendly smile. With a slow gesture he removed a pair of horn-rimmed eye-glasses. He was a tall fellow with a pleasant face, now that he had taken off his spectacles; there was something athletic in the cut of his shoulders that belied the tired scholar's look in his hazel eyes. "Miss Thumm, this is Mr. Gordon Rowe, one of the Britannic's most devoted neophytes. Inspector Thumm."

The young man, who had not taken his eyes from Patience, shook hands with the Inspector. "Hello! Doctor, you know what's good for sore eyes, I'll say that for you. Thumm. . . . Hmm. No, I'm afraid I don't approve the name. Completely inappropriate. Let's see, now. . . . Ah, Inspector! Seems to me I've heard of you."

"Thanks," said the Inspector dryly. "Don't let us disturb you, Mr. What's-Your-Name. Maybe we'd better go off somewhere, Dr. Choate, and leave this young feller to his dime novel."

"Father!" cried Patience. "Oh, Mr. Rowe, please don't mind father. You see, he probably resents your slur upon the name of Thumm." Her color ran high, and the young man, quite unruffled by the Inspector's glare, continued to eye her with cool appreciation. "What name *would* you give me, Mr. Rowe?"

"Darling," said Mr. Rowe warmly.

"Patience Darling?"

"Er—just darling."

"Say—" began the Inspector wrathfully.

"Do sit down," said Dr. Choate with a bland smile. "Rowe, for the Lord's sake, behave yourself. Miss Thumm, please." Patience, who found the young man's steady gaze faintly disconcerting while it for some unaccountable reason fluttered a suddenly conscious artery in her wrist, sat down, and the Inspector sat down, and Dr. Choate sat down, and Mr. Rowe remained standing and staring.

"It's a weary wait," said Dr. Choate hurriedly. "They've just barely begun. The painters, I mean. Haven't touched the upper floors."

"Yeah," growled Inspector Thumm. "Now I'll tell you——"

Gordon Rowe sat down, vaguely grinning. "If I'm intruding," he began with cheerfulness.

Inspector Thumm looked hopeful. But Patience, with a charming glance at her father, said to the curator: "Did I understand you to say that you're included in the general housecleaning, Dr. Choate? . . . Do stay, Mr. Rowe."

Dr. Choate leaned back in the swivel-chair behind his long desk and looked about the room. He sighed. "In a manner of speaking. It hasn't been generally announced, but I'm leaving. Retiring. Fifteen years of my life have been spent in this building, and I dare say it's time I thought of myself." He closed his eyes and murmured: "I know precisely what I shall do. I shall purchase a small English cottage I've had my eye on in upper Connecticut, dig in with my books, and lead the life of a hermit-scholar. . . ."

"Swell idea," said the Inspector. "But as I was saying——"

"Charming," murmured Mr. Rowe, still looking at Patience.

"You certainly deserve your rest, from all Mr. Lane has told me about you," said Patience hastily. "When are you leaving, Doctor?"

"I've not decided. You see, we're acquiring a new curator. He's expected in from England on tonight's boat, as a matter of fact; he'll be docking tomorrow morning and then we'll see. It will take some time before he acclimates himself, and of course I shall stay until he can carry on by himself."

"Social visit, Miss Darling?" asked the young man suddenly.

"I always thought America restricted her borrowing from England to paintings and books," said Patience in some confusion. "I take it your incoming curator is something very special in bibliophiles, Dr. Choate. Is he anyone really important?"

The Inspector fidgeted in his chair.

"Oh, he's built up something of a reputation abroad," said Dr. Choate with a delicate wave of his hand. "I shouldn't say he was first rank. He's been director of a small London museum for many years—the Kensington. His name is Sedlar, Hamnet Sedlar. . . ."

"There's solid roast-beef Britain for you!" said the young man with enthusiasm.

"Personally hired by the chairman of our Board of Directors. James Wyeth, you know."

Patience, annoyed with herself for being suddenly unable to meet the young man's admiring glance, raised her slender eyebrows. Wyeth was a titan among the mighty, a cold, cultured Crœsus with a passionate devotion to knowledge.

"And then, too, Sedlar was warmly recommended by Sir John Humphrey-Bond," continued Dr. Choate amiably. "Of course Sir John's endorsement carried weight. He's been England's most distinguished Elizabethan collector for decades, Inspector, as I suppose you know."

The Inspector started. He cleared his throat. "Sure. Sure thing. But what we——"

"Sure you don't mind my staying?" asked Mr. Rowe suddenly. "I'd been hoping somebody would turn up, you know." He laughed and snicked shut the heavy old folio he had been reading. "This is my lucky day."

"Of course not, Mr. Rowe," murmured Patience; her face was a delicate crimson. "Er—Dr. Choate, I spent a good deal of my adolescence in England——"

"Lucky England, too," said the young man reverently.

"—and it's always been my feeling that most cultured Englishmen consider us rather quaint but slightly offensive barbarians. I suppose the inducement to Mr. Sedlar was sufficiently weighty to——?"

Dr. Choate chuckled in his beard. "Wrong, Miss Thumm. The Britannic's finances didn't permit us to offer Dr. Sedlar even as much as he'd been getting in London. But he seemed genuinely enthusiastic at the prospect of joining us here, and he snapped up Mr. Wyeth's offer. I suppose he's like the rest of us—impractical."

"How true," sighed the young man. "Now if I were practical——"

"How curious," smiled Patience. "It doesn't seem the proper British psychology, somehow."

The Inspector coughed very loudly. "Now, Patty," he said in a chiding tone, "Dr. Choate's a busy man and we can't take up his whole day chinning about something that's not our business."

"Oh, now really, Inspector——"

"I'm sure it's a pleasure for an old fossil like Choate," remarked Mr. Rowe warmly, "to converse with as beautiful a creature as your daughter, Inspector——"

A desperate light began to glitter in Thumm's eye. "What we really came for, Dr. Choate," he said, ignoring the young man, "is to find out about Donoghue."

"Donoghue?" The curator seemed puzzled, and glanced at Rowe, who sat forward with bright eyes. "What's the matter with Donoghue?"

"What's the *matter* with Donoghue?" growled the Inspector. "Why, Donoghue's disappeared, that's what's the matter with him!"

The young man's smile faded. "Disappeared?" he said swiftly.

Dr. Choate frowned. "Are you sure, Inspector? I suppose you're referring to our special guard?"

"Sure! Say, didn't you know he hadn't turned up for work this morning?"

"Certainly. But I thought nothing of it." The curator rose and began to pace the drugget behind his desk. "Burch, our caretaker, did mention something to me this morning about Donoghue's failure to turn up, but it didn't occur to me— Matter of fact, Rowe, you remember I mentioned it to you. You see, we like him here and give him rather more freedom than he would have in another situation. And then the museum's being shut down. . . . What's happened? What's the matter, Inspector?"

"Well, as far as we can find out," replied the Inspector grimly, "he beat it out of here yesterday afternoon while that party of schoolteachers was being shown around and he hasn't been seen since. Hasn't turned up at his rooming house, didn't keep a date with a friend of his last night—just dropped clean out of sight."

"It's rather odd, don't you think, Doctor?" murmured Patience.

Gordon Rowe laid his book down very quietly.

"Quite, quite," said Dr. Choate, who seemed disturbed. "The party of teachers . . . They seemed a harmless enough lot, Inspector."

"When you're a cop as many years as I've been," retorted the Inspector, "you learn not to depend too much on appearances. I understood it was you who took that bunch around the museum."

"Yes."

"How many of them were there, d'ye remember?"

"Really, I don't know. I'm afraid I didn't count, Inspector."

"You didn't by any chance," asked Patience softly, "notice a middle-aged man with a bushy gray mustache and a bluish sort of hat among them, did you, Doctor?"

"I've the failing of most shut-ins, Miss Thumm; half the time I'm unconscious of my surroundings."

"I did," said Rowe with a snap of his lean jaws. "But it was just a glimpse, blast it."

"Too bad," said the Inspector sarcastically. "So you just showed 'em around, eh, Doctor?"

"That's my crime, Inspector," replied the curator with a shrug. "Why do you ask especially after this man in the blue hat, Miss Thumm?"

"Because the man in the blue hat," replied Patience, "was an illegitimate member of the party, Dr. Choate, and because we've every reason to believe that Donoghue's disappearance is connected with him in some way."

"Funny," muttered young Rowe. "Funny. Intrigue in the museum, Doctor! That sounds like Donoghue, with his incurably romantic Irish temperament."

"You mean he might have noticed something strange," said Dr. Choate thoughtfully, "about this chap in the blue hat and permitted himself to be inveigled into a private investigation of his own? It's possible, of course. I'm sure nothing's happened to Donoghue, though. I've every confidence in his ability to handle himself."

"Then where is he?" said the Inspector dryly.

Dr. Choate shrugged again; it was evident he considered the entire affair a trifle. He rose with a pleasant smile.

"And now that your business has been transacted, would you like to look about, Inspector? And you, Miss Thumm? I know you've been through the Britannic before, but we've recently acquired an important benefaction and I'm sure you'll be interested in it. It's housed in what we've named the Saxon Room. Samuel Saxon, you know. He died not long——"

"Well—" snarled the Inspector.

"I'm sure we should love it," said Patience quickly.

Dr. Choate led the way, like Moses, between the painted seas of canvas on the reception-room floor along a corridor to a large reading room whose book-crammed walls were also hung with canvas. Inspector Thumm trudged wearily by his side, and behind them came Patience and the tall young man —an arrangement which was effected with a cool dexterity that brought a new blush to Patience's cheeks.

"You don't mind my trailing along this way, do you, darling?" murmured the young man.

"I've never shunned the company of good-looking men yet," said Patience stiffly, "and I'm sure I shan't start now just to swell *your* head, Mr. Rowe. Did anyone ever tell you that you're an extremely offensive young man?"

"My brother," said Rowe with gravity, "once when I handed him a black eye. Darling, I don't know when I've met a girl——"

Dr. Choate led the way across the reading room to a far door. "As a matter of fact," he called out, "Mr. Rowe has almost more right to do the honors of the Saxon Room than I, Miss Thumm. He was one of those infant prodigies you read about."

"How horrible," said Patience, tossing her head.

"Don't believe a word of it," said Rowe instantly. "Choate, I'll strangle you! What the estimable Doctor means, Miss Thumm——"

"Oh, it's Miss Thumm now, is it?"

He flushed. "I'm sorry. I get this way sometimes. What Dr. Choate means is that it was my good fortune to attract old Sam Saxon's eye. He left a gob of rare books to the Britannic in his will; died a few months ago, you know; and as his protégé I'm here in a sort of semi-official capacity to see that they're started off in their new home properly."

"More and more horrible, Mr. Rowe. I'm chiefly interested in brainless young men with no visible means of support."

"Now you're being cruel," he whispered. Then his eyes danced. "Except for the means of support, I assure you I qualify! Fact is, I'm doing some original research in Shakespeare. Mr. Saxon tucked me under his wing and I'm continuing my researches here, now that he's dead and a good deal of the Shakespearean stuff has been willed to the museum."

They entered a long narrow room which, from its fresh look, turpentine odor, and lack of draping proclaimed it recently redecorated. It contained perhaps a thousand volumes, most of them on open shelves. A small number reposed in wooden cases on slender metal legs, the tops of the cases covered with glass; apparently the more valuable items.

"Just finished," said Dr. Choate. "There are some really unique things here; eh, Rowe? Of course, the contents of this wing have not yet been placed on exhibition; the collection was delivered only a few weeks ago, after we had shut down." The Inspector leaned against a wall near the door and looked bored. "Now here," continued Dr. Choate in a Chautauqua voice, strolling over to the nearest cabinet, "is an item——"

"Say!" exclaimed the Inspector sharply. "What the devil's happened to that cabinet over there?"

Dr. Choate and Gordon Rowe wheeled like startled birds of passage. Patience felt her breath come thickly.

The Inspector was pointing to a case in the center of the room, quite like the others in appearance; but it differed from the others in a signal respect. Its glass top had been shattered, and only a few fragments of jagged glass clung to the frame!

5

The Jaggard Case

The expressions of acute alarm on the faces of the curator and the young man turned instantly to relief.

"Phew!" said Rowe. "Go easy on my heart, Inspector. I thought for a moment something was really wrong. Just an accident we had yesterday, that's all."

Patience and the Inspector exchanged very rapid and illuminated glances. "An accident, hey?" said the Inspector. "Well, well. Glad I decided to soak in a little of your culture at that, Doc. What d'ye mean 'accident,' Rowe?"

"Oh, I assure you that's all it was," smiled the curator. "No significance at all. It's really Mr. Rowe's story. He was working in the reading room next door yesterday afternoon and had occasion to come in here to consult one of the Saxon books. It was he who found the glass top of this case shattered."

"You see," explained Rowe, "the workmen finished this room only yesterday morning, and I've no doubt in coming back for a forgotten tool or something one of them accidentally poked in the glass. Nothing to get excited about."

"Just when yesterday did you discover this, Mr. Rowe?" asked Patience slowly. And this time there was nothing personal in her glance.

"Oh, I should imagine about five-thirty."

"And what time did your visiting delegation from Indiana leave, Dr. Choate, did you say?" she continued. She had quite lost her smile.

Dr. Choate seemed nettled. "Oh, I assure you it's nothing! And I really didn't say, Miss Thumm. The schoolteachers left at five, I believe."

"And the glass was crashed in at five-thirty, Mr. Rowe?"

The young man stared at her. "Miss Sherlocka! I really don't know. Are you a detectress?"

"Cut the comedy, younker," said the Inspector, coming forward; but he said it without rancor and indeed seemed to have regained his good humor. "How's that? You must have heard the glass breaking."

Rowe shook his head sadly. "But I didn't, Inspector. You see, the door to the Saxon Room from the reading room was closed, and then I'm usually so absorbed in what I'm doing you could set a bomb off under my chair and I wouldn't blink an eye. So the accident might have happened any time at all yesterday afternoon, you see."

"Hmm," said the Inspector. He went over to the shattered case and peered in. "Anything stolen?"

Dr. Choate laughed heartily. "Come now, Inspector, we're not children, you know. Naturally it occurred to us that someone might have sneaked in here—there's another door over there, as you can see, which leads into the main corridor, making this room fairly accessible—and made off with one of the three very valuable volumes in the case. But they're still there, as you can see."

The Thumms stared down at the broken cabinet. It's bottom was lined with soft black velvet; three oblong depressions had been artfully built into the velvet, and in each depression reposed a single book, large bulky volumes bound in stained and faded rough old calf. The book to the left was covered in a gold-brown calf, the book to the right in a faded scarlet, and the book in the middle in blue.

"There's a glazier coming in this afternoon to replace the glass lid," continued the curator. "And now——"

"Hold your horses, Doc," said Thumm abruptly. "You say the workmen got through with this room yesterday morning. Didn't you have a guard on duty here in the afternoon? I thought these museums were lousy with guards all the time."

"Why, no, Inspector. We dispensed with our usual staff when the museum was closed for repairs. Donoghue and the caretaker Burch have been enough. Those Indiana people have been the first outsiders permitted here since we shut down. But we didn't think it necessary——"

"Well," said the Inspector in a rumble, "I think I can tell you what happened, and it's not so damned innocent as you make it out."

Patience's eyes were bright. Gordon Rowe looked puzzled.

"What do you mean?" asked Dr. Choate swiftly.

"I mean," snapped the Inspector, "that your guess, Doc, that Donoghue saw something screwy about Mr. Blue Hat and followed him was right. Why did he follow Blue Hat? Because I say Blue Hat smashed this case in, that's why, and Donoghue saw him do it!"

"Then why isn't anything missing?" objected the curator.

"Maybe Donoghue scared him off just before he could take one of these books. You say they're valuable. Plain enough— attempted robbery."

Patience thoughtfully sucked her full lower lip and stared into the shattered case.

"And why didn't Donoghue raise an alarm, Inspector?" murmured Rowe. "And why didn't someone see this chap with the blue hat running out, if Donoghue was scrambling after him?"

"And most important of all," said Patience in a low voice, "where *is* Donoghue? Why hasn't he returned?"

"I don't know," retorted the Inspector savagely, "but I tell you that's what happened."

"I'm very much afraid that what happened," said Patience in a stiff queer tone, "is something rather terrible. And it didn't happen to the man in the blue hat, father. It happened to poor old Donoghue!"

The men were silent. The Inspector began to patrol the flagged floor.

Patience sighed and bent over the cabinet again. A triangular card was propped behind each of the three books in the case. A larger placard in the foreground bore the printed legend:

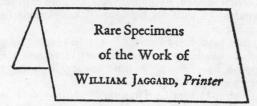

Rare Specimens
of the Work of
WILLIAM JAGGARD, *Printer*

"Elizabethan?" asked Patience.

Dr. Choate nodded absently. "Yes. Interesting items here, Miss Thumm. Jaggard was the famous London printer and publisher who did the First Folio of Shakespeare, you know. These things come from Samuel Saxon's collection—where he got them the Lord alone knows! He was something of a miser."

"I shouldn't say that exactly," remarked Gordon Rowe with a glint in his hazel eyes.

"Oh, purely in the bibliophilic sense," added Dr. Choate hastily.

"Come on," said the Inspector in a gruff tone. "I want to find out something."

But while there was much to find out, literally nothing was found. With Dr. Choate's assistance Inspector Thumm marshaled all the workmen—decorators, painters, masons, and carpenters—in the Britannic Museum and questioned them exhaustively about the events of the day before. No one among them remembered seeing a man in a blue hat enter or leave the Saxon Room, nor did anyone recall the exact movements of the missing Donoghue.

Patience, who had lingered behind in the Saxon Room and had been seized in conversation by young Mr. Rowe, hurried into the reading room where the Inspector had conducted his fruitless examination of the workmen, her face glowing.

"Father! I think there's something. . . . Would you mind terribly if I didn't return to the office with you?"

Forcibly reminded of his fatherhood, the Inspector assumed a stern air, "Where you bound?"

"Luncheon," said Patience gayly, stealing a glance at her profile in her handbag mirror.

"Ha," said the Inspector. "Lunch, hey?" He looked sad.

"With young Rowe, I'll wager," chuckled Dr. Choate. "For a student of such a serious subject as literature that lad is the most incorrigible flibberty-gibbet. Ah, here he is," he said as Rowe marched in with his hat and stick. "Coming back this afternoon, Rowe?"

"If I can tear myself away," grinned the young man. "Shakespeare has been waiting for over three hundred years, so I suppose he can wait a little longer. You don't mind, Inspector?"

"Mind? Mind?" snarled Thumm. "Why the devil should I mind?" And he kissed Patience fiercely on the forehead.

The young couple walked briskly out of the room, deep in a conversation which seemed to have begun in antiquity and would probably continue to eternity. There was a little silence.

"Well," sighed the Inspector, "guess I'll be trottin' along, too. Just keep an eye peeled, will you? And if you hear anything from or about Donoghue, give me a buzz." He gave the curator his card, shook hands rather limply, and stumped out of the reading room.

Dr. Choate stared thoughtfully after his broad simian back. Then he tapped the edge of the card against his bearded lips, whistled softly, and turned back to the Saxon Room.

6

Help Wanted

"I always thought," said Patience over the grapefruit, "that research students of literature were like research chemists—bowed thin young men with a fanatical light in their eyes and a total absence of sex appeal. Are you the exception to the rule, or have I been missing something?"

"*I've* been missing something," asserted Mr. Rowe, swallowing a mouthful of fruit powerfully.

"I notice that that spiritual lack hasn't affected your appetite!"

"Who said it was spiritual?"

The waiter took away the empty rinds and replaced them with cups of *consommé*.

"Lovely day," said Patience hurriedly, and took a hasty sip of soup. "Tell me something about yourself, young man. Pass the biscuits? . . . I mean, make it a personal biography."

"I'd rather make it a cocktail. George here knows me, and even if he doesn't it won't make any difference. George, a couple of Martinis. Dry as hell."

"Shakespeare and Martinis!" murmured Patience, giggling. "How refreshing! I see it all now. That's why you're a scholar and still resemble a human being. You sprinkle the dusty page with alcohol, and somehow it burns, doesn't it?"

"Like the very devil," grinned young Mr. Rowe. "As a matter of fact, you're betraying a most becoming ignorance. I'm deathly sick of lunching intelligent women."

"Well, I like that," gasped Patience. "Why, you insolent B-Bacchus! I've my M.A., I'll have you know, and I wrote a scintillating paper on *The Poetry of Thomas Hardy!*"

"Hardy? Hardy?" asked the young man, wrinkling his firm straight nose. "Oh, the versifier!"

"And just what did you mean by that crack? I'm betraying ignorance of precisely what?"

"The essential spirit of old Will. My dear girl, if you had a really deep-seated appreciation of Shakespeare, you would know that his poetry needs no external stimulant. It burns with its own fire."

"Hear, hear," murmured Patience. "Thank you, sir. I shall never forget this little lesson in æsthetics." There were two fiery pink spots in her cheeks, and she tore a biscuit in half.

He threw back his head and roared, startling George, who was approaching with a tray on which stood two frosty amber-filled glasses. "Oh, good Lord!" he gasped. "She can't take it! I think we're both a little mad. . . . Ah, George. Set them down, my boy. . . . Down the hatch, Miss Thumm?"

"Miss Thumm?"

"Darling!"

"Patience to you, Mr. Rowe."

"Very well, Patience it shall be." They drank gravely; their eyes met over the brims of their glasses and they laughed together, choking over the cocktails. "And now for the autobiography. My name is Gordon Rowe. I shall be twenty-eight come Michaelmas, I am an orphan, I have a pitifully small income, I think the Yankees have a rotten team this year, I see Harvard has bought a swell quarterback, and if I look at you much longer I shall be tempted to kiss you."

"You're a strange young man," said Patience with a furious blush. "No, no, that doesn't mean acceptance, so you'd better drop my hand; those two old ladies at the next table are looking at you with disapproval. . . . Heavens, I'm mortified!

Blushing like any callow schoolgirl at mere mention of a kiss! Are you always so flippant? I'd rather looked forward to an engrossing discussion about the splitting of the infinitive as splat by John Milton, or the domestic problems of the Lepidoptera."

He stared at her, his grin fading. "You're horribly nice," he said, and attacked his chop furiously, and for the moment there was silence. When he looked up they examined each other with searching seriousness, and it was Patience's eyes which fell. "To tell the truth, Pat—I'm glad you let me call you that—this sort of childish vulgarity is my escape. It's not very bright, I know, and I've never felt myself capable of holding my own in the social sense. I've devoted the best years of my young life so far to getting an education, and these last few years to doing something earth-shaking in the line of literary research. I've enormous ambition, you know."

"Ambition never ruined any young man," said Patience softly.

"Thanks for the kind words, young lady. I'm not the creative type, though. Research fascinates me. I suppose I should have gone in for biochemistry, or astrophysics."

Patience devoted herself chastely to her salad. She toyed for an instant with a crisp emerald leaf of cress. "I'm really—oh, it's silly."

He leaned forward and took her hand. "Please tell me, Pat."

"Mr. Rowe, they're looking!" said Patience, but she did not withdraw her hand.

"Gordon, please."

"Gordon. . . . You've hurt me," said Patience tragically. "Oh, I know it was ragging, and all that, but the fact is, Mr. Rowe—very well, Gordon!—I despise most women for their doughy minds."

"I'm sorry," he said contritely. "It was a poor joke."

"No, it's more than that, Gordon. I've been making poor jokes, too. I've never found anything I *really* wanted to do, while you—" She smiled. "Of course, it sounds ridiculous. But the only thing that differentiates us from the lower primates is the power of reasoning, and I don't see why the mere fact that a woman is biologically different from a man should prevent her from cultivating her mind."

"It's the fashion to be horrified at the mere notion," grinned the young man.

"I know it is, and I detest the fashion. I don't believe the full force of the mind's possibilities struck home to me until I met Drury Lane. He's—oh, he tones you up, he makes you *want* to think, to know. And it doesn't prevent him from being a very charming old gentleman, either. . . . But we've strayed from the point." She withdrew her hand shyly and regarded him with earnest eyes. "Do tell me about your work, and yourself, Gordon. I'm really interested."

"There's so little to tell," he said with a shrug of his big shoulders. "It's just work, eat, the gym, and sleep. Work's the most important part of it, of course. There was something special in Shakespeare that gripped me. There never was such genius. Oh, it goes more deeply with me than admiring the polish of a phrase or the acute philosophy behind a Hamlet or Lear conception. It was the man himself. What made him what he was? What was his secret? From what source did he draw his inspiration, or was it just a fire inside himself? I wanted to know."

"I've been to Stratford," said Patience softly. "There's something there. It's in the old Chapel Lane, the Stratford Church, the air——"

"I spent a year and a half in England," muttered Rowe. "It was hellish work. Following a trail so faint it was half imagination. And, by heaven . . ."

"Yes?" whispered Patience, her eyes glowing.

He cupped his chin in his hands. "The most important part of an artist's life is his formative years. It's the period of his intensest passions. His senses are at their fullest vigor. . . . And what do we know about the Maytime in the life of the greatest poet the world has ever produced? Nothing. There's a blank in the story of Shakespeare which must be filled in if we're ever to reach a sensitive and intelligent appreciation of the artist." He paused, and something almost frightened crept into his tired hazel eyes. "Pat," he said in a slightly unsteady voice, "I think I'm on the right track. I think——"

He stopped, and fumbled for his cigarette case. Patience sat very still.

He put the case back into his vest pocket without opening it. "No," he muttered. "It's premature. I don't really know. Yet." Then he smiled. "Pat, do let's talk about something else."

She sighed with minute care, never taking her eyes from him. Then she smiled back. "Of course, Gordon. Tell me about the Saxons."

"Well," he said, slumping boyishly in his chair, "there's precious little to tell. I got old Sam Saxon interested in my— let's call it a hunch. I suppose he took a shine to me; he never had any children. And despite certain defects in his character he was a genuinely passionate lover of English literature. Gruff old boy, but he insisted on financing my researches in the approved way—took me under his wing, into his house. . . . Then he died. And I'm still working."

"And Mrs. Saxon?"

"The incomparable Lydia." He scowled. "Old fuss-budget, and that's a generous estimate. I suppose I shouldn't bite the hand that's feeding me, but she's a little trying at times. Knows absolutely nothing about literature, and even less than that about her husband's collection of rare books. Let's not talk about her. She's an unpleasant female."

"Just because she can't discuss quartos and octavos with you!" laughed Patience. "Who takes care of the Saxon collection? You?"

"Now you're dipping into ancient history," chuckled Rowe. "Fossil by the name of Crabbe. There's poetic justice for you! I? My dear girl! Old Eagle-Eye, I call him, and he is. He was Mr. Saxon's librarian for twenty-three years, and I believe he's more jealous of the stuff in his care than even old Sam himself was." A shadow flitted over his face. "Now he's absolutely king-pin. Mr. Saxon provided in his will that Crabbe continue as curator of the collection. It will be more inaccessible than ever."

"But weren't you working in the Saxon library?"

"Under very close surveillance, I assure you! Crabbe saw to that, and he sees to it now. I don't know one quarter the stuff that's there. For the last few months I've been cataloguing and overseeing the specific items willed to the Britannic; rather set me back in my work, but Mr. Saxon asked me to do it in his will and it was little enough. . . . Look here, Patience, I've bored you stiff. Please tell me about—you."

"Me? There's nothing to tell," said Patience lightly.

"I'm serious, Pat. I—I think you're the most. . . . Oh, very well! But tell me."

"If you insist." She explored the recesses of her handbag for her mirror. "My career may be summed up in a single phrase: I'm a sort of modern Vestal Virgin."

"That sounds formidable," smiled the young man. "I don't think I quite understand."

"I—I've dedicated my life to . . . something." She poked her hair about as she peered into the tiny mirror.

He eyed her keenly. "To cultivation of mind?"

She put the mirror away, and sighed. "Oh, Gordon, I don't really know myself. I'm—I'm a little foggy some times."

"Do you know what your destiny is, young woman?" said Rowe.

"Tell me!"

"You're destined to lead a very prosy life, my dear."

"You mean—marriage, babies?"

"Something of the sort," he said in a low voice.

"How horrible!" Patience rose, the pink blobs annoyingly red. She was conscious of them, for they seemed to be burning holes in her cheeks. "Shall we go, Gordon?"

Inspector Thumm reached his office in a lather of thought. He grunted at Miss Brodie, marched into his sanctum, hurled his hat across the room to the top of the safe, and threw himself into his swivel-chair with a scowl.

He put his large feet on the desk, and then after a moment drew them down. He fished in his pockets for a cigar and, finding none, rummaged in the depths of a drawer until he found an eroded old pipe, which he filled with an evil-looking shag tobacco, lit up, and puffed on sourly. He fingered his calendar. He rose and began to pound his floor. Then he sat down again, cursed beneath his breath, and jabbed a button on the underside of his desk-top.

Miss Brodie hurried in, breathless.

"Any calls?"

"No, Inspector."

"Any mail?"

"Why, no, Inspector."

"For God's sake, didn't Tuttle send me any report on that Durkin case?"

"No, Inspector."

"Damn his pop-eyes— All right, all right, Miss Brodie!"

Miss Brodie's moon eyes were at the full. She gulped: "Yes, Inspector," and fled.

For some time he stood staring out the window at Times Square. The pipe fumed with horrid fecundity.

Suddenly he sprang to his desk, pounced on the telephone, dialed Spring 7-3100. " 'Lo!" he growled. "Put me on to Inspector Geoghan. Yeah, yeah, Geoghan! Listen, flattie, no arguments. This is Thumm talkin'." He chuckled at the police

operator's astonished bellow. "How's the family, John? Your
oldest must be big enough to enter rookie college, I bet! . . .
Fine, fine. Give me Geoghan, you old warhorse. . . . Hello.
Butch? Thumm!"

Inspector Geoghan swore fluently.

"Welcome home," snarled Thumm. "That's a fine reception!
Listen, Butch, and none of your Tenth Avenue lip. . . . Yes,
yes, I'm in the pink. I know *you're* all right, because I saw
that damned gorilla's face of yours in the papers this mornin'
and you looked as disgustingly healthy as usual. . . . Yeah!
Say, what d'ye remember about a cop named Donoghue who
left the force about five-six years ago? I remember he was
attached to H.q. under you when you were a Captain—where
you should 'a' stayed, you Commissioner-suckin' baboon!"

Inspector Geoghan chuckled. "Still the same pleasant old
Thumm. How the hell do you expect me to remember a flat-
foot that far back?"

"Why, he saved your life once, you ungrateful skunk!"

"Oh! *Donoghue.* Why the devil didn't you say so in the first
place? Sure I remember him. What d'ye want to know?"

"Rate him for me. Any black marks against him? What
kind of record did he have, Butch?"

"A-one. None too many brains, as I recall, but so honest he
wouldn't take a fin from a speakie. Too damned honest for his
own good. Didn't play ball, and that kept him from stripes."

"Clean slate, hey?" muttered the Inspector.

"As a whistle. Seem to remember I was sorry to see him go.
Romantic Irishman, Donoghue. Only he got romantic about
the wrong thing—Duty. Ha, ha!"

"Still harpin' on the same smelly old joke, I see," growled
Thumm. "Butch, I'll live to see the day when you're Commis-
sioner. Good-by, damn you, and come up to my office some
time."

He replaced the receiver tenderly and scowled at his calendar. After a moment he picked up the telephone again, repeated his call to Police Headquarters, and asked for the
Missing Persons Bureau.

Captain Grayson, head of the Bureau, was an old friend.
Thumm tersely related the story of Donoghue, the peculiar
circumstances surrounding his disappearance, his description
and habits. Grayson, whose duty it was to investigate all cases
of missing persons under the jurisdiction of the New York
Police Department, promised to institute a quiet inquiry. Then
the Inspector switched his call back to Inspector Geoghan.

"Listen, Butch, I'm in again. Got a line on a smooth crook who makes a specialty of stealing rare books? Guy wore a funny kind of blue lid—I dunno, might be a habit of his."

"Book snatcher, eh?" said Geoghan thoughtfully. "Blue hat . . . Can't remember a mug of that description offhand, but I'll find out and call you back."

"Thanks. I'll be waiting."

A half hour later Geoghan telephoned. There was nothing in the criminal records of the Bureau of Identification which involved a man specializing in the theft of rare books and who moreover had a habit of wearing a blue or bluish hat.

The Inspector stared dismally out of his window. The world seemed very dreary at the moment. Finally he sighed, fished a sheet of notepaper out of his desk, unscrewed the cap of his fountain pen, and began laboriously to write:

Dear Lane:

Here's something I know you'll be interested in. It's that little mystery I told Quacey about over the 'phone this morning. To tell the God's honest truth me and Patty are sort of stuck, and we would like your advice.

Now it seems that an ex-cop named Donoghue . . .

7

"The Passionate Pilgrim"

Miss Brodie stumbled into her employer's sanctum, her vapid young face working. "Oh, Inspector! It's—it's Mr. Lane!"

"What's that?" asked the Inspector blankly. It was Wednesday, and he had quite forgotten having written Lane the day before.

"Now, now, Brodie," said Patience kindly, "get a grip on yourself. What's this about Mr. Lane?"

Miss Brodie made Spartan efforts. She gulped, pointed tremblingly at the door, and said: *"He's outside."*

"Well, for the love of Mike!" bellowed the Inspector, springing for the door. "Why didn't you say so?" He yanked the door open; a tall old man with a mat of pure white hair sat on the bench in the anteroom, smiling at him and Patience by his side. Miss Brodie sucked her thumb nervously in the background. "Lane! It's good to see you. What the devil brings you into town?"

Mr. Drury Lane rose, tucked his blackthorn under his arm, and gripped the Inspector's hand very creditably for a septuagenarian. "Your fascinating letter, of course. Patience! Charming as usual. Well, well, Inspector, aren't you going to ask me in?"

Miss Brodie slipped by, an agitated wraith awed by a higher Presence. Mr. Drury Lane smiled at her in passing, and she gasped faintly. Then the three retired to the Inspector's office.

The old gentleman looked about him with affectionate eyes. "It's been some time, hasn't it? The same stuffy old hole, Inspector. A sort of modern Teach's brig. How are you both?"

"Physically prime," said Patience, "but not so healthy mentally—at the moment. But how have you been, Mr. Lane? The last time——"

"The last time, my dear," said the old gentleman solemnly, "I was slipping on an earthslide into my grave. Today—as you see me. I feel better than I've felt in years."

"Sure makes me feel good to see you sittin' here," growled the Inspector.

Lane spoke with his eyes shifting from the lips of Patience to the lips of Thumm; in a practiced, fluid way they were never still. "The truth is your letter revived me, Inspector. A case! Particularly a case involving my humdrum little Britannic. It seems too good to be true."

"That's the difference between you and father," said Patience, laughing. "Mysteries irritate him and stimulate you."

"And what do they do to you, my dear?"

She shrugged. "I'm the Balm of Gilead."

"The Britannic," murmured Lane. "Patience, have you met young Gordon Rowe?"

Instantly she blushed, and tears of exasperation came to her eyes. The Inspector muttered bitterly to himself. The old gentleman eyed them with a smile. "Oh—oh, yes, I've met him," said Patience.

"So I gathered," said Lane dryly. "Smart young chap, eh?"

"Quite, quite."

The Inspector fidgeted. "Fact of the matter is, Lane, we're in something crazy. I'm not getting any money out of it, it's the nuttiest yarn you ever heard, and I've got to do something about it for old time's sake."

"An unenviable position," chuckled the old gentleman. "I suggest we go at once to the museum. Something in your description of that shattered cabinet in the Saxon Room, Inspector, makes me want very much to examine it."

"Oh!" cried Patience. "Something I missed?"

"It's just a conjecture," said Mr. Drury Lane thoughtfully. "I dare say it's nothing. Shall we go? Dromio is downstairs with the car."

They found Dr. Alonzo Choate in his office deep in conversation with a tall spidery-limbed man dressed in curiously foreign clothes. He possessed the lean hatchety face of a certain physical type of Englishman—very sharp eyes, too, and screwed easily under the brow-ridge of his right eye there was a rimless monocle, from which a slender black silk ribbon fell to circle his neck. There was a bony clean-shavenness about his face which strongly recalled the scholars of the Renaissance. When he spoke it was with a quiet positiveness, and in the charming accent of the cultured Briton. He was perhaps fifty. Dr. Choate introduced him as Dr. Hamnet Sedlar, the incumbent curator, whose boat from England had docked this morning.

"Mr. Lane!" he exclaimed. "This is a genuine pleasure, sir. Ever since I saw you play the Moor in London twenty years ago, I have wanted to know you. And then your scholarly articles on Shakespeare in the *Colophon*——"

"Kind of you, I'm sure," said the old man hastily. "I'm scarcely more than a literary dilettante. I suppose Dr. Choate has told you about the little mystery which preceded your arrival?"

Dr. Sedlar looked blank. "I beg your pardon?"

"Oh, a mere trifle," rumbled Dr. Choate, fingering his goatee. "I'm astonished that you've taken the incident seriously, Mr. Lane."

"The facts present a rather curious superficial appearance, Doctor," murmured Drury Lane. His brilliant eyes darted from Choate to Sedlar and back again. "You see, Dr. Sedlar, an old gentleman obviously disguised managed to worm his way into the museum on Monday—two days ago—and apparently attacked a case in one of the new rooms."

"Really?" said Dr. Sedlar.

"It was nothing," said the curator impatiently. "He didn't get away with anything, and that's the important thing."

"I should think so," agreed the Englishman with a smile.

"If I may interrupt this academic dispute," said the old

gentleman, "may I suggest we examine the evidence itself? Or perhaps you gentlemen would rather——"

Dr. Choate nodded, but the Englishman said: "Dr. Choate and I are, I believe, already quite well acquainted. At the moment I should like nothing better than to see this shattered case." He chuckled. "After all, if I'm to direct the destinies of the Britannic Museum I suppose I should learn something about the methods of your American art-thieves. Eh, Doctor?"

"Er—yes," said the curator, frowning. "As you will, of course."

They passed through the general reading room, which was empty—as Patience observed with a faint twinge of disappointment; where was Gordon Rowe?—and into the Saxon Room.

The cabinet which yesterday had exhibited a broken glass had been repaired. There was nothing to distinguish its fresh gleaming pane from the tops of the other cases about.

"The glazier repaired it yesterday afternoon," said Dr. Choate a trifle stiffly to the Inspector. "Let me assure you that he was not left alone for an instant. I myself stood over him until he had completed his job."

The Inspector grunted.

Mr. Drury Lane and Dr. Hamnet Sedlar looked inquisitively through the glass. Into the eyes of both came a gleam of appreciation.

"Jaggards," said Dr. Sedlar very softly. "Enormously interesting, Mr. Lane. Did I understand you to say, Dr. Choate, that this is a new room and these items a recent benefaction?"

"Yes. The contents of this wing were left to the Britannic by the will of Samuel Saxon, the collector. They will be on exhibition, of course, when the museum reopens."

"Oh, yes! I believe Mr. Wyeth did mention something of the sort to me a month ago in London. I've often wondered what your American Mr. Saxon had in his library. Secretive soul, wasn't he? These Jaggards—exquisite!"

"Dr. Choate," said Mr. Drury Lane dryly, looking up from an unwinking inspection through the glass, "have you a key to this case?"

"Certainly."

"Will you open the cabinet, please?"

The curator stared, looked faintly uncomfortable for an instant, and then complied. They crowded about as the old gentleman raised the lid and propped it back. The three old volumes lay nakedly exposed on the soft black velvet. Under the harsh light of an overhead lamp their faded colors strengthened to titillate the eye. Carefully Lane lifted each calf volume out in turn, inspected its binding closely, opened to the flyleaf. . . . In one instance he spent some time searching the text. When he had replaced the three volumes in their original positions, he straightened, and Patience, watching his chiseled features attentively, saw them tighten.

"Very odd," he murmured. "I can scarcely believe it." And he stared down at the open cabinet.

"What's the matter?" cried Dr. Choate in a thick voice.

"The matter, my dear Choate," said the old gentleman calmly, "is that one of the volumes which originally lay in this case *has been stolen!*"

"Stolen!" they cried simultaneously; and Dr. Choate took a step forward and stopped short.

"That's impossible," he said sharply. "I examined these Jaggards myself when young Rowe found the cabinet bashed in."

"Did you examine them internally?" murmured Lane.

The curator paled. "I didn't see— No. But then the most cursory examination . . ."

"Deceived even your trained eye, I fear, Doctor. As I said, this is the most curious thing in my experience." His silky white brows drew together. "Look here." He pointed a lean forefinger at the triangular placard which stood behind the central volume of the three, the book bound in blue calf. It read:

THE PASSIONATE PILGRIM
By William Shakespeare
(*Jaggard,* 1599)

Extraordinary and unique item from the Samuel Saxon Library. One of the three known copies extant of this rare work in the first edition. Published by the Elizabethan printer William Jaggard in 1599, it was fraudulently assigned by the notorious Jaggard to Shakespeare, although it contained only five poems from the Bard's pen among the twenty in the volume. The residue were by Richard Barnfield, Bartholomew Griffin, and others of contemporary poets.

"Well?" asked Dr. Choate quietly. Hamnet Sedlar stood squinting through his monocle at the central volume; he seemed scarcely to have read the placard behind it.

"Is it—is it a forgery, a dummy?" asked Patience breathlessly.

"No, Patience my dear. I do not claim to be an expert, but I know enough about these things to venture the opinion that the volume you see here is a genuine Jaggard edition of *The Passionate Pilgrim.*"

Dr. Choate grew angry. "Then I don't see—" He picked up the blue-bound book and turned to the flyleaf. His jaw sagged ludicrously. Dr. Sedlar, startled, peered over his shoulder. And he, too, exhibited a shocked surprise that was as intense as it was fleeting.

Lane paced hugely up and down behind the case, head bent.

"Well, but—" began the Inspector, bewildered. Then he threw up his hands and muttered anathemas.

"But if it's a genuine Jaggard," cried Patience, "what——"

"Utterly, starkly impossible. Impossible," murmured Dr. Choate over and over.

"It's mad," said the Englishman in an awed voice.

Together they bent over the volume, searching its pages feverishly. They looked at each other and nodded with something like reverence. Then they returned their attention to the title-page. Patience, peeping over their shoulders, read:

The Passionate Pilgrime, or Certaine Amorous Sonnets between Venus and Adonis. By W. Shakespere. The second edition. Printed by W. Jaggard. 1606.

"I see," said Patience slowly. "This isn't the 1599 Jaggard, then, which was the first edition, but a copy of the 1606 Jaggard, or the second edition. Obviously a less valuable volume——"

"My dear Miss Thumm," said Dr. Choate sharply over his shoulder, "you have never been in greater error."

"You mean it's *more* valuable?"

The Inspector began to exhibit signs of awakened interest. Lane continued to pace the floor, deep in thought.

There was no reply, and Patience, flushing, retreated.

"Patience," said the old gentleman suddenly. She went gratefully to him, and he put his long arm about her shoulders. "Patience, my dear, do you know what makes this incident so astonishing?"

"I haven't the faintest idea, sir."

He squeezed her shoulders gently. "Mr. William Jaggard was a well-meaning patron of the arts. He was apparently in the thick of things in London during the period when Shakespeare, Jonson, Fletcher, Marlowe, and the illustrious rest dripped gold from their quills. There was probably a good deal of competition among the publishers. Mr. William Jaggard sought names, just as some of our current theatrical producers and book publishers seek them today. And so he became something very like a pirate. He printed *The Passionate Pilgrim*. In it he included two previously unpublished sonnets by Shakespeare and three poems drawn from the already published play, *Love's Labour's Lost*. The rest was padding. He assigned them, with colossal nerve, all of them, to Shakespeare. I've no doubt they sold well; and as for Shakespeare, he seems to have been a curiously indifferent dramatist as far as publication was concerned." Lane sighed. "I tell you this to give you something of an appreciation of the background. I'm sure they sold well because after printing a first edition in 1599, he reprinted in 1606, and still a third time in 1612. Now what makes the present situation so amazing is this: There are three copies of the 1599 Jaggard extant. There are two copies of the 1612 Jaggard extant. But until a few moments ago the entire bibliophilic world thought there was *no* copy of the 1606 Jaggard extant!"

"Then this book is priceless?" whispered Patience.

"Priceless?" echoed Dr. Choate absently.

"I said," replied the old man in dulcet tones, "that this was an odd case, my dear. Inspector, I scarcely blame you for being puzzled; although you didn't grasp the full intricacies of the puzzle quite clearly. Patience, my child, the situation becomes slightly insane. Apparently your man of the blue hat went to vast trouble, at great personal risk, to wheedle his way into a closed group, illicitly visit the Britannic Museum, drift away from the group while Dr. Choate expounded on the glories of his museum, make his way to this Saxon Room, smash in the glass of the Jaggard cabinet. . . . Throughout, this odd thief ran the enormous risk of arrest for grand larceny and vandalism—all for what?" Lane's voice sharpened. "To steal one rare and valuable book, and then to leave in its place a book even rarer and more valuable than the one he stole!"

8

The Beneficent Thief

"What's the row?" demanded a cheerful voice, and young Gordon Rowe sauntered into the Saxon Room from the corridor. He grinned at Patience and went to her side at once, like a scrap of iron filing drawn to a magnet.

"Ah, Rowe," said the curator hurriedly. "The very man. The most extraordinary thing's happened!"

"We seem to be attracting marvels like Mr. Barnum's freak show," said young Rowe with a wink at Patience. "Mr. Lane! Glad to see you, sir. Lord, what a solemn congregation! And I see you've been initiating Dr. Sedlar into our little domestic difficulties, Dr. Choate. 'Lo, Inspector. What's the trouble Doctor?"

Dr. Choate mutely waved the blue volume in his hand.

Rowe dropped his smile instantly. "Not—?" He looked around and saw grave faces. Then he took the book from the curator and slowly opened it. An expression of the most intense amazement came over his face. He looked around again in blank confusion. "It isn't— Why, this is a 1606 Jaggard!" he shouted. "I thought there weren't any——"

"Apparently there is," said the old gentleman dryly. "Beautiful copy, isn't it, Gordon? There will be shouting in the streets when the news gets out."

"I know," muttered Rowe, "but— Where in God's good name did this come from? Who found it? You didn't bring it over from London, did you, Dr. Sedlar?"

"Scarcely!" drawled the Englishman.

"You won't believe it," said Dr. Choate with a helpless shrug. "But we *did* have a theft here Monday. Someone left this in the Jaggard case, Rowe, and took away the 1599!"

"Oh," said the young man. "I—" And he threw back his head and roared with laughter. "Lord, this is rich!" he gasped, wiping his eyes. "Wait until divine Lydia hears *this*. And Crabbe. . . . Oh, this is too much!" He gulped hard and composed himself. "I beg your pardon. It just struck me . . . you know. It would be Mrs. Saxon's luck to have a rare book stolen and an even rarer one left in its place. Crazy, that's what it is!"

"I think," said the curator with a nervous tug at his beard, "you'd better get Mrs. Saxon over here at once, Rowe. After all——"

"Of course." The young man caressed the 1606 Jaggard with tenderness, returned it to Dr. Choate, pressed Patience's arm, and left the room with a jaunty air.

"Frightfully boisterous young man," remarked Dr. Sedlar. "I'm afraid I can't share his levity. You know, we can't accept this—this remarkable volume at its face value, Dr. Choate. It will have to be more thoroughly examined. It may be difficult to establish its authenticity——"

The hunter's glare invaded Dr. Choate's eye. "Quite. Quite." And he rubbed his hands. He seemed content to have the stolen volume remain in possession of the thief, so long as the thief did not return and demand the unique volume he had left in the case. "I suggest we get to work at once. We'll have to proceed carefully, Sedlar. We don't want a breath of this to get out! We might call in old Gaspari of the Metropolitan, swear him to secrecy. . . ."

Dr. Sedlar was strangely pale. He kept staring at the ravished cabinet as if hypnotized.

"Or Professor Crowninshield of the Folger," he muttered.

Patience sighed. "We all seem to be assuming that the 1599 Jaggard was stolen by the man in the blue hat. There's really no proof, you know. Why mightn't the thief have been that second stranger on the bus, or one of the seventeen schoolteachers?"

Inspector Thumm threw up his hands and scowled. It was evident that the entire affair was too much for him.

"I scarcely think so, Patience," murmured Drury Lane. "There were nineteen persons on the bus, all of whom apparently entered the museum. Eighteen of them returned to the bus terminal after the visit, the eighteenth being the mysterious second stranger, as you so charmingly have christened him. In other words, our friend, the man in the blue hat, disappeared from the museum. And so did Donoghue. The link is too powerful to have been forged by coincidence. I think it extremely probable that the man in the blue hat stole the 1599 Jaggard, leaving this 1606 in its place, and that Donoghue disappeared in following him."

"Well, well," said the curator briskly, "I've no doubt it will all be explained in time. Meanwhile, Dr. Sedlar, if you'll excuse me, I'll have the museum searched at once."

"For what?" demanded the Inspector bitterly.

"There's the remote chance, you know, that that 1599 Jaggard may not have been taken out of the building."

"Says you," growled Thumm.

"Excellent notion, Doctor," said Dr. Sedlar eagerly. "I—I'll carry on. But when Mrs. Saxon arrives—" Apparently Dr. Sedlar had heard of Mrs. Saxon's potentialities, and was properly apprehensive.

"I shan't be a minute," said Dr. Choate cheerfully. He deposited the blue book carefully in the case and hurried from the room.

The Englishman hovered over the case like a nervous mother-stork over her nest. "Too bad," he muttered. "Too bad. I really should have liked to see that 1599."

Drury Lane stared at him, and then sought a chair and sat down. He shaded his eyes with a white veined hand.

"You sound horribly disappointed, Dr. Sedlar," said Patience.

He started. "Eh? I beg your pardon. . . . Yes, yes, I am."

"But why? Didn't you ever see the 1599? I thought that rare books were common property among bibliophiles."

"Should be," replied the Englishman with a grim smile, "but this one was not. It belonged to Samuel Saxon, you know. That made it quite inaccessible."

"I believe Mr. Rowe and Dr. Choate did say something about Mr. Saxon's—er—secretiveness."

Dr. Sedlar grew excited, and his monocle trembled and then fell, to dangle by its cord on his breast. "Secretiveness!" he exploded. "The man was a bibliomaniac. He spent half his declining years in England bidding in at auctions and quite taking away all our precious things. . . . Sorry. But there were items which weren't universally known. The Lord alone knows where he picked them up. This stolen 1599 Jaggard edition of *The Passionate Pilgrim* was one of the unknowns. Until a short time ago only two copies of this first edition were known to be in existence; then Saxon dug up a third somewhere, but he never permitted scholars so much as a glimpse of it. He stowed it away in his library like so much fodder in a granary."

"That sure sounds tragic," said the Inspector disagreeably.

"Oh, yes," drawled the Englishman. "I assure you it is. I'd really looked forward to examining it. . . . When Mr. Wyeth told me about the acquisition of the Saxon bequest . . ."

"He mentioned that the 1599 Jaggard was included in the benefaction?" murmured Lane.

"Yes, indeed." Dr. Sedlar sighed and bent over the cabinet again. He readjusted his monocle. "Lovely, lovely. I can scarcely wait— What's this?" His thin lips parted with excitement as he seized the third of the three volumes in the case and studied its flyleaf.

"What's the matter now?" asked Lane swiftly, rising and hurrying to the cabinet.

Dr. Sedlar expelled a long whistling breath. "For a moment I thought—I was wrong. I examined this particular copy of *Henry V* in London some years ago, before it was purchased by Saxon. It bears the date 1608—jolly well established as a case of deliberate antedating by Jaggard, who printed it for the stationer Thomas Pavier. It was probably printed in 1619. But I recalled that the leather was a deeper scarlet. Apparently it's faded a bit under the tender ministrations of Saxon."

"I see," said the old gentleman. "You had me jumping, Doctor! How about the *Sir John Oldcastle*?"

The incumbent curator fingered the first volume in the cabinet lovingly. "Oh, that's quite all right," he said seriously. "Hasn't changed hue since I last saw it at Sotheby's in 1913 when it fetched a pretty price at auction—the same golden brown! Mind you, I'm not accusing Saxon of vandalism, please understand——"

Dr. Choate hurried into the room. "I'm afraid I was wrong," he said brightly. "No sign of the stolen Jaggard. We'll keep searching, of course."

Mrs. Lydia Saxon burst into the Saxon Room with the awful irresistibility of an infuriated she-elephant. She was built on the grand scale—an enormous woman with mountainous flanks, a Zeppelin's stern, the bosom of a sea-cow, and the carriage of a frigate. There was a feral glare in her watery green eyes that boded ill for such unfortunate creatures as scholars, curators, and the whole unhappy tribe of beneficiaries. She was followed by Gordon Rowe, grinning cheerfully, and an attenuated, sidling old man dressed in a rusty tailcoat. There was something of the quality of ancient papyrus in this creature: rasping dry skin, almost a rustle of brittle bones as he walked, and the pale predacious features common to Italian seigniors, Spanish pirates, and antiquarians. This old gentleman, who could only be the high-handed librarian of the Saxon Collection, Crabbe, ignored the assembled company and made with a gliding pounce for the Jaggard cabinet, where he seized in his claws the curious gift of the thief and examined it with a very sharp and vulturous eye.

"Dr. Choate!" cried Mrs. Saxon in an unpleasantly shrill soprano. "What's all this about a theft? What's all this nonsense?"

"Ah—Mrs. Saxon," murmured the curator with an uneasy smile. "Yes. Most unfortunate. But there's been an amazing bit of luck too——"

"Rubbish! Mr. Rowe has told me all about that other book. I assure you it doesn't impress me in the least. The fact remains that one of the most valuable items of my husband's bequest seems to have been stolen under your very nose. I demand——"

"Before we go into the distressing details," said Dr. Choate hastily, "may I present Miss Patience Thumm. Dr. Hamnet Sedlar, who is to be our new curator, you know. Mr. Drury Lane——"

"Ah," said Mrs. Saxon, turning her watery green eyes on the old gentleman. "Mr. Lane. How d'ye do, Mr. Lane! And the new curator, did you say?" She regarded the stiff figure of the Englishman with cold curiosity, and sniffed like a monstrous fat tabby.

"And Inspector Thumm——"

"Of the police? Inspector, I demand you find the thief at once!"

"Sure," snarled the Inspector. "And what am I supposed to do—pull him out of my vest pocket?"

She gasped, turning the color of ripe cherries. "Why, I never——"

Crabbe, who had put the blue volume down with a sigh, tapped her arm. "Your blood-pressure, my dear Mrs. Saxon," he whispered with a smile. Then he straightened his crooked old body and inspected with remarkable sharpness the faces about him. "Very peculiar, this theft, it seems to me." There was a personal offensiveness in his tone that caused Dr. Choate to pull his tall figure up with dignity. "I find it——" And Crabbe stopped so suddenly that they started. His roving little eyes had lighted upon the face of Dr. Sedlar. They passed on, and then jumped back as if he had received a shock. "Who's this?" he snapped, jerking a creviced old thumb at the Englishman.

"I beg your pardon," said Dr. Sedlar coldly.

"Dr. Sedlar, our new curator," murmured young Rowe.

"Come, come, Crabbe, don't be rude! Mr. Crabbe, the Saxon librarian, Doctor."

"Sedlar, hey?" grunted Crabbe. "Sedlar, hey? Well, well." And he cocked his thin head and regarded the Englishman with a faintly malicious smile. Dr. Sedlar stared back, offended and apparently puzzled. Then he shrugged.

"If I may be permitted to explain, Mrs. Saxon," he said with a charming smile, stepping forward. "This has been a most—" They moved off to one side, and Dr. Sedlar proceeded to speak rapidly in a low tone. Mrs. Saxon listened with the detached and hostile air of a judge who has condemned the prisoner in advance.

Drury Lane quietly returned to his chair in the far corner of the room. He shut his eyes and stretched his long limbs. Patience sighed and turned to Gordon Rowe, who pulled her aside and proceeded to whisper energetically in her ear.

Crabbe and Dr. Choate went into cold but earnest conference over the quiet carcass of the 1606 Jaggard. Inspector Thumm, wandering about like a lost soul in a special purgatory, groaned with boredom. He caught snatches of the bibliophiles' conversation.

"The inscription on the flyleaf——"

"Halliwell-Phillips said——"

"—inclusion of the pirated sonnets——"

"But was it quarto or octavo?"

"The Bodleian copy——"

"—definitely shows that the two non-Shakespearean poems Jaggard stole from Heywood's *Troia Britannica* appearing in the 1612——"

"The format follows closely——"

"Before 1608 Jaggard was merely the publisher, remember. It wasn't until that date that he purchased James Roberts's press in the Barbican. That would make the 1606——"

The Inspector groaned again, and flung himself about the room in an ecstasy of baffled rage.

Dr. Choate and the saturnine Crabbe looked up, beaming in a temporary truce. "Ladies, gentlemen," boomed the curator, preening his beard, "Mr. Crabbe and I are thoroughly agreed that this 1606 Jaggard is authentic!"

"Hear, hear," said the Inspector gloomily.

"You're positive?" asked Dr. Sedlar, turning from Mrs. Saxon.

"I don't care!" shrilled Mrs. Saxon. "I still think it an extraordinary way to reward Mr. Saxon's generosity——"

"Told you she was an unpleasant female," said young Rowe in a clear voice.

"Hush, you rash young idiot!" whispered Patience fiercely. "The Gorgon will hear you!"

"Let her," grinned the young man. "She's a domineering old whale."

"I really didn't think it would be a forgery," said Drury Lane quietly from his corner, when the bulb-nosed caretaker trudged into the room and shuffled toward Dr. Choate.

"What's this, Burch?" said the curator absently. "That can wait, I'm sure——"

"Suits me," said Burch stonily, and forthwith proceeded to trudge back.

"Just a moment," said Drury Lane. He had risen and was staring intently at the package in Burch's talons. A little wind of intelligence passed over his sharp features. "If I were you, Dr. Choate, I should investigate that package. If this affair is as insane as it appears, there's an incredible possibility . . ."

They all looked blankly from his face to the caretaker's hand.

"You think——?" began Dr. Choate, licking his bearded lips. "Very well, Burch. Let's have it."

Like two faithful guards Dr. Sedlar on one side and Crabbe on the other came swiftly forward to flank the curator.

It was a neat flat package done up in common brown wrapping paper and tied with a piece of cheap red string. A small sticker had been pasted on the wrapper, and Dr. Choate's name and museum address were lettered in blue ink in small clear block letters upon the label.

"Who brought this, Burch?" asked Dr. Choate slowly.

"Young squirt of a messenger," said Burch in a surly voice.

"I see," and Dr. Choate began to undo the string.

"Here, you fool!" roared the Inspector suddenly, leaping forward and snatching the package with hasty but cautious fingers. "There's been so many screwy things happenin' around here. . . . Might be a bomb!"

The men paled, and Mrs. Saxon's bosom heaved like a surging sea as she uttered a piercing shriek. Lane smiled sadly at Thumm.

The Inspector pressed his big red cauliflower ear to the brown paper and listened intently. Then he turned the package over and listened on the other side. Still unsatisfied, he shook it gently, very gently indeed.

"Well, I guess it's all right," he grumbled, thrusting it back into the curator's startled hands.

"Perhaps you'd better open it," said Dr. Choate with a quaver.

"I'm sure it's quite all right, Doctor," said the old gentleman with a reassuring smile.

Nevertheless, the curator's fingers were unwilling as he snapped the string and slowly, very slowly, unfolded the brown paper. Mrs. Saxon oozed toward the door, and Gordon Rowe pulled Patience roughly behind him.

The paper came apart.

Nothing happened.

But if the package had contained a bomb, if it had suddenly exploded in his hands, Dr. Choate could not have shown greater stupefaction. His jaw dropped as his eyes took in what lay exposed, and his fingers fumbled with it, searching out something.

"Why— Good God!" he cried in a strangled voice. *"It's the 1599 Jaggard that was stolen Monday!"*

9

Tale Told by a Savant

No one spoke for a breathless moment. They stared at one another, too overcome by astonishment to utter a 'word. The strange thief had returned his booty!

"Considering the general air of madness about the entire affair thus far," murmured Drury Lane, rising and coming forward, "I suspected that something like this might occur." His cameo face was keen with curiosity. "We're dealing with an intelligent and humorous antagonist. Odd, very odd! Are you sure that's the copy that was stolen, Dr. Choate?"

"Not the slightest question," replied the curator, still dazed. "This is the Saxon Jaggard. Would you care to examine it, gentlemen?"

He placed the blue calf volume, still on its bed of wrapping paper, upon the glass top of the Jaggard cabinet; and Crabbe examined the book with swift absorption. Patience, pressed against young Rowe, caught a glimpse of Dr. Sedlar's face as the Englishman watched Crabbe, and almost cried out with surprise. The man had been wearing a polite mask. Now the mask had dropped away. His expression mirrored a peculiar rage, a rage almost of disappointment; his face was very savage, and its savagery was only enhanced by the cold unwinking glass over his right eye. Then the mask slipped back in a twinkling, and he was carefully interested once more. . . . Patience twisted her head and looked into Gordon Rowe's eyes; their eyes spoke to each other; he had caught the remarkable expression, too, and watched Dr. Sedlar thenceforth with an unwavering intentness.

"That's the Saxon Jaggard," said Crabbe in clipped tones.

"Cripes, what a fool I've been!" shouted Inspector Thumm suddenly, startling them all; and with no further explanation he dashed out of the Saxon Room. They heard his big feet pounding away down the corridor.

"Your father, Miss Thumm," remarked Dr. Sedlar with a slight smile, "seems a very precipitate gentleman."

"My father, Dr. Sedlar," retorted Patience, "is at times a very acute gentleman. He thinks of practical things, you see. I've no doubt he's gone after the messenger, something none of the rest of us thought of doing."

Mrs. Saxon stared at Patience as if she were seeing that angry young woman for the first time. Young Rowe chuckled.

"Yes, yes, Patience," said Drury Lane mildly, "we don't question the Inspector's perspicacity, although I dare say this time it's futile. The point is, gentlemen, that your 1599 Jaggard hasn't been returned in the *status quo ante*. Please examine the back."

His sharp eyes had observed something wrong. Dr. Choate lifted the volume from the wrapping paper and turned it over. They saw immediately what was the matter. A knife had been inserted into the lower edge of the back cover, slitting the leather and the thin leaves of the paper board which made up the body of the cover. The whole lower edge of the binding had been slit in this fashion. Protruding from the slit was the tiny edge of a stiff crisp piece of paper.

Dr. Choate pulled it out cautiously. It was a one-hundred-dollar bill. Pinned to it with a common pin was a small scrap of the same kind of brown paper which had been used in wrapping the book. In the same blue ink, identically block-lettered, were five words:

TO COVER COST OF REPAIRS

There was no signature.

"The cheek of the fellow!" snarled Mrs. Saxon. "Vandalizing my book and——"

Inspector Thumm stamped back, muttering and wiping his brow. "Too late," he growled. "Messenger's beat it. . . . What's this?" He examined the rent in the back cover and read the note with astonishment. Then he shook his head as if to say: "It's too much for *me!*" and turned his attention to the wrapping paper and the string. "Cheap manila," he said. "Ordinary red string. No clue there. Ah, hell! I'm sick of the whole blasted business."

Crabbe fondled the hundred-dollar bill and chuckled: "There's a nice thief for you, Choate. Steals a book, returns it with expenses, and throws in a priceless gift to boot!" Then he stopped chortling and looked thoughtful.

"Telephone the papers," said the Inspector wearily. "Tell 'em about this thing. You'll give the thief an excuse to come back."

"How do you figure that, father?"

"Patty, a crook's a crook even if he's dotty. He left this damned 1606 or whatever you call it, didn't he? He'll come back and claim it."

"I'm afraid not, Inspector," smiled Lane. "He's scarcely as ingenuous as that. No, he has found——"

Mrs. Saxon, who was openly mollified by the unexpected return of the 1599 Jaggard, uttered a startled exclamation which sounded like the siren warning of a ferry-boat. "Why, Crabbe! This is *really* peculiar. It's just struck me. Do you know, Mr. Lane, we had just such an experience as this not long ago?"

"What's this, Mrs. Saxon?" asked the old gentleman abruptly. "What sort of experience?"

Her triple chin quivered with excitement. "Somebody stole a book from my library, Mr. Lane, and then sent it back, too!"

Crabbe shot her a queer look. "I remember, too," he said harshly. And he glanced sidelong at Dr. Sedlar for no apparent reason. "It *is* odd."

"Crabbe!" exclaimed Rowe. "God, what idiots we all are! Of course. It must be the same one!"

Mr. Drury Lane grasped the arm of the Saxon librarian, and the Saxon librarian winced. "Come, come, man, tell us what happened—at once! It may be of the gravest importance."

Crabbe looked slyly about. "In the excitement I forgot . . . About six weeks ago one night I had occasion to work late in the library. The Saxon library, of course, at Mrs. Saxon's. It was when I was recataloguing the collection after the benefaction to the Britannic had been sorted out. I heard a peculiar noise from one of the wings and investigated. I surprised a man in the act of rifling one of the shelves."

"Now we're getting somewhere," said the Inspector. "What did he look like?"

Crabbe spread his dry bony hands, as if to warm them. "*Quién sabe?* It was dark, and he was masked and bundled up in a coat. I got no more than a glimpse of him. He heard me and dashed through one of the French windows and escaped."

"It was dreadful," said Mrs. Saxon grimly. "I shall never forget how upset we all were." Then she chuckled. "Mr. Crabbe ran about like a headless old rooster——"

"Hmm," said Crabbe sourly. "And Mrs. Saxon, I recall, came down in a brilliant red *peignoir*. . . ." They glared at each other. Patience envisioning that mountain of feminine flesh uncorseted, in a loose and floppy wrapper, bit her lip bravely. "Anyway, I raised the alarm and young Rowe here came down in his—he, he!—B.V.D.'s."

"Not quite," said Rowe hurriedly. "Crabbe!"

"Usual thing. Mr. Rowe played the shining knight and chased the thief, and the thief escaped very prettily."

"They were seersucker pajamas," said Mr. Rowe with dignity, "and besides I never even saw the fellow when I chased him."

"And you say he stole a book?" asked Drury Lane slowly.

Crabbe blinked in a crafty way. "You won't believe it."

"Well?"

"He stole a copy of the 1599 Jaggard."

Dr. Sedlar's eyes were fixed upon Crabbe; Dr. Choate looked bewildered; and the Inspector uttered a despairing cry.

"For the love of Mike," he cried, "how many copies of that damned book are there?"

"You mean"—Lane frowned—"that the thief stole this copy of the 1599 Jaggard—before it was turned over to the Britannic—and then returned it to you? That makes no sense at all, Mr. Crabbe."

"No." Crabbe grinned toothlessly. "He stole a *forgery* of the 1599 Jaggard."

"A forgery?" muttered Dr. Sedlar. "I didn't know——"

"A little something Mr. Saxon picked up about twenty years ago," explained the librarian with the same malicious smile. "It was a patent forgery. We kept it as a curiosity. And that's the one the thief took from the open shelf."

"Queer," murmured Lane. "That's the queerest thing that's happened so far. I can't understand it at all. . . . You still had this genuine copy in the library, Mr. Crabbe? I think you said it hadn't been turned over to the museum at that time?"

"Yes, we still had the genuine Jaggard, Mr. Lane. But it was in our private vault at home," chuckled Crabbe. "Very much so! With most of the other rare items. The forgery, being worthless except as a collector's curiosity, we didn't care about. And then, as I said, two days later the forgery was returned to us in the mail, with no explanation."

"Ah," cried Lane. "And was the forgery slit open, as this genuine copy has been slit?"

"No. It was quite intact."

"What kind of paper and string?" growled the Inspector.

"Very much the same as these."

Lane squinted thoughtfully at the Jaggard cabinet. Then he picked up the 1599 Jaggard which had just been returned by messenger and very minutely examined its mutilated binding. At least half the inside back cover—end-paper and top leaf of the inner board—curled away slightly from the remainder of the cover.

"Now here's a curious thing," said the old gentleman contemplatively, and turned to exhibit the flap which had resulted from the thief's slitting. He pulled the flap gently away. Beneath it was disclosed a rectangular depression. It was evident that someone had dug beneath the flap to the thickness of an additional layer of cardboard. The infinitesimal depression thus produced was not more than three inches wide by five inches long.

"Did he cut that, too?" asked Dr. Choate in a scandalized voice.

"I think not. Patience, my dear, you've very keen perceptions. When would you say this strange rectangle had been scooped out of the cardboard?"

Patience dutifully came forward. After a moment she said: "A very long time ago. The edges left by the cutting have a time-glazed appearance. I get the distinct feeling of great age."

"I think that answers your question, Dr. Choate," smiled Lane. "And why, my child, would you say this rectangle had been scooped out of the binding at all?"

Patience flashed a smile at him. "Obviously as a hiding-place for something."

"Hiding-place!" cried the curator. "Preposterous."

"Doctor, Doctor," murmured the old actor sadly, "why must you bookworms sniff at the very exact science of logic? Miss Thumm is quite correct. Something very thin and light— thin because of the shallowness of the depression, light because appreciable weight would have been observed by experts during all these centuries—has been until recently hidden in the back of Mr. William Jaggard's enterprising little venture into piratical publishing. *What but a piece of paper?*"

10

Enter William Shakespeare

There was nothing more to be done at the Britannic Museum. The Inspector especially was in a fever of impatience to be off. They made their adieus and left.

Gordon Rowe went with them to the door. He rapped his knuckles on the bronze beard of Shakespeare. "The old boy's actually smiling. And no wonder! For the first time in centuries something human has happened in a museum, Pat."

"Something tantalizing," said Patience fiercely. "Sir, my hand! I have a very jealous father, and he has eyes in the back of his head. . . . Good-by, Gordon."

"Ah," said the young man, "that was very nice. When may I see you again?"

"I'll think about it," said Patience primly, and turned to follow the Inspector and Lane.

He seized her hand. "Pat! Let me see you now."

"Now?"

"Let me see you to your father's office. That's where you're going, isn't it?"

"Y-yes."

"Mayn't I come, too?"

"Heavens, you're a persistent young man!" said Patience, and for the dozenth time hated herself for blushing. "Very well, if father will have you."

"Oh, he'll have me," said Rowe gayly, and closed the door behind them with a loud bang. He took Patience's arm and walked her briskly across the sidewalk to the others. Dromio,

Lane's red-haired chauffeur, stood grinning beside a sleek black Lincoln limousine at the curb.

"Inspector," said the young man anxiously, "do you mind if I come along? Come, now, you don't mind. I can see it in your eyes!"

Thumm stared icily at him. "Say——"

Mr. Drury Lane clucked a soothing syllable. "Now, now, Inspector, I think it's a splendid idea. I suggest you let me take you all downtown. I've my car here, and I do want a few moments' relaxation. Can't think at all with so many disturbing influences around me. The situation obviously calls for a council of war, and Gordon is a keen lad. Shall we, or are you too busy to be annoyed with us, Inspector?"

"There," said young Rowe, "is a friend."

"The way business is these days," said the Inspector glumly, "I could take a month's vacation and that dumb steno of mine wouldn't even know I'd gone." He glanced sharply at the young man, and then at Patience, who was humming a nervous little tune and trying to appear nonchalant. "All right, younker. Patty, jump in. This is a free ride."

In Thumm's sanctum the old actor sank into a battered leather chair with a sigh. Patience sat down sedately and Rowe leaned against the jam with glittering eyes. "You've apparently taken the admonition of the hundred and twenty-second Psalm to heart, Inspector. 'Peace be within thy walls.' This is good."

"Yes, but not 'prosperity within thy palaces,'" laughed Patience, flinging her pert little toque across the room to the top of the safe. "If business continues as bad as it's been, I'm afraid I'll have to get me a job."

"Women," said Mr. Rowe fervently, "should never work."

"Patty, you shut up," said the Inspector irritably.

"If I could be of any assistance——" began the old gentleman.

"Nice of you, you old scalawag, but we really don't need any. Patty, I'll spank you! Well, Lane, what do you think?"

Lane crossed his fine old legs after a moment's long scrutiny of his companions. "My thoughts are sometimes irrational, Inspector. I will say that this is the most remarkable case in my experience, and that covers a fairly comprehensive reading of criminology. Now you're the practical policeman. What do *you* think?"

"All balled up," said the Inspector with a bitter grin. "Beats hell. First time I ever heard of a crook sendin' back the swag with a bonus to boot! Seems to me, though, that the logical thing to do is try and find out who those two birds are—this guy in the blue hat and that other one, the one with the queer horseshoe ring that the bus-starter told us about. I'll check up again on those seventeen schoolteachers, but I've got the feeling they're all innocent."

"And you, my dear?" murmured the old gentleman, turning to Patience, whose thoughts were far away. "You always have something to contribute."

"It seems to me," said Patience, "we're making a tempest in a teapot. There's been a theft, and the loot has been returned with interest. So far as we know, then, there hasn't even been a real crime!"

"Merely an interesting problem, eh—nothing more vital?"

She shrugged. "I'm sorry if I'm not very brilliant today, but that's all I can get out of it."

"No crime, hey?" said the Inspector sarcastically.

"Ah," murmured Lane with a faint smile, "you think there *has* been a crime, Inspector?"

"Sure! What's happened to poor old Donoghue?"

The old gentleman closed his eyes for an instant. "The missing doorman. To be sure. It looks suspiciously like violence, I agree. But that, after all, is a matter for the police. No, there's something else."

The tall young man at the door looked from one to another of them with his tired eyes. Patience knit her brows, and there was silence for a moment. Then shrugging, Thumm reached for his telephone. "Police matter or not, that's the only thing I'm really interested in. Gave my promise to find the poor Mick, and I'll do my best." He spoke to Captain Grayson of the Missing Persons Bureau; then he was switched to his friend Inspector Geoghan and conversed briefly. "Nothing new on Donoghue. Man's disappeared as if he was shanghaied. I've given Geoghan the serial number of that century-note we found in the returned book. Maybe he can trace it."

"Possible," agreed Lane. "Well, Patience, I see you wrinkling your pretty nose. Have you discovered my 'something else'?"

"I'm trying hard," she said with exasperation.

"Binding," said young Mr. Rowe laconically.

"Oh, Gor—Mr. Rowe, of course!" cried Patience, flushing. "The object that the chap in the blue hat removed from the back cover of the 1599 Jaggard!"

The old gentleman chuckled. "You young people seem to think together. Wonderful, isn't it, Inspector?—and stop scowling; I told you Gordon was an invaluable imp. That's precisely what I do mean, Patience. You see, the superficially erratic conduct of the thief becomes comprehensible when you work from the thin light object which must have been hidden in the secret pocket of the book's binding. Six weeks or so ago someone broke into the Saxon library and stole a copy, presumably, of the 1599 Jaggard. Not a far stretch to say that this antecedent theft was motivated by the same man—our whimsical creature of the blue *chapeau*. But the book was a forgery; it was returned intact. Then the man in the blue hat was searching for a *genuine* copy! Now how many genuine copies of the first edition of *The Passionate Pilgrim* are in existence? Three, of which the Saxon copy is the third, the last to be found. Probably then he has managed to investigate the other two copies. Having stolen the Saxon copy and found it to be a forgery, he must have known that there was still the genuine Saxon copy in existence. Then Saxon made his bequest to the Britannic Museum; in the bequest was the genuine Jaggard. The thief contrived to get into the museum, contrived to steal this third genuine Jaggard. He left an even rarer volume in its place. Two days later he returned the Jaggard. Tell me, Patience, what further conclusions you can draw from these facts."

"I see," said Patience, sucking her lower lip. "It's much clearer stated that way. The fact that he returned the genuine Jaggard to the museum, but sliced its back cover open and removed something from its secret pocket, shows that he's never been interested in the 1599 Jaggard *as such*, but only in the thin light object it concealed. Having removed this object, he had no further use for the book itself, and returned it like a gentleman."

"Brava!" cried Lane. "A masterly deduction, my dear."

"Brilliant," murmured Mr. Rowe warmly.

"And what else?" asked the old gentleman.

"Well," said Patience, flushing a little, "that brings up another queer point. The 1599 Jaggard is valuable. If he were an ordinary thief he would have kept it, despite the fact that he was really after what the book contained. Then he left a hundred-dollar bill to repair the damage to the leather binding. And besides he originally left an immensely valuable volume in place of the one he stole—apparently because it so much resembled the 1599, or because it was a gesture of honesty on his part. All these things point to an essentially honest person, Mr. Lane, who feels forced to commit a dishonest act but tries to make what amends he can in advance."

The old gentleman was leaning forward with sparkling eyes. He sank back when Patience finished and waved a long forefinger at the Inspector. "Well, old blusterer, what do you think of that?"

The Inspector coughed. "Pretty good, I'd say, pretty good."

"Come, come, Inspector, that's niggardly praise. Perfect, my dear! You're a tonic to these old bones. Yes, that's true. We're dealing with an honest, even conscientious, thief—an anomaly unprecedented, I'm sure, in the history of thieves. A veritable Villon! Anything else?"

"I think it's plain enough," said the young man suddenly. "The fact that he returned the forged Jaggard without even slicing the leather binding shows him to be on remarkably familiar terms with rare books. I'm able to tell you, having seen it, that the forgery isn't so clumsy that even a layman would recognize it as such. He examined the volume, saw instantly that it wasn't genuine, and since he was seeking only a genuine 1599 Jaggard, returned the book untampered with."

"That would make him something very like a bibliophile, wouldn't it?" murmured Patience.

"It would, my dear. Gordon, that's excellent reasoning." The old man rose and began to stride about the room on his long legs. "We've painted, then, a very revealing picture. A scholar, an antiquarian, a bibliophile, essentially forthright, who will go to the length of committing robbery to gain possession of—I think there can be no doubt about it—a piece of paper hidden in the back of an extremely old collector's item. Interesting, eh?"

"Wonder what the deuce it could be?" muttered Thumm.

"The opening, or rather the depression," said Rowe thoughtfully, "is about five inches by three. If it's a piece of paper, then, it's probably folded. And it's probably very old, too."

"It would seem so," murmured Lane, "although that last isn't necessarily true. Yes, the situation is considerably clarified. I wonder now . . ." His magnificent voice trailed off, and he paced in silence for some time, white brows knit over his eyes. "I believe I shall engage in a little investigation of my own," he said finally.

"About Donoghue?" asked Thumm hopefully.

Lane smiled. "No, I shall leave that to you; you're infinitely better at that sort of thing than I. I had in mind," he continued with a frown, "a little research. You know I've a rather remarkable library of my own——"

"It's a scholar's paradise," said Rowe dreamily.

"What sort of research?" demanded Patience.

"Well, my dear, it should prove informative, if not actually helpful, to discover whether the present leather binding of the ravaged Jaggard is the original binding—the age of the *reliure* may prove a clue to the age of the hidden object, which from the nature of the repository, as Gordon has said, is most likely a folded document of some sort."

"I may be able to be of some assistance to you there, Mr. Lane," said the young man eagerly.

"Ah," said the old gentleman. "There's an idea, Gordon. You might work independently, and then we can compare notes."

"I should think, too," said Patience, for some unaccountable reason pleased, "that if a document of some sort had been hidden in such an old book, there might possibly be a record of it somewhere. After all, how did the thief know about it, know where to look?"

"A penetrating thought! I had something of the sort in mind. I shall dig through all the known data about the 1599 first edition of *The Passionate Pilgrim*. There may even be dated records. Jaggard had his finger in a good many publishing pies in Elizabethan London, and his name crops out in hundreds of literary connections. Yes, yes, that's undoubtedly the logical step. What do you think, Gordon?"

"I'll help there, too," said Rowe quietly.

"Good! And you intend to follow up on Donoghue, Inspector?"

"Much as I can. I'll let Grayson of the Missing Persons do most of the work."

"Yes, it's really his job. I can't say, Inspector, that I think there's anything in this for you in a monetary way."

"You're damned right," growled Thumm. "But it's got my dander up. I'll play around with it for a while."

"As quaintly stubborn as ever," chuckled the old man. "Then I've a suggestion for you. If you're interested in the case purely as a provocative problem, why not investigate Dr. Hamnet Sedlar?"

The Inspector was startled, and Patience paused in the act

of accepting Rowe's match to her cigarette. "The duke? Why?"

"Call it a hunch," murmured Lane. "But surely you must have noticed the curious look our friend Crabbe threw at Dr. Sedlar?"

"Goodness, yes!" cried Patience. "Gordon, you noticed it, too!"

"Gordon?" rumbled the Inspector.

"Purely a slip," said Mr. Rowe hurriedly. "Miss Thumm's excited. Miss Thumm, please call me Mr. Rowe. . . . Yes, Pat, I did notice it, and I've been wondering about it ever since."

"What *is* this?" scowled the Inspector. "This Gordon-Pat business?"

"Now, now, Inspector," said Drury Lane, "don't bring personalities into this discussion. Do you realize what a fossilized old tyrant you are? Young people today aren't what they used to be."

"Father," said Patience, scarlet.

"In your day, Inspector," said Mr. Rowe helpfully.

"An introduction, a measuring with the eyes, a kiss in a dark corner," continued Lane smiling; "come, come, Inspector, you'll have to become reconciled to it. As I was saying, Crabbe's the secretive kind, and he covered himself with admirable swiftness, but there's something odd there which I think will bear investigation."

"Still and all," muttered the Inspector, "I don't like it. . . . Hey? It passed right over my head. But if that's so, I think maybe we'd better throw a few questions Mr. Crabbe's way."

Patience studied the tip of her cigarette. "Do you know, father," she said in a low voice, "that gives me a notion. Let's not bother Mr. Crabbe at the moment. But why not check up on Dr. Sedlar at the source?"

"You mean England, Patty?"

"Let's start modestly. How about the steamship company?"

"Steamship company? What the devil for?"

"You never know," murmured Patience.

Forty-five minutes later Inspector Thumm put down his telephone and scrubbed his brow with a violently trembling handkerchief. "Well," he sighed at last. "It just goes to show. It's—it's cock-eyed. . . . Know what the purser of the *Lancastria* just told me?"

"Oh, father," said Patience, "you're *provoking*. What did he say, for heaven's sake?"

"There's no record of a Hamnet Sedlar on the passenger list!"

They stared at one another. Then Gordon Rowe whistled and scuffed his cigarette out in the Inspector's ashtray. "So that's the ticket," he murmured. "The famous Dr. Sedlar . . ."

"I like that," murmured Patience. "I like that exceedingly."

"By God, he's a phony!" bellowed Thumm. "Listen, youngster, you keep this under your hat. Not a word! I'll show that——"

"Here, here, Inspector," said Lane mildly; he was slumped in the leather chair and his smooth brow was wrinkled into a hundred tiny lines. "Not so fast. One good scene doesn't make a play, nor does one suspicious circumstance make a guilty man. I saw you describe Sedlar to the purser. What was that for?"

"Well," snorted Thumm, "when he looked over the list and couldn't find a trace of this bird's name, I described Sedlar and asked the purser to check with his stewards. Boat only docked this morning and they're all within call. He got on the job right away. And, by God, not only wasn't Sedlar's name listed, but nobody of Sedlar's description was even on the boat!" He glared. "What d'ye think of that?"

"It begins," said Rowe thoughtfully, "to smell."

"I admit the odor of guilt grows stronger," muttered the old gentleman. "Queer, queer . . ."

"But don't you see," cried Patience, "what this means? It means that Dr. Sedlar has been in this country a very minimum of four days!"

"How do you figure that out, Patty?" demanded her father.

"He didn't fly across the Atlantic, did he? You remember I called the steamship line last Thursday to find out when the next boat from England was due—Sally Bostwick had written me she was crossing, but hadn't told me when. Well, they told me that there was a Saturday boat, and no other boat until today. So, since today's Wednesday, I say this British chap must be in New York a minimum of four days—at the very least since last Saturday."

"Perhaps even longer," suggested Rowe, frowning. "Sedlar! It's incredible."

"You might check up on the Saturday boat," said Lane absently.

The Inspector reached for his telephone. Then he sat back again. "I'll do better than that. Get it all at one crack." He pressed a button and the moon-eyed Miss Brodie popped into the office as if by magic. "Got your book? Good. Take a cable to Scotland Yard!"

"To—to where, Inspector?" stammered Miss Brodie, overcome by the presence of the athletic young man near the door.

"Scotland Yard. I'll show this smooth limey how we do things over here!" The Inspector's face was very red. "You know where Scotland Yard is, don't you? London, England!"

"Y-yes, sir," said Miss Brodie hurriedly.

"Address it to Chief Inspector Trench. T-r-e-n-c-h. 'Want complete history Hamnet Sedlar, ex-director Kensington Museum, London, now in New York City. Give date of departure from England, physical description, affiliations, reputation, record if any. Confidential. Regards.' Send that off right away."

Miss Brodie stumbled toward Mr. Rowe.

"Wait a minute. How'd you spell that name Sedlar?"

"S-e-d-d-l-e-r," stuttered Miss Brodie, pale with emotion.

The Inspector's chest heaved. Then he smiled. "Now, now, Brodie," he said soothingly, "don't faint. It's all right. Only for God's sake can't you even spell? It's S-e-d-l-a-r!"

"Oh, yes, sir," said Miss Brodie, and fled.

"Poor Brodie," giggled Patience. "Father, you always scare her out of a year's growth. Or perhaps it's the strange masculine presence. . . . Why, what's the matter, Mr. Lane?" she cried, alarmed.

The most startling expression had come over the old gentleman's face. He stared at Thumm as if he had never seen him before; and indeed he seemed not to be seeing him now. Then he sprang to his feet.

"Good Lord!" he cried. "So *that's* it!" And he began to stride hungrily about the room, muttering to himself.

"What's it?" asked the Inspector, staring.

"The name, the name! Hamnet Sedlar. . . . Lord, it—it's incredible! There's simply no justice if it's a coincidence."

"The name?" Patience wrinkled her forehead. "Why, what's wrong with the name, Mr. Lane? It seems perfectly sound English, if a little quaint."

Gordon Rowe's mouth was hanging open like the lips of a descending crane. All the mischief had deserted his hazel eyes, to be supplanted by a shocked intelligence.

Lane stopped striding, rubbed his chin, and then burst into a long low chuckle. "Yes, yes, perfectly sound English, Patience; you've a talent for striking at the heart of things. That's precisely what it is. It's English with a history, by Jove! Ah, Gordon, I see the light has burst upon you, too." He stopped chuckling and sat down suddenly. His voice was grave. "I knew that name had struck a responsive note," he said slowly. "It's been annoying me ever since we met the gentleman who bears it. Your spelling it . . . Inspector, Patience, doesn't 'Hamnet Sedlar' mean anything to you?"

The Inspector looked blank. "Not a blamed thing."

"Well, Patience, with all respect to your esteemed father, you've the advantage of a superior education. Didn't you study English literature?"

"Of course."

"Concentrate at all on the Elizabethan period?"

Patience's cheeks bloomed brightly. "It—it's all very remote."

The old gentleman nodded sadly. "There's modern education for you. So you've never heard of Hamnet Sedlar. Strange. Gordon, tell them who Hamnet Sedlar was."

"Hamnet Sedlar," said young Mr. Rowe in a thick dazed voice, *"was one of William Shakespeare's closest friends."*

"Shakespeare!" cried Thumm. "Is that right, Lane? You all going dotty? What's old Shake got to do with this?"

"A great deal, I'm beginning to think," murmured Mr. Drury Lane. "Yes, Gordon, that's right," he said thoughtfully, and shook his head. "Naturally, you would know. Sedlar . . . Lord!"

"I'm afraid I don't understand," complained Patience. "In this, at any rate, I'm one with father. Surely——"

"This Sedlar bird isn't the Wandering Jew, is he?" jeered the Inspector. "What the devil—he can't be over three hundred years old!" and he guffawed heartily.

"Ha, ha," said Mr. Rowe with a profound sigh.

"I'm not suggesting our friend is Ahasuerus," smiled Lane. "There is nothing quite so preposterous in the events to date. But I am suggesting that the present Dr. Hamnet Sedlar, ex-curator of the Kensington Museum in London, incumbent of the Britannic Museum in New York, British, cultured, a bibliophile . . . oh, no, it's not at all impossible that Dr. Sedlar is a lineal descendant of the man who has come down to us in history only by virtue of the fact that Shakespeare called him friend."

"A Stratford family?" asked Patience thoughtfully.

The old man shrugged. "We know next to nothing about them."

"I think," muttered Rowe, "that the Sedlars hailed from Gloucestershire."

"But what connection," protested Patience, "even if Dr. Sedlar is a descendant of Shakespeare's boy-friend, could there possibly be between the old Sedlar family and this 1599 edition of the Jaggard *Passionate Pilgrim* that's been causing all this fuss?"

"That, my dear," said Mr. Drury Lane quietly, "is precisely the question. It was an inspiration, Inspector, as it's turned out, to cable your British friend at Scotland Yard. Perhaps we'll learn. . . . Who knows? *The Passionate Pilgrim* itself can't— But then . . ."

He fell silent. The Inspector sat helplessly, looking from his friend to his daughter. Young Gordon Rowe stared at Lane, and Patience stared at Rowe.

Lane rose suddenly and reached for his blackthorn stick. They watched him in silence.

"Curious," he said. "Very curious," and nodding and smiling a little absently, he left the Inspector's office.

11

3HS wM

Dromio cheerfully cursed a traffic officer beneath his breath and swung the black Lincoln off Fifth Avenue into one of the Forties. He picked his way through a labyrinth of traffic and brought the car to rest at the corner of Sixth Avenue, stopped by a red light.

Mr. Drury Lane sat silently in the tonneau of the car, tapping his lips with the sharp edge of a slip of yellow paper. For the dozenth time he glanced at the message typed upon it, and frowned. It was a telegram, its dateline reading: "June 21 —12.06 a.m." the message had been delivered to The Hamlet in Westchester in the early hours of the morning.

"Queer time for Thumm to send me a wire," thought the

old man. "Midnight! He's never done a thing like that before. . . . Urgent? It isn't possible that——"

Dromio leaned on his klaxon. A car had locked fenders with another at the corner; they were straining at each other like two bulls, and there was an appalling tangle of traffic behind. Lane glanced over his shoulder at the mess extending to Fifth Avenue, and then leaned forward and tapped Dromio's ear.

"I think I shall walk the rest of the way," he said. "It's only a block. Wait for me near Inspector Thumm's office."

He got out of the car, still holding the telegram. Then he put it carefully into the sack pocket of his spruce pongee suit and strode off toward Broadway.

He found the Thumm Detective Avency in a strange state of turmoil. The lunar-eyed Miss Brodie in the anteroom seemed to have contracted the general infection: she sat nervously and stared with mournful uneasiness at Patience, who was striding up and down behind the railing like a fuming regimental sergeant-major, biting her lips and hurling passionate glances at the office clock on the wall.

At the sound of the opening door she jumped, and Miss Brodie uttered a gentle scream.

"So you've come!" cried Patience, grasping the old gentleman's arm in a death grip. "I thought you'd never get here. You're a precious darling!" and to his astonishment she threw her soft arms about his neck and kissed him vigorously on the cheek.

"My dear child," protested Lane, "you're trembling! What on earth has happened? The Inspector's wire was bursting with suppressed portents, but it told me exactly nothing. I trust he's well?"

"As well as might be expected," replied Patience grimly. Then her eyes sparkled and she touched a shining ringlet above her ear and said: "And now let's attack the——the corpse."

She pushed open the Inspector's door and revealed a red-eyed but otherwise pale elderly gentleman who sat stiffly on the edge of his swivel-chair and like a determined boa-constrictor glared at an object on the desk before him.

"Eureka!" he shouted, scrambling to his feet. "Old Faithful, by God. I told you we could depend on the old rascal, Patty! Sit down, Lane, sit down. It's swell of you to come."

Lane sank into the leather armchair. "Heavens, what a reception! You make me feel like the returning prodigal. Now tell me what's happened. I'm perishing of curiosity."

Thumm grasped the object he had been so painfully studying. "See this?"

"I've excellent eyesight, as you know. Yes, I see it."

The Inspector chuckled. "Well, we're going to open it."

Lane stared from Thumm to Patience. "But— Well, do so, by all means. Is this why you wired me to come in, Inspector?"

"We wired you to come in," said Patience quickly, "because some maniac insisted that you be present at the grand opening. Father, *please*. I'll go mad myself if you don't open it this instant!"

It was the long brown manila envelope which the curious gentleman with the dappled beard and blue glasses had left in the Inspector's safekeeping almost seven weeks before.

Lane took the envelope from Thumm's hand and examined it with a swift experimental pressure. His eyes narrowed as he felt the contours of the squarish envelope within. "This mystery calls for an explanation. I should like to know the facts before . . . No, no, my dear, I've told you on several occasions in the past to cultivate—ha, ha—Patience. Proceed, Inspector."

Thumm tersely related the story of the disguised Englishman's visit on the sixth of May. With interpolations by Patience, it was a very complete tale, down to a minute description of the visitor. When the Inspector had finished, Lane glanced thoughtfully at the envelope. "But why didn't you tell me this before? That's not like you, Inspector."

"Didn't think it was necessary. Come on, let's go!"

"Just a moment. I take it, then, that this being the twenty-first of the month, your mysterious client failed to telephone you yesterday on schedule?"

"He called up on the twentieth of May, though," said the Inspector glumly.

"We sat here all the livelong day," snapped Patience, "until midnight yesterday. Not a peep out of him. And now——"

"Did you by any chance make a transcript of the man's conversation?" asked Lane absently. "I know you've a detectograph here."

Thumm jabbed a button. "Miss Brodie. Get that transcript of the envelope case."

They sat in agony while the old man very deliberately read the word-for-word report of the visitor's call.

"Hmm," he said, putting down the report. "Very strange. Quite true, of course, that the creature was disguised. Clumsy, clumsy! No slightest effort, apparently, at realism. The beard . . ." He shook his head. "Very well, Inspector, I think we may proceed. Do the honors."

He rose, tossed the envelope on Thumm's desk, sat down in a chair beside the desk, and leaned forward intently. Patience hurried around the desk to stand behind her father's chair; she was breathing quickly and her usually serene features were pale and agitated. With shaking fingers Thumm pulled out the sliding leaf on the side of the desk near Lane, placed the envelope upon it, and sank into his swivel-chair. He was perspiring freely. Then he looked up at Lane—they faced each other across the utility board—and grinned feebly.

"Well, here goes," he jeered. "And I hope it doesn't jump out at me and say 'April Fool' or something."

Behind him Patience sighed for sheer need of breath.

The Inspector grasped a letter-knife, hesitated, and then plunged the blade beneath the flap of the manila envelope. He cut the flap swiftly, dropped the knife, squeezed the ends of the envelope, and peered inside.

"Well?" cried Patience.

"You were right, Patty," he muttered. "It's another envelope." And he took out a small square envelope, neutral gray in tone, which was in turn sealed. The face was blank.

"What's that on the flap?" asked the old gentleman sharply.

The Inspector turned the envelope over. His face went as gray as the paper.

Patience, scanning the flap over his shoulder, gasped.

Thumm licked his lips. "It says," he said hoarsely, "it says —cripes!—it says: THE SAXON LIBRARY!"

It was the first indication they had had that the visit of the mysterious man with the Joseph's beard might have been connected with the strange events at the Britannic Museum.

"The Saxon Library," murmured Lane. "How curious."

"So that's how it is!" cried Thumm. "Good God, what've we run into?"

"Apparently," said the old man with difficulty, "a coincidence, Inspector. It happens sometimes. With sufficient frequency to make one wonder at—" His voice trailed off, but he did not remove his eyes from the Inspector's lips. Yet they saw nothing, for there was a gloss over them, as if a veil had dropped—a veil to mask the blinding realization that had leaped into them.

"But I can't understand—" began Patience dazedly.

Lane shivered, and the veil disintegrated. "Open it, Inspector," he said, leaning forward and cupping his chin in his hands. "Please."

Thumm picked up the letter-knife again. He inserted the blade behind the flap and slowly exerted pressure. The paper was tough and yielded reluctantly.

Neither Lane nor Patience so much as blinked.

Thumm's large fingers dipped into the envelope and emerged with a sheet of light gray stationery of the same tint as the envelope, neatly folded. He unfolded it. There was printing at one of the short ends of the sheet. The Inspector turned the sheet around; the legend at the top said simply: THE SAXON LIBRARY, in a darker gray printing ink. He spread the paper flat on the sliding board between him and Lane and stared. They all stared, and there was utter stillness in the office.

And reason for it. For if the disguised Englishman had been a mysterious figure, the message he had deposited in the Inspector's care was even more mysterious. More than mysterious, it was cryptic. It made no sense at all.

At the top of the sheet there was the imprint of the Saxon Library. The rest of the sheet was as virgin as the day it had rolled off the printer's press, except for a single inscription, or insignia. Roughly in the center of the sheet below the imprint appeared the following:

3HS wM

And that was all. No intelligible message, no signature, no other pen or pencil mark of any kind.

A fierce suppressed paroxysm seized the aged body of Lane. He crouched in his chair, engulfing the insignia with his staring eyes. The Inspector's fingers suddenly were stricken with palsy; the paper shook as his hand rested upon its lower corner. Patience did not stir. For a long moment none of them stirred. Then the old man tore his eyes slowly from the outspread sheet and looked up at Thumm. There was a queer triumph, almost exultation, in the crystal depths. He opened his mouth to speak.

But the Inspector mumbled: "3HS wM," in wondering

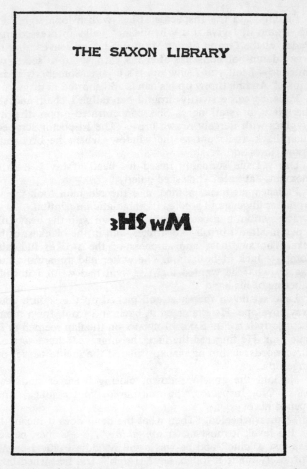

THE SAXON LIBRARY

3HS wM

tones, rolling the syllables on his tongue as if to extract their hidden meaning from the mere sounds.

A faint perplexity came over Lane's face. He glanced swiftly at Patience.

And she said: "3HS wM," like a child repeating the words of a foreign language.

The old man buried his face in his hands, and sat that way without moving.

"Well!" said the Inspector at last with a long sigh, "I give up. Damn it, I give up. When a guy walks in dressed up like Paddy at the Grand Street Masquerade and leaves a string of crazy damnfool nonsense after his yarn about a 'secret worth millions'—I tell you I give up. It's a joke. Somebody's idea of a joke." And he threw up his hands and snorted in disgust.

Patience came swiftly around her father's chair and seized the piece of stationery. She concentrated upon the hieroglyphics with fiercely drawn brows. The Inspector scraped his chair back and went to the window, where he brooded out upon Times Square.

Drury Lane suddenly raised his head. "May I see that a moment, Patience?" he asked quietly.

Patience sat back, baffled, and the old man took the sheet from her fingers and studied its enigmatic inscription.

The symbol had been hastily set down with the heavy nib of a pen in almost brush-like strokes, and in the blackest of black inks. The swiftness and sureness of the strokes indicated a complete lack of hesitation. The writer had apparently known exactly what he wanted to write, and had written it with no faltering of his hand.

Lane set down the sheet and picked up the square neutral-gray envelope. He examined it, back and front, for a moment; the inscription THE SAXON LIBRARY on the flap seemed to fascinate him. He fingered the flap; the engraved characters of the three words, a shining black, titillated the tactile nerves of his fingertips.

He laid the envelope down, closing his eyes and leaning back. "No, Inspector," he murmured, "not a joke." And he opened his eyes.

Thumm wheeled. "Then what the devil does it mean? If it's on the level, it must mean *something*. . . . Cripes, he said it was just a 'clue,' and he was right. Muddiest clue *I* ever saw. Purposely made it tough, hey? Hmph!" and he turned back to the window.

Patience frowned. "It can't be so difficult. Cryptic as he might have desired to make it, he would still make it essentially simple enough to be grasped after a reasonable amount of study. Let's see, now. . . . Of course it might be an original kind of shorthand, mightn't it? Concealing a message of some sort."

The Inspector grunted without turning around.

"Or," continued Patience thoughtfully, "it might be a chemical symbol. *H* is the symbol of hydrogen, isn't it?—and *S* of sulphur. Hydrogen—hydrogen sulphide. That's it!"

"No," said Lane in a low tone. "That would be H_2S, I believe. I don't think HS is chemically possible. No, not chemistry, Patience."

"And then, too," said Patience in despair, "the small *w* and the Capital *M*. . . . Oh lord! it's hopeless. I wish Gordon were here. He knows so many *useless* things."

The Inspector swung about slowly. "Hopeless it is," he said in a strange tone. "For us, Patty. And for your frisky Mr. Rowe, too. But don't forget this mysterious bird said he wanted Lane in on it. So maybe he figured Lane would know what it meant . . . hey, Lane?"

Lane in the face of this palpable challenge sat very still. Then the wrinkles appeared at the corners of his eyes. "Suspicions?" he said. "Yet perhaps I do, old Roman, perhaps I do."

"Well, what the devil does it mean, then?" asked the Inspector flatly, coming forward.

Lane waved a limp white hand. He kept staring at the sheet before him. "The peculiar part of it is," he murmured, "I believe he thought *you* would know what it meant, too."

The Inspector flushed, straightened, and went to the door. "Miss Brodie! Come in here with your book."

Miss Brodie came in quickly, pencil poised.

"Take a letter to Dr. Leo Schilling. Medical Examiner's office. 'Dear Doc: Get busy on this right away. Under your hat. Does the following string of crazy pothooks mean anything to you question mark.' Then put this down: '3 capital H capital S space small w capital M.' Got that?"

Miss Brodie looked up dazedly. "Y-yes, sir."

"Send the same letter to Lieutenant Rupert Schiff, Bureau of Intelligence, Cypher Department, Washington, D.C. Scoot."

Miss Brodie scooted.

"That," said the Inspector savagely, "ought to get results."

He slipped into a chair, lighted a cigar, stretched his columnar legs, and puffed a thoughtful cloud at the ceiling.

"First tack, seems to me," he said, "is the letterhead angle. This guy breezes in, gives us a cock-and-bull story, and leaves a note with this blarney in it. Didn't want us to know it had anything to do with the Saxons; that's why he stuck the small envelope into the manila, which didn't have an identifying inscription. But if anything happened to him, he wanted us to open the envelope. So he wanted us to read *The Saxon Library* and work on that angle. Seems clear enough so far."

Lane nodded. "I thoroughly agree."

"What he didn't figure on is that George Fisher would come in here and tell us about Donoghue, and that that would take us to the Britannic Museum and get us mixed up in that funny business of the stolen books. Where that comes in, I'm damned if I know. Maybe it's just coincidence, this Saxon stationery."

"No, father," said Patience wearily, "I'm sure that's not so. I'm convinced that the man with the false beard and the queer events in the Britannic are connected. And that this symbol written on the Saxon Library stationery is the connecting link. I wonder——"

"What?" asked Thumm with a shrewd squint at his daughter.

Patience laughed. "It's an inane thought. But then the whole thing's inane. . . . I'm wondering if this chap with the false beard mightn't—mightn't have been somebody of the Saxon household dressed in disguise!"

"Not so silly," murmured the Inspector with exaggerated indifference. "I kind of had the same notion, Patty. Take, now, this Rowe feller——"

"Nonsense!" said Patience sharply, and both men looked at her quickly. "It—it couldn't have been Gordon." She had the grace to blush.

"Why not?" demanded Thumm. "Seems to me he was almighty anxious to sit in on our confab that day when we left the museum."

"I assure you," said Patience stiffly, "that his—er—anxiety had nothing to do with the case. It—it—mightn't it have been personal? I'm not exactly an old crone, father."

"Damn' sight rather it *wasn't* personal," snapped Thumm.

"Father! Sometimes you exasperate me to tears. What on earth have you against poor Gordon? He's a very nice young man, and as frank and honest as a—as a child. And besides he has very strong wrists, and the man who came here May sixth didn't."

"Well, he's one of these here, now, bibliophiles, isn't he?" said Thumm belligerently.

Patience bit her lip. "Oh—shoot!"

"Lookin' it over," continued the Inspector, rubbing the tip of his squashed nose, "it couldn't have been Mrs. Saxon, though I did have a crazy feeling at one time it might have been a woman. But Mrs. Saxon's a fat horse, and this bird was skinny. So maybe—mind you, I'm not eliminating Rowe, either!—maybe it was Crabbe."

"That's different," said Patience, tossing her head. "He certainly fits all the physical qualifications."

Mr. Drury Lane, who had been a silent and amused listener to this colloquy, held up his hand. "If I may be permitted to interrupt this profound discussion," he drawled, "may I point out a possible objection to this whole theory? Your visitor maintained, and I see no reason to doubt it, that if he did not telephone on a twentieth it would mean that something drastic had happened to him. If young Gordon Rowe—preposterous, Inspector!—or Crabbe had been your visitor on May sixth, why hasn't one of them disappeared, or turned up murdered, or in some other way incapacitated?"

"That's true, too," said Patience eagerly. "Of course! There you are, father. I lunched with Gordon yesterday, and this morning I spoke to him on the telephone, and he—he didn't say a word about any such thing. I'm sure——"

"Listen, Patty," said the Inspector in a thick alarmed voice. "Listen to your old man for once. Patty, you got a shine on that young squirt? He been makin' love to you? Why, I'll wring his fool neck——"

Patience rose. "Father!" she said furiously.

"Come, come, Inspector," murmured the old gentleman, "don't revert to the Middle Ages. Gordon Rowe's an excellent young man and quite Patience's intellectual equal, which is saying a good deal."

"But I tell you I'm *not* in love with him!" cried Patience. "Father, you're being beastly. Can't I be nice to a man——"

The Inspector looked tragic.

Mr. Drury Lane rose. "Stop squabbling. Inspector, you're an infant. Put this sheet of paper and the envelopes very carefully away into your safe. We must visit the Saxon house at once."

12

Hands Across

Traffic was heavy, and Dromio chafed under the necessity of crawling the Lincoln up Fifth Avenue. But Mr. Drury Lane seemed in no hurry. He glanced quietly from Thumm to Patience. Once he chuckled.

"You're a pair of pettish children. Smile!" They smiled feebly. "A remarkable case," he continued. "I don't believe either of you realizes quite how remarkable it is."

"I've got a headache," grumbled the Inspector.

"And you, Patience?"

"I think," said Patience, gazing steadily at the nape of Dromio's neck, "that the symbol means more to you than it does to us."

The old gentleman actually was startled. He sat forward abruptly, studying her smooth young face with penetration. "Perhaps," he said. "All in good time. Inspector, have there been any developments? So much has happened this morning that I haven't had a chance to ask."

"A lot's happened," said the Inspector wearily. "Brodie took it all down this morning. I knew you'd want to know." He handed Lane a typewritten report.

DONOGHUE: Still missing. No trace.

17 SCHOOLTEACHERS: Gone back to Indiana. All identities checked, and jibe. Careful investigation. Photographs, descriptions, addresses, names—all in order.

$100 BILL: From returned 1599 Jaggard. No success in attempt to trace serial number.

MAN IN BLUE HAT: Still unaccounted for.

19TH MAN IN BUS: Still unaccounted for.

"Is this all, Inspector?" said Lane, returning the sheet; he seemed disappointed. "I thought you had cabled Scotland Yard."

"Never forget, do you, you old fox?" grinned Thumm. "No, that's more like an elephant, isn't it? Yes, I got an answer from Trench at the Yard, and it's a honey. Came late yesterday. Get an eyeful of this."

He handed Lane several sheets of cablegram paper, and these the old man clutched to his breast with avidity. They watched his face. It grew sterner as he read.

The cablegram was addressed to the Inspector, and ran:

REFERENCE HAMNET SEDLAR DESCENDED FROM OLD ENGLISH STOCK DATING TO SECOND CRUSADE ONE HAMNET SEDLAR FAMOUS FOR FRIENDSHIP WITH W SHAKESPEARE PRESENT H S FIVE FEET ELEVEN INCHES TALL ELEVEN STONE THIN WIRY SHARP FEATURES BLUE EYES SANDY HAIR NO IDENTIFYING MARKS KNOWN AGE FIFTY-ONE LITTLE KNOWN OF HIS PERSONAL LIFE HAS LED LIFE OF RECLUSE IN LONDON FOR AT LEAST TWELVE YEARS COMING FROM TEWKESBURY GLOUCESTERSHIRE NOT FAR FROM STRATFORD ON AVON IS BY PROFESSION ANTIQUARIAN CHIEFLY BIBLIOPHILIC WELL-ESTABLISHED REPUTATION IN BIBLIOLOGY PAST TWELVE YEARS CURATOR OF KENSINGTON MUSEUM LONDON RECENTLY ACCEPTED OFFER OF JAMES WYETH AMERICAN FINANCIER AND COLLECTOR TO ASSUME CURATORSHIP OF BRITANNIC MUSEUM NEW YORK ACCEPTANCE CAME AS SURPRISE TO ASSOCIATES FOR SEDLAR HAS OFTEN EXPRESSED HIMSELF AS ANTI-AMERICAN FORMALLY RESIGNED FROM ACTIVE CHARGE OF KENSINGTON MUSEUM ON MAY SEVENTH AT BANQUET IN HIS HONOR IN LONDON GIVEN BY DIRECTORS HAMNET S HAS NO KIN EXCEPT A BROTHER WILLIAM WHOSE WHEREABOUTS ARE UNKNOWN WILLIAM HAS NOT BEEN IN ENGLAND FOR SEVERAL YEARS NOTHING SHADY IN BACKGROUND OF SEDLARS THEY HAVE APPARENTLY LED UPRIGHT AUSTERE SCHOLARLY LIVES HAMNET S LEFT ENGLAND ON S S CYRINTHIA FRIDAY MAY SEVENTEENTH DOCKING NEW YORK ON WEDNESDAY MAY TWENTY-SECOND DEFINITE PROOF H S ON THIS SHIP FROM PURSER'S RECORDS AT YOUR SERVICE IF FURTHER REQUIRED WARMEST PERSONAL REGARDS

TRENCH

"What d'ye think of that?" said the Inspector triumphantly.

"Extraordinary," murmured Lane, returning the cablegram. His forehead was furrowed and his eyes blank.

"It's clear now that Sedlar landed in New York," said Patience, "a full week before he claimed. Seven days! What did he do in New York—if he stayed here—during that week? Why did he lie about it in the first place? I don't like that 'upright' gentleman!"

"I've passed the word along to Geoghan at H.q.," said Thumm, "on the quiet, to try and trace his movements between the twenty-second and the twenty-ninth. It's the same guy, all right—description fits perfectly. But he's got a screw loose somewhere, and I don't like him any more than Patty does."

"Of what, exactly, do you suspect him?" asked Lane.

The Inspector shrugged. "Well, he's clear on one count. He couldn't have been the queer duck with the phony beard and the English accent that left the note with me. According to Trench's information Sedlar didn't leave England until the seventeenth, and my man visited me in New York on the sixth. "But"—and he grinned wolfishly—"he could have been somebody else, by God, and I'd bet dollars to doughnuts he was!"

"Indeed?" said the old gentleman. "And who might that be?"

"This crazy guy in the blue hat throwin' rare books and hundred-dollar bills around!" exclaimed Thumm. "That specimen of insanity came out in the open on May twenty-seventh, and that was five days after Sedlar landed on the q.t. in New York!"

"That's scarcely airtight reasoning, Inspector," smiled Lane. "By the same token the man in the blue hat might have been one of several million persons whose movements on May twenty-seventh cannot be accounted for."

The Inspector digested this and apparently, from the expression on his hardbitten face, did not like its savor. "Yeah, I know, but——"

"Oh, good Lord!" cried Patience suddenly, jumping up and striking her head against the roof of the tonneau. "Ouch! I'm a fool. Why didn't I think of that before?"

"Think of what before?" asked Lane softly.

"The symbol, the symbol! It—oh, how blind I've been!"

Lane regarded her steadily. "What about the symbol, my child?"

Patience fumbled for her handkerchief and blew her nose vigorously. "It's very clear." She put the kerchief away and sat up, her eyes sparkling. "3HS wM. Don't you see?"

"*I* don't see any more now than I did before," growled Thumm.

"Oh, father, the *HS* must stand for *Hamnet Sedlar!*"

Both men stared, and both men broke into chuckles. Patience tapped indignantly with a slippered toe. "I think that's extremely poor manners," she said in an injured tone. "What's wrong with that theory?"

"But what do the other elements of the symbol stand for, my dear?" asked the old gentleman mildly. "I'm sorry I was rude, but your father's chuckle is infectious. How do you explain the 3 and the small *w* and the capital *M?*"

She stared at Dromio's solid red neck, offended—and doubtful.

"Oh, Patty, Patty!" choked the Inspector, doubled up. "You'll be the death of me yet. I'll tell you what it stands for. Ho, ho, ho! It stands for 'three portions of Hamnet Sedlar with Mustard!' "

"That's *so* funny," said Patience frigidly. "I believe we've arrived."

13

The Saga of Dr. Ales

A very English butler with wonderful sideburns admitted them superbly to a Louis Quinze reception room. No, Mrs. Saxon was not at home. No, he had no idea when Mrs. Saxon would return. No, she had left no message. No, she——

"Listen, you!" snarled Inspector Thumm, that violent foe of flunkeyism, "is Crabbe in?"

"Mr. Crabbe? I'll see, sir," replied Sideburns stiffly. "Whom shall I say, sir?"

"Say anybody you blasted please, but get him out here!"

An eyebrow rose, Sideburns bowed slightly, and sailed away.

Patience sighed. "Father, did anyone ever tell you you've atrocious manners? Bellowing at a servant!"

"I don't like these limeys," grumbled the Inspector, slightly abashed. "All except Trench. Only human Englishman I ever met. You'd think he'd been born in the Fifth Ward. . . . Well, well, here's Little Lord Fauntleroy."

Gordon Rowe, passing through the foyer, book under his

arm and hat in hand, started, grinned, and hurried into the reception room. "Avaunt! What ho, visitors! Charming of you to call. Mr. Lane, Inspector—Pat! You didn't tell me over the 'phone——"

"I didn't know," said Patience with dignity.

"Divine ignorance." The young man's hazel eyes narrowed. "On a trail?" he said in a low voice.

"Gordon," said Patience abruptly, "what does 3HS wM mean to you?"

"Patty, for God's sake!" snarled the Inspector. "We don't want——"

"Please. Inspector," said Drury Lane quietly. "There's no reason why Gordon shouldn't know."

The young man looked from Patience to the two men. "Abracadabra to me," he said. "What's it all about?"

Patience told him.

"The Saxon Library," he muttered. "That's the funniest thing— This *is* a problem! I think. . . . Hold it. Here comes Crabbe."

The ancient librarian shuffled quickly into the reception room, holding a pair of gold-rimmed spectacles aloft in one hand and peering inquisitively at his callers. He brightened at once and came forward. Patience would have sworn his bones groaned and creaked in the process.

"Ah, Mr. Lane," said Crabbe with a leathery smile. "And Miss Thumm. *And* the Inspector. Quite a deputation! Rowe, I thought you were going out? Or perhaps the young lady's presence——? Mrs. Saxon is indisposed, you know. Belly-ache. With her girth, of course, that's a major tragedy." He grinned, an *enfant terrible*. "And to what——?"

"For one thing," smiled Lane, before the Inspector could get out what was already growling in the depths of his thick throat, "we should like to see the famous Saxon Library."

"I see." Crabbe stood still, one thin shoulder lower than the other, head cocked on a side, squinting with remarkable keenness at his visitors. "Just a friendly visit of exploration, eh?" He cackled, showing decrepit gums, and swung about. "No reason why you shouldn't," he said with astonishing amiability. "Although really you're the first strangers . . . Eh, Rowe? Shall we break the rule for once?"

"That's human of you," grinned young Rowe.

"Oh, I'm not so bad as I'm painted. Follow me, please."

He led them down several corridors embellished in the

grand French style to what was apparently an east wing of the mansion. He unlocked a heavy door and stood aside with what might have been a welcoming smile, but succeeded only in being the villainous grimace of an *opéra bouffe* Fagin. They entered a vast room with a lofty ceiling ribbed with square oak beams, the walls bristling with full bookshelves. A huge vault frowned from one corner. At the farther side there was an open door through which they could see another chamber apparently quite as large and similarly lined with books. A large desk and one chair stood in the center of the room; there was a billowing Persian rug on the floor; and nothing else.

"Sorry I can't offer you chairs," said Crabbe in his rustling voice, closing the door and going to the desk. "But no one ever uses the library except old Crabbe these days. Rowe's quite deserted me. Ah, youth, always flitting after the will-o'-the-wisp!" He cackled again. "I had Mr. Saxon's desk and chair removed when he died. Now what would you like to——"

He broke off, actually startled. The Inspector, who had been hurling surly glances about, had suddenly pounced forward toward the desk as if he meant to demolish it. "Ha!" he cried. "That's it! That's it!" and he snatched from the desk a sheet of neutral-gray stationery.

"What on earth——?" began Crabbe in astonishment; and then his pointed face screwed up with rage and he darted toward Thumm with something very like a snarl. "You take your hands off things!" he shrieked. "So that's it. It was a trick. Spying——"

"Lay off, runt," growled the Inspector, flinging away the librarian's curving talons. "Keep your shirt on. No one's stealing anything. We just wanted to take a look at your stationery. And by God, it's good-looking, too! Have a squint at this, Lane."

But there was no need for close scrutiny. One glance was sufficient to establish that this was the same stationery as had been employed for the writing of the cryptic symbol by the man with the pied beard.

"No doubt about it, of course," murmured Lane. "You'll excuse the Inspector's rather violent methods, Mr. Crabbe; he's a trifle high-handed in these matters."

"Indeed," sniffed Crabbe, glaring at the Inspector's back.

"Have you an envelope, please?" continued Lane with a smile.

Crabbe hesitated, scratched his wrinkled cheeks, shrugged,

and went to the desk. He produced a small square gray envelope.

"The very same," breathed Patience. "What *can* it—?" and then she stopped and glanced very suspiciously at the old librarian.

Young Gordon Rowe seemed much agitated, for him; and he showed it by remaining perfectly still and glaring at the envelope.

"Sit down, my dear," said Lane softly; obediently she took the lone chair. "Inspector, control yourself. We mustn't alarm Mr. Crabbe. Now, sir, I'm sure you have no objection to answering a few simple questions?"

A shrewd and faintly baffled glint came into Crabbe's beady eyes. "Of course not. Old Crabbe's got nothing to conceal. I haven't a notion what this is about, but if I can be of any service . . ."

"Splendid of you," said the old gentleman heartily. "Now, who exactly uses this stationery with the imprint of *The Saxon Library?*"

"I do."

"Naturally. For the usual library correspondence. But who else?"

"No one, Mr. Lane."

"Ha," said Thumm; and Lane shook his head at him impatiently.

"This is very important, Mr. Crabbe. You're positive?"

"No one but myself, I assure you," replied the librarian with a licking of his thin chops.

"Not even Mrs. Saxon?"

"Oh, Lord, no. Mrs. Saxon has her own stationery—half a dozen kinds. And since she never bothers with the library, you see——"

"Quite so. But how about you, Gordon? You've been living here for some time. Can you throw a little light on the subject?"

Patience watched the young man anxiously, and the Inspector eyed him with what he fancied was detached coolness.

"I?" Young Rowe seemed startled. "Ask friend Crabbe. He's cock of this walk."

"Oh, Mr. Rowe rarely if ever comes here, Mr. Lane," squeaked Crabbe, his torso curved like a melting candle. "Our young friend has been doing some research in Shakespeare, as I suppose you know, but it's been a rule of the household— Mr. Saxon's own rule, you understand—and . . . When he's wanted anything, he's asked me and I've given him the requested volumes."

"I hope," said Mr. Rowe huffily, "that that answers your question, Mr. Lane."

The old gentleman smiled. "Down off your horse, Gordon. You know that's a very infantile attitude. You would say, then, Mr. Crabbe, that aside from yourself no one in this house has access to the Saxon Library stationery?"

"I would say so, yes. It's kept only here, you know. Of course, if someone really wanted to——"

"Yes, yes, Mr. Crabbe, we thoroughly understand that. Gordon, please smile. I take it these rooms have been forbidden territory for years. Now——"

"How about the servants?" asked Patience suddenly, avoiding the misery in Rowe's eyes.

"No, Miss Thumm. That's been a strict rule. I clean these rooms myself. Mr. Saxon insisted on it."

"When the books left to the Britannic were packed off," asked Lane, "were you present, Mr. Crabbe?"

"Certainly."

"I was, too," muttered Mr. Rowe morbidly.

"Every moment?"

"Oh, yes," said Crabbe. "Mr. Rowe fussed about the truckmen, but I had my eyes open, I assure you." Crabbe snapped his toothless gums together viciously. That he had kept his eyes open, that he would always keep his eyes open, seemed unquestionable.

"Well!" smiled Lane. "All this, Inspector, seems to establish that it's difficult to get one's clutches on a sheet of this stationery. Doesn't seem to wash, does it?"

"You're tellin' me?" grinned Thumm.

Lane gazed squarely into the old librarian's eyes. "There is no mystery about this, Mr. Crabbe," he said quietly. "We have come into possession of a sheet of Saxon Library stationery—and an envelope—the source of which it is necessary for us to trace. You're innocently making it difficult. . . ." Suddenly a thought struck him, for he smacked his forehead and exclaimed: "How stupid I've been! Of course!"

"Piece of my stationery?" said Crabbe, puzzled.

The old gentleman tapped Crabbe's shoulder. "Do you often have visitors?"

"Visitors? To the Saxon Library? He, he! Tell him, Rowe."

"This prime sample of fossilized wormwood," said Mr. Rowe with a shrug, "is the world's most faithful watchdog."

"Come, come, you must have some. Please think! Has there been any visitor to this room in recent months whom you have reason to recall?"

Crabbe's eyes blinked. His scraggly jaw opened a little, and he stared at his inquisitor without seeing him. Then astonishingly he doubled in laughter and slapped his scrawny shanks. "Ho, ho! That's—that's one on me!" and he straightened and wiped his rheumy eyes.

"Ah," said Lane. "I believe we have struck oil. Well, sir?"

Crabbe stopped laughing as abruptly as he had begun. He half-turned his reptilian head and rasped his dry palms together. "So that's it, eh? Well, well. Wonders never cease. . . . Yes, there was one. Yes, indeed. A very interesting gentleman. He called several times before I would see him. Then when I did see him, he begged—very prettily, he, he!—if I would not permit him just a glimpse of the famous Saxon collection."

"Yes?" said Lane sharply.

"He was a book fancier, he said, and he'd heard so much— You know. As a matter of fact," continued Crabbe slyly, "the man knew books. So I let down the bars once—he looked harmless enough—and showed him this room. He was working on something, he said, and was most anxious to consult a certain volume. It would take just a moment, he said. . . ."

"What was the book?" demanded Rowe with a frown. "You never told me about this, Crabbe!"

"Didn't I, my boy? I must have forgotten," chuckled Crabbe. "It was the 1599 edition of the Jaggard *Passionate Pilgrim!*"

For a moment they were silent, scarcely daring to look at one another.

"Go on," urged Lane softly. "And you brought it out for him?"

Crabbe grinned an ugly grin. "Not Crabbe! No, sir. Couldn't, I said. Standing rule, I said. He nodded as if he'd sort of expected that. Then he looked about a bit. I began to get a little suspicious, but he jabbered on about books. . . . Finally he got back to the desk here. There was some stationery—paper and envelopes—on it. A queer look came into his eye and he said: 'Is this your Saxon Library stationery, Mr. Crabbe?' and I said yes, it was. So he turned to me with an appealing look. 'Ha, ha!' he said. 'Very interesting. This is a deucedly hard place to get into, you know. I'd wagered a friend of mine, you know, that I could gain entrance to the Saxon Library, and by the Lord Harry I've done it!' 'Oh, you did, did you?' I said. 'And,' he said, 'now that I'm really here, would you be a good chap and let me collect my wager? I'll need proof that I've been here. Ah, yes,' he said, just as if it had struck him at that moment, and he picked up a sheet of the stationery and an envelope and fingered 'em, 'the very thing! This will prove it. Thank you, Mr. Crabbe, a thousand times!' and before I could say anything he ran out!"

The Inspector had listened to this remarkable story with open mouth. When Crabbe had finished with smacking lips, he thundered: "Of all the hogwash! You let him get away with that? Why, it——"

"So that's how our man secured the stationery," said Patience slowly.

"My dear," said Lane in a low voice, "let's not take any more of Mr. Crabbe's valuable time than is absolutely necessary. Mr. Crabbe, can you describe this extraordinary visitor?"

"Oh, yes. Tall, thin, middle-aged chap. Rather English."

"Good God," said the Inspector hoarsely. "Patty, that's just——"

"Please, Inspector. Exactly when did this man call? On what day?"

"Let me think. Four, five—about seven weeks ago. Yes, I remember now. It was early in the morning, on a Monday. May sixth."

"The sixth of May!" exclaimed Patience. "Father, Mr. Lane, did you hear that?"

"I heard it, too, Pat," complained Mr. Rowe fretfully. "You make it sound like the Ides of March. Queer!"

Crabbe's bright little eyes darted from one to another of them; there was a repressed and malicious mirth in their depths, as if he were holding in an immense joke by main force. "This man, then, a tall thin Englishman of middle age," murmured Lane, "called on May sixth and managed by a none too credible ruse to get hold of a sample of your stationery. Very good, Mr. Crabbe, we've progressed. There's one thing more and then I believe we shall have finished. Did he give a name?"

Crabbe regarded him with that irritating half-smile. "Did he give a name, eh? You *are* a card for asking pertinent questions, Mr. Lane! Did he give a name? Certainly he gave a name. How it all comes back to me." And he chuckled. He scudded like an aged crab around the desk and began exploring various drawers. "Excuse me, Miss Thumm. . . . Did he give a name!" and he chuckled once more. "Ah, the very thing!" He handed a small pasteboard to Lane. Patience rose very quickly and the four of them read the name upon it together.

It was an extremely cheap calling card. On it was printed in bold black characters the name:

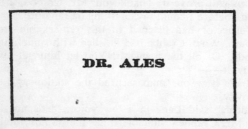

There was nothing more—no address, no telephone, no given name.

"Dr. Ales!" said Patience with a frown.

"Dr. Ales!" said the Inspector with a grunt.

"Dr. Ales!" said Rowe with a thoughtful look.

"Dr. Ales!" nodded Crabbe with a leer.

"Dr. Ales," said the old gentleman, and something in his voice made them look at him swiftly. But he was staring at the card. "Heavens, it doesn't seem possible. Dr. Ales. . . . Patience, Inspector, Gordon," he said abruptly, "do you know who Dr. Ales is?"

"Totally unfamiliar name," said Patience with a keen glance at his intent face.

"Never heard of him," said the Inspector.

"There's *something* about it," said Rowe thoughtfully.

"Ah, Gordon. I might have known he would strike a responsive chord in the student's memory. He——"

Crabbe made a grotesque dancing movement, like a trained monkey. His gold-rimmed spectacles slipped down the bridge of his nose and he grinned in a horrible way. "*I* can tell you who Dr. Ales is," he said, pursing his shriveled lips like a perfumed old dandy.

"You can, eh?" said Lane quickly.

"I mean I can tell you who he *really* is, where he is, and everything!" cackled Crabbe. "Oh, it's an enormous joke! It came over me all of a sudden."

"Well, for God's sake," said the Inspector harshly, "who *is* he?"

"I knew him the minute I saw him that day at the museum. Oh yes," gurgled the old librarian. "Did you see him look away? He knew I knew him, the precious scoundrel! I tell you the man who visited me seven weeks ago and left this card, the man who called himself Dr. Ales, is—*Hamnet Sedlar!*"

14

A Battle of Bibliophiles

Over the luncheon table in a private dining room at one of the midtown hotels they tried to collect their scattered thoughts. Crabbe's ironical and triumphant revelation had left them, for the moment, witless. Hamnet Sedlar the mysterious Dr. Ales! Crabbe had seen them to the door in a perfect ecstasy of lip-licking exultation, and the last glimpse they had of him was his spare angular figure framed in the Ionic doorway of the Saxon house, his hands scratching ceaselessly against each other like the hindlegs of a cricket. Yes, his cocked little head had seemed to say as he watched them speed off, your worthy Dr. Sedlar is also your Dr. Ales; and what do you think of that? Old Crabbe's no fool, eh? For there was a personal triumph in his entire bearing which baffled them, a cruel and smug satisfaction like the powerful mass pleasure of a mob bent on lynching.

Gordon Rowe, who had despite his preoccupation managed to insinuate himself into the little party, sat very quietly watching the sun on Patience's hair as it pulsed in through the window of the limousine. But for once he did not seem to see it.

"There's something remarkably peculiar here," said Mr. Drury Lane when they had seated themselves at their table. "I confess it's beyond me. That terrible old creature impressed me—with all his dramatic grimaces—as essentially truthful. He's the sort who delights in rubbing the truth in, especially if he knows that it will hurt. And yet—Hamnet Sedlar! Of course, it's impossible."

"If Crabbe said that his visitor was Sedlar," remarked young Rowe with a grim muttering, "then you can bet your crusading boots it *was* Sedlar."

"No, Gordon," sighed Patience. "Sedlar couldn't possibly have been the man who called on Crabbe May sixth. We've learned that the directors of the Kensington Museum in London had given a farewell banquet in Dr. Sedlar's honor on May seventh. Dr. Ales called on Crabbe in New York on May sixth. The man isn't a spirit. He couldn't have crossed the Atlantic overnight."

"Oh! That's damnably queer. I know Crabbe, and I tell you he wasn't lying. He always gets that devilishly satisfied air when he's rubbing the truth in, as Mr. Lane says."

"Crabbe was so *certain*," said Patience, jabbing at her chop in pure exasperation. "He said he'd swear it was Sedlar on a stack of Bibles."

"What's all the fuss about?" growled the Inspector, eying young Mr. Rowe with disfavor. "The old bird's lying, that's all."

"Hmm," said Lane. "It's possible, of course, that he invented the tale out of sheer malice. These old bookworms have a capacity for professional jealousy— Come, come, we'll never get anywhere this way. The whole thing's uncommonly mysterious. . . . There's something I must tell you. About Dr. Ales."

"Oh, yes!" cried Patience. "You were going to say when Crabbe interrupted. . . . Then the name isn't fictitious?"

"Lord, no! That's what's so extraordinary about it, my dear. Gordon, you seemed to be hovering on the verge of recollection back at the house. Do you remember now who Dr. Ales is—or was?"

"Sorry, sir. I thought I did. I may have run across his name in connection with my work somewhere."

"Quite possible. The fact is that I never met Dr. Ales in the flesh, and I know nothing whatever about him personally; but one thing I do know. Unless it's an astounding coincidence, such a man actually exists, and moreover is a very clever and well-informed student of research literature." The old gentleman chewed thoughtfully on a sprig of parsley. "Some years ago—oh, eight or ten years—an article appeared in *The Stratford Quarterly*, a publication devoted to the advancement of book knowledge. . . ."

"Oh, of course!" cried Rowe. "I got it regularly in my undergraduate days."

"That accounts for the faint recollection. The point is that this article was signed 'Dr. Ales.' "

"An English magazine?" demanded Thumm.

"Yes. I don't recall the precise details, but this Dr. Ales was writing on a new development in the fatuous and eternal Baconian controversy, and there were some things he said with which I took violent issue. I wrote a lengthy rebuttal to the *Quarterly*, which appeared under my name; and Dr. Ales, quite nettled, replied in the correspondence columns of the publication. We wrangled back and forth through the *Quarterly* for several issues." He chuckled at the memory. "A sharp pen, my adversary! He called me everything but a doddering old idiot."

"I remember now," said Rowe eagerly, thrusting his firm jaw forward. "The fur flew. That's the chap, all right!"

"Know where he lives?" inquired the Inspector abruptly.

"Unfortunately, no."

"Well, we can find out through this magazine——"

"I'm afraid not, Inspector. Mr. Rowe can undoubtedly tell you that *The Stratford Quarterly* collapsed five years ago."

"Damn! Well, I'll cable Trench again and make another pest of myself. Do you think——"

"By the way, Gordon," said the old gentleman, "have you had time to look into those little matters we talked about? About the binding of the 1599 Jaggard, and traces of a possible secret connected with the binding?"

Rowe shrugged. "I haven't been too successful. I succeeded in tracing the binding back about a hundred and fifty years—it's been a hellish job. The present binding is at least that old. As for the document hidden in it—blank. Haven't run across a clue."

"Hmm." Lane's eyes flashed for an instant, and then he lowered them and devoted himself to his salad.

Patience pushed her plate aside. "Oh, I can't chew," she said fretfully. "This persnickety case is getting on my nerves. It's preposterous, of course, this business of Dr. Sedlar being Dr. Ales, but it keeps going round and round in my head in the most frightful fashion. And yet other things are so clear. . . ."

"As for instance?" said the Inspector with a scowl.

"The trail left by Dr. Ales. It *was* Dr. Ales, you know," she said suddenly, "who was the bearded man in our office May sixth, father."

"And how do you arrive at that?" murmured young Rowe.

"He visited the Saxon place early that morning. There he got hold of the Saxon Library stationery. He must have cached his ridiculous disguise somewhere in midtown. Perhaps a hotel washroom. He wrote down the symbol—damn that symbol!—got into his doohickeys, and hurried up to father's office. That much is clear." Her blue-water eyes appealed to Lane.

"It seems probable," said the old gentleman.

"He didn't expect to be—to be bumped off," said Patience, biting her lip. "He thought no one knew his secret, the secret worth millions. Doesn't it sound silly? . . . But he's a canny devil and he wasn't taking any chances. If he called on the twentieth, if he was all right, there was no harm done; the envelope would remain unopened. If he didn't call we'd open the envelope, see the Saxon stationery, hunt up Crabbe, find out about this queer Dr. Ales—he must have told Crabbe that impossible story purposely, so that Crabbe would remember it —and be in a very advanced position to pursue the hunt for him. Because by the time we did we would know the name of the man we were looking for, something of his profession. . . ."

"What an appallingly logical analysis!" said young Rowe with a feeble grin.

"That was why he asked you not to open the envelope except in my presence," said Drury Lane quietly. "He knew I would remember our *Quarterly* controversy. So I was asked in to supply the confirmation that Dr. Ales is a bibliophile."

"He must have planned it from the start. *If* something went wrong, as it apparently has. We've got to search now for a Dr. Ales, a bookworm or something, and how we're to begin——"

"Easy," said the Inspector with an absent look. "That's my job, Patty. He said if he didn't call something would have happened to him, didn't he? That means that besides having a description of him, his name, his business or profession, we also know he's either disappeared from his regular haunts—he must hang out somewhere!—or been pipped."

"Bravo, Inspector," murmured Lane. "You've hit it exactly. You must procure an official report of all murders, kidnapings, and other disappearances from May twentieth, the day he 'phoned you on schedule, until a few days ago."

The Inspector scowled. "I know, I know. Realize what a job it is?"

"Not quite so formidable as it seems, Inspector. You've very specific information to go on, as Patience has pointed out."

"All right," said Thumm gloomily. "I'll do it, by God, but

what I'm getting out of it is beyond me. I've got to live, too, don't I?—I'll get Grayson and Geoghan on the job right away. . . . I s'pose you kids are goin' to run off somewhere?"

When Mr. Drury Lane deposited Inspector Thumm at his office and Miss Patience Thumm and Mr. Gordon Rowe in the leafy haven of Central Park, he signaled Dromio silently and sat back with a wonderfully thoughtful look on his face. Now that he was unobserved a multitude of faint quick expressions chased one another across his mobile features and he sat dead in the tonneau, clutching the knob of his stick and staring sightlessly at Dromio's neck. Unlike most old men he had never acquired the habit of speaking aloud to himself, perhaps because his pale stony ears forbade even the birth of the habit. Instead he thought in pure pictures, and some of them were so extraordinary that he shut his eyes to see them better.

The Lincoln catfooted its way uptown, bound for Westchester.

The old man opened his eyes after a long while and started at the sight of crisp green trees and a curving, park-bound driveway. He leaned forward and tapped Dromio's shoulder.

"Didn't I tell you, Dromio? I want you to stop at Dr. Martini's first."

Dromio, that faithful dragoman, stiffened and half-turned his red head so that his employer might see his lips. "Anything the matter, Mr. Drury? Don't you feel well again?"

The old gentleman smiled. "Perfectly well, my boy. This is a visit in the interests of pure science."

"Oh," said Dromio. He scratched his left ear, shrugged, and pressed the accelerator.

He brought the car to a stop near Irvington, before a small cottage half-hidden by trees and smothered with vines and late June roses. A portly man with white hair smoked a pipe at the gate.

"Ah, Martini," said Lane, alighting and stretching his legs. "Lucky to have found you in this time of day."

The portly man stared. "Mr. Lane! What are you doing down here? Come in, come in."

Lane chuckled and swung the gate to behind him. "Don't look so startled, you old bone-setter. I'm in perfect health." They shook hands. Dr. Martini's tired eyes swept over him with professional penetration. "Look all right, do I?"

"Splendid. How's the heart?"

"Pumping magnificently. I can't say as much for the stomach." They entered the physician's cottage; a woolly dog sniffed at Lane's ankles and then walked away indifferently. "I can't understand why, in my senescence, it should give out——"

"A lifetime of theatrical menus, my dear Malvolio," said Dr. Martini dryly, "isn't conducive to clockwork digestion in the latter years. Sit down. I managed to sneak off from the hospital for a few hours. Maddening routine. I haven't had a really interesting case——"

Lane chuckled. "I have one for you."

The physician took the pipe out of his mouth. "Ah. I might have known. Not yourself?"

"No, no."

"For something really knotty," remarked Dr. Martini with a dreamy smile, "I'd forgo even this afternoon's bucolic pleasures——"

"Needn't." The old man leaned forward. "This is a case which—I trust—can be diagnosed from the armchair." He looked about suddenly. "I think you had better close the door, Martini."

The physician stared. Then he rose and shut out the sunlight.

"You're acting horribly mysterious," he said, returning to his chair. The pipe dangled unheeded from his jaws. "Confidential, eh? A criminal case, I suppose. But there's no one about to hear——"

Lane fixed him with a stern and glittering eye in his best Ancient Mariner style. "When a man is deaf, Martini, even walls have ears. . . . Old friend, I've become involved in one of the most incredible adventures that ever fell across the path of man. A great deal hinges upon a certain point. . . ."

Dromio, who had been nodding at the wheel, flicked a bee off his lapel and started. The heavy scent of the roses had drugged him. The door of Martini's cottage, which had remained shut for half an hour, had opened, and the tall spare figure of his employer had appeared. Dromio heard Dr. Martini say in an absent tone: "I'm afraid that's the only solution, Mr. Lane. I must see the paper before I can give you an opinion. And even then, as I've told you——"

"You scientists!" Dromio heard Lane say in a lightly impatient voice. "I had hoped that the issue would be clearer. However—" He shrugged and extended his hand. "Kind of you to show this interest. I fancied there might be something in my inspiration. I shall have the paper for you this evening."

"Hmm. Very well. I'll be at The Hamlet tonight."

"Oh, rubbish! That's really putting you to too much trouble. I'll come back here——"

"Nonsense. The drive will do me good, and then I want to have a look at Quacey. Last time I saw him I didn't like the antics of his arteries."

Dromio, puzzled, held the door open. His employer, walking quickly down the path, stopped short. He eyed Dromio with a sudden bunching of white brows and said sharply: "Have you seen anyone prowling about here?"

Dromio gaped. "Prowlin', Mr. Drury?"

"Yes, yes. Did you see anyone?"

Dromio scratched his ear. "I guess I did snooze for a couple of minutes, sir. But I didn't think——"

"Ah, Dromio," sighed the old gentleman, climbing into the car, "when will you learn that vigilance . . . I suppose it doesn't matter." He waved his hand at Dr. Martini cheerfully. "Stop in Irvington, Dromio. The telegraph office."

They drove off. In Irvington Dromio found a Western Union office and Drury Lane went in. He stared thoughtfully at the wall clock, and then sat down at one of the tiny tables and reached for a yellow pad and the chained pencil. For an instant he regarded the lead tip; it was well sharpened; but he did not see it, for his level eyes were fixed on something far beyond the range of physical sight.

He penciled a message on the blank slowly, pressing hard under the vitality of his thought.

The message was addressed to Inspector Thumm at his office:

IMPERATIVE HAVE PAPER WITH SYMBOL TONIGHT COME
FOR DINNER URGENT   D L

He paid for the telegram and returned to the car. Dromio was waiting, faint excitement in his Irish eyes.

"We may go home now, Dromio," sighed the old gentleman, and relaxed with gratefulness against the welcoming cushions.

As the long Lincoln disappeared in the direction of Tarrytown, toward the north, a tall man in a dark topcoat with the collar turned up to his ears—despite the hot sun—detached himself from the shadow of a long black Cadillac sedan parked at the curb across the street, looked about quietly, and then with quick strides headed for the telegraph office. He looked about again, his hand on the doorknob, and then went in.

He made directly for the table at which Lane had written his wire, and sat down. Out of the corner of his eye he looked beyond the counter. Two clerks were busy at desks. He returned his attention to the yellow pad. There were faint impressions on the top sheet, impressions made by Lane's unconsciously heavy strokes on the sheet on which he had written the message to Inspector Thumm. The tall man hesitated; then, picking up the chained pencil, he held it between his fingers almost horizontally to the paper and began to draw light even lines from side to side. Under the gray mass Lane's message began to appear in clear yellow strokes. . . .

After a moment the tall man rose, ripped the yellow blank off the pad, crumpled it, put it into his pocket, and quietly walked out of the office. One of the clerks gazed after him, puzzled.

He made directly for the big Cadillac across the street, got in, released his emergency brake, and with a powerful purr of gears made off toward the south . . . toward New York City.

15

Alarums and Excursions

It was late afternoon when Miss Patience Thumm returned to the Thumm Detective Agency from a modest but highly satisfactory shopping tour to find Miss Brodie in a state mildly bordering upon insanity.

"Oh, Miss Thumm!" she cried, causing Patience to drop all her bundles, "I've had the most *dreadful* time! I'm so glad you've come back! I was going almost *frantic*——"

"Brodie, I'll shake you," said Patience firmly. "What on earth's happened? Why the hysterics?"

Miss Brodie, wordless, pointed dramatically at the open door of the Inspector's sanctum. Patience dashed in. The office was empty, and on the Inspector's desk lay a yellow envelope.

"Where's my father?"

"Somebody came in with a case, Miss Thumm. Jewel robbery or something, and the Inspector said to tell you he didn't know *when* he'd be back. But the telegram——"

"Brodie," sighed Patience, "You've the common bourgeois fear of telegrams. It's probably an advertisement." Nevertheless she frowned as she ripped open the envelope. She read Mr. Drury Lane's laconic message with wide eyes. Miss Brodie hovered in the doorway, wringing her stubby-fingered hands like a professional mourner.

"Stow it, Brodie," said Patience absently. "You always act like the living figure of Tragedy. Go out and get properly kissed or—or something." And to herself she said: "I wonder what's happened *now*. What *could* have happened? It's only *hours* . . ."

"Has—has something happened?" asked Miss Brodie fearfully.

"Don't know. At any rate, it's nothing to get in a stew about. Relax, child, while I dash off a note to father. Relax, darn you!" and she slapped Miss Brodie vigorously upon a buxom backside. Miss Brodie blushed and retreated to her desk in the anteroom to relax.

Patience sat down in the Inspector's chair, seized a sheet of paper, moistened a pencil-point on the tip of her red tongue, and proceeded to engage the muse of creative composition:

Dear Roughneck: Our beloved friend the Sage of Lanecliff has wired you in most peremptory fashion to bring the Papuh to The Hamlet this evening. It seems that something's brewing, but he doesn't say what. Poor Brodie's had a conniption here this afternoon dithering about the fringes of the telegram, not daring to open it and not knowing where either of us was. She tells me that you are now engaged in earning some more money for me to spend; and indeed after Mr. Rowe took me walking in the Park and regretfully—I hope—went back to work at the Britannic, I proceeded to Macy's in pursuit of the most fascinating investigation into a new scanty (pants to you, darling); so you see I *am* co-operating. I shall of course carry on in the best Thumm Detective Agency manner during your absence. I am taking the Scooter now, and I promise to take very good care of the Papuh, too. Call me at The Hamlet when you get in. Dear old Drury's extended a dinner invitation and if worst comes to worst I'm sure he won't mind my

wrinkling the sheets of one of his nice old beds. Be careful, darling.

PAT

P. S.—That's a lonely ride up through them thar hills. I
do believe I shall ask Mr. Rowe to accompany me. Now
doesn't that make you feel better?

She folded the sheet with a flourish, slipped it into an envelope, and tucked the envelope into one of the flaps of the
Inspector's desk blotter. Then, humming, she went to the safe,
tinkered with the dials for a moment, pulled the heavy door
open, rummaged about, came out with the broken-sealed manila envelope, and shut the safe. Still humming she made sure
that the contents of the manila envelope were intact; and then
she opened her linen handbag, a large and mysterious recep-
tacle crammed with feminine gewgaws, and tucked the envelope safely away inside.

She dialed a number. "Dr. Choate? . . . Oh, I see. Well, it
doesn't make any difference. I really wanted to speak to Mr.
Rowe. . . . Hellð, Gordon! Do you mind my bothering you
again so soon?"

"Angel! Bother me? I'm—I'm *overwhelmed*."

"How's the work?"

"Progressing."

"Would you greatly mind slowing the wheels of progress for
the rest of the day, sir?"

"Pat! You know what I'd do for you."

"I've got to make a rush trip up to The Hamlet with—with
something, Gordon. *Could* you come along?"

"Please attempt to stop me, lassie."

"Very well. In front of the Britannic in ten minutes or so."
Patience replaced the receiver, tucked a vagrant curl behind
her ear, and went into the anteroom. "Brodie," she announced, "I'm off."

"Off, Miss Thumm?" Miss Brodie was alarmed. "Where
to?"

"To Mr. Lane's in Westchester." Patience examined herself
very critically in a mirror behind Miss Brodie's desk. She
powdered her little nose, touched her lips with rouge, and
investigated her person thoughtfully from above. "Oh, dear,"
she sighed, smoothing her white linen suit, "and I haven't time
to change. Linen gets *so* wrinkly!"

"Doesn't it, though," exclaimed Miss Brodie with a trace of
animation. "I know I had a linen suit last year, and I spent

'more in having it *cleaned* . . ." She stopped abruptly. "What shall I tell the Inspector, Miss Thumm?"

Patience adjusted her preposterously small linen turban with its blue polka-dot band on her honeyed curls, fingered her polka-dot tie expertly, and murmured: "I've left a note for him on his desk, *and* the telegram. You're staying, of course?"

"Oh, yes. The Inspector would be furious——"

"It's very important," sighed Patience, "this business of holding down the fort, Brodie. I'll pick up my packages to-morrow. Be a good girl!"

Satisfied with her complete inspection, she smiled at Miss Brodie, who waved a limply mournful hand, clutched her linen bag tightly, and left the office.

At the curb downstairs a small blue roadster stood waiting. Patience scanned the sky anxiously; but it was bluer than her eyes. She decided not to put up the top. Jumping in, she tucked her bag securely between the leather seat and the back beside her, turned on the ignition, released her brake, threw the car into first gear, and rolled slowly off toward Broadway. She went into neutral at once; there was a red light at the corner; the car coasted softly along.

And then a strange thing happened. Patience, rapt in darkly feminine thoughts, for once was unobservant. It was a little thing in itself, scarcely calculated to arouse apprehension; but it was significant and grew more dangerous with every passing moment.

A large closed black car, a Cadillac, parked on the opposite side of the street, hummed into life the instant Patience stepped into her blue roadster. It slipped almost noiselessly into gear as Patience rolled off, and it followed her like a grim black shadow. It was precisely behind her in the clutter of the traffic waiting at the red light; it nosed after her as the light turned green; it swung right into Broadway as she swung right into Broadway, followed her on a right turn, up to Sixth Avenue, up to Fifth Avenue, into Fifth Avenue . . . never once faltering in its easy pursuit of the roadster.

It acted like a live thing when Patience suddenly pulled in at the curb near Sixty-Fifth Street. It hesitated, shot ahead, slowed down, and finally cruised very slowly indeed up to Sixty-Sixth while young Gordon Rowe, flushed with pleasure, gayly dropped into the seat beside Patience. It idled along until the roadster passed; and then again took up the trail.

Patience was unaccountably in a gala mood. Her color was

lovely, the turban set off the pertness of her features, the roadster obeyed beautifully, the sun was warm and there was a cool little breeze blowing; and moreover the occupant of the adjoining seat was young and male and particularly exciting. She permitted Rowe to see the envelope in her bag, told him about Lane's telegram, and then chattered on about nothing whatever while the young man, his arm on the edge of the upholstery behind her, sat in silent scrutiny of her face-front piquancy. . . .

All through crowded Manhattan the Cadillac dogged the heels of the roadster, and all through crowded Manhattan Patience and her escort were unconscious of· its presence behind them. Then, as they left the city behind, it slipped a little to the rear; and despite the fast pace at which Patience drove the car, the Cadillac sedan seemed merely to loaf along in her wake.

Then, with the city limits left far behind, young Mr. Rowe's eyes narrowed and he glanced briefly over his shoulder. Patience chattered on.

"Step on it, Pat," he said casually. "Let's see how much speed you can get out of this tin can."

"Oh, you want speed, do you?" said Patience with a grim smile. "Remember, you pay the fine, young man!" and she pressed hard on the accelerator. The roadster leaped ahead.

Rowe looked back. The Cadillac, without effort, maintained precisely the same distance as before.

Patience drove in oblivious silence for some time, lips tight, intent on giving Mr. Rowe his fill of speed. But Mr. Rowe was not appreciably alarmed; his chin was set a trifle, and his hazel eyes were screwed into slits, but that was all.

Suddenly he said: "I see a side road there, Pat. Dash into it."

"What? What's that?"

"Into that road, I tell you!"

She was offended, and glanced angrily at his face. It was half-turned away. Slowly she glanced into her mirror.

"Oh," she said, and the blood drained from her face.

"We're being followed," said Mr. Rowe quietly, and there was no levity in his voice. "Into that road, Pat. Let's see if we can't shake the beggar off."

"All right, Gordon," said Patience in a small voice; and with a twist of the wheel hurtled the roadster off the main highway into a narrow road.

The Cadillac shot by, stopped, turned about in a flash, and roared into the road after them.

"I think," whispered Patience, her lips trembling slightly, "that we've made a mistake. There—there's no outlet, Gordon."

"Keep driving, Pat. Keep your eyes on the road."

It was indeed a narrow road apparently with no outlets, and there was no time for her to turn the roadster about and flee in the direction from which they had come. Patience's toe squeezed the accelerator violently, and the little machine sprang forward like a wounded animal. Rowe watched the road behind intently. The Cadillac was creeping forward. And still it made no serious attempt to overtake them; perhaps because the sun was still too high, or the driver of the big sedan feared a premature attack.

Patience's heart throbbed like a drumstick against the tom-tom of her breast. In a flood of wild blind feeling she thanked her little gods for the impulse to ask Gordon Rowe to accompany her. His physical presence, the warmth of his big body next to her, steadied her nerves; she gritted her teeth and bent lower over the wheel, eyes wide and steady on the poor road ahead. This was no concrete highway, but a badly chopped and battered macadam; they bounced and rattled in their seats. The Cadillac came on.

The road grew worse, narrowing even more. Ahead loomed a tangle of trees overhanging the road. There was no habitation within hailing distance. Pictures of "lonely woods"—"girl attacked"—"escort murdered"—"horrible crime in Westchester"—her torn body lying by the roadside, Rowe bleeding and dying beside her—flashed through her brain. . . . And then, in a mist, she saw the black car hurtling along by her side, making no effort to pass. . . .

"Keep going!" shouted Rowe, rising in the seat and crouched against the driving wind of their passage. "Don't let him scare you, Pat!"

A long black-sleeved arm in the dark recesses of the car made unmistakable motions. The Cadillac itself began to lunge perilously close to her rocketing little machine, as if to force her off the road. She realized in a cold dash of reason that her pursuer wanted her to stop.

"Wants to fight, does he?" muttered Rowe. "All right, Pat. Stop and let's see what this bird wants."

For a moment, as she shot a quick glance up and saw the

young man perched by her side, ready to spring, she contemplated with the desperation of panic-born courage driving the roadster deliberately into the Cadillac, to wreck both cars. She had often read of such things and had never questioned either the impulse or the act. But now that she was confronted by the real situation, she knew with a sudden rush of tears to her eyes that she did not want to die, that there would be a curious sweetness in living. . . . She cursed herself for a fool and a coward, but despite all she could do the wheel remained steady in her hands.

And so, after a long tremulous moment, her toe relaxed its pressure on the accelerator and sought blindly for the footbrake, and then the roadster slid to a long slow grudging stop.

"Keep down, Pat," said Rowe quietly. "Don't you mix into this. I have the feeling he's an ugly customer."

"Oh, Gordon, don't—don't do anything rash. Please!"

"Down!"

The Cadillac had shot past, slued about so that its rakish body barred the road, ground and growled its way to a stop: and then a dark muffled figure—Patience gasped—masked, brandishing a revolver, leaped from the car and ran up to the roadster.

With a formless cry Gordon Rowe sprang out of the little car into the road, directly in the path of the masked man. He lunged toward the revolver.

Patience stared in a blur of weakness. It wasn't *possible*. It's like a—a movie, she thought. There was something unreal about the menace of the shining bluish weapon directed at the young man in the road.

And then she cried out. Smoke and a vicious spat of fire came out of the muzzle and Gordon Rowe dropped on the muddy macadam, toppling like a falling tree. His body jerked a little. Blood stained a few fragments of rubble near his body.

The smoke licked out over the muzzle, like a demon licking its chops. The masked man leaped nimbly on the running-board.

"You—you *murderer!*" screamed Patience, struggling to get out of the car. He—he was dead, she thought. Quite dead in the road. Oh, Gordon! "I'll *kill* you," she panted, and clawed for the gun.

It came down sharply on her knuckles, and she was flung back against the seat, stunned with pain, for the first time really understanding what was happening. The end of Patience Thumm?

A thick disguised voice came from behind the mask. "Keep still. Sit there. Give me the paper." The revolver wove and wove before her eyes in a mist.

She looked dazedly at her hand; the knuckles were bleeding. "What paper?" she whispered.

"The paper. The envelope. Hurry." There was no least expression in that thick dead voice. Suddenly, for the first time, she grasped it all. The Saxon stationery! The cryptic symbol! This was why Gordon Rowe had died. . . .

She felt for the bag. The man on the running-board cuffed her aside, pounced on the bag, backed off quickly, the revolver still menacing her. Patience began to climb out of the roadster. Gordon . . . There was an incredible noise close to her ear; it sounded like the world exploding; a whine. . . . She sank back, half-unconscious. He had fired at her! . . . When she opened her eyes again, struggling for mastery of her whirling senses, the Cadillac was moving. An instant later the big car roared in reverse, squealed about, and shot past her like lightning, hell bent in the direction from which they had come. . . .

Patience managed to crawl out into the road. Rowe was still lying in the rubble, pale and still. She fumbled beneath his coat for his heart. It was beating!

"Oh, Gordon, Gordon!" she sobbed. "I'm so glad. I'm so glad."

He groaned and opened his eyes, started up, sank back with a wince. "Pat," he said hollowly. "What happened? Did he——"

"Where are you hurt, Gordon?" cried Patience. "I must get you to a doctor. I'll have to——"

He sat up weakly and together they investigated. His left arm was bloody. Patience pulled his coat off; he winced again. A bullet had passed through the fleshy part of his upper arm.

"Hell," he said disgustedly. "Fainted like a woman. Here, bind this up, Pat old girl, and we'll chase that damned murderer."

"But——"

"Don't need a doctor. Just bind it up. Come *on*."

Kneeling in the rubble, she tore away part of the tail of his shirt and bound the wound tightly. He refused her assistance in rising; indeed, shoved her roughly in the driver's seat and sprang into the car himself.

Patience turned the car about and made off, a little tremulously, after the Cadillac. A half-mile down the road Rowe commanded her to stop and rather weakly clambered out to pick up something lying in the middle of the road. It was Patience's linen bag, open.

The long manila envelope with its cryptic symbol written on the stationery of the Saxon Library was gone.

And so was the Cadillac.

An hour later, sobbing against Mr. Drury Lane's aged and concerned breast, Miss Patience Thumm related in tumbling syllables the story of the hold-up and their incredible adventure. Gordon Rowe sat by on a bench in the gardens, white-faced but quite calm. His coat lay on the grass, and the bandage about his arm was stiff with blood. Little Quacey, Lane's ancient retainer, was scurrying away for warm water and bandages.

"Now, now, my dear," soothed the old gentleman, "don't take it so hard. Thank heaven it wasn't worse. Gordon, I'm dreadfully sorry! I never dreamed, Patience, that you would come out here with the envelope. I recognized a certain theoretical element of danger, but I knew the Inspector always goes armed. . . . Quacey!" he called after the old man, "telephone Inspector Thumm at his office."

"But it's all my fault!" sniffled Patience. "See, I've got your jacket all wet. Gordon, are you all right? . . . Oh, I've lost the envelope. I could *strangle* that beast!"

"You're both very fortunate children," said Lane dryly. "Obviously your assailant wasn't the sort who would be stopped by mere considerations of humanitarianism. . . . Yes, Quacey?"

"He's *frothing*," said Quacey in a trembling voice. "Falstaff is coming with the water."

"Falstaff!" said Gordon Rowe bitterly. "Oh, yes." He passed his good hand slowly over his eyes. "I'm going to see this thing through, sir," he said to Lane.

"Indeed. The first thing you need, young man, is medical attention. Here comes Dr. Martini in his runabout, by George! . . . Patience, speak to your father."

Patience went to Rowe, hesitated, they looked at each other for an instant, and then she turned and ran toward the house.

A small battered Ford clattered up the main driveway and the white head of Dr. Martini leaned out in greeting.

"Martini!" called Mr. Drury Lane. "How fortunate. I've a patient for you. Gordon, sit still. You always were an impetuous youngster. Doctor, have a look at this young man's arm."

"Water," said the physician briefly, after one glance at the crusted blood.

A little pot-bellied man—Falstaff, in person—hurried up with a huge basin of warm water.

The black Cadillac was found abandoned at the edge of a road near Bronxville late that night, as a result of Inspector Thumm's raging efforts and the assistance of the Westchester police. It proved to be a rented car. It had been hired from a transparently innocent dealer in Irvington during the morning before by a tall silent man well muffled in a dark topcoat. No, that was all he could remember about the man.

On Lane's suggestion, the clerks of the Irvington telegraph office were questioned. One of them recalled the brief visit of the tall man in the dark topcoat.

The Cadillac was found. The manner in which the tall man had learned of the accessibility of the envelope was thus cleared up. But of the tall man himself and the stolen envelope there was not the faintest trace.

16

The Horseshoe Ring

A silent company left The Hamlet the next morning—which was, Patience thought, incredibly only Saturday—in Mr. Drury Lane's car. Patience's roadster was left behind. Young Mr. Rowe, his left arm in a sling, sat sulkily between Lane and Patience, frowning and refusing to talk. Lane was deep in thought, and Patience was near tears.

"My dear child," said the old gentleman after a while, "don't blame yourself so bitterly! It wasn't your fault. I haven't forgiven myself for causing you to run into danger."

"But I lost the paper," wailed Patience.

"It isn't really cosmic. I fancy we can manage without it."

"Then why," said Rowe suddenly, "did you wire for it?"

Lane sighed. "I had a thought," he said; and lapsed into silence.

Dromio stopped at Dr. Martini's cottage, and the physician without a word climbed into the tonneau to join them. A quick digital examination of the young man's wounded arm, and he nodded, sat back, closed his eyes, and proceeded to fall asleep.

When they entered the city limits, Mr. Drury Lane roused himself. "I think we had better take you home first, Gordon."

"Home!" said Mr. Rowe bitterly.

"Dromio, the Saxon house. . . . Look at Martini. Fast asleep!" The old man chuckled. "That comes of having a pure heart, my boy. If you hadn't played Romeo to Patience's Juliet . . ."

They found the Saxon mansion as usual forbidding and deserted. The butler with the wonderful sideburns was sorry once more; Mrs. Saxon was "out." His stony eyes widened a trifle at the sight of Rowe's bandaged arm, and for an instant he looked almost human.

Old Crabbe, however, apparently considered a bullet in a young man's arm a great jest; for after a long stare he broke into his disagreeable chortle and wheezed: "That's for meddling! Who broke your arm, you young devil?" and all the while he glanced sidewise at Lane's calm face and the imperturbable countenance of Dr. Martini.

Rowe flushed, and his one good fist tightened.

"We should like to see," said Mr. Drury Lane hastily, "a sheet of your Saxon Library stationery, Mr. Crabbe."

"What, again?"

"Please."

Crabbe shrugged and scurried off, to return shortly with a blank sheet of stationery from the library.

"Yes, that's precisely like the other," murmured Lane to Dr. Martini, taking the sheet from Crabbe's talons. "What do you think?"

The physician fingered the paper thoughtfully. Then he took it to one of the reception-room windows, jerked aside the heavy drapes, and examined the paper with narrowed eyes. Once he held it at arm's length; once he brought it to within two inches of his eyes. . . . He dropped the drapes and sauntered back, to place the sheet of gray paper on a table. "Yes," he said quietly, "what you suspected is very likely true."

"Ah!" said Lane with a curious inflection.

"As I told you, we know very little about—what you brought up. This must be an extremely rare case. I should really like to see him."

"So should I," murmured Lane. "So should I, Martini. Well!" He eyed the young couple with a twinkle. "Shall we go? *Au revoir*, Gordon——"

"No," said Mr. Rowe. "I stick." His jaw protruded very handsomely.

"I don't think you should," said Patience. "A nap—" But she was watching Dr. Martini in a puzzled way.

"Dear, dear," said Crabbe, rubbing his hands. "The possessive instinct of the female! Beware, Rowe. . . . Would you mind telling me, Mr. Lane, what all this rigmarole means?"

But the old gentleman was gazing fondly at Patience and Rowe, and since his affliction was well known, he merely murmured: "I fancy a call upon the Inspector is in order. Doctor, I shall send you home in my car. Send Dromio back. We'll taxi downtown, children. . . . Ah, Mr. Crabbe! So kind of you. Good day."

"What happened to you?" demanded the Inspector of Rowe, after he had embraced his daughter and been properly embraced in return.

"Stopped a bullet, sir."

"Oh, sure! Patty did tell me last night." Thumm grinned. "Well, that'll teach you to stick your two cents in, younker. Sit down, the lot of you. A stick-up, hey? By God, I wish I'd been there!"

"You'd have stopped a bullet, too," said Mr. Rowe shortly.

"Hmm. Any idea who this bird was, Patty?"

Patience sighed. "He was all bundled up, father. And I'm afraid I wasn't in the observant mood at the moment, with—with Gordon lying bleeding in the road."

"How about his voice? You told me he asked for the envelope."

"Disguised. I could tell that much."

"Fired at you." The Inspector sat back dreamily. "Now that's more like it. He's coming out in the open. I like that." Then he sighed. "But I'm afraid I shan't be able to mess around with this thing much longer. I'm in a jewel-robbery case up to my neck——"

"Have you done anything about that list of disappearances?" asked Lane. "That's really why I've come in, Inspector."

Thumm picked up a bulky sheaf of typewritten papers and tossed it across the desk. "Can't find a single record here of a murdered or missing man connected with books or the book world."

The old gentleman examined the list himself. "Odd," he

muttered. "One of the oddest features of the whole affair. Yet what else could he have intended?"

"That was my hunch, too, you'll remember. Well, I'm ready to call quits. It's all too deep and dirty for me."

The telephone rang in the anteroom outside. Miss Brodie's tragic voice could be heard appealing for information. Then the Inspector's instrument rang, and he took up the receiver.

"Hello! . . . Oh. . . . *What?*"

The angry red which flushed Thumm's granite face like a danger-signal when he became excited surged into evidence. His eyes bulged. The others looked at him, puzzled.

"Be right over!" He banged the receiver and sprang from his chair.

"What's happened, father? Who was that?" asked Patience swiftly.

"Choate! At the museum," shouted Thumm. "Something's happened over there and he wants us to come over at once!"

"Now what?" said Rowe, rising. "This is the *craziest* business!"

The old gentleman rose slowly; his eyes snapped. "It would be extremely curious if . . ."

"If what?" asked Patience as they hurried out to the elevator.

Lane shrugged. "Every event, as Schiller said, is a judgment of God. Let's wait and see. I have great faith in the consistency of the divine order, my child."

She was silent as they stepped into the elevator. Then she said: "Just what did Dr. Martini's examination of that sheet of Saxon stationery mean? I've been trying to think——"

"Don't, Patience. It's interesting and pertinent, but scarcely important at this stage. Some day—who knows?—it may serve a useful purpose."

They found the Britannic Museum seething with excitement. Dr. Choate, the hairs of his goatee bristling, met them behind the bronze head of Shakespeare. "Glad you came," he said fretfully. "This has been the most annoying day. . . . Rowe, what's happened to your arm? Accident, eh? . . . Come in, come in!"

He hurried them through the reception room to his office. There they found a strange company. Tall Dr. Sedlar, his lean face flushed, paced the floor with a frown; a burly policeman was planted solidly behind a chair; his hand gripped his riot-stick; and in the chair sat a tall, dark, Latinish creature with sullen eyes in which lurked a beady demon of fear. His clothes, badly rumpled as if by a struggle, were of clamorous design; a natty pearl-gray fedora lay ignominiously on the floor beside him.

"What's this?" growled Inspector Thumm, stopping in the doorway. Then a hard grin lifted his lips. "Well, well," he said softly. "Look who's here."

Simultaneously there were two swift intakes of breath. One came from Gordon Rowe, the other from the Italian in the chair.

"Hullo, Coburn," said the Inspector genially to the policeman behind the chair. "You still poundin' a beat?"

The officer's eyes widened. "Inspector Thumm! Ain't seen you in a dog's age!" He saluted with a grin.

"Haven't been around in a dog's age," remarked the Inspector in a cheerful voice. He advanced and took his stand three feet before the man in the chair, who cowered and sullenly dropped his eyes. "Well, well, Joe, and what are you doin' in a museum? Graduated from the ranks of dips? Don't tell me you're goin' to college! Last time I ran across you you were liftin' leathers. Stand up when I talk to you!" The words crackled and, startled, the Italian jumped out of the chair to stand fingering his shrieking cravat and studying the Inspector's shoes.

"This man," said Dr. Choate in an agitated voice, "somehow got into the museum a few minutes ago and Dr. Sedlar caught him in the Saxon Room prowling about and disturbing the books."

"Indeed?" murmured Mr. Drury Lane, advancing into the room.

"We called in this officer, but the man refuses to tell who he is, how he managed to get into the building, or what he was after," complained the curator. "Lord, I can't understand what's happening to us!"

"Precisely what was he doing, Dr. Sedlar," asked Lane, "when you surprised him in the Saxon Room?"

The Englishman coughed. "Most amazin' thing, Mr. Lane. You would say—ah—a creature of his intellectual level would scarcely be the sort to go after rare books. And yet I'm positive he meant to steal something. He was, as Dr. Choate has said, prowling among the cases."

"The Jaggard case?" asked Lane sharply.

"Yes."

"Won't tell his name, hey?" said the Inspector with a broad grin. "Well, we can help there, hey, Joe? This prime hunk of sneakin' devilment is Mr. Joe Villa, one of the best pickpockets in the game when I knew him, recently turned second-story man—general sneak-thief, dip, stool-pigeon, and everything that stinks. Right, Joe?"

"I ain't done nuttin'," croaked the Italian.

"How'd you get in, Joe?"

Silence.

"What's the pay-off? Who sent you? It's a cinch that dumb piece of cauliflower you call a brain didn't think up *this* stunt!"

The man licked his lips; his small black eyes shifted rapidly from face to face. "Nobody put me up to this job!" he cried passionately. "I—I just come in, 'a's all, just come in for a look aroun'."

"To read a book, hey?" chuckled Thumm. "You know this heel, don't you, Coburn?"

The policeman blushed. "Why, no, Inspector, can't say I do. I—I guess he's been layin' low since you left the Department."

"Tsk, tsk, what's the world coming to?" clucked the Inspector sadly. "Well, Joe, you goin' to talk or do we have to take you down to H.q. and give you a taste of the pipe?"

"Ain't done nuttin'," mumbled Villa surlily, but his face blanched.

Gordon Rowe stepped forward; his wounded arm flapped a little. "I think," he said calmly, "that I can help, Inspector." Villa darted a glance at him; he seemed bewildered; then he searched Rowe's face wildly as if seeking some familiar feature. "He was in that group of schoolteachers who visited the museum the day the 1599 Jaggard was stolen!"

"Gordon, you're sure?" cried Patience.

"Positive. I knew him the moment I stepped into this room."

"Gordon," said Lane swiftly, "which was he?"

"I don't know, sir. But he was in the group. In the museum that day, I'll swear."

Dr. Sedlar was studying Villa as if he were a laboratory specimen under the microscope. Then he retreated and effaced himself against the drape of one of the long windows.

"Speak up, Joe," said Thumm grimly. "What were you doing here when you horned in on that schoolmarm party?

Don't tell me you've got a license to teach school in Indiana!"
Villa's thin lips clamped together. "All right, wise guy. Dr.
Choate, may I use your 'phone?''

"What you gonna do?" asked Villa suddenly.

"Put the finger on you." Thumm dialed a number. "Mr.
Theofel? Thumm, of the Thumm Detective Agency. Is George
Fisher around? . . . Swell. And how about Barbey, your
starter? Behavin' himself? . . . Say, can you spare the boys
for a half-hour? . . . Fine. Send 'em up pronto to the Britannic Museum on Fifth and Sixty-Fifth."

Stalwart George Fisher and the red-faced bus-starter
tramped in with rather pallid faces. They took in the silent
company, and then both men riveted their attention upon the
cowering man in the chair.

"Fisher," said the Inspector, "do you recognize this scum?"

"Sure do," drawled Fisher. "He's one of the two guys got in
with the schoolteachers."

Villa snarled: "Nerts! 'Is's a frame!"

"Shut up, Joe. Which one, Fisher?"

Fisher shrugged. "Don't remember, Chief," he said regretfully.

The Inspector swung on Barbey. The bus-starter was nervous and kept stroking his jowls with a flabby hand. "You
ought to know, Barbey. You actually must have talked to this
weasel. He was one of the two men who bribed you to let 'em
get on the bus, wasn't he?"

Villa stared venomously at the bus-starter. Barbey muttered: "Yeah. Yeah, I think so."

"You *think* so! Was he or wasn't he?"

"Yes, sir. He was."

"Which one?"

"The second."

"The nineteenth man!" whispered Patience to Rowe.

"Sure? No mistake about it?"

Barbey lunged forward, and a squealing sound came from
Villa's dark throat. For a moment they were stunned, staring
at the scuffling men. Then the policeman leaped into the fray,
and Thumm.

"For the love of Mike," panted the Inspector, "you gone
nuts, Barbey? What's the big idea?"

Coburn secured a stranglehold on the sneak-thief's collar
and jerked him viciously three times. The man gagged and

became limp. Barbey snatched at Villa's left hand, gripping the sallow wrist. The yellow-brown skin twitched.

"The ring," said Barbey heavily. "The ring."

On the little finger of Villa's left hand there was a curious circlet of platinum, displaying a small horseshoe of the same metal set with twinkling diamond chips.

Villa moistened his dry lips. "A' right," he croaked. "You got me. I was the guy."

17

Accusation No. 2

"Ah," said the Inspector. "Coburn, let go. He'll talk now."

Villa looked about with despairing eyes. Everywhere he met grim faces. He nodded almost wearily.

"Sit down there, Joe, and take it easy," continued Thumm with a wink at the officer. Coburn pushed the chair against the backs of the man's legs, and he sat down heavily. The others made a ring about the chair, watchful and unsmiling.

"So you were the nineteenth man in the bus, Joe," began Thumm in an easy tone. Villa shrugged. "You gave Barbey here a five-spot to let you join the party, hey? Why? What was the game?"

Villa blinked and said carefully: "I was on a tail."

"Oho," said the Inspector. "So that's it! Followin' this bird in the blue hat, hey?"

Villa started. "How the hell—!" His eyes fell. "Yeah."

"All right, Joe, that's oke for a starter. Tell us some more. Did you know this bird?"

"Yeah."

Patience sighed with excitement; Rowe gripped her hand, cautioning her to silence.

"Well, well, Joe! I'm not talkin' for my health."

Villa croaked: "I know this guy, see. He gives me a C to do a little job about two mont's ago, see——"

"What kind of job?" asked the Inspector quickly.

Villa writhed in the chair. "Just a—a job, 'a's all."

Thumm gripped the thief's shoulder; Villa sat very still. "Take it easy, will ya?" he whined. "I'm— You'll let me off if I come clean?"

"Spill it, Joe."

Villa dug his pointed chin into the folds of his blazing necktie and mumbled: "House. Fift' Avenoo. He tells me to get in, see, an' swipe a book——"

Mr. Drury Lane's thrilling baritone rang clear over Villa's averted head. "Whose house, and what book?"

"Saxon's the handle. An' the book—" Villa jerked a dirty thumb at Rowe. "This bozo said it a while back. Jag—Jag——"

"The 1599 Jaggard?"

"Yeah. 'A's it."

"Then this man," cried Patience, "must be the one who broke into the Saxon Library and stole the forged Jaggard!"

"Apparently," muttered Gordon Rowe. "So you're the scoundrel I chased that night!"

"Let's get this straight," said the Inspector. "Joe, this bird in the blue hat—had a bushy mustache, too, hey?—hired you to break into the Saxon house on Fifth Avenue a couple of months ago and steal a book. What was the title, just to make sure?"

"Well," said Villa with a dark frown, "it was somepin' 'bout a pil-grim. Some kind o' "—he licked his lips—"o' sex book."

Patience giggled. *The Passionate Pilgrim!*

"Yeah! 'A's it!"

"And that's all he told you to hook?"

"Yeah. He says: 'Git into the lib'ary, see, an' look aroun' for a book in a kind o' blue leather binding, see, an' it's called *The Passionate Pilgrim* by this bird Shakespeare, see, an' it says inside it was printed by a bozo called Jag—Jaggard in 1599,' he says."

"And he gave you a hundred bucks for the job?"

" 'A's right, Chief."

"So you hooked it, hey, and forked it over?"

"Well," muttered Villa, "maybe I did take a good look at it before, see. A lousy book! This boid was noivous, see, an' I'm wise to him. He didn't want no lousy book, no, sir! Somepin' in 'at book, I says to m'self. So I gives it the old o-o. But there wasn't nuttin'. He wasn't foolin' Joe Villa, though. I knew 'ere was somepin' about 'at book. So 'at's why——"

"I see," drawled the Inspector. "I get it now. You couldn't find anything in the book, but you figured there was somethin' about it that was ready dough if a man was willing to pay you a hundred bucks to steal it. So that's why you followed this bird in the blue hat!"

"Figgered if there was cush . . . I tailed 'm aroun'. I says to m'self I'll lay low, see, an' keep my eyes open, an' maybe I'll get the lunch-hooks into what this guy's after. Then 'at day when he acts so damn' funny, an' I sees him slip this bus-starter here a green boy, I says to m'self: 'Joe,' I says, 'here's somepin' doin'.' So I does the same, see, an' I tails him all the way to this here dump, an' I sees him smash in the glass of one o' the cases in 'at room——"

"Ah," said Lane. "The truth at last. What else did you see?"

"He takes a book outa his pocket an' he puts it in the case in place of a blue book he takes out, see. Then I says to m'self: 'Joe,' I says, 'you're hot. 'At's the same kind o' book you hooked for this guy before,' I says. So when he finishes I starts to tail him, see, an' I gets mixed up in the mob of highbrows an' I don't see him for a couple o' minutes, an' 'en when I fades outside he's gone. So I goes back with the mob. 'At's all, Inspector, cross me heart!"

"You haven't got a heart," said Thumm genially. "You kept on the tail, Joe. Why lie?"

Villa's little eyes fell. "Well, maybe I did go back to this bird's hangout after. I hangs aroun', see, but I don't see nut-tin', an' I goes back the next day an' I don't see nuttin'. So 'a's why I comes back here t'day to see maybe I can find out what the hell it's all about."

"You poor sap! What could you expect to find?" It was pathetically apparent that Villa, an unintelligent animal with the lowest variety of cunning, had been plunged into an adventure whose implications were far above his low-browed head. "Now listen to me, Joe. That day when you lost this man, did you notice the special cop on duty here?"

"Yeah. I snuck by. Looked kinda familiar. He didn't spot me."

"That was Donoghue, an ex-cop. Didn't you see Donoghue following your man around?"

Villa gasped. "Cripes! 'A's right! 'A's why I couldn't tail 'm, see? This special dick, he had his eyes open. But then I lost 'em both."

"Have you seen Donoghue since that day?" asked Lane slowly.

"Naw."

"How did you come to be hired by this man in the blue hat?"

"He—he looks me up downtown, see?"

"Recommended by the fraternity," said the Inspector with heavy sarcasm. "By God, we're gettin' somewhere! Joe,

where's he hang out? You delivered the book to him somewhere, so don't say you don't know."

"He met me in town, Chief, honest to Gawd."

"Yes, but you trailed him that day to the bus. Where's he
live?"

"He's got a dump of a shack up the line, Inspector. Between
Irvington an' Tarrytown."

"Know his name?"

"Tol' me his handle was Dr. Ales."

"Dr. Ales, hey?" said Thumm softly. "Lane, we're in luck.
All ties up. Ales set this rat to robbin' the Saxon house, saw
the book was a forgery, came here after the real one, evidently
got it . . . Same bird who left that note with me, who visited
the Saxon house and swiped the stationery. Swell! Listen, heel,"
he said fiercely to Villa, "what's this Dr. Ales look like? I want
a damn' good description of him!"

Villa rose suddenly from the chair. It was as if before this
he had been biding his time, as if from the beginning he had
expected this question and had been preparing himself with a
species of wolfish exultation for it. His lips curled back from
his gums in a snarl, disclosing hideous black-flecked yellow
teeth. He whirled so quickly that Patience cried out a little,
and the Inspector took a swift step forward. But Villa merely
shot his dirty finger, on which the horseshoe ring glittered
evilly, over his shoulder.

"Describe him?" he shrilled. "Ain't 'at a pleasure! 'Ere's
your Dr. Ales! 'At wise guy there!"

He was pointing squarely at Dr. Hamnet Sedlar.

18

Contradiction in Terms

Dr. Alonzo Choate's tufted jaw waggled toward his chest;
his eyes opened to their widest dimensions, and he goggled at
Joe Villa. Dr. Sedlar blinked a little; then he turned quickly
pale, and little bunches of muscle ridged themselves along his
lean jawline like the spinal column of a hairless animal.

"I say," he began harshly, "that's a bit thick." He glared at
Villa. "You swine," he snarled, "that's not true and you know
it!"

Villa's beady eyes glittered. "Come off that perch, Yer

Lordship. You know damn' well you're the guy hired me to swipe that book!"

For a moment it seemed as if the Englishman contemplated physical assault upon the malignant dark visage of the Italian. No one spoke. To Lane, to Patience, to Rowe, to Inspector Thumm, Villa's accusation had come only as a mild shock; and they waited quietly, allowing the drama to play itself out. Dr. Choate seemed paralyzed.

Dr. Sedlar sighed at last, the blood returning to his thin cheeks. "This is, of course, utterly preposterous," he smiled. "The man is either a maniac or a willful liar." He studied the faces about him, and lost his smile. "Lord," he cried, "you don't really believe him?"

Villa snickered; he seemed very sure of himself.

"Pipe down, rat," said the Inspector softly. "The funny part of it is, Dr. Sedlar, that this isn't the first time we've been told you were a man who used the name of Dr. Ales."

Sedlar drew himself up. "I am beginning to think that this is a damnable conspiracy. Dr. Choate, what do you know about this?"

The curator passed a trembling hand over his goatee. "Well, really . . . I don't know what to think. This is the first I've heard——"

"And who is this other person who has accused me of being"—the Englishman's eyes flickered—"Dr. Ales?"

"Crabbe, Mrs. Saxon's librarian. He says that on May sixth you visited the Saxon house, giving the name of Dr. Ales."

"May sixth?" said Dr. Sedlar haughtily. "You see what utter rot this is, Inspector. On May sixth, as you may discover by cabling my former associates at the Kensington Museum, I was in London. In fact, on May seventh I attended a farewell banquet there in my honor."

Beneath the Inspector's politely inquiring air there was deep bafflement. "Well, I s'pose that lets you out, then. On the Crabbe count." His bleak eyes flashed suddenly. "But how about the day of the theft in the museum?"

"I tell you that's the guy!" screamed Villa in a rage.

"Damn you, Joe, shut up," said Thumm fiercely. "Well, Doctor?"

The Englishman shrugged. "I'm afraid I'm stupid, Inspector. I don't understand the question. Surely you know that on the day this—this creature invaded the Britannic Museum I was on the high seas?"

"That would be swell if it were true. But it's not!"

Dr. Choate gasped. Dr. Sedlar blinked for the third time, and his monocle fell to his breast. "What do you mean?" he said slowly.

"This Dr. Ales rifled the Jaggard cabinet on these premises on May twenty-seventh. . . ."

"Bah!" roared Dr. Choate. "I think this has gone far enough. I see no point in badgering Dr. Sedlar further. His boat from England did not make port until midnight of the twenty-eighth and didn't dock until the morning of the twenty-ninth. So you see it's impossible, even in theory, for him to have been the man who stole—I beg your pardon, Doctor!—the 1599 Jaggard."

Dr. Sedlar said nothing. He acknowledged the curator's heated defense with a faint smile and looked inquiringly at the Inspector.

Thumm frowned. "That's the queer part of it, Dr. Choate. If that were true, I'd kick our friend Villa in the slack of the pants and forget the whole thing. But it isn't. Because Sedlar here wasn't on that boat!"

"Not on the boat!" gasped the curator. "Dr. Sedlar, what— why—?"

The Englishman's shoulders sagged and a tired look crept into his eye. But he still said nothing.

"Well, were you, Dr. Sedlar?" asked Thumm quietly.

Dr. Sedlar sighed. "I see now how an innocent man may become entangled in a web of incriminating circumstances. . . . No, Doctor, I was not on that boat, as the Inspector says. Although how he found——"

"Checked up on you. You left England on the *Cyrinthia* Friday, May seventeenth, which docked in New York Harbor on Wednesday, May twenty-second. That means you were in New York a full week earlier than you pretended. That makes you a damned good possibility, I'll tell you!"

"I see," murmured the Englishman. "Most distressin', to be sure. Yes, that's quite correct, gentlemen. I arrived in New York a week earlier than I publicly claimed. But still I fail to see——"

"What's the game? Why'd you lie?"

Dr. Sedlar smiled. "An ugly word, Inspector. I see that I'm on what you Americans so vigorously term 'the spot.' " He leaned suddenly against Dr. Choate's desk and folded his arms. "You're entitled to an explanation. I know Dr. Choate will forgive the prevarication, but the point is that I wanted a week in New York to myself. Had I announced my arrival, I should have been constrained to get in touch with the Britannic at once, which would have hampered my movements. To avoid the necessity of—ah—rather tedious explanations, I simply said that I'd crossed a week later than I did in actuality."

"What was this week's vacation in the city for?"

"That, Inspector," replied Dr. Sedlar with a courteous smile, "I'm afraid I must refuse to answer. It was purely a personal affair."

"Oh, yeah?" sneered Thumm. "I thought——"

Mr. Drury Lane said gently: "Come, come, Inspector, a man has a right to a certain amount of privacy, you know. I see no purpose in heckling Dr. Sedlar. He has explained away a curious detail——"

Joe Villa bounced to his feet, his features writhing with passion. "Sure! I knew it!" he screeched. "Sure you'll believe *him!* But I tell you 'at's the guy hired me to pull the Saxon job an' the guy I tailed here that day! Gonna let him get away with it?"

"Sit down, Joe," said the Inspector wearily. "All right, Doctor; only I'm telling you right now it looks screwy to me."

Sedlar nodded a little stiffly. "I'm sure you'll find it all a mistake. At that time I shall of course expect an apology." He screwed the monocle back under his eyebrow and stared icicles at Thumm.

"If I may ask a question," said Patience in a charming voice in the silence. "Dr. Sedlar, do you know this man who calls himself Ales?"

"Child—" began Lane.

"Oh, it's perfectly all right, sir," said the Englishman with a smile. "Miss Thumm no doubt has the right to ask. No, I can't say I do. It strikes a faintly reminiscent note——"

"He used to write for *The Stratford Quarterly*," said Rowe suddenly.

"Ah! No doubt that's why I thought I had heard it somewhere."

"And now," interrupted the curator, coming nervously forward, "I'm sure we've had enough of accusations and recriminations. Inspector, I suggest we all forget today's little unpleasantness. I see no point in pressing a charge against this man Villa——"

"No, no," agreed Dr. Sedlar politely. "No harm done at all."

"Here, wait a minute," objected Coburn, the policeman.

"I've got my duty, gentlemen. This man's got a charge of attempted burglary against him, an' I can't just let him go. And then he's just confessed to breakin' into Mrs. Saxon's mansion . . ."

"Good heavens," sighed Patience to her young companion. "We're getting mixed up again. My head's spinning."

"There's something uncommonly rotten about all this, darling," muttered the young man. "All right, Pat, not darling! But I feel there's just one little key to the whole business, a clarifying element——"

Joe Villa stood very still, his vulturous head swaying from side to side, his little eyes gleaming darkly.

"Well—" began Thumm doubtfully.

"Inspector," murmured Lane. Thumm looked up. "One moment, please." The old gentleman took him aside and for a moment they conferred in low tones. Thumm continued to look doubtful; then he shrugged and beckoned Coburn. The officer reluctantly relinquished his grip on Villa and stalked over to listen with a grim expression to the Inspector's gruff voice. The others looked on in silence.

Finally Coburn said: "Well, okay, Inspector, but I'll have to hand in my report just the same."

"Sure. I'll make it all right with your lieutenant."

Coburn touched his visor and pounded out.

Joe Villa sighed and relaxed against the table. Thumm left the room in search of a telephone, ignoring the instrument on the desk. The curator began an earnest murmur of conversation with Dr. Sedlar. Mr. Drury Lane dreamily regarded a crisp old engraving of the Droeshout portrait on Dr. Choate's wall. As for Patience and Rowe, they stood shoulder to shoulder without speaking. It was as if they all waited for something to happen.

The Inspector stamped back. "Villa," he said shortly. The thief snapped to attention. "You're my baby. Come along."

"Where—where you takin' me?"

"You'll find out soon enough." The scholars had stopped talking and were regarding Thumm with anxious, solemn eyes. "Dr. Sedlar, you remaining here?"

"I beg your pardon?" murmured the Englishman, astonished.

"We're taking a little jaunt out to this Dr. Ales's house," explained the Inspector with a sly smile. "I thought you might like to come along."

"Hey—" croaked Villa.

Dr. Sedlar frowned. "I'm afraid I don't quite understand."

"Dr. Sedlar and I have many things to go over today," said Dr. Choate frigidly.

"Quite so." Lane moved suddenly. "Inspector, please. I shudder to think of what Dr. Sedlar will think of our American hospitality after this ghastly affair. By the way, Doctor, where are you stopping in the event we need you in an—ah—emergency?"

"At the Hotel Seneca, Mr. Lane."

"Thank you. Come along, Inspector. Patience, Gordon, I suppose we can't shake you off, eh?" The old gentleman chuckled. "Ah, inquisitive youth," and he shook his head sadly and moved toward the door.

19

The House of Mystery

At the sullen direction of the dark Italian, Dromio swung the Lincoln off the main highway between Irvington and Tarrytown into a narrow road, little more than a gravelly lane bordered by overhanging trees. From a humming concrete world they plunged suddenly into a cool wilderness. Birds and insects stirred the leaves above and about them. There was no sign of human life anywhere. The road wound and pirouetted through the green trees like a live thing.

"Sure this is it?" asked Thumm fretfully.

Villa nodded in a wary way. "I oughta know."

They drove through what seemed an interminable forest, and all were pale and silent. Dr. Ales at last! It did appear as if the perplexities of the past few weeks would be cleared away. Tensely they watched the trees flow by.

Then, without warning, the foliage fell away and they came upon another lane—the first exit they had encountered since turning off the main road a mile behind. This lane was a rough driveway branching snakily off to the left, running through thick dusty underbrush to what appeared to be a house set some fifty yards away. They could see a crumbling, patchwork, gabled roof through the trees.

"Turn off here," croaked Villa. "This is it. Now can I—?"

"You sit tight," said the Inspector grimly. "Take it easy, old boy," he ordered Dromio, who had brought the big car to rest. "We don't want to scare anybody away. Quiet, everybody."

Dromio nosed the machine into the narrow side-lane, handling it as if it were a feather. The car crept softly along; the lane widened a trifle; and then it emerged into a small clearing before a weatherbeaten wooden house which looked like the grandfather of all neglected old houses. Its paint, once white no doubt, was now a dirty gray-yellow; it hung in curled slivers from the walls, giving the structure the disagreeable appearance of a peeling potato. There was a tiny porch before the house, and the wooden steps leading up to it sagged crazily. All the visible windows were tightly shuttered, and these seemed stout enough. The trees on the sides brushed the walls. On the left side of the house leaned a tired old woodshed. Not ten feet from the shed there was a dilapidated little one-story building, apparently a garage; its double door was closed. Telephone and electric wires stuck out from the house and the garage and plunged mysteriously into the wilderness beyond.

"What a lovely old ruin!" exclaimed Patience.

"Ssh!" said the Inspector vehemently. "All right, Drome. You stick here, you people, while I do a little scoutin' around. No funny business, Joe. If you're on the level about this, I'll see you don't suffer."

He climbed quickly out of the car, crossed the clearing, and with amazing lightness for a man of his bulk mounted the steps to the porch. The door was a solid one, although it suffered from the same paint disease which afflicted the walls; there was an electric bell-button to its side. He avoided this, creeping about the porch, trying to peer into the window which looked out upon it. But the shutter effectually prevented peeping; and he softly retreated down the steps and disappeared to the left side of the house. After three minutes he appeared from the right, shaking his head.

"Damn' place looks deserted. Well, let's see." He boldly mounted to the porch and jabbed at the push-button.

Instantly—so quickly that he must have been watching them through some peephole of his own—a man opened the door and stepped out. As the door swung open a bell jangled —an antiquated device at the top of the door coiled on a spring which shivered and tinkled at the least movement of the door. The man was a tall gaunt old fellow, shrunken within his somber clothes, with a seamed and pitted face of remarkable pallor. His faded gray eyes rested briefly upon the Inspector, peered out in the bright sun toward the car, and then swung back.

"Yes, sir?" he said in a shrill voice. "What can I do for you?"

"This house occupied by a Dr. Ales?"

The old man bobbed his head eagerly; for an instant he was animated. He smiled and scraped. "Oh, yes, sir! You've heard from him, then? I was beginning to get worried——"

"Oh," said the Inspector. "I see. Just a minute." He stumped to the edge of the porch. "Better come up here, folks," he called out in bitter tones. "It looks as if we're in for a long session."

The gaunt old man led them through a narrow hallway to a tiny parlor. The interior of the house was dark and cool. The parlor was furnished with solid old pieces glazed with age, old carpets, and older hangings. A musty odor, like the cold stale smell of a crypt, assailed their nostrils. Seen in the light of day as the old man hastened to push back the shutters and pull up the blinds, the room was threadbare and repulsive.

"First thing we want to know," began the Inspector curtly, "is who *you* are."

The old man smiled cheerfully. "My name is Maxwell, sir. Been working for Dr. Ales as sort of general man around the house. Cook, clean, chop firewood, shop in Tarrytown——"

"Handyman, eh? You the only servant?"

"Yes, sir."

"Dr. Ales isn't home, you say?"

Maxwell's grin changed into an expression of alarm. "I thought— Didn't you know? I thought maybe you had news of him, sir."

"And that," sighed Patience, "just goes to show. Damn! You were right, Mr. Lane. Something's happened to him."

"Hush, Patty," said her father. "Maxwell, we're looking for information, and we've got to locate this employer of yours. When——"

Maxwell's faded eyes clouded with suspicion. "Who are you?"

Briefly the Inspector revealed a glittering shield; it was his old one which he had neglected to turn in upon his retirement; and he kept it to flash upon such occasions as he felt demanded a judicious show of authority. Maxwell retreated. "The police!"

"Just answer my questions," said Thumm sternly. "When was Dr. Ales last home?"

"I'm glad you've come, sir," murmured Maxwell. "I've been very worried. Didn't know what to do. Dr. Ales often took little trips, but this is the first time he's been away for such a long time."

"Well, for God's sake, how long has he been away?"

"Let's see, now. Today is June twenty-second. Oh, it's over three weeks now, sir. May twenty-seventh it was; yes, sir, May twenty-seventh on a Monday when Dr. Ales went off."

"The day of that funny business at the museum," muttered Thumm.

"Di'n' I tell you?" cried Joe Villa.

Mr. Drury Lane took a short turn about the parlor; Maxwell watched him with anxiety. "Suppose," he said slowly, "suppose you tell us what happened here, Maxwell, on the twenty-seventh. I have a notion it's an interesting tale."

"Well, Dr. Ales left the house early morning, sir, and he didn't come back till late in the afternoon; toward evening, I'd say. He——"

"How did he seem?" asked Rowe curiously. "Excited?"

"That's right, sir! Excited, although he is a very cold sort of person and never shows any—any . . . you know what I mean, sir."

"When he returned, was he carrying anything?" Rowe's eyes gleamed.

"Yes, sir. A book, it looked like. But then he'd gone off with the same book in the morning, so——"

"How do you know it was the same book?"

Maxwell scratched his chin. "Well, it looked the same."

The old gentleman said softly: "It all fits admirably. He went off Monday morning carrying the 1606 Jaggard, and returned with the 1599 Jaggard he had taken from the Britannic, after having left the 1606 in its place. Hmm . . . Go on, Maxwell. What then?"

"Well, sir, Dr. Ales was no more in the house than he told me: 'Maxwell, I shan't want you any more tonight. You can have the night off,' he said. So, seeing that I'd left supper for him all prepared, I went away—walked down the lane to the main pike and caught the bus there for Tarrytown. I live in Tarrytown; have folks there."

"And that's all you know?" grumbled Thumm.

The man looked crestfallen. "Well, I— Oh, yes, sir! Before

I went he told me he was leaving a package in the hall for me to send the next morning. Not to mail, he said, though; when I got back Tuesday morning I was to take the package into Tarrytown and send it off by messenger, he said. Well, when I got back Tuesday morning, sure enough, Dr. Ales wasn't there but the package was, so I took it into Tarrytown and sent it."

"What sort of package was it?" asked Lane sharply.

Maxwell looked blank. "Why, a package. Flat, I guess——"

"Could it have contained a book?"

"That's it! Just the right shape, sir. It must have been a book."

"Let's clear up one thing at a time," growled the Inspector. "When Ales got back that Monday night, was he alone? Did you notice ánybody prowling around outside?"

"Oh, he was alone."

"You didn't see a tough Irisher, middle-aged, ugly red map, hangin' around, did you?"

"No, sir."

"Funny. What the devil happened to the blasted Mick?"

"Don't forget, father," said Patience, "that Maxwell was sent away shortly after Dr. Ales got home. It's possible that Donoghue was hiding outside behind a bush, saw Maxwell go away, and then——"

"Then what?"

Patience sighed. "I'd give a cookie to know."

"Did you notice the address on the package?" asked young Rowe.

"Oh, yes, sir. This gentleman"—Maxwell inclined his gray thatch toward Lane—"mentioned the name a minute ago. Britannic Museum, it was. Fifth Avenue and Sixty-Fifth Street, it said, New York City."

"Brown wrapping-paper, and the address printed in blue ink?"

"Yes, sir."

"Well," said Thumm, "it clears up a lot, anyway. No question now but that the man in the blue hat was Ales; he stole the book, put the 1606 in its place, and the next day returned the 1599 by messenger."

"It's in the bag," said Villa with a gloating grin.

"Yes, yes," murmured Lane; his brow was corrugated. "By the way, Maxwell, do you recall mailing a similar package about two months ago?"

The remarks about theft had disturbed Maxwell; he fidgeted. "I—I hope," he said nervously, "I've not done anything wrong. I didn't know—Dr. Ales always seemed such a gentleman. . . . Yes, sir. I did mail a package like that once before; it was addressed to a Mr. Crabbe, I think, in care of Saxon, on Fifth Avenue——"

"Nothing wrong with your eyesight, eh?" said the Inspector dryly. "Well, Joe, you've got the luck of the devil. It all checks."

"Amazing thing," muttered young Mr. Rowe. "It all seems to revolve about this Dr. Ales. Not only was he *deus ex machina* of the events at the Britannic, but he seems also to have inspired that night-raid on the Saxon Library. What the deuce *was* in that book?"

Joe Villa hunched his thin shoulders, his beady black eyes shining. Then he saw the Inspector looking at him and he relaxed rather elaborately. "If you know what's good for you, Joe, you'll lay off," said the Inspector mildly. "Now listen, Maxwell. How long have you been workin' for this Dr. Ales?"

Maxwell licked his shriveled lips. "Why, just about three months. He came to Tarrytown at that time—it was the end of March—and advertised in the *Tarrytown Times* for a man to do general work. I applied for the job and got it. Reason I know when he came is because Jim Browning, the renting agent of this property in Tarrytown, is a sort of friend of mine, and he told me. Dr. Ales took this house and paid cash in advance for six months' rent, no lease, no questions asked, no references. The way things are these days, Jim said . . . So we came out here and that's all. He—he was always very nice to me."

"No questions asked, eh?" said Patience grimly. "How romantic! We'll be finding out next that he's Prince Fidelio of Zuringia, in the United States incognito on a lark—tra-la! Tell me, Maxwell, did this charming employer of yours have many visitors?"

"Oh, no, miss. Nobody— No, I'm wrong. There *was* one."

"Ah," said Lane softly. "When?"

Maxwell frowned. "It was a week before he went away—I don't recall the exact day. It was a man, but he was all bundled up and, seeing that it was at night, I couldn't see his face very well. He wouldn't give a name and insisted on seeing Dr. Ales. When I told him there was a gentleman in the parlor to see him, Dr. Ales got very excited and at first he wouldn't come out. But then he did, and he went into the parlor and was there for quite a time. Then he came out, leaving the gentleman in the parlor, and told me—he was nervous, I think

—to take the night off. I did, and when I got back the next morning the other gentleman wasn't there."

"Ales never referred to this man, Maxwell? He didn't say anything later to you about him?" demanded Rowe.

"Me, sir?" Maxwell giggled. "No, sir. Not a blessed word."

"Now who the deuce could that have been?" muttered the Inspector. "It couldn't have been this mug here, could it, Maxwell?" and he clamped his meaty hand on Villa's shoulder.

Maxwell stared, and then broke into a long chuckle. "Oh, no, sir! This gentleman doesn't speak like—like *that* gentleman. The other talked like Dr. Ales. I mean—sort of like an actor."

"An actor!" Mr. Drury Lane stared. Then he laughed heartily. "I dare say you would think that," he chuckled. "You mean an Englishman, I take it?"

"Englishman—that's it, sir!" cried Maxwell excitedly. "They both did."

"Strange," murmured Patience. "Now who in the world could that have been?"

Mr. Gordon Rowe drew his brows forbiddingly together. "Look here, man, the afternoon of the twenty-seventh when Ales sent you packing, didn't he say anything about going away?"

"Not a word, sir."

"And when you got back the next morning and found the package but Ales gone, wasn't there even a note from him to explain where he'd gone, or something?"

"No, sir. I didn't think much of it, sir, but when the days passed and he didn't come back——"

"That's why, Inspector," remarked the old gentleman, "you drew a blank on that list of missing persons Captain Grayson supplied you. Had Maxwell reported the disappearance of Dr. Ales when it occurred, you would have got a line on him. Unfortunate!" He shrugged. "It may be too late now."

"Dr. Ales is—missing?" faltered Maxwell.

"Apparently."

"Then what shall I do?" The old man wrung his hands. "This house and all the furniture——"

"Oh, yes," said Thumm. "The furniture. Was the house furnished when Ales rented it?"

"No, sir. He bought it second-hand in Tarrytown——"

"Doesn't jibe with a bird who throws hundred-dollar bills around," mused Thumm. "Evidently he didn't mean to park permanently." His gray eyes studied Maxwell shrewdly. "What did your man look like? Maybe we can get a good description of him now, anyway!"

"Why, he was tall, and rather thin——" Maxwell scratched his chin. "I've got a snapshot of him, sir; I'm sort of an amateur photographer and I took his picture one day when he wasn't looking——"

"Good glory!" shouted Rowe. "A photo!" He leaped out of the horsehair chair in which he had been restlessly sitting. "Produce it, old fellow, for heaven's sake!"

They stared at one another while Maxwell pattered off toward the rear. The musty odor seemed stronger; Villa with a quivering of his dark knife-like nostrils suddenly lighted a cigarette. Lane paced quietly up and down, hands loose behind his back.

"A snapshot," murmured Patience. "Now—hear ye! once and for all time—we'll settle the tantalizing question of . . ."

The gaunt servant hurriedly re-entered, carrying a small photograph. Thumm snatched it and held it up to the light. One devouring glance, and he cursed in astonishment. The others crowded about.

"There!" shrilled Villa. "Wha'd I tell you?"

The photograph revealed a tall slender middle-aged man in a dark sack suit of unfamiliar cut. It was a clear, well-focused picture.

There seemed no doubt, despite the absence of a monocle, that the man in the photograph was Dr. Hamnet Sedlar.

" 'At lets me' out," said Villa complacently, and he sucked at his cigarette with evil enjoyment.

"The dirty lying devil," said Gordon Rowe in a passionate undertone; and his jaw hardened. "So he *was* lying! I'll pay that murdering scoundrel back for the bullet in my arm if it's the last——"

"Here, here," murmured Lane. "Don't let your emotions carry you away, Gordon. We've proved nothing against Dr. Sedlar, remember."

"But Mr. Lane," cried Patience, "you can't get away from the evidence of this photograph!"

"Only one thing to do," muttered the Inspector. "Clamp the bracelets on him and sweat the truth out of him."

"Coerce an English citizen, Inspector?" asked the old gentleman dryly. "I ask you all again to keep your heads.

There's too much here that completely baffles rational explanation. If my opinion carries any weight, you will proceed very slowly indeed."

"But——"

"At any rate," continued Lane quietly, "there is still work to be done. I suggest we examine the house very scrupulously. There's no telling what we may find." Then he gave a little chuckle; Maxwell gaped from one to another of them, plainly confused. "As Bedford said in Orleans: 'Unbidden guests are often welcomest when they are gone.' Another pearl from our mutual oyster, Gordon. . . . So lead on, Maxwell, and we'll relieve you of our burdensome presence with the utmost expedition!"

20

A Beard and an Anagram

Old Maxwell shuffled before them into the odorous little hall, turned right a few paces and then left, crossing before the lowest riser of a decrepit wooden staircase, badly carpeted, which led apparently to the sleeping quarters upstairs. He descended two stone steps to an alcove and stopped before a massive oak door. The door was closed. He opened it and stood aside. "Dr. Ales used to work in this room."

It was a spacious study paneled from floor to ceiling in dark oak, and lined with built-in shelves for the most part empty. Only a few of the lower shelves held books, a sparse scattering of odd volumes.

"From the appearance of his library," remarked Gordon Rowe, "he never did intend this house as anything but a temporary hideout."

"It would seem so," murmured Lane.

The ceiling was low and an ancient chandelier of hideous colored glass hung above a battered desk in the center of the study. On the far wall stood a fireplace with a sturdy oak mantel above it made out of a single thick slab of wood; in the blackish grate there was a residue of charred logs and ashes. On the desk lay an old quill, a bottle of India ink, a powerful reading glass, and a clutter of odds and ends.

The Inspector and Patience both exclaimed at once and pounced upon the desk.

"What is it?" cried Rowe, darting forward.

There was an ashtray upon the desk, a poor chipped thing of colored porcelain decorated with an impossibly buxom mermaid sporting among several grinning and ugly little dolphins. In the well of the tray lay five grayish-white fragments of clay; two of the largest were concave, and the in-curved surfaces presented a burnt appearance. Clots and scraps of dried dottle made a bed for the clay pieces.

"Looks like the remains of a cheap clay pipe," said Rowe with a puzzled air. "What's all the *huzza*-ing and *banzai*-ing for?"

"Donoghue," muttered the Inspector.

Patience's blue eyes shone. "There's evidence!" she cried. "Gordon, Donoghue always smoked a clay pipe. We know he must have followed Dr. Ales that day from the museum. This virtually proves he's been here!"

"Maxwell," said Thumm harshly, "I thought you said a tough-lookin' Irishman hadn't been in this house recently. How'd the pipe get here?"

"I don't know, sir. I've not been in this room since the day after Dr. Ales went away. I saw the pieces on the floor in front of the desk that morning before I sent the package off and picked them up and put them in the ashtray with the little pieces of ash and tobacco."

Lane sighed. "Did you notice the fragments the night before, when Dr. Ales sent you away?"

"They weren't there when I left, I'm positive."

"Did Dr. Ales smoke a clay pipe?"

"Dr. Ales didn't smoke at all. We found the ashtray in some old rubbish in the woodshed when we got here." Maxwell blinked. "I don't smoke, either," he said rather tremulously.

"Then I think, Inspector," remarked the old gentleman with a note of weariness, "that we can reconstruct events with a certain degree of assurance. After Ales sent Maxwell away the evening of the twenty-seventh, Donoghue, who had followed Ales from the city and was lurking in the bushes outside, entered the house. He was face to face with Ales in this room; of that we may be certain. What happened then is conjectural."

"That's a swell word," said Thumm with a scowl. "Let's look over the rest of this dump."

They mounted the creaking staircase and found themselves in a narrow upper hallway punctuated by doors. They investigated the rooms in order. Two were empty and festooned with spider-webs; apparently Maxwell was not the most conscientious of housekeepers. One was Maxwell's own room; and it contained nothing but an iron bedstead, an old-fashioned washstand, a chair, and a chest of drawers resurrected from the cellar of some second-hand dealer's establishment. The fourth was the bedroom of Dr. Ales—a small, not too clean room as poorly furnished as Maxwell's although here a braver effort had been made to banish dust. The ancient bed, a scratched but hardy walnut piece, was neatly made up.

Patience examined the bedclothes with a feminine eye. "Did you do this up?" she asked severely.

"Yes, miss. The last time," Maxwell gulped, "the morning of the twenty-seventh——"

"Indeed?" murmured Lane. "How is that? When you returned on the morning of the twenty-eighth to find Dr. Ales gone and the package in the hall downstairs, didn't you also find this bed mussed?"

"No, sir. That's how I knew Dr. Ales must have gone away the night before, the same night he sent me off to Tarrytown. Because on Tuesday morning I saw he hadn't slept in his bed."

"Why the dickens didn't you say so before?" snapped Thumm. "That's important. It means that whatever happened here that Monday night happened before Ales turned in. I mean—before Sedlar turned in."

"Here, here, Inspector," smiled the old gentleman. "Let's not become involved. Suppose for the time being, at any rate, we continue to refer to the missing tenant of this establishment as Dr. Ales. . . . Dr. Ales." He smiled again, queerly. "Odd name, eh? Has it struck any of you how odd it is?"

Gordon Rowe, who was rummaging through a wardrobe closet, straightened up. "It's struck *me* how odd it is," he said sharply, "and if there is any sense or pattern to the phenomenon of this benighted world, its oddity makes the Inspector right and you wrong, Mr. Lane!"

"Ah, Gordon," said Lane with the same queer smile. "I might have known it wouldn't escape that terrier's pertinacity of yours."

"What do you mean?" cried Patience.

"Escape what?" roared the Inspector, crimson with exasperation.

Joe Villa dropped disgustedly into the single chair, as if he were bored to tears with the antics of these maniacs. As for Maxwell, he stared at them with his mouth half-open, the picture of idiocy.

"The fact," snapped Rowe, "that Dr. Ales has six very peculiar letters to his name. Think *that* over."

"Letters?" echoed Patience blankly. "A-l-e-s. . . . Oh, Gordon, I'm so stupid!"

"Oh, yeah?" mumbled the Inspector. "A-l-e-s. . . ."

"Not A-l-e-s," said Lane. "D-r-a-l-e-s."

"Drales?" frowned Patience.

Rowe shot a strange look at Lane. "So you *did* see it! Patience, don't you understand that the letters of the name 'Dr. Ales' make a perfectly gorgeous anagram?"

Patience's eyes widened, and she went a little pale. She breathed a name.

"Exactly. The letters of the name 'Dr. Ales' spell with the simplest sort of rearrangement the name . . . 'Sedlar'!"

"How true," murmured the old gentleman.

For a moment there was silence. Then Rowe very quietly returned his attention to the wardrobe.

"Say!" exclaimed the Inspector. "You're not so dumb after all, youngster! Well, Lane, you can't get around *that*."

"Perhaps it doesn't require getting around," smiled Lane. "No, I agree with Gordon that the anagram 'Dr. Ales' is much too felicitous to be a coincidence. There's design there. But what sort of design, springing from what source, with what purpose . . ." He shrugged. "I've learned one thing since the time I began to investigate the vagaries of the human mind. And that is never to leap at conclusions."

"Well, I am ready to leap at this one," began the Inspector harshly, when there was a satisfied grunt from young Rowe.

He backed out of the wardrobe, muttering to himself. Then he turned quickly and thrust his unwounded hand behind him.

"Guess what I've found," he said with a grin. "Dr. Ales, old boy, you're a rotten and slightly mildewed Machiavelli!"

"Gordon! What have you found?" exclaimed Patience, taking a hasty step toward him.

He waved her off with his bandaged arm. "Now, now, little lady, live up to your name." He dropped his grin abruptly. "This ought to interest you, Mr. Lane," and he brought his sound arm forward. Among his fingers flowed a green-and-blue mat of false hair, neatly shaped. It was beyond question the extraordinary beard which Inspector Thumm's client had worn on his memorable visit to the Thumm Detective Agency on the sixth of May.

Before they could recover from their stupefaction, Rowe

turned and dug again into the wardrobe. He brought out in succession three other objects—a fedora hat of a peculiar shade of blue, a pair of blue-tinted spectacles, and a luxuriant gray mustache.

"This is my lucky day," chuckled the young man. "Well, what do you think of these little exhibits?"

"I'll be eternally damned," said the Inspector blankly, regarding Rowe with grudging admiration.

"Oh, Gordon!"

Lane took beard, spectacles, mustache, and hat from Rowe. "I suppose there's no doubt," he murmured, "that the beard and glasses are the same?"

"Listen," growled Thumm. "There couldn't be two brushes like that in the whole world. Can y' imagine a sane man *wearin'* that thing?"

"Certainly." Lane smiled. "Under certain very odd circumstances. Maxwell, have you ever seen these articles before?"

The servant, who had been staring at the beard with horrified fascination, shook his head. "Except for the hat, I never saw them, sir."

The old gentleman grunted. "The hat . . . Villa, is this the hat Dr. Ales was wearing the day you followed him to the Britannic? And the mustache?"

"Sure. I tol' you this guy's up to somepin'. I ain't——"

"Tangible proof," Lane said in a musing way. "There's no doubt but that the man who left the envelope with you on May sixth, Inspector, and the man who burglarized the Britannic on the afternoon of May twenty-seventh, were identical. On the face of it——"

"On the face of it," said the Inspector with a bitter savagery, "it's a clear case. With this evidence, and with the testimony of Crabbe and Villa and the swell proof of that snapshot, there's nothing to it. I tell you there's no Sedlar in this case at all!"

"No Sedlar? Inspector, you astonish me. What do you mean?"

"But there is a Sedlar," objected Rowe, and Patience frowned at her father.

Thumm grinned. "I've busted the back of this mystery, by God! It's simple as pie. The man who showed up at the museum claiming to be the new curator they hired, Dr. Sedlar, isn't Dr. Sedlar at all! He's Dr. Ales, whoever *he* is! But I'll bet you a good smack in the whiskers that Ales managed to *do away with Sedlar* when Sedlar landed in New York and before the English johnnie could make tracks for his new job, took Sedlar's place—impersonating him maybe on the basis of a superficial resemblance, in build, height, and so on; these limeys look all alike anyway—and then started the whole train of monkeyshines. I tell you your slippery Dr. Ales is not only a thief but a *murderer.*"

"The question, it seems to me," remarked Rowe, "is: Who *is* Dr. Ales?"

"You could put your theory to a very simple test, you know," said Lane with a twinkle. "Simply cable your friend Trench of Scotland Yard to dig up a photograph of Hamnet Sedlar and send it to you."

"There's an idea!" cried Patience.

"Come to think of it, I'm not so sure——" began Lane.

The Inspector, whose underlip had been creeping forward by marked degrees during this interlude, suddenly turned scarlet and threw up his hands. "Nuts!" he roared. "I'm finished with this whole damned case. I'm not going to do another lick of work on it. I'm through, I tell you. It's got me so I can't sleep nights. The hell with it. Patty, come on!"

"But what shall I do?" asked Maxwell helplessly. "I've got some of Dr. Ales's money left, but if he isn't coming back——"

"Forget it, old boy. Close up the joint and go home. Patty——"

"I think not," murmured Mr. Drury Lane. "No, Inspector, I think not. Maxwell, it might be an excellent idea for you to remain on the premises quite as if nothing had happened."

"Yes, sir?" said Maxwell, scratching his doughy cheeks.

"And if Dr. Ales should return—which is not at all without the realm of possibility—I'm sure the Inspector will be glad to hear the news."

"Yes, sir," said Maxwell with a sigh.

"Damn it, I won't——" grumbled the Inspector.

"Come, you old thunderer," smiled Lane, "give Maxwell one of your cards. . . . That's better!" He linked his arm in Thumm's. "Remember, Maxwell, the instant Dr. Ales returns!"

21

Wickedness in Westchester

And then, as suddenly as if a blight had fallen upon it, the case died. For over a week it lay supine in death; nothing happened, nothing new was learned, and moreover no one seemed greatly to care.

The Inspector was as good as his word; he definitely threw up the case. His investigation into the jewel robbery he had mentioned—a sensational affair involving a valuable rope of pearls and an assault upon a languorous *demimondaine* nesting in the clouds above Park Avenue—consumed the Inspector's whole attention; he rarely appeared at his office and when he did it was merely for a snatched glance through his mail. The Thumm Detective Agency, except for an occasional visit by Patience, was left to the tearful mercies of Miss Brodie.

As for Patience, she had suddenly acquired a passion for learning. She haunted the Britannic Museum, to the mute approval of various gentlemen of the trades who were still busy applying architectural and ornamental cosmetics to that sadly battered edifice; and she and young Mr. Rowe applied themselves with all outward signs of diligence to research in Shakespeare. The Bard, it was to be feared, did not yield many of his secrets during this collaboration in literary history. Between discussing the enigmatic Dr. Sedlar and themselves Patience and Rowe made little progress in Rowe's labors.

But the least concerned of all, it seemed, was Mr. Drury Lane. He sequestered himself in his conveniently impregnable fortress, The Hamlet, and for nine days preserved a monastic silence.

There were picayune interludes. During the week, for example, two letters arrived at the Inspector's office which had a direct bearing upon the all-but-abandoned investigation. One was from Dr. Leo Schilling, Chief Medical Examiner of New York County, the medico-criminological terror of Manhattan's murderers. As a chemical symbol, the worthy physician wrote, the characters *3HS wM* were absolutely meaningless.

At first he had thought of splitting the symbol into its components. *3HS* might mean three parts of hydrogen and sulphur; but unfortunately there was no such chemical compound, since one molecule of hydrogen had from Priestley's day, and before, stubbornly refused to combine chemically with one molecule of sulphur. As for the small *w,* it possessed various chemical interpretations, Dr. Schilling continued; such as *watt,* the electrical term, and *wolframite,* which is a rare mineral. Capital *M* being the generic sign for "metal," there might be a connection between the *M* and the *w,* if the *w* stood for wolframite. "In general, however," the Medical Examiner's report concluded, "my opinion is that this hodgepodge of number plus small and capital letters is plain nonsense. It has no scientific meaning at all."

The second letter was from Lieutenant Schiff, cipher expert at the Bureau of Intelligence in Washington. Lieutenant Schiff excused himself for the delay in replying to Inspector Thumm's curious inquiry; he had been very busy; perhaps he had not given the symbol the proper study; but it was his opinion that "as a cipher or crypt it is so much abracadabra." He did not believe it could be broken down, if it was intended as a cipher; if anything, it was possibly the kind of cipher for which prearranged secret code-meanings had been assigned to the individual characters. An expert might spend months searching for the key or code and still be unsuccessful.

Patience was near tears; she had secretly spent many sleepless nights puzzling over the odd symbol. Rowe comforted her rather helplessly; he had had no better luck.

Other reports trickled in, similarly unenlightening. One was a confidential note from Inspector Geoghan: detectives from headquarters had spent fruitless days endeavoring to pick up Dr. Hamnet Sedlar's trail in New York City between May 22, the day on which the *Cyrinthia* had docked, and May 29, when he officially presented himself at the Britannic Museum. Inquiry at the Hotel Seneca, where the Englishman had then taken up residence, merely revealed that a Dr. Sedlar had engaged a room on the morning of May 29—an obvious development, since it was the natural step to take after the man's false story of having arrived from England on the twenty-ninth. He had had bulky luggage. He was still living at the Seneca, a quiet middle-aged Englishman who took his meals alone in the Hunting Room and, on those occasions when he happened to be in the hotel afternoons, ordered four o'clock tea which he consumed in the staid seclusion of his room.

The unfortunate Irish guard, Donoghue, was still missing. Not the faintest clue to his fate had turned up.

Dr. Ales also had vanished without a trace.

Italian Mr. Villa had come in for his share of official surveillance. The Inspector explained one afternoon to Gordon Rowe—having apparently amended his opinion of the young man since Rowe's encounter with the masked man and his subsequent discovery of the false beard—that when Villa had been apprehended in the museum he, sharp old warrior that he was—ahem!—had excused himself and sought out a telephone. Yes, perhaps it *had* been at Mr. Drury Lane's suggestion. At any rate, the purpose of this procedure had been to prepare the hounds to take up the trail of the saturnine Mr. Villa when the Inspector should have finished with him. The particular hound had been one Gross, an employee of the Thumm Detective Agency; and Gross had quite invisibly followed the entire party from the Britannic to Dr. Ales's house near Tarrytown, had quietly waited outside until the party emerged, and had then shadowed Villa with his considerable skill, sticking to the Italian's trail like the shadow of a Comanche. But Gross had nothing to report. The thief had apparently abandoned his attempt to fathom the "secret worth millions."

Dr. Sedlar came and went at the museum. As did Dr. Choate. Crabbe fondled his books at the Saxon mansion. Mrs. Saxon went about fatly and damply in the late June heat, preparing the exodus of her household to Cannes for the summer season. . . . Everybody performed his normal function. Everybody seemed as innocent as Patience's blue eyes. As Inspector Thumm remarked to one of his operatives in a moment of relaxation from the rigors of the jewel investigation: "It's just about the screwiest business I've ever had a hand in."

Maxwell, it was assumed, still held down the lonely fort at Dr. Ales's house.

Then the call came.

It came on the first of July, a broiling Monday morning which found the Inspector two days absent, off on a mysterious hunt connected with his latest investigation; Gordon Rowe peacefully asleep in the family-hotel quarters he had taken during the week—having with dignity packed his meager belongings and left the Saxon house, as he stated to Patience, "for the rest of my natural life"; Miss Brodie in the usual spiritual lather in the anteroom of the Inspector's office; and Patience at the Inspector's desk frowning over a note from her father postmarked Council Bluffs, Iowa.

Miss Brodie shouted in through the open door: "Will you take this call, Miss Thumm? Can't make him out. He sounds drunk or something."

"Oh, dear," sighed Patience, reaching for the telephone. Miss Brodie was at times difficult. "Hello," she said wearily, and then stiffened as if the wire had shot her full of current.

The voice on the other end was unquestionably old Maxwell's. But what a voice! Choking, weak, wild—it babbled on and on, and Patience could not make out more than a chance word. "Help—at the house—terrible—Inspector Thumm—come"—all amid a mumble of crazy syllables that made no sense.

"Maxwell!" cried Patience. "What's happened? Did Dr. Ales come back?"

For an instant the old man's voice, while feeble, was clear. "No. Come," and there was a hollow thud, as if something heavy had fallen. Patience stared at the receiver. Then she jangled frantically. There was no reply. "Maxwell!" But it was soon evident that poor Maxwell was in no condition to hear or answer her plea.

Patience scrambled into the anteroom, her straw hat askew on her curls. "Brodie! Get Quacey at The Hamlet for me. . . . Quacey! Patience Thumm. Is Mr. Lane there?" But Quacey was desolated: Mr. Drury, he reported, was somewhere about the estate—exactly where he did not know; however, he would find his master as soon as he could and transmit Patience's message to proceed immediately to the Ales house. . . . Then Patience rang up Gordon Rowe's new number.

"Good God, Pat! That sounds serious. Wait till I get the sleep out of my brain. . . . Have you telephoned the police?"

"Police? What police?"

"The Tarrytown police, ninny! Pat, my girl, your wits are addled this morning. For heaven's sake, get help to that poor old fellow!"

"Oh, Gordon," wailed Patience, "I'm such a fool. I'm so sorry. I should have thought of that. I'll notify them at once. Pick you up in twenty minutes."

"Put some pep into it, darling!"

But the head of the Tarrytown police, a man named Bolling, was out when Patience called; and a fatigued assistant who seemed to have difficulty understanding the urgency of the situation finally promised to "send somebody out."

As the difficulties mounted, Patience's lips became grimmer. "I'm going out," she announced tragically to Miss Brodie. "Lord, what a mess! And poor Maxwell w-weltering there in his blood for all I know. 'By!"

Patience jerked her roadster to a stop just outside the entrance to the lane. Gordon Rowe stood up and squinted hard up the road.

"I think that's Lane's car coming now."

A long black limousine hurtled toward them at breakneck speed. It shrieked to a stop in front of them and they both sighed with satisfaction. The daredevil at the wheel was Dromio. The door of the tonneau opened and Lane's tall spare figure leaped nimbly out.

"Children!" he cried. "I'm frightfully sorry. You've just come? I was out swimming and Quacey, poor fool, couldn't find me. Have you telephoned the police?"

"They should be there now," said Patience with a gulp.

"No," murmured the old gentleman, keenly eying the gravel of the lane. "It poured during the night; the gravel is still black and soft; no marks of tires. . . . For some reason they've failed. We'll have to see this out ourselves. Your arm, I see, Gordon, is healed. . . . Proceed, my dear. Not too fast. There's no telling what we may find."

He returned to his car and Patience swung the roadster into the lane. Dromio followed with the bigger machine. The trees closed in over their heads. The early-morning downpour had washed the gravel and its bed of earth clean; it was like an uncontaminated sheet of paper. The young man and the young woman were silent, Patience intent on the whimsies of the narrow road, Rowe's eyes straining ahead. They did not know what to expect. Had an armed man jumped out of a clump of bushes, or a gang appeared ahead bristling with machine guns, neither would have been surprised. The two cars crashed along; and nothing happened.

When they reached the entrance of the narrow driveway which led to the Ales house, Patience stopped. Lane got out behind them, and the three held a council of war. The countryside was cheerful and brisk with the usual summer noises; but there was no sign or sound of human proximity. They decided to leave the two cars in the lane in Dromio's charge and proceed on foot.

They walked down the driveway cautiously, Rowe in the van, Lane holding up the rear, and Patience nervously between them. The trees thinned and they peered into the clearing before the house. It was quite deserted. The front door was solidly closed, the windows were as before shuttered, the garage door was closed—nothing seemed amiss.

"But where's Maxwell?" whispered Patience.

"Let's get into the house and see. I don't like the look of this," said Rowe grimly. "Stick close, Pat; no telling what we may run into."

They crossed the clearing quickly and mounted the rickety steps to the porch. Rowe pounded hard on the thick panels of the door. He pounded again, and again. But there was no answer. They glanced at Lane; the old man's lips were set in a thin line and there was a curious glitter in his eyes.

"Why not force the door?" he suggested mildly.

"Bully idea." Rowe moved back to the edge of the porch, waved them aside, braced himself, and then took a long leaping step forward. His right foot came up sharply and crashed against the lock in a vicious kick that shivered the stout wood and set up a faint jangling above the door inside. He returned to the edge of the porch and tried again. On the fifth attempt the door burst inward, its lock shattered, while the coiled-spring bell above it set up a wild protest.

"The *savate*," panted Rowe triumphantly, springing through the doorway. "A French wrestler taught it to me in Marseilles last spring . . . For the love of God!"

They stopped short beyond the threshold, stricken dumb by what they saw. The tiny hall was a wreck; it looked as if a twister had played with it. An old chair which stood near an umbrella-stand lay broken into four pieces. A mirror which had hung above the wall carpeted the hall floor with glass fragments. The umbrella-stand had rolled crazily down the hall. A small table lay overturned, like a dead beetle.

In silence they went into the parlor. It was demolished.

They looked into the study, and Patience paled. It was as if an elephant, or a family of famished tigers, had swept through it. Not a single piece of furniture was left standing. There were peculiar gashes all over the walls. The chandelier had been demolished. Books were scattered over the floor. Glass. Splinters. . . . In the same silence they investigated the kitchen at the rear. It had been left comparatively untouched; comparatively only, for its table-drawer had been turned out,

and the shelves of its closets had been ravaged, dishes and
pans being scattered over the floor.

Upstairs the same condition prevailed. The gashes . . .

They returned to the ground floor. There was no slightest
sign of Maxwell in the house, although his clothes were in his
bedroom.

"Wasn't there a garage outside?" murmured Lane thoughtfully. "It's barely possible——"

"Let's see," said Rowe; and they went outside. Rowe
prowled about the garage. It had only one window, and that
was so crusted with dirt and carbon that it was opaque. Lane
hammered on the thin door, from whose hasp hung a rusty
lock. There was no response.

"I'll have to smash the window in," said the young man.
"Pat, stand off; don't want you hurt by flying glass." He found
a heavy stone and tossed it at the window. The glass shattered,
and he fumbled with the catch inside. Then he scrambled
through the window and an instant later called out: "Get
away from the door!" The door burst outward, its hasp
wrenched from the wood. . . . Gordon Rowe, his lean face
flushed, stood in the doorway without moving. Then he said
tightly: "He's here, all right. But I think he's dead."

22

The Hacker

A battered automobile stood in the garage, which was
strewn with rusty bolts, oily rags, wooden cases—a litter of
evil-smelling *débris*. An ancient chair stood between the win-
dowed wall and the car, and festoons of ragged rope hung
from it. Between the chair and the double door lay the body
of Maxwell, black garments streaked with dust; he was lying
prone, his legs crumpled beneath him. There was no sign of a
wound, although the knot of a bound cloth was visible at the
nape of his neck. Two feet from his outstretched right hand
there was a paint-smeared taboret on which lay an extension
telephone. Its receiver dangled at the end of the cord. Patience
dully replaced it on the hook.

Rowe and Lane knelt by the side of the still figure and
turned it over. Maxwell's gaunt face was a creamy white;
beneath his chin like a bib there was a thickly folded cloth,

apparently a gag which he had managed to work loose after freeing himself from the ropes which had held him tied to the chair beyond. Then, incredibly, his face began to twitch, and he uttered a croaking groan.

"Why, he's alive!" cried Patience, flying to his side. She went down on her knees, ignoring the grime of the concrete floor, and patted the old man's cheeks. His eyes flickered open, and closed again. Rowe scrambled to his feet and made for a greenish tap at the rear of the garage; he soaked his handkerchief in water and returned. Patience bathed the white face gently.

"Poor fellow," said Lane slowly. "I think between us, Gordon, we can manage to get him into the house."

They lifted the limp sharp-boned body carefully and carried it across the clearing through the shattered front door into the parlor. Patience struggled with an overturned sofa, managing to right it; its upholstery had been slashed to strips. They laid Maxwell upon it and stood silently looking down on him. His eyes fluttered open again, and a faint tinge of color began to suffuse his withered cheeks. There was fear and horror in his eyes; but when he saw the concerned faces above him he sighed and began to lick his lips.

At this moment there was the roar of a motor outside and they quickly went out onto the porch. A thick-set man with a red face, dressed in a blue uniform, was hurrying up the steps, two policemen at his heels.

"I'm Chief Bolling of Tarrytown," he snapped. "Were you the one that called my office this morning, young lady? . . . Couldn't find this damned place and that's why we're late. Now tell me what's happened here."

When introductions and explanations had been made, and Maxwell had been sufficiently revived, they gathered about the old man in the shattered parlor and listened to his story.

On the previous night at 11:30—a dark threatening Sunday night—Maxwell had been alone in the house playing solitaire when the doorbell rang. He had hurried to the door, a little apprehensive; it was pitch-black outside, he was alone, far from a human habitation. . . . Who might a visitor be at this time of night—to this house which had had so few visitors? Then the thought came to him that perhaps it was Dr. Ales returning; and at the insistent demand of the bell he had opened the door. Instantly a foot had slipped over the threshold and in the dim light of the hall he had seen a tall man muffled to the eyes. Maxwell started back with a squeal of alarm, but the visitor pushed something small and round and hard against Maxwell's quivering belly and he realized with a weakening of his knees that he was being threatened with a revolver. Then, as the man advanced and the feeble light fell directly upon him, Maxwell saw with a convulsion of horror that the man was masked.

"I—I was so scared," said Maxwell in a cracked voice, "that I thought I'd faint. He turned me around and made me march out of the house in front of him, keeping the gun pressed into my back. I shut my eyes; I thought he—he was going to shoot me. But he only made me go into the garage, and he found some old rope and tied me to the broken old chair there, and he gagged me with a piece of cloth. Then he went off. But he came back right away and searched me. I knew why. When we'd left the house the front door had clicked shut; it's got a spring-lock. He couldn't get back into the house. But I had a duplicate key in my jeans—Dr. Ales had the original—and he took it from me. Then he went away and locked the garage door and I was left in the dark. Everything was so quiet. . . . I was in the garage all night, hardly breathing." He shivered. "The ropes hurt. I couldn't sleep. I felt strained, and my arms and legs sort of fell asleep. But in the morning I finally managed to loosen the ropes, and I took the gag out of my mouth, and then I found in my pocket the card Inspector Thumm left with me. So I called up on the extension 'phone. . . . I guess I must have fainted. That's all I know."

They went over the house thoroughly, Maxwell tottering after them. They began with the study.

It was evident at once that Maxwell's captor had been incredibly ruthless in the pursuit of whatever purpose had brought him to the lonely country house. The room had been devastated in the search. Not only had furniture been overturned and glass objects broken, but the paneled walls showed unmistakable evidence of having been attacked in places by some sharp instrument. The instrument was very quickly found by Chief Bolling. It was a small hand-ax, and it lay on the floor near the fireplace.

"That's our ax," said Maxwell, licking his lips again. "It comes from the tool-box in the kitchen. I used it for chopping wood for the fireplaces."

"Is it the only ax on the premises?" asked Patience.

"Yes, miss."

The woodwork and paneling had been viciously attacked: long splinters lay on the molding at the base of the walls. Even the floor had been hacked in one place, where a scatter-rug had lain, according to Maxwell. The rug now lay crumpled in a corner, as if it had been violently hurled aside. An ornate grandfather-clock of Victorian vintage which had stood in another corner now lay prone on the floor in a litter of glass. Examination showed that the wielder of the ax had deliberately smashed its case, torn away the brass pendulum, tipped the clock over, and then hacked away its back and sides, revealing its intricate gears and works. The hands stood at precisely twelve o'clock.

"Was this clock going last night?" asked Rowe sharply.

"Yes, sir. I was in here playing solitaire when—when the doorbell rang, so I know. It had a very loud tick. It was going, all right."

"Then he attacked the clock at midnight," murmured Patience. "That might be useful."

"I don't see for what," grunted Bolling. "We know he came at half-past eleven from Maxwell's story, don't we?"

Mr. Drury Lane, wrapped in a mantel of reverie, stood quietly to one side, watching. Only his eyes were alert—deeply sparkling.

Patience moved slowly about the room. She surveyed the desk, whose drawers had been pulled out and their contents scattered; on the top lay strewn playing cards. Then she caught sight of something across the room and her eyes narrowed. It was a cheap tinny alarm-clock, and it stood on the oak mantel above the fireplace.

"What is it, Pat?" asked Rowe, noticing her preoccupation.

"That alarm-clock. Queer thing to be in a study," and she walked over and picked it up. It was ticking away cheerfully.

"I brought that in here, miss," said Maxwell apologetically; he seemed to have recovered from his shock and was watching the proceedings with curious eyes.

"You did? But why did you need the small clock when there was the big grandfather-clock in the room?" demanded Patience suspiciously.

"Oh, for the alarm," Maxwell hastened to reply. "I had a slight cough the last few days, miss, and I'd got some cough medicine in Tarrytown on Saturday. The druggist told me to take a teaspoonful every four hours, you see. I'd taken one at eight last night but I'm sort of absent-minded, miss"—he smiled weakly—"and I thought maybe I'd forget to take it again before I went to sleep. So I brought the alarm in here while I was playing solitaire and set the alarm to ring at midnight to remind me to take the medicine, and then I was going to bed. But before I could——"

"I see," said Patience; the story seemed innocent enough, for there was a small bottle of brown liquid on the mantel near the clock, three-quarters full, and a sticky spoon. She looked over the clock and found, quite as Maxwell had said, that its alarm was still set to go off at twelve o'clock; its little lever was pushed against the end of the slot marked *Alarm*. "I wonder now—" she murmured; and consulted her own tiny wrist-watch. It was 11:51. "What time have you, Gordon?"

"Just about eleven-fifty."

"Have you the time, Mr. Bolling?"

"Eleven-fifty-two," snapped Bolling. "What's all this—?"

"I was just wondering how correct this clock was, that's all," said Patience with a faint smile; but her eyes were perturbed. "As you see, it's on the dot." And indeed the hands of the cheap alarm-clock stood at 11:51.

"Ah—Patience," murmured Lane, coming forward. "May I see that for a moment, please?" He examined it briefly, set it back on the mantel, and returned to his corner.

"What the deuce is that?" asked Rowe wonderingly; he had been wandering about among the wreckage, poking things. His head was thrown back and he was gazing at something high on one of the walls.

This wall differed from the others in that its built-in bookshelves ran almost to the ceiling whereas the others ran only halfway to the ceiling. A sliding ladder, such as is used in shoe stores and libraries, ran along a metal track at the foot of this wall, evidently put in by the original owner of the house to provide easy access to the uppermost shelves out of normal reach. Above the topmost shelf there was a series of walnut panels, like the paneling on the other three walls. They were narrow and carved in the gingerbread style of a bygone generation. What had caught Gordon Rowe's eyes was one of these panels. It was swung away from the wall, quite as if it were a door.

"Looks like a secret compartment, by George," chuckled the young man. "In another minute I'll expect the Count of Monte Cristo to pop out of the fireplace." He ran lightly up the ladder, which stood directly below the opening in the panel near the ceiling.

"What the devil've we run into?" groaned Bolling. "Secret compartment! Sounds like one of these, here, now, detective stories. . . . Maxwell, did you know about this?"

The old man was staring upward open-mouthed. "N-no, sir! That's the first time I ever saw it. Why, it's a little door——"

"Empty," announced Rowe grimly. "Swell hiding-place! It's about—let's see now—eight inches wide by two inches high by two inches deep. . . . Ales must have made it, and a clever job he did, too! It's of recent vintage; you can still see the fresh chisel-marks inside." He squinted about, while they watched him intently. "Whoever demolished this place was unlucky. He didn't find the hole. See?" And he pointed to the narrow strip of paneling above the topmost shelf. Here and there the blade of the ax had bitten savagely into the wood; but when Rowe swung the little door shut they could see that it bore no marks of any kind. "Missed it clean! Clever, isn't it? Now how the devil do you get it open again?"

"Let me up there, young fellow," said Bolling grimly.

Rowe reluctantly descended, and the police chief mounted with a heavy caution. The secret compartment, as Rowe had said, was ingeniously made. Now that the little door was swung to, there was no sign of its existence. The cracks had been so contrived that they came at the edge of the frame of carving and were thus undetectable. Bolling pushed and pulled until his red face became redder; but the door remained shut and the panel outwardly innocent, although it gave out a hollow sound when he rapped it with his knuckles. The frame of this panel, as uniformly of the others, was set with tiny wooden rosettes. Bolling panted: "Some trick to it," and began to finger the rosettes. Then he exclaimed aloud. One of them had turned in his fingers. He revolved it once, and nothing happened. He revolved it again; and the door flew open with such coiled vigor that he almost fell off the ladder. . . . He took the door off and examined the interior. It contained a crude but clever mechanism of catch-and-spring.

"Well," he said, descending to the floor, "no use worrying about that. Whatever was in it, if anything ever was, is gone. Mighty small space, hey? Let's take a look around upstairs."

Dr. Ales's bedroom was as badly hacked as the study downstairs. The bed had been taken apart, mattress sliced open, furniture split, floor attacked—obviously the wielder of the ax, not having found what he was seeking downstairs, had mounted to Dr. Ales's bedroom to continue his search. There was a small gilt clock in the bedroom; and, oddly enough, this had been damaged also in the tornado which had swept the room, having fallen to the floor from the night-table, perhaps when the hacker had upset the table in his haste to get the bed apart. The hands had stopped at 12:24.

Patience's eyes sparkled. "Our friend's left almost a time-table of his activities," she exclaimed. "This proves that he attacked the lower part of the house first. . . . Maxwell, do you know if this clock kept correct time?"

"Yes, miss. All the clocks were good ones, even if they were cheap, and I regulated them so that they corresponded all the time."

"That's very fortunate," murmured Lane. "How stupid this man was!"

"What?" asked Bolling sharply.

"Eh? Oh, nothing, Mr. Bolling. I was just commenting upon the essential imbecility of criminals."

A bass voice rolled upstairs. "Hey, Chief! Look what I found!"

They tumbled down the stairs in their haste. One of the policemen was standing in the hall, focusing a flashlight on a dark and dirty corner. In the rays of the light they saw three pieces of glass, to one of which was attached a long loop of black silk ribbon, torn in one place.

Lane picked up the pieces and took them into the parlor. He fitted the three pieces together; they made a perfect circle of glass.

"A monocle," he said quietly.

"Good Lord," muttered Rowe.

"A monocle?" Maxwell blinked. "That's funny, sir. Dr. Ales didn't wear any, and I've never seen one about the house. And of course I——"

"Dr. Sedlar," said Patience gloomily.

23

A Matter of Symbolism

There was nothing more to be done on the scene. Maxwell was advised to forget his employer and return to Tarrytown to resume the sadly broken thread of his hitherto peaceful life.

Bolling, an energetic if plodding executive, placed the house under guard, leaving his two men to watch both the lane leading to the house and the rear, although the rear was inaccessible unless one plowed through a tangle of underbrush and treacherous leaf-mold. Of one point young Rowe, who had been progressively more silent with the discovery of the secret compartment in the study, made certain: Maxwell had stated that due to his being alone at night in the country he had on the previous night, as always, locked all doors and windows. Rowe then personally toured the house; he found that with the exception of the front door all doors and windows were locked from the inside. As for the cellar, it was not necessary to examine it, since there was no entrance to it except through the staircase near the kitchen inside the house. . . . The bell contrivance on the front door jangled derisively after them as they left the house.

On the old gentleman's invitation—Bolling took Maxwell into Tarrytown in the police car—Patience and Rowe followed Dromio's limousine bound for The Hamlet. The young people retired gratefully to rooms assigned them by the Falstaffian little major-domo of the household, scrubbed themselves clean, and came down to a late luncheon refreshed in body if not in spirit. The three ate alone in the more intimate atmosphere of Lane's private quarters. There was little said during the repast; Patience was fretfully quiet, Rowe thoughtful, and Lane devoted himself to mild conversation and a complete silence on the events of the morning. After luncheon he placed them in the hands of Quacey, excused himself, and retired to his study.

Patience and Rowe wandered idly about the vast acreage of The Hamlet. When they came to a lovely little garden, they flung themselves by tacit consent full length on the grass. Quacey peered at them, chuckling, and then vanished.

Birds sang, and the grass smelled hot and sweet. Neither spoke. Rowe twisted about to study the face of his companion. She was flushed a little with the warmth of the sun and her exertions; her slim body lay outstretched, healthily curved. To Rowe, watching her with a curious eagerness, she seemed at once enticing and remote. For her eyes were closed and there was a faint white line between her straight brows that did not invite either badinage or love-making.

Rowe sighed. "What do you make of it, Pat? For heaven's sake, don't frown that way! I like my women vapid."

"Am I frowning?" she murmured; and she opened her eyes

and smiled at him. "You're such a child, Gordon. I've been thinking——"

"I suppose I'll have to get resigned to a brainy wife," said the young man dryly. "The point is, so have I—so that makes two."

"Wife? That's *not* funny, young man! I've been thinking that Dr. Ales's house last night was invaded not by one person but by *two*."

"Ah," said Rowe; and he lay back suddenly and plucked a blade.

She sat up, her eyes warm. "So you saw it, too, Gordon? One was the wielder of the ax. The condition of the house clearly shows that he was searching for something; he didn't know where it was and wanted desperately to find it—witness his systematic demolition of furniture and things with the ax. The important point is that the man *wasn't* Dr. Ales."

Rowe yawned. "Naturally not. If he'd been Ales he would have known exactly where to find something that he himself— surely it was Ales who made that little compartment in the wall—had hidden there." Rowe yawned again. "And the other?"

"Don't act so disinterested," laughed Patience. "You know you're thinking furiously. . . . I don't know. You're right about the reason. The hacker is one of our unknowns; Dr. Ales wouldn't have had to chop the place to kindling wood— he would have *known* where to find whatever the hacker was looking for. On the other hand, the thing the hacker sought *was actually found:* witness the secret compartment which we found open, and which therefore was *left* open by someone."

"And that makes you think two people were in the house last night? Why couldn't the hacker—confound that clumsy word!—have found the compartment himself, after he'd done the dirty work with the ax?"

"Well, smarty," snapped Patience, "for one thing the compartment as you saw was very cleverly hidden. Only the fact that Bolling knew a compartment was in precisely that spot by seeing the open door led him to find that rosette. With the door closed and the wall a blank, the chances would be a million to one that a searcher would pick the right panel, and then the right rosette, and then would know enough to twist the rosette completely around *twice,* as Bolling had to do to open the door. In other words, the aperture couldn't have been found by *accident.* Had the hacker known the secret of the rosette and the aperture there would have been no necessity for hacking. So I say it wasn't the hacker who twisted the rosette, opened the compartment, took out what was in it, and left the door open. If it wasn't the hacker it was someone else, and that makes two people, my man. Q.E.D."

"A veritable lady-sleuth," chuckled Rowe. "Pat, you're a jewel. That's excellent logic. And there's another conclusion, too. When did the other man—if it was a man—go to the compartment? That is, did he precede the hacker or follow him?"

"Must have followed, teacher. If the man who rifled the compartment had been first, then the hacker, coming second, would have seen the open door of the compartment and therefore would have known at once where the hiding-place was. Result: he wouldn't have chopped the house to little bits *looking* for the hiding-place. . . . Yes, Gordon, the hacker came first, which must mean he was the man who held up Maxwell and left him trussed in the garage. And then a second man came, and what happened then goodness only knows."

They were silent for a long time. They both lay on the grass and stared up at the wool-flecked sky. Rowe's brown hand stirred and touched hers. It remained there, and she did not draw her hand away.

After an early dinner the three repaired to Lane's study, an old English-style room which smelled of leather and books and wood-sparks. Patience sat down in the old gentleman's armchair and, taking a piece of paper, idly began to scribble. Lane and Rowe seated themselves before the desk, relaxed in the half-light of the lamp on the desk.

"You know," said Patience suddenly, "before dinner tonight I wrote down a few things that—well, bothered me. They might be called the specific mysteries. Some of them annoy me dreadfully."

"Indeed?" murmured Lane. "My child, you possess a pertinacity positively amazing in a woman."

"Sir! That's my chief virtue. Shall I read my little essay?" She slipped a long sheet of paper out of her bag and unfolded it. And began to read in a clear voice.

"(1) It was Dr. Ales who left the sealed envelope with the symbol in it with us—proof, the beard and glasses found in his closet; proof, he is a 'missing bibliophile.' It was Dr. Ales who sent Villa to steal the 1599 Jaggard in the Saxon house. It was Dr. Ales who joined the bus party and rifled the Jaggard cabinet in the Britannic—Villa's confession brings this out, and it is confirmed by finding the blue fedora and the false gray mustache in Ales's bedroom. BUT who *is* Dr. Ales? Is he Hamnet Sedlar, as Crabbe and Villa both claim, or someone else entirely? Is there somehow a confusion of identities?

"(2) Who is the man known as Hamnet Sedlar? That a Hamnet Sedlar exists we know from Scotland Yard and the fact that such a person was hired to be the Britannic's new curator. But is the man who presented himself at the Britannic as Hamnet Sedlar really Hamnet Sedlar, or someone masquerading as Hamnet Sedlar, as father thinks? He is definitely on the shady side; he lied about the true date of his arrival. Is the real Hamnet Sedlar dead? Did this man take his place and his name? What was his motive in lying about the arrival date? What was he really doing between the date of his real arrival and the date of his pretended arrival?"

"Phew!" said young Mr. Rowe. "What a tortuous mentality!" Patience glared at him and continued:

"(3) If Hamnet Sedlar is not Dr. Ales, what's happened to Dr. Ales? Why did he disappear?

"(4) What really happened to Donoghue?

"(5) Who held Gordon and me up and stole the envelope?

"(6) Who was the hacker? He was not Dr. Ales, but might have been anyone else.

"(7) Who was the person who followed the hacker and actually rifled the secret compartment? It might have been Dr. Ales himself—he knew the secret of his own hiding-place, naturally."

"One moment, Patience," said Lane. "How do you know the wielder of the ax was not Dr. Ales, or that there were two persons in the Ales house last night?" Patience explained. Lane eyed her lips fixedly, nodding. "Yes, yes," he murmured when she had finished. "Extraordinary. Eh, Gordon? And perfectly true. . . . Is that all?"

"No. There's one more," said Patience, frowning, "and it's the most important and puzzling of all." She continued:

> "(8) What are all these confused mysteries revolving about? Undoubtedly the 'secret worth millions' Dr. Ales mentioned. But the secret worth millions is tied up with the symbol Ales left in father's keeping. So everything depends on this last question: *What does the symbol mean?*"

And she put down the paper and resumed her idle scribbling at the desk. Neither man spoke for some time. Then Rowe, who had been watching absently the gyrations of Patience's pencil, stiffened and half-rose from his chair. Patience and Lane looked at him curiously.

"What are you writing there?" demanded the young man sharply.

"What?" Patience blinked. "That blankety-blank symbol. 3HS wM."

"Eureka!" shouted Rowe. He sprang to his feet, eyes shining. "I've got it, I've got it! How perfectly, childishly simple it is after all!"

Mr. Drury Lane rose and went to the desk. His face leaped out of shadow, and every line was etched in fine black. "So you've seen it at last," he murmured. "I saw it, knew it, the day we sat in your father's office, Patience, and he unfolded the original sheet of Saxon stationery to disclose what was written on it. Tell her, Gordon."

"I don't understand you two," complained Patience.

"How was I sitting when you just jotted the symbol down?" said Rowe.

"In front of the desk, facing me."

"Exactly! In other words, I saw the characters of the symbol just as Mr. Lane must have seen them at the time he faced your father across the desk when the Inspector unfolded the original sheet. I saw them *upside down.*"

Patience uttered a faint cry. She snatched up the sheet and turned it around. The symbol now read:

She repeated slowly: "Wm SHe," the individual characters, mouthing them as if to extract their essential flavor. "That looks—that looks like a signature of some sort. "W-m. . . . William—" Both men watched her keenly. *"William Shakespeare!"* she cried, springing to her feet. *"William Shakespeare!"*

A little later Patience seated herself on the rug at the feet of the old gentleman; his long white fingers played with her hair. Rowe sat slumped opposite them.

"I've gone through that mentally many times since that day," Lane wearily explained. "It seems clear enough from the analytical standpoint. Dr. Alēs was not copying a facsimile of A Shakespearean autograph; a facsimile would have been Elizabethan script. He was jotting down in his own way—probably with some fantastic notion of making it clearer—the *capital letters* of this unusual Shakespearean signature. What makes it unusual is the small-sized *m* and the script *e*. But why the capital *H*? Probably a vagary of Alēs's mind. It isn't important."

"What is important," muttered Rowe, "is that this *is* one variation of the Shakespeare autograph. Queer!"

Lane sighed. "As you know even better than I, Gordon, there are only six fully authenticated signatures of Shakespeare extant."

"Talk about queer," remarked the young man. "One of them is written *Willm̄ Shak'p'.*"

"Yes. But there are a number of the so-called 'doubtful' autographs, and among these is one spelled like the Alēs symbol—a capital *W*, a small *m* aligned with the top of the *W*, space, then a capital *S*, small *h*, and a small script *e* also aligned with the top."

"Like the old English style of writing 'ye'?" asked Patience.

"Exactly. This doubtful autograph appears in the Aldine edition of Ovid's *Metamorphoses*, now at the Bodleian Library in Oxford."

"Saw it when I was in England," snapped the young man.

"I have checked with the Bodleian Library," continued the old man quietly, "and the *Ovid* is still there. I had thought, you see, that this entire affair was mixed up perhaps with a theft of that volume. It was ridiculous, of course." Patience felt his fingers stir on her head. "Let me go into this more deeply. Dr. Alēs said the 'secret' was worth millions; he left this copy of the autograph of William Shakespeare as the key to the secret; so we must begin from there. Do you see now what the secret must be?"

"Do you mean to say," asked Patience in an awed voice, "that all this stealing and mystery and everything revolve about the discovery of a *seventh genuine Shakespeare signature?*"

"Looks like it, doesn't it?" Rowe laughed bitterly. "Here I've squandered my youth—ha, ha!—messing about old Elizabethan records, and I've never even run across a hint of such an extraordinary thing."

"What else?" murmured Lane. "If the secret is indeed worth millions, then Dr. Ales had reason to believe the signature was authentic. How would it be worth millions? Ah, there's a fascinating question."

"In itself," said the young man softly, "it would be priceless. It would have incalculable historic and literary value."

"Yes, a newly discovered and fully authenticated seventh Shakespearean autograph would bring even in auction, as I've read somewhere, a cool million or more. And I don't know whether my authority meant dollars or pounds sterling! But no signature exists without purpose. Signatures are generally affixed to some type of *document.*"

"The paper in the book!" cried Patience.

"Hush, Pat. That's true, although not always," said Rowe reflectively. "The six authentic signatures are documented, of course: one is on a legal deposition in a suit in which the old boy was involved; one on the purchase deed of a house he bought about 1612; another on a mortgage deed involving the same house; and the last three on the three sheets of his will. But it might be on the flyleaf of a book, you know."

"I think not, as Patience has already seen," said Lane. "Would this seventh signature appear on a document—a deed, a lease—in which event the document itself would have comparatively small historic value? Well, perhaps . . ."

"Not small," said Rowe defensively. "If it were a deed or a lease it might have tremendous importance. It might show where Shakespeare was at a certain date—clarify all sorts of issues."

"Yes, yes. I meant small from the human side. But suppose it is on a *letter?*" Lane leaned forward, and his fingers gripped Patience's curls so tightly she almost cried out. "Think of the possibilities! A letter signed, written by immortal Shakespeare!"

"I'm thinking," muttered Rowe. "It's almost too much. To whom might it have been addressed? What did it say? Autobiographical data. A genuine Shakespearean holograph——"

"Certainly it's within the realm of possibility," continued the old gentleman in a queerly choked voice. "If it appears at the bottom of a letter, the letter would be worth almost more than the signature! No wonder respectable old scholars are apparently at each others' throats. It would be like—like finding, by heaven, one of the original epistles of Paul!"

"That document was in the 1599 Jaggard," whispered Patience fiercely. "Dr. Ales evidently searched the first two existing copies of the 1599 Jaggard and, finding nothing, made every effort to get hold of the third, which was in the Saxon collection. And he did! Is it—could it be possible . . . ?"

"It looks that way," grinned Rowe. "He's found it, lucky dog!"

"And now somebody's stolen it. Oh, dear! I'll bet it was in that compartment in Dr. Ales's study."

"That's very probably so," said Lane. "There's another thing. I have discovered that this third copy, stolen and then returned, was originally bought by Samuel Saxon from Sir John Humphrey-Bond, the British collector."

"The man who recommended Hamnet Sedlar to Mr. Wyeth?" cried Patience, aghast.

"The same." Lane shrugged. "Humphrey-Bond is dead; he died only a few weeks ago. No, no," he said with a smile as they both started, "don't be alarmed. It was a perfectly natural death, in the sense that it was caused by no human agency. The Lord God, as usual, was the executioner. He was eighty-nine and died of pleural pneumonia. But my correspondent on the other side cabled me also that the Jaggard, bought by Saxon from Humphrey-Bond, the one that's been causing all this trouble, had been in possession of the Humphrey-Bond family since Elizabethan times. Sir John was the last of his family; had no heir."

"He couldn't have known there was such a document hidden in the back cover of the Jaggard," remarked Rowe, "or he wouldn't have sold the book in the first place."

"Naturally not. The chances are that for many generations none of the Humphrey-Bonds even suspected the existence of such a document in one of their books."

"But why," demanded Patience, "was the document hidden in the binding at all? And who hid it there?"

"There's a question," sighed Lane. "I suppose it's been nestling there for centuries; it might have been addressed to a contemporary; who knows? But the fact that it was hidden at

all points to an extra value or significance connected with the
document itself. I believe——"

Old Quacey slipped into the study. His ancient face was
wrinkled in a thousand places, and each place was the repository of bad news. He tugged at his master's sleeve. "Man
named Bolling," he complained. "Policeman from Tarrytown,
Mr. Drury."

Lane frowned. "Eternally Caliban! What *are* you talking
about?"

"He 'phoned. He said to tell you that an hour ago"—the
clock on the study wall showed seven o'clock—"the house of
Dr. Ales was destroyed in a mysterious explosion!"

24

Holocaust and a Discovery

The house was a burning, smoking ruin. Tenuous sheets of
thick yellow smoke still clung to the charred trees about, and
there was a pervasive sulphurous odor which gripped the
throat. The old wooden structure had been razed to its foundation; fragments of wall and roof strewed the road; the house
had collapsed over the cellar and now lay, a smoldering heap,
in the cindery clearing. State troopers prowled about keeping
back a curious crowd. Firemen from Tarrytown were keeping
the blaze under control, concentrating their efforts on prevent-
ing the flames from spreading to the dry woods. But there
were ineffective water facilities, and auxiliary tanks had been
rushed from Tarrytown and Irvington. The tanks soon ran
dry; and onlookers were pressed into service to fight the
flames.

Chief Bolling met Patience, Rowe, and Lane at the edge of
the clearing. His red face was speckled with cinders and he
was panting. "Devilish damn' thing," he shouted. "My two
men were badly injured. Good thing nobody was in the house
when it happened. Blew up at six o'clock."

"Without warning?" muttered Lane; he was strangely agitated. "No possibility of a bomb dropped from aircraft, I
suppose?"

"Not a chance. There hasn't been a 'plane near here all
day. And my two men both say not a soul came near the
place since we left a couple of hours ago."

"It must have been a bomb planted in the house, then," said Rowe grimly. "Lord, what a narrow escape!"

"Why, it might have exploded while we——" Patience went white. "It——it's just a little staggering. A *bomb!*" and she shuddered.

"Probably planted in the cellar," remarked Lane absently. "That's the one place in the house we didn't search this afternoon. Stupid!"

"The cellar——that's the way I figure it, too," grunted Bolling. "Well, I've got to see that my two men are carted off to the hospital. Lucky devils! They might have been blown to little pieces. We'll have a look at the ruins tomorrow, when the fire's out."

In the old gentleman's car on the way back to The Hamlet, all three were very quiet, rapt each in his own thoughts. Lane especially was meditative, fingering his lower lip and gazing into space.

"You know," said Rowe suddenly, "I've been thinking."

"What?" said Patience.

"There seems to be a nest of people involved in this thing. No question but that the Shakespearean document, whatever it is, is at the bottom of everything. We're agreed, I think, that Dr. Ales found it in the 1599 Jaggard he stole from the museum. That makes one protagonist——Ales. Another one is the gentleman who wielded the ax last night; what was he looking for if not the document? There's two, then. And there was the person who came after the hacker, the one who left the secret compartment-door open; that's three. And now the explosion; someone set a bomb. There's four, by heaven, and it's enough to give you a pain in the cervix."

"Not necessarily," said Patience argumentatively. "One or two of these protagonists of yours——you're so *technical!* ——might have been repeaters. The second visitor to the house might have been Dr. Ales; that would cut them down to three. The hacker might have set the bomb; that would make two. . . . We'll not get far on that tack, Gordon. But there *is* one thing. Now that I've had time to think over this appalling explosion, I've got the queerest idea." The film dissolved over Lane's eyes and curiosity crept into them. "We've been assuming that whoever is after the document wants it for *itself*—— to steal it, keep it, or dispose of it for money——the usual crime for gain."

Rowe chuckled. "Pat, you're the most contrary wench! Of course. That's the normal explanation of a scramble after something valuable!"

Patience sighed. "Perhaps I'm going daffy, but I can't help thinking that if the bomb was set in advance of last night, it's a possibility that the one who set it *knew the document was in the house!*"

The old gentleman blinked. "Yes, Patience?"

"Oh, I suppose it's insane, but we're dealing with violent events—attacks, thefts, explosions. . . . Only Maxwell was living in the house; surely the bomb-setter knew that. It's preposterous to think that the bomb was meant for that harmless old servant. Then what *was* it meant for? We've been supposing that a person or persons were after the document to keep it; I tell you there's somebody after it to *destroy* it!"

Rowe gaped for a moment, and then he threw back his head and guffawed. "Oh, Pat, you'll be the death of me. Talk about woman's arguments . . ." He wiped his eyes. "Who the devil would want to destroy a document of such historic and monetary value? It's insane on the face of it!"

Patience flushed. "I think you're being miserable."

"Patience's alternative, Gordon," said Lane shortly, "is strictly logical. You won't get far, my boy, challenging this young woman's intellect. I should say that if only the Shakespearean signature were involved, then only a madman would wish to destroy it. But there's more than the signature involved; there's the document to which the signature is appended. The bomber therefore might have been moved by a desire to keep the document, with whatever message it contained, *from becoming public knowledge.*"

"There, smarty," said Patience.

"But to destroy—!" Rowe grimaced. "I can't imagine what sort of secret old Shake could have written which would induce a twentieth-century being to go to such lengths to keep it from becoming public. What on earth could it be? It doesn't make sense."

"That's exactly the point," said Lane dryly. "What can it be? If you knew that— As for it's not making sense, that's another story."

Had Patience been asked, she would probably have said that this day, which had begun with a weird telephone call, which included an assaulted old man, a mysteriously vandalized house, and ended with a violent explosion, could hold no further surprises. But there was still another awaiting her—and Rowe and Lane—at The Hamlet.

It was growing dark. There was a firefly of light on the drawbridge; Quacey's gnomish old face gleamed leathery and wrinkled before an ancient lantern.

"Mr. Drury!" he cried. "Was anyone hurt?"

"Not badly. What's the matter, Quacey?"

"There's a gentleman in the hall. He telephoned just after you left. Then he came out himself, about an hour later. He seems frightfully upset, Mr. Drury."

"Who is he?"

"He says his name is Choate."

They hurried into the manorial hall, like the building itself faithful to the medieval English castle from which it had been copied. The rushes sighed beneath their shoes. Far at the other end, his hands clenched behind his back, was the bearded figure of the Britannic's curator, striding up and down below the huge mask of Tragedy which it had been Lane's fancy to install at that end of the hall.

The three crossed to him eagerly. "Dr. Choate," said Lane slowly. "Sorry to have kept you waiting. Something unexpected happened. . . . Your face is as tragic as that mask! What's the trouble?"

"Something unexpected?" Dr. Choate was agitated. "Then you know?" He scarcely nodded to Patience and Rowe.

"The explosion?"

"Explosion? What explosion? Heavens, no! I'm talking about Dr. Sedlar."

"Dr. Sedlar!" they all exclaimed together.

"He's disappeared."

The curator leaned against an oak table. His eyes were bloodshot.

"Disappeared?" frowned Patience. "Why, we saw him only Saturday, didn't we, Gordon?"

"Yes, yes," said the curator hoarsely. "He was in for a few minutes Saturday morning. He seemed quite all right. I asked him before he left to telephone me at my home Sunday—last night—about a certain matter connected with the museum. He promised. Then he went away."

"He didn't call?" murmured Lane.

"No. I tried to get him at the Seneca; he wasn't there. All day today I waited for him, or for word from him. But there was nothing." Dr. Choate raised his shoulders. "It's so—so imbecilic! He said nothing about going away. I thought perhaps he might be ill. I called again this afternoon, and discovered that he hadn't been seen at the hotel since Saturday morning!"

"That doesn't necessarily mean he disappeared Saturday," muttered Rowe.

"I suppose not. But it's strange. I didn't know *what* to do. Call the police or— I tried to get in touch with your father, Miss Thumm, but the girl in the office said . . ." The curator sank into a chair, groaning.

"First Donoghue, then Dr. Ales, now Sedlar," said Patience tragically. "All these disappearances! It's—it's indecent."

"Unless Sedlar is Ales," pointed out Rowe.

Dr. Choate seized his head. "Good God!"

"I wonder," frowned Patience, "if it mightn't mean that Dr. Ales *is* Sedlar, that he's got the document, and that he's skipped out!"

"My dear Miss Thumm. The hotel people say all his effects are still in his room. That's scarcely consistent with an escape, I should say! And what document are you—?"

Lane looked very tired; there were deep rings under his eyes and his skin was like creased parchment. He shook his head wearily. "These speculations get us nowhere. Unexpected development . . . The only thing I can suggest is that you try to find out what's happened to Sedlar."

It was very late when Patience and Rowe reached the city. They parked the roadster outside the Hotel Seneca and sought out the manager. After some delay they were permitted to see Dr. Sedlar's room. It seemed quite orderly; English-cut clothes hung stiffly in the wardrobe, the bureau was full of fresh linen, and the man's two trunks and three bags were unpacked. The manager, who seemed eager enough to keep the police out of it, glanced again at Patience's credentials—which belonged, of course, to the Inspector—and wearily permitted a search of the room.

The luggage and clothing were uniformly English; there was some correspondence, postmarked "London" and addressed to "Dr. Hamnet Sedlar." It was of an innocent nature, apparently from former associates of the Briton. The passport, properly viséd, was found intact in one of the bureau drawers; it was made out to Dr. Hamnet Sedlar and bore a small familiar photograph.

"Sedlar, all right," scowled Rowe. "This thing is beginning

to get on my nerves. There's certainly no indication here that the man intended to skip the country."

"Bother!" groaned Patience. "Gordon, take me home and— and kiss me."

25

Murder

The sun beamed and the fire was out. The smoke had dissipated overnight. Only the charred embers, the heap of wreckage like a prehistoric mound, and the scorched trees remained to tell of the explosion the evening before. Firemen and police were busy digging about in the ruins. One man, dark quiet fellow with a sharp eye, was directing operations. He seemed particularly anxious to get the *débris* cleared away so that he could descend into what remained of the cellar.

They looked on from the edge of the trees, a warm early-morning wind blowing their clothes about. Bolling watched the workmen grimly.

"See that bird over there with the eagle eye? He's a bomb expert. Thought I might as well do this right while I was doing it. I want to know how this damn' thing *happened*."

"Do you mean to say he'll find something in that rubbish?" demanded Rowe.

"That's what he's here for."

The workmen made huge progress. In a short time the wreckage had been cleared out of the hole in the ground and passed from hand to hand to make a ragged heap thirty feet away. When the cellar had been sufficiently excavated to permit descent, the quiet man scrambled into the pit and disappeared. He emerged after ten minutes, looked about as if measuring the circumference of the explosion, and vanished again, this time among the trees. When he returned he dived into the cellar again. On his third appearance he wore a look of quiet satisfaction, and he carried in his two hands a heterogeneous mess of small iron fragments, rubber, glass, and wire.

"Well?" demanded Bolling.

"Here's the evidence, Chief," said the bomb expert casually. He held up a small piece of clock-like apparatus. "Time-bomb."

"Ah," said Mr. Drury Lane.

"Crude, home-made. Set by a clock to go off at six. Swell charge of trinitrotoluol—TNT."

The same question leaped to the lips of Patience, Rowe, and Lane. It was Lane, however, who said sharply: "When was the bomb planted?"

"Six p.m. Sunday, if this went off at six last night. It was a twenty-four hour bomb."

"Six o'clock Sunday," repeated Patience slowly. "Then it was planted before Maxwell was assaulted Sunday night!"

"Looks as if you were right, Pat," murmured Rowe. "If whoever set the bomb knew the document was in the house, then he planted it to destroy the document. That means he knew it was in the house but didn't know exactly where. It's hard to take——"

"Focal point of the explosion," said the expert, spitting at a blackened rock, "was the cellar."

"Ah," said Lane again.

"The second visitor, the one who got the document out of the little secret compartment," said Patience with a thoughtful squint at Lane, "couldn't have been the one who set the bomb. That's obvious. That second visitor *knew* where the document was; the bomb-setter didn't, as you've just said, Gordon . . ."

She was interrupted by a hoarse shout from one of the workmen digging in the ruins of the cellar. They all turned quickly.

"What's the matter?" cried Bolling, breaking into a run.

Three men were stooping over something, their heads just visible above the lip of the excavation. One of them turned, white and shaking. "There—there's a body in here, Chief," he croaked. "And from the—the looks of him he was *murdered.*"

The young people dashed through the blackened ashes to the rim of the foundation. Lane followed slowly behind, pale and worried.

Rowe took one look and turned to shove Patience roughly away. "No good, Pat," he said huskily. "You'd better go off there under the trees. It's—not nice."

"Oh," said Patience; and her nostrils flared nervously. Without another word she obeyed.

The men stared, fascinated, down into the pit. One workman, a young red-cheeked policeman, crept off to a corner of the cellar and bent double, trembling and sick. . . . The remains were fearfully charred, wholly beyond semblance to human form; a leg and an arm were horribly missing, and the clothes were completely burned away.

"How do you know," asked Lane harshly, "that he's been murdered?"

An older man in uniform looked up, lips compressed. "He wasn't so burnt I can't see the *holes*," he said.

"Holes?" choked Rowe.

The man sighed queerly. "Three holes. Neat as hell in his belly. Those are bullet holes, mister, and don't forget it."

Three hours later Lane, Chief Bolling, Patience, and young Rowe were seated silently in the office of the district attorney at White Plains. A hurry call had been sent through for a vehicle and arrangements made to cart the corpse off to the Medical Examiner's office in White Plains, the county seat. Bolling would permit no one to touch the body beyond the handling necessary to assemble the scattered remains. A search had been conducted for fragments of clothing, particularly buttons, which might provide a clue to the murdered man's identity in the absence of more specific identification; but the body had been in the vortex of the explosion and the searchers soon gave up. It was a miracle, the bomb expert said cheerfully, that the body had not smashed to atoms.

They sat about the district attorney's desk staring at the object upon it. It was the only article taken from the dead body which might be construed as a clue. It was a wrist-watch of British manufacture, a cheap timepiece with a leather strap; it would have been futile to attempt to trace it. Nothing remained of the crystal except a single triangular bit of glass clinging to the frame. The alloy metal of which the watch was made had not suffered from the explosion, aside from its smoky blackish appearance. There was one thing about it, however, which was odd. The hands stood fixed at 12:26; and there was a deep gash on the face. This gash had not only bitten into the number *10* but extended beyond the *10* into the very metal of the frame.

"That's a funny one," said the district attorney, a youngish man with worried eyes. "Didn't you tell me, Bolling, that the body was found face down and the arm on which this watch was strapped was folded *under* the body?"

"That's right."

"Then the gash on the edge of the dial wasn't made by the explosion."

"There's something else too," murmured Patience. "The explosion occurred at six o'clock; if it had caused the watch to stop then the hands should show six o'clock. But they don't."

The district attorney surveyed her with admiration. "Right! I never thought of that, to tell the truth. Inspector Thumm's daughter, did you say?"

The Medical Examiner came in hurriedly—a bald little man with a pink face and tender jowls. "Hello, hello! Well, I suppose you want the good news. I've just finished looking over that mess inside."

"He was murdered, wasn't he?" asked Rowe eagerly.

"Yes, indeed. Of course in the condition of the corpse it's hard to tell, but it's my opinion that he's been dead about thirty-six hours, which would make the time of death approximately midnight Sunday."

"Midnight Sunday!" Patience stared at Rowe, and he stared back. Mr. Drury Lane stirred a little.

"That checks pretty well with the wrist-watch," remarked the district attorney. "Twelve-twenty-six. The watch must have stopped during the murder-period. He was killed at twenty-six minutes past twelve early Monday morning."

The bald little man continued: "He was shot from the front, at very close range. Three slugs." He tossed three smashed and shapeless bullets on the desk. "Funny thing about the gash on that watch. There's a corresponding gash on the wrist which cut pretty deep. The wrist-gash starts just where the gash on the watch leaves off."

"In other words," asked Rowe, "you think the same blow caused the gashes on both wrist and watch?"

"That's the ticket."

"Then there's our ax-wielder," muttered Rowe with a hard glitter in his eyes. "Or at least it's somebody who used an ax. . . . Doctor, could these gashes have been caused by a small ax?"

"Sure. Couldn't have been a knife. Anything with a broad blade and a handle for leverage."

"Then that's settled," grunted Bolling. "Somebody used an ax to carve this bird, hit him over the wrist, broke his watch and stopped it, wounding the wrist at the same time; and then, I suppose in a fight, filled his belly full of lead."

"There's something else, too," said the doctor. He produced from his pocket a small key wrapped in tissue paper. "One of your men, Bolling, just brought this in. Found in a scrap of trouser-pocket they managed to dig up in the ruins near the body. It's been identified by somebody——"

"Maxwell?"

"Man who took care of the house? Yes. Maxwell identified it as the original key to the front door."

"The *original!*" cried the young people in chorus.

"Funny," muttered Bolling. "Hold on a minute." He seized the district attorney's telephone and called his headquarters in Tarrytown. He spoke shortly to someone, then replaced the receiver. "Sure enough. My man tells me Maxwell said this was Dr. Ales's key. The one that the masked man took from Maxwell the night he tied him up in the garage was just a duplicate."

"The only original?" breathed Patience.

"That's what Maxwell said."

"Then I don't think there's any doubt about it," said the district attorney with a sigh of satisfaction. "The corpse must be that of Dr. Ales."

"Indeed?" murmured Lane.

"You don't think so?"

"A key, my dear sir, doesn't make an owner. However, I suppose it's logically possible."

"Well, I'm busy," said the Medical Examiner. "Only one other thing. I suppose you want a description of this cadaver. Five feet eleven, sandy or blond hair, must have weighed somewhere around a hundred and fifty-five pounds, and he was anywhere from forty-five to fifty-five years old. I couldn't find any identifying marks."

"Sedlar," whispered Patience.

"On the dot." Rowe spoke brusquely. "One of the men involved in this case, an Englishman, Dr. Sedlar, disappeared from his hotel in New York City on Saturday. That description fits him perfectly!"

"You don't say!" growled Bolling.

"I do say. At the same time there seems to be a confusion of identities. This man Sedlar has been accused of being Dr. Ales——"

"Then there's the answer," said Bolling hopefully. "Don't forget the corpse was carrying around Dr. Ales's key. If Sedlar was Ales, then everything's hunky-dory."

"I'm not so sure, on second thought," muttered Rowe. "There are really only two possibilities, and we're muddling about here because we haven't analyzed thoroughly enough. The first possibility is that Sedlar and Ales are the same man, as you say, Mr. Bolling, in which case the corpse—which is remarkably like both—clears up the major mystery of both men's disappearance. But if Sedlar and Ales aren't the same, then there's only one conclusion to come to: they bear an uncanny resemblance to each other! We've been evading that conclusion because it seems—er—pulpy and penny-dreadful-ish; but you can't get around it."

Lane said nothing.

"Well," grumbled Bolling, struggling to his feet, "all this talk may get you people somewhere, but it leaves me with a headache. All I want to know is: Whose corpse is this, Dr. Ales's or that bloody Englishman Sedlar's?"

On Wednesday morning two things of importance occurred. Inspector Thumm returned victorious from Chillicothe, Ohio, his jewel thief caught and safely behind bars; and the mystery of the "uncanny resemblance" was solved.

26

Resurrection

"The reason we're up here again—Patty tells me she and this young brute have practically been living here!" said the Inspector genially to Lane the next morning as the two old men and the young couple sat under a spreading oak in one of Lane's serene gardens, "is that we've got some interesting news for you."

"News?" The old gentleman shrugged; he looked listless and wan and tired. Then he smiled feebly; a bit of the sonorous vigor of old time leaped into his voice. " 'Ram thou thy fruitful tidings in mine ears, that long time have been barren.' I trust they're fruitful?"

The Inspector grinned; he was in high good humor. "Judge for yourself." He dug into his pocket and produced an envelope. "Heard unexpectedly from good old Trench this morning."

The message said:

FURTHER INVESTIGATION INTO HAMNET SEDLAR REVEALS
INTERESTING DEVELOPMENT IN LAST CABLE I INFORMED
YOU H S HAD A BROTHER WILLIAM WHOSE WHEREABOUTS

WERE UNKNOWN WE HAVE NOW FOUND THAT WILLIAM
AND HAMNET ARE TWINS WILLIAM HAS BEEN TRACED TO
THE UNITED STATES HAVING EMBARKED FROM BORDEAUX
FOR NEW YORK ON A SMALL TRAMP IN LATE MARCH HE
IS WANTED BY BORDEAUX POLICE DEPARTMENT OF GI-
RONDE ON CHARGE OF ILLEGAL ENTRY AND FELONIOUS AS-
SAULT HAVING BROKEN INTO PRIVATE LIBRARY OF WEALTHY
FRENCH BIBLIOPHILE OF BLAYE AND APPARENTLY AT-
TEMPTED TO STEAL A RARE BOOK FRENCHMAN WAS FOUND
BADLY BEATEN HAD SURPRISED WILLIAM IN ACT OF MUTI-
LATING BINDING BOOK A 1599 JAGGARD EDITION OF QUOTE
THE PASSIONATE PILGRIM UNQUOTE BY WILLIAM SHAKE-
SPEARE ACT IS PECULIAR SINCE WILLIAM SEEMS TO BE A
MAN OF MEANS HE IS A BIBLIOPHILE LIKE HAMNET AND
HAS WRITTEN LITERARY ARTICLES UNDER THE PSEUDO-
NYM OF DOCTOR ALES BEFORE HIS DISAPPEARANCE FROM
ENGLAND THREE YEARS AGO HE HAD ACTED AS EXPERT AT
RARE BOOK AUCTIONS BUYING FOR MILLIONAIRE COLLEC-
TORS HIS BEST PATRON WAS SIR JOHN HUMPHREY-BOND
RECENTLY DECEASED NO FINGERPRINTS OF EITHER WIL-
LIAM OR HAMNET AVAILABLE NOR DISTINGUISHING MARKS
KNOWN ALTHOUGH FROM INFORMATION AT HAND WILLIAM
IS IMAGE OF HIS BROTHER HOPE THIS INFORMATION IS OF
ASSISTANCE TO YOU IF YOU FIND TRACE OF WILLIAM SED-
LAR ALIAS DOCTOR ALES NOTIFY PREFECT OF POLICE BOR-
DEAUX FRANCE REGARDS AND GOOD HUNTING

                                        TRENCH

"That explains it, don't you see?" cried Patience. "Being
twin brothers Hamnet and William must have been as alike as
two peas in a pod. That's why everybody's been mixing them
up!"

"Yes," said Lane softly. "This is exceedingly valuable information. It's clear, then, that Sedlar was Sedlar, and Dr.
Ales was William, Sedlar's brother, the fugitive from French
justice." He placed the tips of his long fingers together. "But
the *embarras de choix* still remains to plague us. Whose body
was found—Hamnet's or William's?"

"And then there's this business of William trying to get his
hooks into a copy of the 1599 Jaggard in Blaye," remarked
Rowe. "You must have heard of that old Frenchie, Mr. Lane.
Pierre Gréville. In fact, I visited him last year." Lane nodded.
"He's the owner of the second copy. Saxon had the third, and

the other is Lord knows where. Mutilating the binding, eh? Nonsense. He was looking for that Shakespeare holograph!"

"Figure it out, kids," chuckled the Inspector. "I've washed my hands of *this* case. But it's beginning to show improvement, hey?"

"Do you want to know," said Patience suddenly, smoothing her frock with absent fingers, "who murdered that man in the cellar?" They all started, and Patience laughed. "Oh, I can't give you any names. It's like an algebraic problem where you're dealing with a flock of unknowns. But of one thing I'm sure: the murderer was the wielder of the ax!"

"Oh," said Rowe, and sank back on the grass.

"We know he was in the study at midnight from the evidence of the grandfather-clock. At twelve-twenty-four he was upstairs in the bedroom, still hacking—evidence of the broken bedroom clock. The murder occurred at twelve-twenty-six— only two minutes later! And the murderer was wielding an ax —evidence of the deep sharp gash on the victim's wristwatch and wrist. Which was to be proved."

"I see," said Lane, and looked up at the blue sky.

"Isn't it right?" asked Patience fretfully.

But Lane was not watching her lips; he seemed intent on the frowzy contour of a curiously formed cloud.

"There's another thing," said Rowe crisply. "There's that monocle we found in the hallway of the house. That's pretty good evidence that Sedlar was in the house. Was he the victim or the murderer? Offhand it would seem he was the victim. The corpse corresponded to his specific description. . . ."

"Unless," said Patience, "the corpse was Dr. Ales's."

"But who set the bomb?" demanded the Inspector.

Quacey came pattering up before a mahogany-faced man in uniform.

"You Inspector Thumm?" demanded the stranger.

"Yeah."

"I'm from Chief Bolling of Tarrytown."

"Oh, yes! I called him this morning to tell him I'd come back."

"Well, he said to tell you people that a man's been found wandering on the pike between Irvington and Tarrytown sort of dazed. Looks nigh starved, too. Bum physical condition. Half-dotty. Won't tell his name but keeps mumbling something about a blue hat."

"Blue hat!"

"Yep. They've taken him to the hospital in Tarrytown. If you want to see him, the Chief says, hop to it."

They found Bolling striding hugely up and down in the waiting room of the hospital. He shook Thumm's hand heartily. "Haven't seen *you* in a good many years, Inspector! Well, this is just getting messier day by day. Want to see him?"

"You bet. Who is he?"

"Search me. They're just getting him out of it now. He's a husky old boy, but he's so thin you can see his ribs. Starved."

They followed Bolling along the corridor with mounting excitement.

Bolling opened the door of a private room. A middle-aged man lay very still on the hospital bed. A heap of tattered dirty clothing lay on a chair nearby. His face was emaciated, deeply lined and covered with a ragged short beard; and his eyes were open, staring at the wall.

Inspector Thumm's jaw dropped. "Donoghue!" he roared.

"Is that the Irishman who disappeared?" asked Bolling eagerly.

Mr. Drury Lane quietly closed the door. He approached the bed and looked down upon the old Irishman. The eyes suddenly filled with pain, and the head turned slowly. They met Lane's gaze blankly, shifted to the Inspector's face. . . . Recognition sparked at once. He licked his lips. "Inspector," he whispered.

"The same," said Thumm heartily, approaching the bed. "Well, you cantankerous old Mick, you've led us one hell of a chase. Where've you been? What happened to you?"

A slight flush suffused the thin cheeks. Donoghue croaked once before he could find his voice. "It's—it's a long story." And he tried to grin. "They've been feedin' me here through a dum' pipe, bedad! I'd give me right arm for a juicy steak. How—how'd ye find me, Chief?"

"We've been looking for you since you took that runout powder, Donoghue. Feel strong enough to talk?"

"Sure, an' it'll be a pleasure." Donoghue rubbed his bearded cheeks and then in a steadily strengthening voice told a fantastic story:

On the afternoon when the Indiana party had visited the Britannic Museum, he had noticed a tall thin mustached man carrying a peculiar blue fedora slipping out of the building with something under his arm—it looked like a book. On the alert always for thieves, Donoghue had not had time to give the alarm but had dashed after the man. His quarry had jumped into a cab, and Donoghue had trailed him in another. The chase had led by devious means of transportation out of the city to a ramshackle wooden house about a mile from the main highway between Tarrytown and Irvington. He had hidden in the shrubbery while an old man in black clothes left the house; and had then mounted the porch. A name-plate under the bell had told him that this was the house of a Dr. Ales. He had rung the bell and the man himself had come to the door. Donoghue recognized him despite the fact that he had discarded his hat and no longer wore the bushy gray mustache. The mustache, then, had been a disguise! Donoghue had been in a quandary. He had no proof that the man was a thief; perhaps it had been his imagination. Yet the absence of the mustache was promising. . . . Having no authority to make an arrest, he had permitted himself to be courteously invited into the house. He was ushered into a study lined with books. Taking the bull by the horns, Donoghue had then accused his host of having stolen a book from the museum.

"He was a mild divil," said Donoghue, his eyes bright. "Admitted th' charge! Then he says he'll make full restitootlon, says he'll pay for it an' all that blarney. I took out me dickey-pipe an' begun to smoke, thinkin' I'll kid him along till I can git to a 'phone an' sic the nearest police onto him. But I was nervous an' I broke me pipe on the floor. So he shows me out of th' house, smooth as ye please, an' I'm walkin' down that lane thinkin' hard, when all of a suddin somethin' cracks down on th' top of me shkull an' that's all I know for a long, long time."

When he awakened, he found himself bound and gagged in a dark room. He had thought at the time that Dr. Ales had followed and attacked him; he had held to this theory all along until today, when on making his escape he had discovered that his prison had not been Dr. Ales's house but a totally different house which he had never seen before.

"You're sure of that? But then, sure. The Ales house went up," muttered the Inspector. "Go on, Donoghue."

"I'd no idee how long I'd been trussed up like a dum' pig," continued the resurrected Irishman comfortably. "What's t'day? Well, it makes no diff'rence. I was fed oncet a day by a masked man with a gun."

"Was it Dr. Ales?" cried Patience.

"No, mum, that I can't say. Th' light was niver good. But his voice was kind of the same—spoke like a blinkin' Britisher, he did, an' well I know that accent, me havin' seen an' heard many of thim in the ould country. Divil th' day if he didn't go an' threaten me time after time with torture, bedad!"

"Torture?" gasped Patience.

"Th' very same, miss. On'y threaten; niver did it. He wanted me to tell him 'where is th' documint.'" Donoghue chuckled. "So I says: 'Are ye daft?' an' he threatens me some more. *I* didn't know what he meant by documint, ye see."

"Strange," said Rowe.

"Some days he didn't feed me a-tall," complained Donoghue. "Cripes, for a leg o' mutton!" He licked his lips and continued the odd tale. At one time—long ago, he said, although he could not place the exact date or period since he had lost all track of time—he had heard a commotion somewhere in the building. He heard the sound of a heavy body being dragged and apparently dumped in a room near his; and then a man's groans. A few moments later he heard the faint slam of a door. He attempted to communicate by signal with his neighbor, whom he took to be a fellow-prisoner, but bound and gagged as he himself was, his attempt was unsuccessful. For the past three days Donoghue had not been fed, nor had he seen his masked captor. This morning, after days of agonizing effort, he had managed to rid himself of his bonds; he had forced the lock on his door and found himself in a dark, dirty, smelly hall. He listened, but the house seemed deserted. He had tried to locate the room which held his companion prisoner, but all doors were locked and he could get no reply to his rappings. Weak himself, afraid his captor might return, he had crept out of the house and made his escape.

"Do you think," said Inspector Thumm fiercely, "you could find that dump again, Donoghue?"

"Sure, an' I'll niver forget it."

"Just a moment," protested a white-clad young man near the door. "This man is still very weak. I strongly advise against his moving."

"Advise an' be dum'ed to ye!" shouted Donoghue, attempting to sit up in bed. Then he sank back with a groan. "I ain't as spry as I used to be. Give me another swig o' your soup, Doc, an' I'll lead the rescuin' party. Whisht, Inspector, 'tis like ould times!"

At Donoghue's direction Lane's car, followed by Bolling with a squad of men in another, proceeded to the point where he had been found wandering by a trooper earlier in the day. Thumm assisted him from the limousine, and the doughty old Irishman stood squinting up the road.

"This way," he said finally, and the two men got back into the car. Dromio drove slowly. Not a hundred yards away Donoghue shouted something, and Dromio turned the car into a narrow drive. It was a side-road no more than a mile from the lane which led to the Ales house.

The two cars proceeded cautiously. Three cottages slipped by, set far back from the road, when Donoghue suddenly cried out "There!"

It was a small old house, no more than a shack, as lonely and dilapidated as an archæological exhibit. There was no sign of life; the place was boarded up and looked as if it had not been occupied for years.

Bolling's men made short shrift of the feeble barriers. An old log served as a battering ram and the front door crumpled in like the shell of a rotten nut. They swarmed through the house, guns drawn. It was empty, hollow, dirty, and, except for the room in which Donoghue had been kept prisoner, unfurnished. They crashed in door after door. And finally they came upon a black sour-smelling cubicle provided with a cot, a basin, and a chair. Upon the cot lay the bound body of a man.

He was unconscious.

Bolling's men carried him out into the sunlight. They all stared at the man's drawn yellowed face. The same question was mirrored in all their eyes. Was this victim of foul air and starvation Hamnet or William Sedlar? For that he was one or the other they could not doubt.

Donoghue, his work done, uttered a faint groan and collapsed in the Inspector's arms. An ambulance which had trailed the two cars sped up, and Donoghue was deposited inside. An interne bent over the limp figure of the unconscious Englishman.

"He's just fainted. Tight bonds, lack of food, rotten air—general debilitation. He'll come around with a little attention."

The thin cheeks were covered with a silky blond stubble. The young doctor applied restoratives and the man's eyes fluttered open. But they were dazed, and he returned blank stares to the Inspector's shouted questions. Then he closed his eyes again.

"All right," grumbled Bolling. "Take 'em both to the hospital. We'll talk to this bird tomorrow."

As the ambulance shot away, a car drove up and a hatless young man jumped out. He was, it proved, a reporter drawn to the scene by that mysterious undercurrent of rumor which seems to serve the gentlemen of the press as a happy vehicle. Bolling and Thumm were overwhelmed with questions. Despite all of Lane's frantic signs the news came out: all they knew about Dr. Ales, the "fugitive from French justice," the dramatic story of Donoghue, the confusion of identities concerning the Sedlar twins. . . . The young man dashed away grinning with triumph.

"That," said Lane coldly, "was an error of judgment, Inspector."

Thumm blushed. At this moment a man came up to Bolling and reported failure to turn up the slightest clue to the identity of the two prisoners' captor despite a thorough search of the house.

"I called Tarrytown, too," he reported, "and located the owner of this property. He didn't even know anybody was living here. He says it's been 'vacant' for three years."

The two parties clambered into their respective automobiles in silence. It was a full ten minutes later that Gordon Rowe said wearily: "Talk about puzzles!"

27

The 300-Year-Old Crime

"The first thing we want to settle," said Inspector Thumm grimly, "is who you are."

They were congregated about the Englishman's bed the next morning in the Tarrytown hospital. A call from the House Physician had informed them that the patient was in good enough condition to talk; careful nourishment, sedatives, and a sound night's sleep had worked wonders with him. He had been shaved, and there was a slight flush on his flat cheeks, and his eyes were remote and intelligent. They had entered the room to find the man propped in bed, a profusion of morning newspapers strewn on the coverlet, talking amiably to Donoghue in the next bed.

The Englishman's sandy brows lifted. "Was there any doubt? I'm afraid I don't understand." He looked keenly from one to another of them, as if weighing them in some secret balance of his own. The voice was weak, but had a familiar timbre. "I am Dr. Hamnet Sedlar."

"Ah," said Lane. "This will be excellent news for Choate."

"Choate? Oh yes, Dr. Choate! He must have been worried," said the Englishman smoothly. "Horrible time! Your friend Donoghue here thought I was his quarry of the blue hat. Ha, ha! The resemblance is—was startling." He sobered. "He was my twin brother, y'know."

"Then you do know he's dead?" cried Patience. Lane glanced once at the Inspector, and the Inspector grew very red.

"I've been besieged by reporters all morning. And then these newspapers— They told me everything. From the Medical Examiner's description of the corpse, it must have been my brother William. He used the pseudonym Dr. Ales, y'know, in his professional writing."

"Hmm," said Thumm. "Look here, Dr. Sedlar. It looks very much as if this case is solved. But what the solution is I'm blamed if I know. We've learned, as we told you, some suspicious things about you—and now about your brother— and we want the truth. If your brother's dead there's no longer any reason to keep quiet."

Dr. Sedlar sighed. "I suppose that's so. Very well, I shall tell you everything." He closed his eyes; his voice was very feeble. "You and the papers have made a great point about my untruth concerning the date of my arrival in this country. The fact is that I came here in secret before my announced arrival in an attempt to avert a dishonorable act. My brother William's act." He stopped; no one spoke. He opened his eyes. "There are too many people here," he said abruptly.

"Oh, come now, Doctor," said Rowe. "We're all in this thing together. And as far as Donoghue is concerned——"

"I'm deaf, dumb, an' blind," grinned the Irishman.

The story came out reluctantly. Some years before, when William Sedlar had been actively engaged in England as a representative of book collectors, he had been friendly with Sir John Humphrey-Bond, the famous British bibliophile. William had been instrumental in effecting the deal whereby Samuel Saxon had purchased from Sir John's library one of the three existing copies of the 1599 Jaggard edition of *The Passionate Pilgrim*. Some months later William, who had access to Sir John's enormous library, ran across an old manuscript —not in itself valuable and utterly unknown to the bibliophilic world—which stated that a personal letter written and signed in the hand of William Shakespeare and containing a strange secret had been in existence as late as 1758, the date of the manuscript William found. This Shakespearean letter, went on the manuscript, because of its hideous secret, had been hidden in the back-cover binding of a 1599 edition of the Jaggard *The Passionate Pilgrim*. Excited by his discovery, William ascertained that Sir John had never read the manuscript and, his collector's cupidity aroused, had purchased it from his patron without revealing its contents. He had taken Hamnet, then curator of the Kensington Museum, into his confidence and had shown him the manuscript. Hamnet had scoffed at it as an old wives' tale. But William, drunk with the extraordinary historic, literary, and monetary value of this long-lost document the manuscript spoke of, had gone on the prowl—despite the fact that he realized that most of the first-edition Jaggards of *The Passionate Pilgrim* had disappeared in the course of three centuries and that only three were left. He satisfied himself after a three-year search that two of the copies—the second of which was in possession of Pierre Gréville, the French collector—did not contain the rumored holograph. Having to flee France with the *gendarmerie* at his heels, he embarked for the United States almost in despair, but savagely intent on examining the third and last copy, which ironically enough he himself had been instrumental in putting into the hands of Samuel Saxon. He had written his brother Hamnet secretly before leaving Bordeaux.

"He wrote me about his attack on Gréville," said Dr. Sedlar faintly, "and I realized that his pursuit of the document had become an obsession with him. As luck would have it I had agreed to Mr. James Wyeth's proposal to come to America only a short time before. I saw my opportunity to look William up and try to avert another crime, if I could. Consequently I caught an earlier boat and on my arrival in New York placed an advertisement in the personal columns of the newspapers. William got in touch with me readily enough, meeting me at the cheap hotel where I had taken temporary quarters under an assumed name. He told me he had rented a house in Westchester under his old alias of Dr. Ales; that he was on the track of the Saxon copy, but had had ill luck since the book among others had been left in Saxon's will to the Britannic Museum and he had not been able to get hold of it. He told me also about having hired a common thief named Villa to break into the Saxon mansion and steal the volume; but Villa had bungled, stealing a worthless and palpable forgery, and William had returned it anonymously. He was in a fever of impatience; the museum, he told me, was closed for repairs; the Jaggard had been delivered among the others in the benefaction; he must get into the museum! I saw he was mad with cupidity and I tried to dissuade him; the situation was desperate; I myself was becoming curator of the museum. But William was adamant and our first conversation got nowhere; he went away."

"It was you, I suppose," said Lane slowly, "who visited your brother's house in secret one night—the muffled visitor your brother's man told us about?"

"Yes. But it did no good. I was beside myself with consternation and fear. Not a pleasant position for me, y'know." The Englishman drew a deep breath. "When the Jaggard was stolen, I knew at once that William must have been the man in the blue hat. But I could not talk, obviously. William got in touch with me secretly that same night, telling me gleefully that beyond all hope he had actually discovered the document in the binding of the Saxon Jaggard and was sending the book itself back to the museum, having no further use for it. Because he was after all no petty thief, he had left his own copy of the 1606 Jaggard—I had not even dreamed of its existence and where he got it I do not know—in place of the stolen Jaggard as a salve to his own conscience and because, I suppose, he thought it would delay discovery of the theft. It superficially resembled the 1599."

"But how about this business of being made prisoner?" growled Thumm. "Where does that come in?"

Dr. Sedlar bit his lip. "I'd never dreamed he would go to such rascally lengths, you know. He caught me quite off guard. My own brother! . . . On Friday last I received a note in the post at the Hotel Seneca, making a secret appointment near Tarrytown, not at his own house. He was very mysterious about it, and I was not suspicious because—" He stopped and his eyes clouded. "At any rate Saturday morning I went to the rendezvous from the museum, where I'd left Dr. Choate. It's—it's a little painful, gentlemen."

"He attacked you?" said Bolling sharply.

"Yes." The man's lips trembled. "Virtually kidnaped me—his own brother! And he stuffed me, bound and gagged, into a filthy hole. . . . You know the rest."

"But why?" demanded Thumm. "I can't see the sense in it."

Sedlar shrugged his thin shoulders. "I suppose he was afraid I'd give him away. I *had* in desperation threatened to give him up to the police, y'know. I imagine he wanted me out of the way until he could slip out of the country with the document."

"Your monocle was found in the Ales house after what we know now to have been a murder," said Thumm sternly. "Explain that."

"My monocle? Oh, yes." He waved a weary hand. "The press did have something to say about that. I can't explain it. William must have taken it from me when— He did say he was returning to the house to get the document, which he had hidden there; and then he meant to skip out. But I suppose he ran afoul of his murderer and in some way the monocle slipped out of his pocket and was crushed during the struggle. Unquestionably he was slain for possession of the document."

"And it's now in the hands of your brother's murderer?"

"What else?"

There was a little silence. Donoghue had frankly gone to sleep, and his snores punctuated the silence like a rattle of musketry. Then Patience and Rowe looked at each other, and both rose and leaned over the bed on opposite sides.

"But the secret, Dr. Sedlar," pleaded Rowe, his eyes feverish.

"You *can't* just let it go at that!" cried Patience.

The man on the bed regarded them with a smile. "So you want to know, too?" he said softly. "Suppose I told you that the secret revolved about . . . *the death of Shakespeare?*"

"The death of Shakespeare!"

"Well, well?" said Rowe hoarsely.

"But how can a man write about his own death?" asked Patience.

"A very pertinent question," chuckled the Englishman. He shifted suddenly in bed, his eyes flaming. "What did Shakespeare die of?"

"No one knows," muttered Rowe. "But there's been speculation and some attempt at scientific diagnosis. I remember reading an article in an old copy of *The Lancet* which ascribed Shakespeare's death to a fantastic complication of causes—typhus, epilepsy, arterio-sclerosis, chronic alcoholism,

Bright's disease, locomotor ataxia, and the Lord knows what else. I think there were thirteen altogether."

"Indeed?" murmured Dr. Sedlar. "How interesting. The point is that according to this old manuscript"—he paused—"*Shakespeare was murdered.*"

There was an appalled silence. The Englishman went on with a faint odd smile. "It seems that the letter was written by Shakespeare to a certain William Humphrey——"

"Humphrey?" whispered Rowe. "William Humphrey? The only Humphrey I've ever heard of in connection with Shakespeare was Ozias Humphrey, who was commissioned by Malone in 1783 to prepare a crayon drawing of the Chandos portrait. Ever hear of this Humphrey, Mr. Lane?"

"No."

"It's a name new to Shakespeareana," said Dr. Sedlar. "The——"

"By George!" exclaimed Rowe, staring. "W.H.!"

"I beg your pardon?"

"W.H. The W.H. of the Sonnets!"

"There's an inspiring thought. It's possible; there never was a clear conclusion on that point. At any rate we know this: William Humphrey was a direct ancestor of Sir John Humphrey-Bond!"

"Explaining," said Patience in an awed voice, "how the book with the letter in it came to be in possession of the Humphrey-Bond family."

"Precisely. Evidently Humphrey was a close friend of the poet's."

Young Rowe sprang to the foot of the bed. "You've *got* to be clear about this thing," he rasped. "What was the date of the letter? When was it sent?"

"April twenty-second, 1616."

"God! The day before Shakespeare's death! Did you—did you see this letter?"

"I'm sorry to say I did not. But my brother told me about it, unable to keep it to himself." Sedlar sighed. "Strange, eh? In this letter Shakespeare wrote to his friend William Humphrey that he was 'fast sinking,' that he was in 'sore bodily distress,' and that he was convinced someone was slowly poisoning him. The next day—he died."

"Oh, good Lord," said Rowe again and again, and he fingered his necktie as if it choked him.

"Poisoned, hey?" said the Inspector, shaking his head. "Who the hell would want to poison the old boy?"

Patience said stiffly: "It looks horribly as if we'll have to solve a three-hundred-year-old murder before . . ."

"Before what, Patience?" asked Lane in a curious voice.

She shivered a little, avoiding his eyes, and turned away.

28

The Clue of the Bells

A remarkable change had come over Miss Patience Thumm. The Inspector was openly worried. She ate like a bird, slept little, and went from the Thumm apartment to the office day after day like a slender little ghost, pale and thoughtful. Occasionally she complained of headache and retired to her room for hours at a time. When she emerged she invariably looked tired and depressed.

"What's the matter?" asked the Inspector shrewdly one day. "Had a run-in with the boy-friend?"

"With Gordon? Nonsense, father. We—we're just very good friends. Besides he's busy at the Britannic these days and I don't see him much."

The Inspector grunted, but he watched her with anxiety. That afternoon he telephoned the museum and spoke to Gordon Rowe. But the young man sounded characteristically preoccupied. No, he had no idea— The Inspector hung up, a sorely tried father; and for the rest of the day he made Miss Brodie's life miserable.

About a week after the events at the Tarrytown hospital, Patience appeared at her father's office dressed in fresh linen and looking more like herself than she had in days. "I'm off for a little jaunt," she announced, pulling on white mesh gloves. "Into the country. Mind, darling?"

"Gawd, no!" said the Inspector hastily. "Have a nice time. Going alone?"

Patience examined her face in her mirror. "Of course. Why shouldn't I go alone?"

"Well, I thought—this Rowe boy—Patty, he's been neglectin' you, isn't that it?"

"Father! No doubt he—he's very busy. Besides, why should

I mind?" And she kissed him lightly on the smashed tip of his nose and sailed out of the office. The Inspector muttered a ferocious curse on the head of the recalcitrant Mr. Rowe and rang for Miss Brodie viciously.

Patience's airy manner vanished as she climbed into her roadster downstairs and rolled off. The frown that had been perched between her brows for days deepened. She passed the Britannic Museum on Fifth Avenue without a glance; but when she had to stop at the corner of Sixty-Sixth Street for a red light, she could not keep from stealing a peep into her windshield mirror. There was, of course, nothing to be seen; and she sighed and drove on.

It was a long lonely drive to Tarrytown. She gripped the wheel in her gloved hands, driving with absent skill; her eyes were on the road, but her thoughts were far away.

She stopped before a drug store in the heart of the town, went in, consulted a telephone directory, asked the clerk a question, and went out again. She drove off, turned into a narrow side-street, and coasted slowly along watching the street-numbers. In five minutes she found what she was seeking—a ramshackle one-story frame house with a scratchy garden in front and a staggering fence whose pickets were twined with ivy.

She mounted the porch and rang a bell which sounded hoarsely and faintly through the house. A middle-aged woman with tired eyes opened the screen-door; she wore a wrinkled house-dress and her hands were red and sopping with sudsy water. "Yes?" she said sharply, eying Patience with a sort of defeated hostility.

"Is Mr. Maxwell at home?"

"Which one?"

"Are there more than one? I mean the gentleman who until recently took care of Dr. Ales's house."

"Oh. My brother-in-law." The woman sniffed. "Just wait on the porch. I'll see if he's around."

The woman vanished and Patience sat down with a sigh in a dusty rocker. A moment later the tall white-topped figure of old Maxwell appeared; he was pulling a coat on over his sweaty undershirt, and his scraggly throat was bare.

"Miss Thumm!" he said in a cracked voice. His bleary little eyes searched the street as if seeking others. "You want to see *me?*"

"Hello, Mr. Maxwell," said Patience cheerfully. "No, I've come alone. Sit down, won't you?" He seated himself in a rickety chair which was peeling like burnt skin and studied her anxiously. "I suppose you've heard all about the explosion?"

"Oh, yes, miss! Terrible thing, that was. I was telling my brother and sister-in-law how lucky I was. If you hadn't come that day and—and made me get out of the house, I'd have been blown to smithereens." He squirmed nervously. "Have they found out—who did it?"

"I believe not." Patience eyed him sternly. "Maxwell, I've been thinking and thinking about this case. And in particular about your story. I've been unable to get over the feeling that you left something out!"

He was startled. "Oh, no! I told the truth. I swear——"

"I don't mean that you deliberately lied. Look out for that bee! . . . I mean you neglected to mention something that may be important."

He brushed his skull with shaking fingers. "I—I don't know."

"Look here." Patience sat up briskly. "Everybody—but me —has apparently overlooked one thing. The walls of the garage in which the masked man tied you up were quite thin. The garage was only a few feet from the front door of the house. It was night-time in the country and every sound must have been distinctly audible." She leaned forward and lowered her voice. *"Didn't you hear the bell over the door ring?"*

"Judas!" he gasped, staring. "So I did!"

Patience burst into her father's office to find Mr. Drury Lane stretched out in the best chair, and the Inspector in a state of nervousness. At the window stood Gordon Rowe, staring gloomily out upon Times Square.

"What's this—a conference?" demanded Patience, stripping off her gloves. Her eyes were starry with news.

Young Mr. Rowe whirled. "Pat!" He darted forward. "The Inspector had me worried. You're all right?"

"Perfectly, thank you," said Patience coldly. "I——"

"I've had the most rotten luck," said the young man dejectedly. "I've just about come to the end of my rope. The work's a frost, Pat."

"How interesting."

"Yump." He sat down opposite her and assumed the classic pose of *The Thinker*. "I was all wrong. On the wrong trail. My grandiloquent research into Shakespeare is *kaput*. Oh Lord," he groaned, "all these wasted months and years . . ."

"Oh," said Patience; and her face softened. "I'm so sorry, Gordon. I didn't realize— Poor boy."

"Cut that stuff," growled the Inspector. "Where you been? We were just goin' without you."

"Where?"

"To see Sedlar. Mr. Lane's come in with an idea. Maybe you'd better spill it, Lane."

The old gentleman was studying Patience keenly. "That can wait. Patience, what is it? You are displaying every symptom of suppressed exultation."

"Am I?" Patience laughed nervously. "I've always been a rotten actress. The point is, I've just found out the most *marvelous* thing." She took out a cigarette deliberately. "I've been talking to Maxwell."

"Maxwell?" scowled Thumm. "What for?"

"He wasn't sufficiently questioned the last time. I thought of something no one asked him. . . . He knows how many visitors there were to the Ales house the night of the murder!"

"So," said Lane after a pause. "Interesting if true. How is that?"

"He was in the garage, conscious, during the entire period when the house was being ransacked by the masked man and the murder was taking place. I remember that the front door was equipped with one of those old-fashioned thingamajig arrangements by which a bell attached to the top of the door jangles every time the door is opened."

"Ah!"

"I saw that Maxwell must have heard the jangles—*all* the jangles! I asked him, and he remembered that he had. It seemed unimportant. . . ."

"That's fiendishly clever, my child," murmured Lane.

"I was stupid not to have thought of it before. At any rate, Maxwell traced back in memory what happened. After the masked man left him in the garage—after he'd taken Maxwell's key to get back into the house—Maxwell distinctly heard two clangs of the bell. A short interval; only a few seconds."

"Two?" said Thumm. "That would be when he opened the door and when it shut after he went in."

"Exactly. That put the masked man in the house, alone. After that there was silence—for more than half an hour, Maxwell judges. Then there were two quick jangles again. And a short time after that another two jangles. And that was the last he heard all blessed night!"

"I should imagine," said Lane oddly, "that was sufficient."

"Bully for you, darling," cried Rowe. "That's getting somewhere! The first two, as you said, meant the masked man reentering the house. The second two meant a second person entering the house. The third set meant one of the two leaving. No further sounds of the bell, so only two persons were in the house during the murder-period—the masked man and the visitor!"

"Gordon, that's it to a T," exclaimed Patience. "That's exactly as I figure it. The masked man we know was the hacker from the evidence of the clocks, and the hacker was the murderer from the evidence of the gash on the corpse's wrist-watch and wrist. So the visitor was the victim, left behind dead in the cellar!"

"Reducing it to two," said Lane dryly, "certainly clarifies the issue, eh, Inspector?"

"Wait a minute," growled Thumm. "Not so fast, m'lady. How do you know that second set of bell-sounds was made by the second guy comin' in? How do you know it wasn't made by the masked man *going out,* leavin' the house empty? And the third set made by the second man coming in——"

"No. Don't you see that's fallacious?" cried Patience. "We know someone was killed in the house in that period. Who was it? If the second man came in after the masked man left, what have you got? A victim without a murderer. The second man must have been the victim; he didn't leave the house, no sound of the front-door warning bell and all doors and windows found locked from the inside. But if he was the victim and alone in the house, who killed him? No, it's as Gordon said. The man who left was the murderer, and the murderer was the masked man."

"And where does that get you?" murmured Lane slowly.

"To the murderer."

"Yes!" cried Rowe.

"I'll show you—you hush, Gordon! There were two men in the house that night. One of them, the victim, was one of the Sedlar brothers—dead man's make-up too perfect to admit of coincidence. Now, one of the two who visited the house knew exactly where the document was: he went to the secret compartment in the study; the other did not: he hacked the house almost to bits looking for the compartment. Now who would be the most likely person to *know* where the hiding-place was?"

"This Ales bird—William Sedlar," said the Inspector.

"Right, father. Because it was he who had created the hiding-place and hidden the paper. So, since the second visitor knew the hiding-place—the first being the hacker, who didn't—then Dr. Ales was the second visitor. This is confirmed at once by the fact that the second visitor got into the house without trouble; the door locked automatically; Maxwell's duplicate was in possession of the first visitor; yet the second man got in. How but by Dr. Ales's original key?"

"Who do you figure the masked man was?" demanded her father.

"There's evidence for that. We found the fragments of a monocle in the hall. Dr. Sedlar was the only person involved who wore a monocle. Maxwell had never seen a monocle in the house before. This would indicate that Hamnet Sedlar was in the house on the night of the murder! If Hamnet was in the house then he was one of the two, the other being his brother William, Dr. Ales. But since William was the victim, as I've just shown, then Hamnet must have been his brother's murderer!"

"I'll be damned," said Thumm.

"No, no, Patience," said Rowe, springing to his feet. "That's——"

"One moment, Gordon," said Lane quietly. "On what basis do you adjudge Dr. Hamnet Sedlar a protagonist in this case, Patience?"

"I say," replied Patience with a defiant look at the young man, "that Hamnet is one of those after the Shakespearean document on several counts. One is that he's a bibliophile; he admits William told him all about that manuscript; I claim he's got too much the scholar's blood to let slip a chance to get his fingers on an authentic Shakespeare letter. Another is his remarkable action in suddenly relinquishing his situation as curator of a London museum to take a similar situation in despised America *at a lower salary*—a situation, incidentally, which would give him legitimate access to the Saxon Jaggard! And finally, his coming to New York in secret before he was expected to arrive."

Lane sighed. "That's masterly, Patience."

"Besides," continued Patience eagerly, "the theory of Hamnet as the hacker is bolstered by the fact that of the two brothers he would *not* know where the hiding-place was, and therefore would have had to search blindly as the wielder of the ax actually did. . . . With the two Sedlars in the house, it's easy to reconstruct the scene. While Hamnet was hacking away in William's bedroom upstairs, William came in and got the document out of the hiding-place in the study. They met shortly after and Hamnet, seeing the paper in William's hand, swung with the ax, causing the cut on watch and wrist. In the struggle Hamnet's monocle fell and was broken. Hamnet shot William, deposited the body——"

"No!" shouted Rowe. "Patience, shut up. Mr. Lane, listen to me. I agree to everything up to a certain point—that William and Hamnet were the two men in the house, that William was the one who retrieved the document and Hamnet the masked man and hacker. But in the struggle for possession it wasn't William who was killed by Hamnet but Hamnet who was killed by William! The body from the ruins might be that of either man. I believe that the man who claims to be Hamnet, the man we found apparently 'starving' in that house, is really William!"

"Gordon," snapped Patience, "that's—that's asinine. You're forgetting that the original house-key was found on the corpse. That in itself makes the corpse William's."

"Ah, no, Patience," murmured Lane. "That isn't logical. Go on, Gordon. What makes you think this ingenious theory is correct?"

"Psychology, sir; I'll admit there's little evidence to support it positively. I believe the man in the hospital lied about his identity because, being William Sedlar, he's wanted by the French police. Naturally, as the survivor, it's he who has the document now and he wants freedom of movement to dispose of it. Don't forget that he had all the facts at his disposal; the Inspector's chat with the reporter the night before had splashed all the facts in the papers, and the rest he got from the reporters themselves the next morning."

Lane smiled queerly. "I grant the soundness of the motive, Gordon, hypothetically; it's a clever theory. But who set the bomb?"

Patience and Rowe looked at each other. Then they both hastily agreed that the bomb had been set twenty-four hours before the murder by a third person altogether, whose only purpose was to destroy the document for reasons unknown; and this third protagonist, after setting the bomb, disappeared from the scene thinking his work done.

The old gentleman grunted. "How about the kidnapings? Why should the survivor, whether he is William or Hamnet, deliberately involve himself in a tangled scheme to be found 'helpless' by the police? The man we found was legitimately starved and exhausted, remember."

"That's easy," retorted Patience. "No matter whether it was William or Hamnet, the purpose was the same: to lay the blame for a fictitious kidnaping on the dead man and so bolster the appearance of the plotter's own innocence." And Rowe nodded, although doubtfully.

"How about Donoghue?" demanded the Inspector.

"If Hamnet's the survivor," said Patience, "then it was he who kidnaped Donoghue because he'd seen Donoghue leave the Ales house and thought he was an accomplice of William's. By kidnaping him he might have thought he could wrest from him—remember his threats of torture—the secret of the hiding-place."

"Whereas if William is the survivor," pointed out Rowe sharply, "it was he who kidnaped Donoghue because Donoghue had followed him and was a potential menace to his plans."

"The question, then," murmured Lane, "revolves about this: you agree that Hamnet and William Sedlar were the two persons involved in the crime; but you disagree upon the essential problem of who killed whom. Very pretty, I must say!"

"By God," burst out the Inspector, his eyes popping, "this sure comes at a swell time."

"What do you mean, father?"

"Well, Patty, before you came Lane was tellin' us that he'd thought there might be a possibility the Englishman was lying about who he was, and that there was a way of telling whether he was lying or not!"

"A way of telling?" frowned Patience. "I fail to see——"

"It's really very simple," said Lane, and he rose. "It entails a trip to the Britannic. Gordon, you left the man who calls himself Hamnet Sedlar there?"

"Yes, sir."

"That's splendid. Come along. This will take only five minutes."

29

The Optical Illusion

They found the man who called himself Hamnet Sedlar at work with Dr. Choate in the curator's office. The curator looked faintly startled when they entered; but the Englishman rose quickly and came forward with a smile.

"Quite a delegation," he said with cheerful inoffensiveness. Then his smile faded as he saw the solemnity of their expressions. "I trust nothing's wrong?"

"We all do," growled the Inspector. "Dr. Choate, will you be good enough to let us chin a while with Dr. Sedlar—alone? This is kind of confidential."

"Confidential?" The curator, who had risen at his desk, stood still and stared from one to another of them. Then he looked down and fumbled with some papers. "Ah—of course." A slow tide of red rose from the hairs of his goatee. He circled the desk and swiftly left the room. Dr. Sedlar had not moved, and for a moment there was silence. Then Thumm nodded to Lane, and Lane stepped forward. The Inspector's heavy breathing was the only sound in the room.

"Dr. Sedlar," said Lane with no expression whatever, "it has become necessary, in the interests of—let us say—science, to put you to a very simple test. . . . Patience, your bag, please."

"Test?" A scowl appeared on the Englishman's face, and he thrust his hands into the pockets of his sack suit.

Patience quickly handed Lane her bag. He opened it, looked inside, took out a gayly colored kerchief, and snapped the bag shut. "Now, sir," he said quietly, "please tell me what color this kerchief displays."

Patience gasped, her eyes widening with a sudden shock of intelligence. The others stared stupidly.

Dr. Sedlar flushed. A remarkable mixture of emotions seemed to be struggling for mastery on his hawkish face. He took a little backward step. "This is the most frightful rubbish, you know," he said harshly. "May I ask the purpose of this childish demonstration?"

"Surely," murmured Lane, "there can be no harm in identifying the color of this innocent little handkerchief?"

There was a silence. Then the Englishman said, without turning, in a flat voice: "Blue."

The handkerchief was green, yellow, and white.

"And Mr. Rowe's necktie, Dr. Sedlar?" continued Lane, without changing expression.

The Englishman swung slowly about, his eyes tortured. "Brown."

It was turquoise blue.

"Thank you." Lane returned handkerchief and bag to Patience. "Inspector, this gentleman is not Dr. Hamnet Sedlar. He is William Sedlar, sometimes known as Dr. Ales."

The Englishman sank suddenly into a chair and buried his face in his hands.

"How the Great Horn Spoon did you know?" gasped Thumm.

Lane sighed. "Elementary, Inspector. You see, it was Dr. Ales, or William Sedlar, who visited your office on May sixth, leaving the envelope in your care. That man could not have been Hamnet Sedlar, as he himself once pointed out; Hamnet Sedlar was in London on May seventh attending a banquet in his honor. Now Dr. Ales, who brought the sealed envelope, was of course the man who had written down the symbol in the envelope—he admitted as much to you that morning in your office. What did the paper and symbol show?"

"Why, just a—a . . . Hell, I don't know," said the Inspector.

"The paper," explained Lane wearily, "was neutral-gray in hue, and the letterhead inscription of the Saxon Library at the top of the sheet was printed in a darker gray ink. That, combined with the manner in which the symbol had been written, struck me at once."

"What d'ye mean? We just looked at it the wrong way, that's all. And by luck you happened to look at it the right way."

"Precisely. In other words, William Sedlar had written the characters W^m SH^e upside down! That is, when you read the symbol correctly, *the letterhead inscription was at the bottom of the sheet,* upside down. That was enormously significant. When a person picks up a letterhead with the intention of writing something upon it, instinctively he will turn the sheet rightside up—which is to say, with the name and address at the top. Yet the writer of the symbol had picked up the sheet and done exactly the opposite! Why?" Lane paused, took out a handkerchief, and dabbed at his lips. The Englishman had removed his hands from his face and now sat slumped in his chair staring bitterly at the floor.

"I know now," sighed Patience. "Unless it was pure accident, *he simply didn't see that line of printing!*"

"Yes, my dear, that's precisely right. It seems on its face impossible. It was much more probable that Dr. Ales had been in haste and had simply written the characters with the sheet upside down, not realizing that it would make a difference to those who read the symbol later. But the other possibility logically existed, and I could not ignore it. I said to myself: By what miracle could this phenomenon, if it's true, have come about? Why didn't Dr. Ales see that line of dark-gray printing on the sheet of Saxon stationery? Was he *blind?* But that was inconceivable; the man who visited your office, Inspector, gave every evidence of possessing good eyesight. Then I remembered another thing, and I saw the answer in a flash. . . . *The beard.*"

The Englishman raised agonized eyes; there was a fleeting curiosity in them now. "The beard?" he muttered.

"You see?" smiled Lane. "To this moment he does not know that there was anything wrong with the false beard he wore! Mr. Sedlar, the beard you sported that day was appalling, a monstrosity! It was streaked with blues and greens and heaven only knows what else."

Sedlar's mouth fell open; he groaned. "Good God. I purchased it at a costumer's. I suppose I didn't make myself clear and the creature thought I wanted a—a *comic* beard for a masquerade, or something as insane as that. . . ."

"Very unfortunate," said Lane dryly. "But the beard and the stationery confirmed each other. I felt the excellent possibility that the writer of the symbol was *totally color-blind.* I had heard of such things and consulted my physician, Dr. Martini. He told me that cases of total color-blindness are extremely rare; but when they occur the victim sees the entire spectrum in varying tones of gray, like a pencil drawing. There was a possibility, he said, that instead of being totally color-blind the victim had suffered a complete loss of color-sense; which would account even better than color-blindness for the fact that the printing and the shade of the paper were so much alike to his eyes that the printing virtually became invisible. When Dr. Martini examined a sheet of the stationery at the Saxon house, he felt fairly certain that some such optical condition afflicted the writer of the symbol."

The Englishman stirred. "I have never," he said hoarsely, "seen a *color*."

They were all silent for a while. "Dr. Ales, then," continued Lane with a sigh, "was color-blind, I was morally convinced. You, sir, have just demonstrated that you are afflicted with the same condition; you guessed wildly at the colors of Miss Thumm's kerchief and Mr. Rowe's necktie, not having the faintest notion what their true colors might be. Now you claim to be Hamnet Sedlar. But Hamnet Sedlar was *not* color-blind! The first day we met him, in the Saxon Room of this museum, he looked over the repaired case from which the 1599 Jaggard had been stolen and plainly and correctly distinguished not only various antipathetic colors of the bindings of the books in the cabinet, but shades of the same color, since he designated one binding as *golden* brown, a subtle differentiation impossible to a color-blind person. Since you are either William or Hamnet, then, and Hamnet had normal eyesight while William was color-blind, and you are color-blind, obviously you must be William. It's the simplest sort of syllogism. I suggested the test to determine whether you lied or not. You lied. Most of the tale you told us in the hospital was fabrication, although I suspect much of it is true. Now please be good enough to give my friends the complete story."

He sank into a chair, dabbing at his lips again.

"Yes," said the Englishman in a low voice, "I am William Sedlar."

He had first visited the Inspector as Dr. Ales, leaving the symbol in the Inspector's hands as a clue should anything happen to him in his pursuit of the Shakespearean document —an eventuality which at that time he considered remote. The reason he had not telephoned on June twentieth was that he could not; the remote eventuality had occurred. His brother Hamnet who, as William now knew, had accepted the curatorship of the Britannic Museum for the sole purpose of getting closer to the Saxon copy of the 1599 Jaggard, had kidnaped him the very evening of the day on which William had stolen the Jaggard from the museum. This was only shortly after the visit of Donoghue, and the same night on which Donoghue had been kidnaped by Hamnet, the Irishman's sense of time having been warped by his ignorance of how long he had been unconscious. . . . William had been *hors de combat*, therefore, from the day of the museum theft until the day the police rescued him from the isolated shack where he had been kept a prisoner!

He had despite all Hamnet's threats refused to divulge the hiding-place; Donoghue, of course, being ignorant of even the existence of the document, could tell Hamnet nothing. Hamnet, whose visits to the house of captivity were perforce hurried and spasmodic, due to the necessity of visiting the museum and maintaining a cloak of innocence, finally became desperate. He told William one day that, knowing the document to be in William's house, he had set a bomb in the cellar to explode and destroy the house with the document in it!—a bomb which he himself had had made secretly by an underworld chemist. It was only then that William realized what his brother's real purpose was in pursuing the Shakespearean document; not to save it but to *destroy* it!

"But why?" roared Rowe, his hands clenched. "That's— that's the most barbaric sort of vandalism! Why destroy it, for the love of God?"

"Was your brother insane?" cried Patience.

The Englishman's lips tightened; he flashed a look at Lane, but the old gentleman was gazing quietly into space. "I don't know," he said.

Hamnet had set the time-bomb for twenty-four hours. Realizing that by permitting the bomb to go off the document would be irrevocably lost, William at the last moment capitulated, reasoning that any delay would be better than none; he might be able to free himself and save the document. So he told Hamnet where the secret compartment was and how to open it. He had, however, been unable to escape. Hamnet had exclaimed with gloating that he intended to return to William's house and actually destroy the document with his own hand; there was plenty of time. He would pull the teeth of the bomb. . . . Hamnet had left with William's key, the original, and William had never seen him alive again. He knew nothing whatever of what had happened until he was rescued by the police after Donoghue's escape. In the hospital he read the newspapers and listened to the talk of reporters; it was then that he learned of the explosion and the discovery in the ruins of a body thought to be that of one of the Sedlar brothers. He realized in a flash what must have happened: while Hamnet was in the house getting the document he must have had a fatal encounter with still a third person after the document, this third person must have killed Hamnet over possession of the document—ignorant of the fact that the bomb was ticking away in the cellar—and made away with the precious sheet of paper. With Hamnet dead there was no one who knew of the bomb except William, who was helpless in the house where he was a prisoner; the explosion occurred on schedule, destroying the house.

"I saw at once," said the Englishman in a wrathful voice, "that there was still a third person gaddin' about who now actually possessed the document. I have sacrificed so much— so many years of my life—in pursuit of that holograph. . . . I had thought the document destroyed; now I was sure it still existed, unharmed! I had to start over again, solve this mystery of who murdered my brother, get back my document. To have acknowledged myself William Sedlar would have been fatal to this plan; I am wanted by the police of Bordeaux. By the time I had been extradited to France and had faced the charge, the document would probably have been lost to me forever. So, taking advantage of the fact that the police did not definitely know which of our bodies had been found in the ruins, and the fact that my brother and I were striking twins— even to the voice—I decided to say I was Hamnet. I'm sure Dr. Choate has been suspicious; I've been treading on dangerous ground all week."

By the time he had finished they knew that it had been Hamnet who had held up Patience and Rowe on the road to The Hamlet. Having followed Lane and read Lane's wired instructions to Thumm to bring the document to The Hamlet, he had thought the sealed envelope contained the precious paper itself.

The Inspector was grim-lipped, and Patience was in the glummest of moods. Rowe paced up and down, frowning. Only Lane sat quietly.

"Listen here," said Thumm finally. "I'll tell you right now I don't believe you. I'm willing to believe you're William, but that doesn't prove *you* weren't the second man in the house that night! I say there's a good chance you're lying. I say there's nothing to show you didn't escape from the place where your brother had you tied up, trailed him to your own house, and killed him for the paper. I claim this business of a third person killing Hamnet and getting the paper is all poppycock—don't believe there's a third person or ever was!"

William Sedlar went pale by degrees. "Oh, I say—" he began in a shocked voice.

"No, father," said Patience wearily. "You're wrong about

that. Mr. Sedlar is innocent of his brother's murder and I can prove it."

"Ah," said Lane, blinking. "You can, Patience?"

"We know now he is William; we know now that since the dead man was one of the two Sedlar brothers the dead man must be Hamnet. The question is: was Hamnet the first or second man to visit the house on the murder-night? We know that the first man had been forced to appropriate Maxwell's key in order to get back into the house after imprisoning the old man in the garage. The first man, then, *didn't* have a key when he arrived. But Hamnet Sedlar did have a key when he arrived—the original he had taken from his brother William, and which we later found on the body. Then Hamnet must have been the second visitor.

"Hamnet being the second visitor, was therefore murdered by the first, since there were only two involved according to Maxwell's bell-testimony. Who was the first, the masked man?" Patience's lips parted eagerly. "We proved long ago that the first man was the wielder of the ax, the hacker. Then Hamnet was killed by the hacker. Could William have been the hacker, as you've just maintained, father? I say no, because William knew better than anyone else in the world where the secret compartment was; he wouldn't have had to hack the place to splinters under any circumstances! So I say William Sedlar was *not* the hacker, wasn't in the house at all that night, didn't kill his brother, and there *is* a third man in this case—the wielder of the ax, the man who did not know where the document was, the man who killed Hamnet after Hamnet had taken it from the hollow panel, the man who put Hamnet's body into the cellar and escaped with the document!"

"Swell," said young Rowe quickly. "But who is he?"

"We'll have to start all over again, I'm afraid," said Patience, shrugging. She fell silent, frowning deeply. Suddenly she uttered a choked cry and her face became white as death. "Oh!" she said, and got uncertainly to her feet. She swayed a little, and Rowe with an expression of alarm leaped to her side.

"Pat, for God's sake. What's the matter? What's happened?"

The Inspector brushed him roughly aside. "Patty. Don't you feel well, darling?"

Patience moaned faintly: "I—I— It was the strangest

feeling. I—I really think I'm ill. . . ." Her voice trailed off; she staggered and fell against her father's arm.

Lane and the Englishman sprang forward. "Inspector!" said Lane sharply. "She's going to . . . Look out!"

Rowe darted forward and caught her knees as she began to slip to the floor.

When Thumm and Rowe had departed with Patience, bound in a cab for the Thumm apartment, Patience weeping queerly in a quiet hysteria, Mr. Drury Lane and William Sedlar found themselves alone in the curator's office.

"It must have been the heat," muttered Sedlar. "Poor girl."

"No doubt," said Lane. He was on his feet, tall as a pine topped with snow; and his eyes were two bottomless pits, dark and deep.

Sedlar shivered suddenly. "I suppose it's all up, eh? The end of the quest," he said bitterly. "I shouldn't care half so much if——"

"I quite understand your feelings, Mr. Sedlar."

"Yes. I suppose you'll turn me over to the authorities——"

Lane regarded him inscrutably. "Why should you suppose that? I'm not a policeman, nor is Inspector Thumm connected with the police any longer. Our little group are the only ones who know. There is really no charge against you; your thefts have been paid for; you are not a murderer.". The Englishman stared at him with a flaring hope in his haggard eyes. "I can't very well speak for the Inspector, but as one of the directors of the Britannic Museum I suggest you submit your resignation to James Wyeth at once and . . ."

The man's thin shoulders drooped. "I quite understand. It seems hard. . . . I know what I must do, Mr. Lane." He sighed. "I never thought when we conducted that erudite battle in the columns of *The Stratford Quarterly*——"

"That it would come to this very dramatic end?" Lane eyed him for a moment and then grunted noncommittally. "Well, good day," he said and, picking up his hat and stick, walked out of the room.

Dromio waited patiently at the curb with the car. The old man got into the tonneau very stiffly, as if his joints ached, and was driven away. He closed his eyes at once, so sunken in thought that he seemed to have fallen fast asleep.

30

Mr. Drury Lane's Solution

The Inspector was not a subtle man; his emotions were raw and spontaneous, like the leaping juice of a squeezed lemon. He had accepted fatherhood with a mixture of bewilderment, delight, and trepidation. The more he saw of his daughter the more he adored her and the less he understood her. Consequently she kept him in a stew of excitement; the poor man never succeeded, no matter how desperately he tried, either in anticipating her next mood or grasping the mystery of her last one.

In the turbulent depths of his misery he was suddenly glad to turn over to Mr. Gordon Rowe the task of calming the young woman so inexplicably stricken with hysteria. And Mr. Gordon Rowe, who until now had loved only books, realized with a despairing groan what it meant to love a woman.

For Patience remained a puzzle, neither to be grasped nor solved. When her weeping had run its course, she dried her eyes on the young man's breast-pocket kerchief, smiled at him, and retired to her room. Neither threats nor pleas moved her. She advised Mr. Gordon Rowe to go away. No, she would not see a physician. Yes, she was perfectly well; just a headache. And not another word out of her in response to the Inspector's frantic bellowings. Mr. Gordon Rowe and his prospective father-in-law looked gloomily at each other, and then Mr. Rowe went away, already obeying orders.

Patience did not emerge for dinner. She uttered a choked "good night" without opening her door. During the night the Inspector, finding his old heart strangely pounding, rose from his bed and went to her room. He heard a wild sobbing. He raised his hand to knock on her door and then dropped it helplessly. He returned to bed and stared bitterly at the black wall for half the night.

In the morning he peered into her room; she was asleep, traces of tears still on her cheeks, her honey-colored hair tumbled about the pillow. She stirred restlessly, sighing in her sleep; and he retreated in haste to a lonely breakfast and his office.

He moved listlessly through the routine work of the day.

Patience failed to make her appearance in the office. At 4:30 he uttered a loud curse, grabbed his hat, dismissed Miss Brodie for the day, and returned to the apartment.

"Pat!" he called anxiously from the foyer.

He heard a movement from her room, and he quickly crossed the living room. She was standing, pale and strange, before the closed door of her bedroom dressed in a severe suit, a dark little turban over her curls.

"You goin' out?" he rumbled, kissing her.

"Yes, father."

"Why've you got the door closed that way?"

"I'm—" She bit her lip. "Father, I'm *packing*."

His huge jaw dropped. "Pat! Darlin'! What's up? Where you going?"

She opened her door slowly. The Inspector saw through a sudden mist a full suitcase lying on her bed. "I'm going away for a few days," she said in a quivering voice. "I—it's very important."

"But what——"

"No, father." She snapped the case shut and buckled the straps. "Please don't ask me where or why. Or anything. Please. Just for a few days. I—I want to . . ."

The Inspector sank into a living-room chair and stared at her. She snatched up the suitcase and ran across the room. Then she dropped the bag with a little choked cry, ran back to him, and flung her arms about his neck and kissed him. Before he could collect his stupefied wits she was gone.

He sat there limply, in the empty apartment, a dead cigar in his mouth and his hat still on his head. The slam of the apartment-door kept thundering in his ears. In his slow deliberate way, as he calmed down, he thought things over. And the longer he thought the more uneasy he became. His lifetime of dealing with criminals and policemen had given him a certain shrewd insight into human nature. When he forgot that Patience was flesh of his flesh he began to appreciate the especial oddity of her conduct. His daughter was a level-headed, grown woman. She was not given to the customary feminine tantrums or emotional storms. The strangeness of her actions . . . He sat in the darkening room for hours, without moving. At midnight he rose, switched on the light, and made himself a cup of strong coffee. Then he went heavily to bed.

Two days passed with agonizing slowness. Gordon Rowe made his life miserable. The young man telephoned, he dropped into the office at odd hours, he clung to the Inspector with the grim tenacity of a leech. He did not seem even remotely satisfied with Thumm's grunted explanation that Patience had gone away for a few days "for a rest."

"Then why didn't she call me up, or drop me a note, or something?"

The Inspector shrugged. "I don't want to hurt your feelings, younker, but who the hell are you?"

Rowe flushed. "She loves me, damn it all!"

"Looks like it, doesn't it?"

But when six days had passed and there was no word, no smallest sign, from Patience, the Inspector caved in. He dropped his tightly casual air and for the first time in his life experienced real terror. He forgot his elaborate pretenses at working; he paced his office floor with slow wavering steps; and finally on the sixth day he could bear the agony no longer. He took his hat and left the building. Patience had not taken her roadster; it stood as she had left it in the public garage near the Thumm apartment. The Inspector climbed in wearily and headed its nose toward Westchester.

He found Drury Lane sunning himself in one of the crisp little gardens of The Hamlet; and for an instant the Inspector was shocked out of his own misery at the old gentleman's appearance. Lane had aged incredibly in less than a week. His skin was waxy yellow and exhibited the appalling texture of crumbling chalk; he sat wrapped in an Indian blanket, despite the hot sun, as if he were cold. His body seemed to have shrunken; and Thumm, recalling the astonishing vigor and youthful vitality of this man only a few years before, himself shivered and sat down with averted eyes.

"Well, well, Inspector," said Lane in a feeble, almost croaking voice. "It's good of you to come here. . . . I suppose you're sickened by my appearance?"

"Uh—no, no," said the Inspector hastily. "You look fine."

Lane smiled. "You're a poor liar, old friend. I look ninety and feel a hundred. It comes over you suddenly. Do you remember Cyrano in that fifth act seated beneath the tree? How many times I've played that part, a withered old buckaroo, while underneath my doublet my heart beat with the surging strength of youth! Now . . ." He closed his eyes for an instant. "Martini is openly worried. These medical men! They won't recognize the fact that old age is, in Seneca's phrase, an incurable disease." He opened his eyes. Then he said sharply: "Thumm, old man! What's happened? What's the matter?"

The Inspector buried his face in his hands. When he took them away his eyes were like wet marbles. "It's—it's Patty," he muttered. "She's gone—Lane, for the love of God, you've got to help me find her!"

The old gentleman's pallor deepened. He said slowly: "She's—disappeared?"

"Yes. I mean no. She went off by herself." The story tumbled out. A score of wrinkles appeared about Lane's unwavering eyes as they watched the Inspector's lips. "I don't know what to do. It's my fault. I see now what must have happened," cried Thumm. "She got a clue, some damn' notion that sent her off on a wild chase. It might be dangerous, Lane. It's about a week now. Maybe . . ." He faltered and stopped, unable to phrase the horrible uncertainty in his mind.

"You think, then," murmured Lane, "that she was perilously close to the truth, somehow. That she's gone off on the trail of the third man, the murderer. That he has possibly turned on her . . ."

The Inspector nodded dumbly; his big gnarled fist was pounding the seat of the rustic bench in a steady tattoo.

Both men were silent for a long time. A robin perched on a nearby bough burst into song; from somewhere behind them Thumm heard Quacey's querulous old voice raised in argument with a gardener. But Lane's dead ears heard nothing; he sat studying the grass at his feet. Finally he sighed and laid his veined hand on Thumm's, and Thumm looked at him with tortured hope.

"Poor old friend. I can't tell you how sorry I feel. Patience . . . Shakespeare once said a remarkable thing. He said:

> " 'O most delicate fiend!
> Who is't can read a woman?'

You're much too honest and primitively masculine, my friend, to understand what has happened to Patience. Women have an inexhaustible capacity for concocting exquisite tortures for their menfolk, many times in all innocence." Thumm's haggard eyes devoured his face. "Have you a pencil and paper about you?"

"Penc—— Sure, sure!" The Inspector fumbled in an agony

of eagerness in his pockets and produced the requested articles.

He watched his friend fiercely. Lane wrote steadily. When
he had finished he looked up.

"Insert this in the personal columns of all the New York
newspapers, Inspector," he said quietly. "Perhaps—who
knows?—it may do good."

Thumm dazedly took the paper.

"And let me know the moment anything happens."

"Sure, sure." His voice broke. "Thanks a lot, Lane."

The queerest spasm of pain twisted the old gentleman's pale
face for an instant. Then his lips curled in a smile that was
just as queer. "It's little enough." He gave Thumm his hand.
"Good-by."

" 'By," muttered Thumm. Their hands clasped. The Inspector strode abruptly off toward his car. Before he started the
motor he read the message Lane had scribbled:

"Pat. I know everything. Come back. D.L."

He sighed with relief, grinned, sent the engine roaring,
waved his hand, and disappeared in a cloud of gravel and
dust. Lane had risen and smiled very peculiarly until the car
was gone. Then he shivered a little and sat down again, wrapping the blanket more closely about him.

The next afternoon found two men seated opposite each
other, an old man and a young; and both were haggard and
biting their nails. The apartment was cool and quiet. An ashtray at each man's elbow was filled with dead butts. Between
them, on the floor, lay a tumbled heap of morning newspapers.

"Do you think she will—?" said Gordon Rowe hoarsely for
the twentieth time.

"I don't know, son."

And then they heard the scrape of a key in the lock of the
front door. They sprang to their feet and dashed into the
foyer. The door opened. It was Patience. With a little cry she
fell into the Inspector's arms. Rowe waited quietly. Not a
word was said. The Inspector was uttering formless little
noises that had no meaning, and Patience began to sob. She
seemed harried, exhausted; white and drawn, as if she had
undergone unbearable suffering. The suitcase lay on the sill
keeping the door open.

Patience looked up, and her eyes widened. "Gordon!"

"Pat."

The Inspector turned and went into the living room.

"Pat. I never knew until now——"

"I know, Gordon."

"I love you, darling. I couldn't stand it——"

"Oh, Gordon." She placed her hands on his shoulders. "You're a dear sweet boy. I was foolish to do what I did." He seized her suddenly and held her so tightly that she could feel his heart straining against her breast. They stood that way for a moment, and then they kissed.

Without another word they went into the living room.

The Inspector whirled; he was all a-grin, and a fresh cigar spurted smoke from his mouth. "All made up, hey?" he chortled. "That's swell, just swell. Gordon, my boy, congratulations. Now, damn it all, we'll have some peace——"

"Father," whispered Patience; and he stopped and the joy went out of his face. Rowe gripped her lifeless hand; she returned the pressure faintly. "He knows everything? Really?"

"Everything? Who—oh, Lane! Well, that's what he said, Patty." He came forward and put his long ape-like arms about her. "What the devil's the difference? The point is you've come back, and that's all that counts with me."

She pushed him back gently. "No. There's something——"

"He told me," frowned Thumm, "to let him know the minute you returned. Maybe I'd better put in a call. . . ."

"He did?" Patience's pallor fled; her eyes were suddenly feverish. Both men stared at her as if she had gone insane. "No, I tell you! It's better if we tell him personally. Oh, what a stupid, whining, revolting *fool* I've been!" She stood fiercely biting her lower lip. Then she sprang toward the foyer. "He's in the most horrible danger!" she cried. "Come *on!*"

"But, Pat—" protested Rowe.

"Come on, I tell you. I might have known. . . . Oh, we may be too late!" and she turned and raced out of the apartment. Rowe and Thumm looked at each other, their faces mirroring a sudden disturbance; and then they grabbed their hats and darted after her.

They squeezed into the roadster and were off. Young Rowe drove; and if he was a gentle bookworm under a lamp, at the wheel he was a fiend. For some time—until they fought clear of the city traffic—they were all silent; Rowe grimly intent on the rushing road ahead, Patience white and, from the peculiar expression in her eyes, faintly nauseated, big Thumm watchful as the Sphinx.

It was he who broke the silence when the city lay behind them and the open road stretched like white elastic before them. "Tell us all about it, Patty," he said quietly. "Evidently Lane's in trouble. I don't get you at all. You should have told me——"

"Yes," she said in a cracked voice. "It's all my fault. . . . It's not fair that you shouldn't know, father. And you, Gordon. It's important that both of you know, now. Gordon, faster! There's—there's blood ahead, I tell you!"

Rowe's lips tightened; the roadster fled like a chased hare.

"Toward the end," began Patience, her nostrils quivering inexplicably, "—but you saw it, too. We had come to the point of saying that the victim and the murderer were the Sedlars. We thought one of them had killed the other in the house. But then it changed. Last week—in the museum—it changed. We knew then that the dead man in the ruins was Hamnet, that the survivor was his brother William, and that William couldn't have been one of the two men in the house on the murder-night; you remember how I proved that: by the keys. So that meant our theory was exploded; we knew the victim, Hamnet Sedlar, but we didn't know the first visitor to the house that night, the man who tied up Maxwell, the hacker. . . . And when that struck me, I went back in my mind to things half-forgotten, never wholly grasped at the time they happened or I saw them. It was like a—like a streak of lightning."

She kept her eyes on the road ahead. "The whole problem resolved itself, then, into discovering if possible the identity of that first visitor to the house. What had happened? After leaving Maxwell bound and gagged in the garage, this man had re-entered the house, using Maxwell's duplicate key. The door had shut behind him automatically, due to its spring lock. He had taken the small ax from the wood-box in the kitchen and attacked the study, obviously on the theory that the study would be the most likely hiding-place for the document which he was seeking. He hadn't the faintest idea where the document might have been hidden in the study: witness his indiscriminate attack on all sorts of objects. First, presumably, he had looked through the books, thinking the paper might be in one of them. Not finding it, he had attacked the furniture with the ax—the wood-paneled walls, the floor. At precisely midnight, we know from the position of the hands, he shattered the clock, I suppose thinking it might have been the repository of the paper. But he was completely baffled; he could not find it in the study. Nor in the rest of the ground floor. So he went upstairs to William Sedlar's bedroom as the next most likely location."

"We know all that, Pat," said Thumm, looking at her strangely.

"Please, father. . . . We know he was in the bedroom at twelve-twenty-four from the smashed bedroom clock. Now Hamnet was killed in that house at twelve-twenty-six, according to his smashed wrist-watch—only two minutes after the hacker shattered the bedroom clock upstairs. The question was: At what time had Hamnet entered the house? He had to unlock the door, go to the study, see the wreckage there, go to the hollow panel above the bookshelves, take out the document, descend the ladder, perhaps examine the paper, then encounter his murderer, struggle, and be killed. Certainly this involved more than two minutes! Certainly, then, Hamnet must have entered the house *while the hacker was still in the house.*"

"Well, well?" growled Thumm.

"I'm getting there," said Patience dully. "We know from William Sedlar's last statement that Hamnet was the one who wanted the document only to destroy it. What would Hamnet do, then, when he finally did lay hands on it in the study? Proceed immediately to destroy it. How? Well, by fire as the surest and quickest means. He must have struck a match, holding the document in his hand, and started to touch the flame to the paper." She sighed. "This is only a theory, of course, and accomplishes nothing except to clear up one point. *It explains the presence of the slashes on Hamnet's wrist-watch and wrist.* For if at the moment Hamnet applied the match to the document the hacker came downstairs from the bedroom and saw what was happening, he would naturally —being interested in the salvation, not the destruction, of the document—attack Hamnet to *prevent* its destruction by fire. Therefore he would have swung like a flash at Hamnet's hand with the ax he still carried, striking Hamnet's wrist and wrist-watch, causing the vandal probably to drop both document and match. Undoubtedly Hamnet then put up a fight; in the struggle the hacker shot him dead. The struggle probably started in the study, where the hacker dropped the ax, and moved by degrees into the hall, where we found Hamnet's shattered monocle and where Hamnet was probably shot to death. . . . The hacker dragged Hamnet's body downstairs into the cellar not knowing the bomb was there, and then—if the document hadn't been consumed before he struck at Hamnet's wrist—took the document and left the house. The important thing about the slash and the struggle is that the hacker was willing to go to any lengths—physical combat, *murder*—to preserve that document."

The steep ascent to the cliff-tops on which The Hamlet was perched occupied young Rowe's whole attention; and Patience fell silent as the young man skillfully wrestled the roadster around the hairpin turns. Then suddenly they came to the outpost of the estate; and were passed across the quaint little bridge. The tires sang against the gravel road.

"I still don't see," said Rowe with a frown, "even if all this is true, Pat, where it gets you. You're still as far from the murderer as you were before."

"You think so?" cried Patience. She closed her eyes and winced, like a child swallowing bitter medicine. "I tell you it's all clear as—as sin! The man's characteristics—his characteristics, Gordon. They're betrayed *by what happened in the house*."

The two men looked at her blankly. They were through the main gates now, bowling along the curving main driveway. The gnomish little figure of Quacey, his hump a leathery knob on his shoulders, popped out of a clump of syringa, stared, then broke into a thousand-wrinkled grin, waved, and darted into the road.

Rowe stopped the car. "Quacey!" said Patience in a stiff voice, half-rising between the two men. "Is—is Mr. Lane all right?"

"Hullo, Miss Thumm!" squeaked Quacey cheerfully. "He's better today, thank you. Feeling almost chipper. Inspector, I was just going to mail this letter to you!"

"Letter?" echoed Thumm, puzzled. "That's funny. Let's have it." Quacey handed him a square large envelope and he tore an edge off.

"Letter?" said Patience in the blankest of voices, and she sat down between the two men again and stared up at the blue sky. Once she murmured: "Thank God, he's all right."

The Inspector read it silently; and then, with a deep pucker between his brows, read it aloud:

"Dear Inspector:
  "I trust Patience has returned none the worse for her

harrowing experience. My 'personal' will bring her safely back to you, I know. While you are waiting, you may wish to distract your mind by learning the answers to some of the mysteries which have confounded your investigation of the case.

"The chief puzzle, as Patience and Gordon both remarked, is certainly this: Why should a sane, intelligent, and cultured man like Hamnet Sedlar have wished to destroy an authentic holograph so rare, so precious, so irreplaceable, as a letter written in the immortal hand of William Shakespeare? I can tell you the answer, having solved the mystery in my own way.

"The letter, written to an ancestor of Sir John Humphrey-Bond's, evidently a dear friend of the poet's, besides saying that the writer—Shakespeare—suspected he was being slowly poisoned, actually added in Shakespeare's own script the *name* of the suspected poisoner. . . . This is a strange, strange world. The man Shakespeare accused of poisoning him was named *Hamnet Sedlar*. Hamnet Sedlar, Inspector, from whom the brothers Hamnet and William Sedlar are directly descended!

"Strange, eh? It is now comprehensible why this student, this man of culture, this earnest and enlightened antiquarian, this proud Englishman, should against every dictate of education and scientific instinct have desired to keep from the world, even at the expense of what will become one of the world's dearest treasures, the knowledge that the immortal Shakespeare, the Bard of Avon, whom Carlyle characterized as 'the greatest of intellects' and Ben Jonson as 'not of an age but for all time,' revered and worshiped by over three centuries of sensitive mankind, was murdered by Hamnet Sedlar's own ancestor; a forbear who—horror of horrors—bore his own name! Some will find in his passion a touch of madness, and others will not believe; but pride of ancestry is, like old age, an incurable disease, and it consumes itself in its own cold flame.

"William was not touched with this disease; in him the scientific spirit rises triumphant. But he too was afflicted with the touch of earth; he wanted the document not for posterity but for himself. The third man, who entered the case as a protagonist for the first and only time on the night of the murder, was willing to take even human life to preserve the document for the world.

"Please tell Patience, Gordon, and whoever else may be interested—the truth will be known soon enough, old friend—that they may have no fears about the safety of the document. I have myself seen to it that it is on its way to England where it belongs, to become the property of England legally and the world spiritually; since its legitimate owner, the late Humphrey-Bond, is dead without issue or heirs and his properties have reverted to the Crown. If I have had anything to do with this work of restoration, Inspector, I know my friends will always think of me kindly. I prefer to think, in the customary egotism of all men, that even in the twilight of my life I have been of some service to humanity.

"Patience and Gordon, if I may presume to intrude an old man's concern into your very intimate affairs—I think you will both be happy together. You have a communion of interests, you are both intelligent young people, and I know that you will respect each other. May God bless you. I have not forgotten you.

"My dear Inspector, I am old and so tired that there no longer seems . . . I shall be going away soon, I think, for a long rest; which is what prompts this inordinately long letter. And since I leave unattended, as it were, and without your knowledge, I shall say to myself these shining farewell words:

"'They say he parted well, and paid his score;
And so, God be with him!'

"Until we meet again—

"DRURY LANE"

The Inspector wrinkled his flat nose. "I don't see——"

Rowe looked about quickly. But the scene was peaceful; the spires and turrets of The Hamlet loomed serenely above the treetops.

Patience said in a strangled voice: "Where is Mr. Lane, Quacey?"

Quacey's batrachian little eyes twinkled. "Sunning himself in the west gardens, Miss Thumm. He'll be surprised to see you, I dare say. I know he wasn't expecting anybody today."

The men jumped out of the roadster and, rather stiffly, Patience stepped down to the gravel. Between them, with

Quacey pattering quietly along at their heels, she began to stroll across the velvet grass toward the west gardens.

"You see," she said so softly that they had to strain their ears, "the hacker did betray himself. He made no mistakes; he didn't know he was making mistakes; fate made them for him. Fate in the shape of a cheap alarm-clock."

"Alarm-clock?" muttered the Inspector.

"When we examined the study and came upon Maxwell's alarm-clock on the mantel above the fireplace, we saw that its alarm *was still set*. What did this mean? That the alarm went off at the time it was set for—twelve o'clock, midnight, of the night before (because we examined it before noon of the following morning and Maxwell had set it before midnight the previous evening). The little lever still pointed to *Alarm*, you'll remember, when we examined it. But if we found the lever still pointed to *Alarm*, then the alarm must have *rung*. But what's significant about the fact that the alarm rang? The fact that, if it rang and we found the alarm still set, *then it must have rung itself out*. Had it been stopped while it rang by a human hand, we should have found the little lever at *Silent*, not *Alarm*. So it was *not* turned off; the alarm rang and rang until it exhausted itself, the spring of the alarm unwinding; and died off, spent, with its lever still set at *Alarm*. . . ."

"But what the devil does that mean, Patty?" cried Rowe.

"Everything. We know the hacker was in the room precisely at midnight; so he must have been in the room when the alarm began to ring. We know this from two facts: Maxwell said he kept all the clocks perfectly synchronized, and the grandfather-clock had been shattered exactly at twelve."

Rowe stepped back a little, quietly; he was very pale.

"All right, I'll follow along," growled the Inspector. "Why didn't this ax-wielder of yours turn off the alarm when it started to ring? Must have made him jump! Anyone prowling about somebody else's house would have jumped like a shot and turned it off, whether there was anyone to hear it or not."

They paused under an ancient oak and Patience felt rather blindly for the rough bark. "Exactly," she whispered. "The fact remains that even though he was in the same room, even though every instinct would have impelled him to turn the alarm off, *he didn't*."

"Well, it's too much for me," muttered Thumm. "Come on. Come on, Gordon," and he strode past the tree. The others followed slowly. Not far away, over a low wall of privets, they saw the quiet shrunken figure of Lane seated on a rustic bench, his back to them.

Patience made a sick little sound and the Inspector turned sharply. Rowe, death in his eyes, bounded forward and caught her about the waist.

"What is this?" said the Inspector slowly.

"Father, wait," sobbed Patience. "Wait. You don't understand. You don't see. Why didn't the hacker discover that ticking bomb in the cellar when he took Hamnet Sedlar's dead body down there? Why did he hack at the walls of the study in the first place? He was obviously looking for hollow places. What's the normal way of looking for hollow places? Rapping for them, rapping for them, father! Why didn't he tap those paneled walls?"

Thumm looked from one to the other, baffled, uneasy. "Why?"

Patience put a trembling hand on his big arm. "Please. Before you—see him. The hacker didn't stop the alarm-clock's ringing, he didn't investigate the ticking of the bomb in the cellar, he didn't tap the walls—for the same reason, father. Oh, don't you see? It struck me so hard, such a horrible blow, that I ran, blindly, like a child; I wanted to get away, anywhere. . . . He couldn't *hear* the alarm. He couldn't *hear* the tick of the bomb. He couldn't *hear* a hollow sound even if he did tap. HE WAS DEAF!"

The little glade was quiet. The Inspector's jaw dropped like the iron floor of a portcullis; a concentrated horror of realization charged into his eyes. Rowe stood stonily, his arm a rigid brace about Patience's quivering torso. Quacey, hovering in the background, suddenly uttered a choking, squealing animal cry and sank like dead to the grass.

The Inspector took an unsteady step forward and touched Lane's quiet shoulder. Patience whirled and buried her face in Rowe's coat, sobbing as if her heart would break.

The old gentleman's head was sunken on his breast; there was no response to Thumm's touch.

More swiftly than it seemed possible for a man of his bulk and weight, the Inspector charged around the bench and grasped Lane's hand.

It was icy cold, and a small stained empty vial dropped from its white fingers to the green grass.